Colin Forbes
Year of the
Golden Ape

Pan Books
in association with Collins

For Jane

First published 1974 by William Collins Sons & Co. Ltd
This edition published 1975 by Pan Book Ltd,
Cavaye Place, London SW10 9PG
in association with William Collins Sons & Co. Ltd
19 18 17 16 15 14
© Colin Forbes 1974
ISBN 0 330 24627 5
Made and printed in Great Britain by
Richard Clay (The Chaucer Press) Ltd, Bungay, Suffolk

Year of the Golden Ape

Colin Forbes, born in Hampstead, London, writes a novel every year. For the past twenty years he has earned his living solely as a full-time writer.

An international bestseller, each book has been published worldwide, including the United States. He is translated into twenty languages.

He is an enthusiastic traveller and visits all locations appearing in his novels. 'It is essential for an author to see everything for himself to achieve vivid atmosphere and authenticity.'

He has explored most of Western Europe, the East and West coasts of America, and has made excursions to Africa and Asia. He lives with his wife in Surrey.

Surveys have shown that his readership is divided almost equally between men and women.

Contents

Part one The terrorists

1

In January two major assassinations took place in the Middle East. The new, thirty-year-old King of Saudi Arabia was murdered as he made love to one of his numerous wives, skewered through the back so savagely as he lay prone that the knife blade penetrated the body of the girl beneath him, piercing her heart. An alleged cousin promptly assumed nominal power and issued a statement that he would not rest until Arab troops patrolled the streets of Jerusalem. The statement reassured everyone east of Suez – it showed that the King's heart was in the right place, that he was bent on the extinction of the State of Israel.

But the significant figure in this drama was the man who planned it. Sheikh Gamal Tafak immediately took over the posts of Oil and Finance Minister from his predecessor, who with so many other moderates had fled the country for his life. Tafak, a brilliant fanatic, sincerely believed that to recover Palestine for the Arabs, the oil weapon which chance had placed in their hands must be wielded ruthlessly. It was from this moment that the power of the sheikhs was really exerted against the West.

The oil tap was turned off in January – at the height of a savage European winter – and Tafak himself visited western capitals to inform his nervous hosts that this time, unlike in 1973, there would be no concessions . . .

'The West must no longer support Israel with so much as a glass of water,' he informed European foreign ministers. 'Until this condition is fulfilled we are cutting the flow of oil to Europe and America by fifty per cent. We are declaring a state of blockade . . .'

Tafak was in London when the gentle, statesmanlike President of Egypt was assassinated, beaten to death with rifle butts as he slept, by the urgent hammerblows of young soldiers under the direct orders of Colonel Selim Sherif who personally emptied his revolver into the already dying president. Within hours Col Sherif was proclaimed as the new President of Egypt. He reassured the Cairo mob with a speech from a balcony.

'The traitor who sat down with our enemies at the same table

8

is dead. In the West they call us apes – we will now show them the real power of the ape . . .'

Sherif's reference was to an article by an exasperated Washington correspondent who had dubbed certain autocratic sheikhs as 'golden apes, gold piling up in their treasuries while their people still roam the desert . . .' Sherif, a clever propagandist, seized on the phrase and broadened it to include the entire Arab nation.

What the West had most feared had happened. The moderate Arab leaders who had struggled valiantly to ease their way forward to cooperation with the rest of the world had been swept aside, buried. As so often happens when vast power is there for the taking, the extremists had climbed into the saddle. In London, shortly after Col Sherif's balcony speech, Sheikh Gamal Tafak made his own speech at a City of London banquet – much to the consternation of his hosts.

'This time there will be no favoured nations as in 1973. The whole of the West must suffer as we are suffering in Palestine – where an alien race oppresses our people, steals their land, turning them into refugees who are stateless persons without a country, without hope . . .'

The Year of the Golden Ape had begun . . .

2

By March the new fifty per cent oil cut was squeezing the life out of Europe, America and Japan. The price had climbed to thirty dollars a barrel. Gold, the bellwether of international disaster, was approaching the five hundred dollars an ounce level. And Sheikh Gamal Tafak was flying back to Jeddah from Washington, having told the Americans that he could offer no hope of a respite yet.

For some people it was a nightmare, for others a dream – the destruction of Israel. For Gamal Tafak, a handsome man with dark hair and a dark fringe of beard, it was a dream close to realisation. In only a few months the Arab armies – under the overall command of Col Sherif – would advance and overwhelm the enemy, occupying his country. The occupation would have to be followed by stern measures – to persuade three million Israelis to leave Palestine for ever.

The key to Tafak's plan was to immobilise the West at the critical moment, to make it impossible for them to supply fresh arms to Israel when she was on the point of extinction. As he looked down from the jetliner, now passing over the Aegean, Tafak thought how curious it was – that the plan which would make him the most famous Arab of the twentieth century depended at this stage on two Europeans – an Englishman – and a Frenchman . . .

Jean Jules LeCat was forty-two years old, a man with a violent past, an unpromising present and a hopeless future. He was intelligent enough to know this, so he was relieved when he was approached secretly by Sheikh Gamal Tafak's right-hand man in Algiers, Ahmed Riad, one week after his unexpected release from the Santé prison in Paris. Riad offered him two hundred thousand dollars to carry out a massacre.

'The English adventurer, Winter, will nominally be in control of the operation,' Riad explained, 'but you will kill the hostages. We do not think Winter is capable of such detachment . . .'

'He is not,' LeCat replied. 'We worked together for two years in the Mediterranean before I was betrayed and ended up in the Santé. I know Winter. He is squeamish . . .'

To the average person the proposal might have sounded barbaric, but to LeCat it was a highly dangerous operation Riad had proposed and one to be undertaken because the compensation was so high. His violent past made him view the transaction clinically.

LeCat was the product of a brief liaison between an Arab girl and a French army captain before the Second World War. When the child was born in Constantine, Algeria, LeCat took his son away from the girl who was glad to receive a few hundred francs on condition she never saw the child again. Applying for leave,

Jules LeCat, the father, took the baby back to France.

Its birth was registered in Toulon where LeCat persuaded a girl friend to pretend to be his wife. A cosmopolitan girl, she was amused by the deception – especially as LeCat's estranged wife was at that moment living in Bordeaux. A doctor, a *piednoir*, was bribed to provide the requisite documentation, and Jean Jules LeCat became a French citizen.

Brought up by an aunt in Algiers, who was never told the truth – Jules LeCat's real wife conveniently got herself killed in a motor accident shortly after the registration of the birth – the boy went into the Army in 1950 when he was seventeen. His rapid promotion came years later during the ferocious fighting in Algeria when the Arabs were struggling for their independence.

It was an experience which suited his nature. At twenty-seven he became skilled at locating terrorists, at laying traps for them, at torturing information out of the men he caught. He was quickly promoted to captain, his father's old rank. 'To trap a terrorist you must learn to think like him' was one of his favourite sayings. Later, he added a new maxim. 'You must become a terrorist . . .'

His father died at the height of the terrible war, and on his deathbed he made a bad mistake. He told Jean Jules the truth about his origins. 'Your mother was an Arab girl out of the Casbah . . .'

He got no further because Jean Jules, proud of his French citizenship, despising the men he captured and tortured as no more than animals, slapped the dying man hard with the back of his hand. Jean Jules had been two days without sleep and there was still blood on his jacket from a savage engagement in the hills. When he recovered from the shock of what his father had told him, the old man lay dead. He called the doctor, who signed the death certificate without a second thought; after all, the patient had been dying.

LeCat became even more savage in his battles with the terrorists; from then on he used his skill as an explosives expert to lace the hillsides with boobytraps. No farm building, no outhouse, not even an animal's drinking trough was safe to touch. His commanding officer was impressed with his subordinate's ferocity.

'LeCat, you seem determined to kill every Arab in north Africa . . .'

11

'Then, *mon colonel*, there will be no terrorists left,' LeCat replied.

When De Gaulle decided to give Algeria independence and the OAS, a secret organisation pledged to keep Algeria French, revolted, LeCat joined it. His maxim, 'You must become a terrorist', came true. He became one. Had there been two dozen men like him in Algeria, De Gaulle might have failed. LeCat turned half Algiers into a minefield, but only half . . . When the end came he fled to Egypt to survive.

Speaking fluent Arabic – as well as French and English – LeCat merged with his Egyptian background, changing his name and telling everyone how he had worked against the OAS. He earned a little money – and the friendship of certain Arabs, including a certain Ahmed Riad – by going to Tel Aviv and spying on the Israelis. He also earned a reputation for being a good man to send on a killing party.

For ten years LeCat drifted, living in the Middle East, in Quebec, in America, engaged in various criminal activities, never staying anywhere so long that he was caught. In 1972 he returned to the Mediterranean where he joined the Englishman, Winter, in smuggling operations. For two years he had a profitable existence, then he was arrested in Marseilles, tried for smuggling and serious assault against the police, sentenced to a long term of imprisonment in the Santé prison in Paris.

Released later under mysterious circumstances, he came out of prison to be met by an Algerian who provided him with an air ticket to Algiers, a sum of money, and the address of a café where he met Ahmed Riad.

Riad explained the nature of the vast operation to create an incident which would outrage the West. What Riad did not explain was the ultimate plan whereby Sheikh Gamal Tafak, exploiting the outcry from the West, would persuade every Arab oil producer to cut the oil flow a second time – and this time to zero. Then, with the West hamstrung, the way would be open for the final, annihilating attack on Israel.

It was in March, in what came to be known as the Year of the Golden Ape, that LeCat put into operation the first part of the plan to create the terrible incident which would appal and outrage the West. He went about organising the production of a nuclear device.

On March 10, France, like so many other countries, was half-paralysed by the huge Arab oil cut when Jean-Philippe Antoine, a small, self-contained man of thirty-five, walked confidently along a street in Nantes in western France. Stopping, he glanced up and down the street, then pressed the bell on a dentist's front door. The door opened a few inches, a pair of eyes stared at him. The Frenchman's confidence cracked.

'For God's sake, let me in . . .'

The pair of eyes disappeared and the door opered wider, just wide enough for him to step inside. Standing in the hallway, Antoine blinked in the gloom. At ten o'clock on a March morning it was still only half-light inside the old house; the lamp had not been turned on as an energy-saving measure. The front door closed behind him, the key turned in the lock. Antoine's lips trembled as he gazed at the short, wide-shouldered man who had let him in.

'Surely we should hurry?' Antoine demanded. 'Which way do I go?'

'You are nervous?' LeCat lit a Gitane and for a few seconds Antoine caught sight of his face in the match-flame; a cruel face, hardened by grim experience few men have to endure in their lifetime, a moustache curved down almost to the corners of a wide mouth, the eyes half-closed against the match-flame, eyes which calmly studied Antoine who had not replied. '*Oui*, you are nervous, my friend. Go down the hall and through the doorway. The man who is waiting there will take you to the car.'

'I've changed my mind . . .' The effort the words caused Antoine made them come out in a near-hysterical rush. 'I can't go on with this thing.'

'But you have to . . .' LeCat blew smoke through his nose. 'You see, they are dead already – in there . . .'

Gesturing towards a half-open door leading off the hall, LeCat gripped Antoine's arm. 'Give me everything in your pockets and then *move*!' He took the identity card Antoine extracted from his pocket, grabbed the wallet, replaced the card inside it. He took a

13

key-ring, a notebook, a pen. 'Now, that ring on your finger . . .'

'I must have the wallet . . .' Antoine was removing the ring from his finger, protesting and obeying at the same time. 'My ring is gold . . . there is one thousand francs inside the wallet, some photos . . .'

LeCat took the ring. 'A gold ring may survive. The wallet may get blown a hundred metres away by the explosion. If that happened, if the wallet survived also, your identity would be confirmed. Which would be excellent, would it not?' The face came closer in the gloom as Antoine shivered from the chill in the hall. 'I told you, my friend, they are already dead. Go!'

LeCat waited until Antoine had disappeared, then he walked inside the room beyond the half-open door. It was a dentist's surgery and the chair was occupied by a patient wearing his overcoat, a small, lean man about the height and build of Jean-Philippe Antoine. LeCat went over to the chair, placed the ring carefully on the limp hand lying in the patient's lap. The head was slumped forward and a smear of blood showed at the back of the skull.

The dentist's nurse lay on the floor face downwards, her legs curled, her white coat rumpled. It was cold inside the surgery and the window which faced the back garden was rimed with frost. No oil had arrived for a fortnight and the tank in the back garden was empty. LeCat finished distributing Antoine's possessions among the dead patient's pockets he had earlier emptied, then took one last look around the bleak room.

The dentist, wearing a white jacket and dark trousers, was sprawled at the foot of the dental chair. Like his nurse and his patient, he was also dead. A quarter of an hour before Antoine had arrived this frozen tableau had been alive. The dentist had been attending to his new patient, quite unaware that this stranger who had made his appointment to arrive just before Antoine's own appointment was a miserable Parisian pickpocket.

LeCat had searched Montmartre to find the right man, someone who was approximately the height, build and age of Antoine, someone not too bright who could be persuaded to make a dental appointment in exchange for the payment of a small sum of money. He had gathered from LeCat that the dentist was playing mothers and fathers with his nurse, who happened to be LeCat's

14

wife, so a witness was needed. Not for any sordid court case where the pickpocket's record would be exposed, LeCat had assured him, but simply to teach the adulterer a lesson.

Everything was now correct, LeCat decided. He glanced at the patient's record files where a drawer was half-pulled out of the filing-case, patted his breast pocket to feel the bulge of record cards inside his jacket. Everything correct. Walking back into the gloomy hall, he bent down and turned a switch on a large box. Three minutes to detonation. He checked his watch where the sweep hand moved clearly round on the illuminated dial. He went quickly along the hall, through the doorway at the end and out of the back door. Then he started running, keeping below the level of the garden wall, through the open gate at the bottom and along the frosted track beyond until he reached the car parked behind a copse of evergreens.

The engine of the Renault was running and Antoine was sitting in the back beside another shadowy figure. LeCat climbed in behind the wheel, closed the door quietly, checked his watch. Sixty seconds . . . He drove rapidly along the track, away from the house hidden by the evergreens. He was turning on to a main road when they heard the b-o-o-m. In the back seat Antoine gave a little cry of horror which LeCat ignored. He felt the shockwave push the side of the car, which he also ignored.

The time-bomb, two hundred pounds of gelignite, had totally demolished the house and little that was identifiable was left of the three corpses which had lain inside it. Six people in Nantes knew that Jean-Philippe Antoine had a dental appointment at ten in the morning – he had been careful to tell them this – and it was obvious he had died in the explosion. The force of the bomb was so great it shattered the patient's body, making it impossible to check identity by the most foolproof method known to science – by Antoine's dental records. No teeth were found to check, and in any case his dental records were inside LeCat's jacket pocket.

There were good reasons for the precautions LeCat had taken. In France the Direction de la Surveillance du Territoire (counter-intelligence) does not like it when key security risks go abroad on unexplained visits. And France had just lost one of her more promising nuclear physicists.

*   *   *

Travelling under different names and carrying false papers, LeCat and Antoine arrived at Dorval airport, Montreal, during a blizzard. There is nothing conspicuous about two Frenchmen arriving in Montreal, a city where French is widely spoken. A car was waiting to take them away the moment they had passed through Immigration and Customs.

LeCat handed Antoine over to André Dupont, who escorted the nuclear physicist to a motel for the night. Dupont and Antoine did not linger in eastern Canada; the following morning they caught a CPR train and stayed aboard until it reached Vancouver on the Pacific coast. On arrival they went straight to a house in Dusquesne Street.

Nor did LeCat linger. Inside the car which met them at Dorval airport was an American, Joseph Walgren, a fifty-year-old ex-accountant LeCat had got to know rather well when he was living in Denver in 1968. Walgren, a round-faced man with wary eyes, had given up accountancy years earlier when he muddled up a client's money with his own bank account. Since then his method of earning a living had not been completely legal. Twenty-four hours after LeCat's arrival in Montreal, Walgren drove him over the border into the States. They were heading for Illinois, a part of America Walgren knew well. They had the man to make the nuclear device. Now they needed the material.

3

Extract from transcript of Columbia Broadcasting System's television '60 Minutes' report, August 10 1973·

Dr John Gofman: 'Any reasonably capable physicist, say, getting out of a university with a Ph.D., I would estimate would be able to come up with a design to use plutonium in a bomb in a very short time...'

Carole Bannermann was driving too fast for the road, for the weather, for her own safety. In Illinois, ten miles from the city of

Morris, the highway was awash from an earlier flash-flood as rain swept across it, great driving sweeps of rain which passed her headlight beams in the night like moving curtains. Recklessly, because she was late for the party, she kept her speedometer needle at sixty, five above the regulation fifty-five.

At nine in the evening in March the highway was deserted; few people took the car out at night during the present energy crisis – not since gas had been rationed. Carole, fair-haired – her mother had named her after Lombard – had no patience with the gas situation. You were twenty only once in a lifetime and she was going to make the most of her natural resources. To hell with the energy crisis. She pressed her foot down, the speedometer climbed, the rain curtains whipped past her headlights probing the darkness.

She was reckless, but she had split-second reflexes, and she believed in watching the road ahead. Beyond her headlights another light was flashing, like a torch waving up and down as it signalled frantically. Hell, some hitch-hiker nut – standing in the middle of the highway. She lost speed, getting ready to pick it up again, to drive round the man in the night when she could locate him precisely. Pick up a guy at this hour, after dark – in the middle of nowhere? He must be out of his crazy mind . . .

Carole's eyes narrowed and she lost more speed, travelling at less than thirty as the headlight beams hit the silhouette of an armoured truck parked broadside on across the highway. It must have skidded, turned through ninety degrees, and then stopped like a barricade across the highway. The beams shone on a driver or guard standing on the highway, wearing helmet, leather tunic and boots, which gave him a para-military look. She felt reassured as she stopped and the man walked towards her in the rain, staying inside the headlight beams.

A security truck is reassuring – like a security guard or a highway patrolman. He was still carrying the heavy torch he had flashed as he came closer, rain streaking his visor which hid the upper half of his face. Carole was reassured, but still conscious enough of the loneliness of the place to keep her motor running. She lowered the window as he came up on her side and leaned an elbow on the cartop while he looked down at her. He had, she noticed, glanced into the back of her Dodge.

Rain from his visor dripped on the short, wide-shouldered man's chest as he looked down without speaking. She kept her hand on the brake. 'We hit a flash-flood,' he explained. 'Jo braked too hard and there we were – turned on a dime like you see us. With the motor stopped . . .'

He spoke with an accent she couldn't place and she frowned. What did he expect her to do? She seemed to have heard that these security trucks carried a radio link, so why did he need help? She was still uncertain, not sure why she was uncertain, when the security man moved. He brought down the heavy torch he had been holding as he leaned against the cartop with a crushing blow. It struck her on the temple with such force she died instantly.

Studying her for a moment as she lay slumped in the seat, LeCat opened the door, and hauled her half way out of the car, propping her head against the wheel. Then he stood up and flashed the torch three times rapidly in the direction of the parked truck.

The second armoured truck was moving down the highway at fifty-five miles an hour, keeping inside the regulation limit as its headlights shone on the driving rain. The driver, Ed Taglia, was not wearing his helmet, which lay on the seat beside him, which was against regulations. Beyond the helmet sat Bill Gibson, who always wore his helmet.

'This speed limit chews me up,' Taglia said as he stared at the highway ahead. 'Why build freeways and then make us crawl? Screw those A-rabs . . .'

'There's an energy crisis . . .'

'Screw that. I want to get home . . .'

'With what we have aboard, fifty-five is fast enough,' the older man observed. 'If you turn her over and the truck busts open . . .'

Taglia was tired and didn't reply. When you got old, you got old. You slowed down with women and you slowed down with cars. Gibson was all of fifty years old. Screw Gibson for coming on the trip. On his own Taglia would have pressed his foot down and to hell with it. He squinted through the windscreen where the wipers were just coping with the cloudburst.

'Trouble,' Gibson said quietly. 'Don't stop – just drive slow until we see what it's made of . . .'

'Stop leaning on me – I know the routine . . .'

Like Carole Bannermann had done, he was reducing speed as he came up closer to the flashing torch waving about in the middle of the highway. With one hand he jammed the helmet on his head and snapped the catch under his jaw. Gibson reached for the mike, switched it on. 'Angel One calling Roosevelt . . . Angel One calling Roosevelt . . .' He repeated the call back to base in Morris several times and then gave a grunt of disgust. 'Must be the storm – Goddam thing is full of static . . .'

Taglia was moving slowly now, approaching what lay ahead with extreme caution. Then he whistled. 'One of us . . .' In front his lights picked out a grisly scene. Another armoured truck sat broadside across the highway, its hood tucked inside the rear door of a green Dodge. The front door of the car was open and a blonde-haired girl lay sprawled half in and half out of the car, sprawled on her back with her head propped up against the wheel.

It was a tableau which immediately aroused Gibson's suspicions – the classic set-up for a hi-jack. First, the seeming car accident with the girl lying on the highway, apparently injured. A classic set-up except for two things – the second armoured truck, the sight of which reassured Gibson to some extent, and the appearance of the girl. 'Drive a little closer,' Gibson ordered as he leaned close to the windscreen. The lights played over the sprawled girl and Gibson saw her face. He told Taglia to stop as a helmeted figure appeared from behind the other truck.

'What do you think?' Taglia asked.

'I think it's OK. Look at her face, for God's sake. Keep trying to raise Roosevelt,' he added as he opened his door.

The security man with the helmet and visor waited for him in the rain with one hand behind his back as Gibson jumped down beside him.

Behind the wheel Taglia was getting a lot of static on the radio link. The security man whose face Gibson couldn't see had a shaky voice. 'She was hitting seventy, I swear to God she was. She just came out of nowhere . . .'

'They always do,' Gibson said as rain hit his face. 'And they end up nowhere. She has to be dead, of course?'

'I'm not sure . . .' The security man sounded in a bad way, in a state of shock, Gibson guessed. 'I thought I felt a pulse at the side of her neck. Trouble is we can't get through to the base – the static is hell tonight . . .'

'Same problem.' Gibson glanced over his shoulder to see how Taglia was getting on, then something rammed into his stomach. He looked down and saw the Colt .45 as the helmeted man pulled the trigger. The heavy bullet threw him against the cab as the man stepped back and raised the revolver. Inside the cab Taglia, the mike still in his hand, stared in disbelief at Gibson, at the man holding the Colt. The man whose face they never saw fired twice at Taglia, lowered the gun, fired once more at Gibson. Both men died inside fifteen seconds.

Another man wearing security guard uniform came from behind the truck which appeared to have crashed into the Dodge and ran forward. 'I was monitoring their set – they didn't get through the jamming . . .'

'Stop jabbering, Walgren, and get this thing open . . .'

LeCat found the keys inside Gibson's pocket and used them to open the back of the truck. Rows of steel boxes were stacked along either side of the truck and each box had a legend stencilled across its lid. LeCat started on the difficult task of levering off the padlock from one of the boxes with a wrench. 'Keep an eye on the bloody road,' he told Walgren as he strained at the heavy padlock. Then the hasp cracked. LeCat switched on his torch again, lifted the lid cautiously, stared inside. The box contained two large steel canisters, each protected with foam rubber to minimise travel shake.

LeCat lifted one canister out by its handle, grinning sourly as the American stepped away from the truck. 'Frightened, *mon ami*? This stuff is as safe as milk -- until our associate, Antoine, has treated it. One five-kilogram canister would be more than enough, he said . . .'

He slid the canister carefully inside a reinforced carton Walgren had placed on the floor of the truck, a carton which was the right size because the American had known in advance the exact dimensions of the canister. Like the steel boxes, the canister carried the

20

same warning legend. *GEC, Morris, Illinois. Highly Dangerous – Plutonium.*

On the night when LeCat attacked the armoured truck in Illinois, the plutonium was flown across the United States border aboard a Beechcraft piloted by Walgren, who had served with the US Army Airforce during the war. So while a huge dragnet was spread out south of the border, the plutonium canister was taken across Canada to Vancouver by car. As a precaution, LeCat kept the canister inside a house in Winnipeg for a few days, then, when it was clear that the Royal Canadian Mounted Police had not spread its own dragnet, he completed his journey across the continent.

Antoine had to wait two weeks for the canister's arrival, but for the French physicist it was a busy fortnight. He constructed his laboratory in the large basement of the house from equipment LeCat had arranged to be delivered there. For a man of Antoine's background it was not too difficult; Walgren, using Arab money, had earlier found the engineering workshop by the simple process of consulting the 'for sale' section in trade magazines. There were plenty to choose from with so many small firms going bankrupt through the mounting energy crisis. And the nuclear physicist had just completed his preparations when LeCat delivered the plutonium late one evening at the end of March.

It took Antoine seven months to make the nuclear device.

During that time he never left the house on Dusquesne Street. He worked a twelve-hour day, working alone except for an ex-OAS engineer, Varrier, who produced the required metal casing and parts under Antoine's instruction. There was one other man in the house, forty-four year old André Dupont, the man who had met them with Walgren when they arrived in Montreal. Dupont doubled up as cook and housekeeper. It was a régime most men could never have endured, but Antoine was a scientist who lived only for work and reading the novels of Marcel Proust. And the cuisine was good – Dupont in his youth had once served an apprenticeship in the kitchens of the Ritz in Paris before he was

21

discovered trying to blackmail a wealthy woman of a certain age staying at the hotel.

LeCat had delivered to Antoine no more than five kilograms of reprocessed plutonium – used fuel refined back to its original energy-producing state at the GEC plant at Morris, Illinois. This plutonium had been on its way back to a nuclear power plant when it was hi-jacked by LeCat. Antoine's task was to design a nuclear device and insert the charge inside it. The public, with memories of the vast plant required to make the first atomic bomb, still imagined that something on the same scale was necessary to make a nuclear device. But that vast plant had been required to process the plutonium – and Antoine had in his possession the end-product which came from Morris, Illinois.

Antoine's agreed price for this dangerous assignment was fifty thousand tax-free dollars, together with the passport to enable him to start a new life in the province of Quebec once his work was finished. Being a solitary man, he probably enjoyed the seven months it took him to complete his task.

Following LeCat's detailed instructions, he constructed a device which was the size of a largish suitcase. In fact, when the device was ready, he fitted it inside a specially reinforced suitcase and then plastered the outside with hotel labels from different parts of the world which André Dupont supplied. The case was very heavy – the plutonium charge was packed inside a heavy steel shell to maximise its power on detonation and weighed almost two hundred pounds. But a man of exceptional strength like LeCat could carry it short distances as though he were transporting an ordinary suitcase. When Antoine completed his work in late October, LeCat was informed and flew direct to Vancouver from London on a BOAC flight.

'Show me how it works,' LeCat demanded when they stood in the basement laboratory with the suitcase open on a work-bench.

'This activates the trigger . . .'

'I shall need to attach a time mechanism . . .'

'I would suggest . . .'

LeCat listened only to the first part of the explanation. As an explosives and boobytrap specialist, the Frenchman knew before Antoine explained how he was going to deal with the problem –

he simply wanted confirmation that he would be going about it the right way. After all, the nuclear physicist had produced a bomb large enough to destroy a medium-sized city.

Antoine had carefully not enquired to what purpose the device would be put; he believed he knew – that it would be handed over to either Israel or one of the Arab states for a large sum of money. The Frenchman had managed to persuade himself that he was going into business like any other armaments manufacturer; if he did not supply the device, someone else would. It was the way of the world, and fifty thousand dollars was a sum he would never have seen all his life had he remained in the service of his own government.

'You are leaving tonight,' LeCat said abruptly. 'You will be driven from here after dark.'

Antoine was surprised at the suddenness of his departure, and a worry he had been nursing for some time came to the surface. 'The fifty thousand dollars...'

'I shall bring it here in a few hours. We do not want you travelling back the same way you came – across Canada. I have to drive you into the States by a devious route to Seattle. From there you will catch a train to Chicago and you will enter Canada again from America. Then we are finished with you.'

Antoine, clever enough at his own job, did not fully understand the reasons for this, but the complexity of the plan impressed him. Except for one question. 'I can enter America without a visa?'

'Of course! You forget – you are now a Canadian citizen with your new passport. Canadians can go across the border as often as they like – they only have to show their passport. I will see you this evening...'

LeCat left the house with the suitcase and drove to the ferry point where he crossed to Victoria. He took a cab to the wharf where the trawler *Pêcheur* was anchored and spent some time aboard the vessel. Most of the time he spent chatting to the French captain while the hours passed, and during his stay he enjoyed a typically French meal of endless duration. It was after dark when he arrived back at the house on Dusquesne Street with another suitcase.

'You can count it if you like,' LeCat said, 'but we have a long journey ahead of us...'

23

Fifty thousand dollars. Antoine opened several of the hundred dollar bill packets inside the suitcase and checked the currency with a feeling of embarrassment – and relief – which amused Le-Cat. Then he closed the case, locked it, put the key inside his wallet. 'I suppose I'd better bank it a little at a time?'

'That's right,' LeCat said amiably. 'Keep the rest inside a safety deposit. And now, if you're ready . . .'

LeCat suggested putting the suitcase in the boot of the car, but Antoine said he would prefer to ride in the back with the case beside him. LeCat shrugged, climbed behind the wheel, and they drove off, leaving Dupont and the engineer, Varrier, to remove the laboratory equipment Antoine had dismantled and packed up. They drove east out of the city in the darkness, up into the mountains.

LeCat shot Antoine three times through the chest when they had stopped by the side of a lake. He weighted the body with chains he had concealed under canvas in the boot, put it inside a small boat moored to the water's edge, and rowed the boat far out. Antoine was dropped in the lake, which at this point was over one hundred feet deep, and LeCat returned to the car and the suitcase containing fifty thousand dollars.

LeCat did not take the money for himself: it was part of the arrangement with Ahmed Riad – who had hired him in Algiers – that this amount would be used to pay the French crew of the trawler *Pêcheur*; one-third to be paid now, the balance of two-thirds to be handed over when the trawler had served its ultimate purpose.

When he returned to the *Pêcheur*, André Dupont was waiting for him, and a powerful launch was putting out to sea in the middle of the night with the crates of laboratory equipment aboard. Like the man who had used the equipment, the crates would be dropped overboard in deep water. A perfectionist for detail, LeCat checked to make sure Dupont had not overlooked anything.

His subordinate had not overlooked anything. While LeCat had driven off with the nuclear physicist, Dupont had thoroughly dusted the rooms in the house Antoine had used, wiping away all fingerprints. He had then Hoovered the basement and the other rooms to remove any particles or clothing threads a police scientist might find interesting – the police scientist, if he ever came, would himself use a special Hoover in search of the evidence Dupont had so carefully removed. The Hoover went overboard with the laboratory equipment.

Nor was it likely that the police would visit the building on Dusquesne Street for the next few months, because LeCat had taken a year's lease on the premises. After checking the place personally the following morning, LeCat locked it up and went back to the trawler with Dupont.

The cognac has been delivered.

LeCat cabled the message to an address in Paris from where it was sent by a devious route to Sheikh Gamal Tafak who was at that moment at Jeddah, in Saudi Arabia. For 'cognac' Tafak read the phrase 'nuclear device'. Earlier he had received two other similarly cryptic messages from LeCat, one reporting the 'death' of Antoine in Nantes, the other confirming the seizure of the plutonium canister. The day after he had sent his latest message, LeCat flew back to Europe. It was November, time to bring the Englishman, Winter, into his stage of the operation.

4

Winter.

The background of the English adventurer with whom LeCat had previously worked for two years was totally unknown. He had appeared in the Mediterranean one day, materialising out of nowhere, a man looking for a job which paid well, where the rewards would be tax-free, a job with a hint of excitement to ward off the boredom which was always threatening to assail him. He had first met LeCat in Tangier.

No one ever knew his real name, and no one ever came close enough to call him by his first name, whatever that might have been. In the Mediterranean underworld where this Englishman

25

earned his living he was simply known as Winter.

Over six feet tall, in his early thirties, he was lightly built and walked with a brisk step. There was a coldness in his steady brown eyes his associates found disconcerting, an aloofness of manner which discouraged any attempt at intimacy, but within a few minutes of first meeting him, people formed the impression that this glacial Englishman was clever. His personality had a certain hypnotic effect; an adventurer, he always seemed to know exactly what he was doing.

At that time LeCat was looking for a partner he could trust, which automatically ruled out all his previous associates. And Winter had reduced the problem the Frenchman outlined to its bones in a few words. 'You want to smuggle cigarettes from Tangier to Naples? Forget powerboats and yachts – everyone uses them. Be different – use a trawler.'

'A trawler?' LeCat had been staggered as they drank wine in a bar overlooking Tangier harbour. 'This is crazy – a trawler has no speed. Anyone can catch you.'

'If they are looking for you . . .'

Winter worked it out for LeCat inside ten minutes, the new twist to cigarette smuggling which proved so profitable. The Italian police and security services knew exactly what type of vessel to look for – as LeCat had said, you used a power-boat or a fast yacht. Winter proposed obtaining a 1,000-ton trawler, a vessel where a large consignment of cigarettes, say as much as one hundred tons, could easily be hidden under eight hundred tons of fish.

No attempt would be made to get the consignment ashore in the dark from small boats, the normal technique – instead they would sail into Naples in broad daylight as a bona-fide fishing vessel. Who would suspect a trawler? As everyone knew, for smuggling you needed a fast boat . . .

When Winter raised the question of finance, LeCat admitted he was an agent for the French Syndicate, a group of Marseilles businessmen who were not always over-concerned with legality. In a very short time LeCat purchased a 1,000-ton trawler, *Pêcheur*, with funds provided by the French Syndicate, and the crew of so-called fishermen were largely made up of LeCat's ex-OAS terrorist friends. The smuggling operation proved highly profitable – until the Italian Syndicate began making menacing noises.

'One night these people will meet us off the Naples coast,' LeCat warned. 'They think we are poaching on their preserve. And their method of discouraging opposition is likely to be swift and permanent . . .'

Again Winter worked out a plan while they sat at a table in the bar overlooking Tangier harbour. The idea was submitted to the French Syndicate whose top men were impressed once more by Winter's plan, a little too impressed for LeCat's liking. By this time the Englishman had organised the smuggling out of Italy on the return trips to Tangier, valuable works of art stolen from Italy. These paintings fetched high prices from certain American and Japanese millionaires.

Winter had the foremast removed from the trawler and a platform built over one of the three fish-holds. On this platform an Alouette helicopter could land and take off with ease. LeCat grumbled about the expense, but the French Syndicate chiefs over-ruled him, which did not increase his affection for Winter.

The *Pêcheur* made further trips to Naples without incident. No one was worried about the presence of the helicopter on the main deck after Winter had casually mentioned to an Italian Customs man that this was the new fishing technique – the helicopter was used to seek out fish shoals from the air. Then the rival smuggling organisation, the Italian Syndicate, struck.

The *Pêcheur* was within twenty miles of the Italian coastline when Winter saw through field-glasses a powerful motor vessel approaching at speed. It was full of armed men and made no reply to *Pêcheur*'s wireless signals. Winter, a skilled pilot – no one ever knew where he acquired the skill – took off in the machine with the most resourceful of LeCat's ex-OAS associates, André Dupont. Flying over the Italian Syndicate vessel the first time, Dupont dropped smoke bombs on its deck. On the second run, while Winter held the machine in a steady hover barely fifty feet above the smoke-obscured deck, Dupont dropped two thermite bombs. The vessel was ablaze within seconds; within minutes the armed smugglers had taken to their small boats. When Winter landed again on the *Pêcheur* he had to exert the whole force of his personality to stop LeCat ramming the helpless boatloads of men. The Frenchman was giving the order to the *Pêcheur*'s captain as Winter came back on to the bridge.

'Change course! Head straight for them! Ram them!'

'Maintain previous course,' Winter told the captain quietly. 'The object of the exercise,' he informed LeCat, 'is to let them see it is unprofitable to tangle with us. Those people are Sicilians – kill them and you start a vendetta. They'll have enough trouble getting home as it is.' He started walking off the bridge, then turned at the doorway to speak to the captain. 'If you don't maintain course,' he said pleasantly, 'I'll break your arm . . .'

The incident was significant on two counts. It set a precedent Winter was later to utilise on a far vaster scale, and it pointed up the vast chasm that opened between LeCat and Winter where human life was concerned. To the Englishman, killing was abhorrent, to be avoided at all costs unless absolutely unavoidable. To the Frenchman it was a way of life, something you did with as little compunction as cleaning your teeth.

A few months later, sensing that so much success could not continue for ever, Winter withdrew from the smuggling operation. Settling himself in Tangier, he proceeded to enjoy the profits he had made; staying at one of the two best hotels, he shared his luxury suite with first an English girl, later with a Canadian girl. To both of them he explained at the outset that marriage was an excellent arrangement for other people, and it was while he was relaxing that the first oil crisis burst on the world in 1973.

Winter observed with some cynicism the way the Arab sheikhs ordered Europe about, telling foreign ministers what they could and could not have, and he admired their gall. What he did not admire was world reaction, the scramble for oil at any price, and personally he would have dealt with the new overlords in a very different manner.

His judgement that the smuggling operation could not last for ever was vindicated when LeCat, having extended the operation to the south coast of France, was caught with a consignment in Marseilles. He was arrested, but only after a flying chase through the streets of the city when he managed to break the leg of one gendarme and fracture the skull of another. He was tried, given a long prison sentence and incarcerated in the Santé in Paris. Later, Winter heard the Frenchman had been released in mysterious circumstances. He shrugged his shoulders, never expecting to see LeCat again.

Winter, who knew his Mediterranean, did hear that the *Pêcheur*, which put out to sea before LeCat's arrest, later sailed through the Straits of Gibraltar for an unknown destination. What he did not know was that LeCat, using Arab funds this time, had bought the vessel off the French Syndicate. The trawler made the long Atlantic crossing to the Caribbean, passed through the Panama Canal, and then made its way up the Californian coast to the port of Victoria in Canada. It had been anchored in Canadian waters less than a month when the approach was made to Winter.

For several weeks Winter had known he was being watched. He made a few discreet enquiries, a little money changed hands. He learned that the men who shadowed him were Arabs, and since he had never done anything to arouse Arab hostility, he assumed someone was considering making him a proposition. The name of Ahmed Riad was mentioned.

Riad, he had heard, had some link with Sheikh Gamal Tafak, although they had never been seen together in public. By this time Winter's opinion of the West was simple and brutal: it had lost the will to survive. When the sheikhs first cut off the oil the West depended on for its very existence, the European so-called leaders had panicked, scuttling round like headless chickens in a desperate attempt to scoop up all the oil they could find, paying any price the sheikhs cared to fix at their OAPEC (Organisation of Arab Petrol-Exporting Countries) meetings, receiving the sheikhs in their various capitals like Lords of Creation. Seeing the writing on the wall, Winter took his decision – he must make one great financial killing and get to hell out of it.

One million dollars was the sum he had decided on – even with inflation it should last out for the rest of his life. And in the 1970's that kind of money could come from only one source – from the sheikhs themselves. So when Ahmed Riad met him in November, Winter was more than receptive to his approach – providing Riad

29

would pay him one million dollars. From where Riad sat on the Tangier rooftop, Winter appeared to be anything but receptive after thirty minutes' discussion.

'You are asking me to undertake an operation most men would find impossible, Riad,' Winter said coldly.

Riad, wearing western clothes, was a hard-faced, plump little man with sweat patches under the armpits of his linen suit. He sat facing the sun, an arrangement Winter manoeuvred by the simple process of hauling out a certain chair when the Arab arrived. It was not only the heat which was making him sweat: he was uncomfortable in the presence of the Englishman.

Earlier Winter had compelled him to explain what was needed by refusing to discuss terms until he knew exactly what he had to do. Riad had lied convincingly, assuring Winter he would be in complete command of the operation, that LeCat, who had already been approached, would be his subordinate. The plan was, he said, to bring pressure on Britain and America to stop more arms being sent to Israel. A British ship would be hi-jacked off the West Coast of America, would be taken to an American port, and there the demand that no more arms be sent to Israel would be made. The British crew of the seized ship would be hostages until the demand was met.

It was a shrewd piece of power-play, Winter saw at once. The Americans would hesitate to take a strong line with the lives of another country's men apparently at stake – and if they tried to take a strong line the British government would intervene. 'There is, of course, no question of actually harming the hostages . . .' Riad went on. And this, too, made sense: certain Arab statesmen were trying to drive a wedge in between Britain and America, so the last thing they would wish to do would be to antagonise Britain.

'Your idea – LeCat's idea – of how to hi-jack a ship is, of course, a joke,' Winter pointed out at one stage. He outlined his own idea which had occurred to him while he was listening. The flicker in Riad's eyes told Winter he had just scored a major point. This was the moment when he told the Arab, 'You are asking me to undertake an operation most men would find impossible . . . so the fee must be reasonable,' Winter continued.

'Reasonable?' Riad blinked in the sun. They had said this man was a hard negotiator.

'From my point of view,' Winter said coldly. 'Otherwise it is not worth the risk. The fee for my controlling this operation will be one million dollars.'

'That is impossible!' Riad half-rose out of his chair.

'Are you going?' Winter enquired bleakly.

'It is quite impossible,' Riad repeated, sinking back slowly into his chair. 'We could not even discuss a sum like that . . .'

'I agree. I'm not prepared to discuss it myself. Accept it – or forget the whole idea.'

'You insult me . . .' Riad was perched at the edge of his chair as though on the verge of imminent departure. 'You are like all Westerners used to be – before they discovered they would die without oil, our oil . . .'

'It's not your oil. Your ancestors just happened to pitch their tents in the right place. We had to find and dig it out for you.' Winter poured some more black coffee and then left the pot in the middle of the table. 'If you want more coffee, there's some in the pot . . .'

They must need me badly he was thinking. Arab pride had lately become overweening; had, in fact, reached the stage where only Arab pride existed as far as the sheikhs were concerned. A dangerous combination – supreme economic power allied with fierce pride. Couldn't the West see this?

'We are prepared to pay you a fortune for your cooperation,' Riad said stiffly. 'We are prepared to pay you the sum of six hundred thousand dollars. Not one cent more.'

'If you think my figure of one million is negotiable, forget it.' Winter's manner was icy and Riad, who had been staring into the unblinking brown eyes, looked away. To Riad, a shrewd man, it was beginning to get through: Winter meant what he said.

'You cannot fix the figure just like that,' the Arab said with a show of spirit. 'We are employing you! It is up to us to fix the fee . . .'

'That's right.'

'I beg your pardon?'

'It's up to you to decide what you can afford.' The Englishman paused as the Arab's eyes flickered at the implication that he might be short of funds. 'On the other hand, I don't believe you. To your masters one million is something they could lose on the way to the bank and not bother to go back for . . .'

'It is a fortune . .'

'To you, Riad . . .'

'You insult me again . . .'

'Then get to hell off this rooftop and leave me alone,' Winter said viciously. 'I'm beginning to wonder whether I want to get mixed up in this thing – the risks are enormous.'

The viciousness of the outburst startled Riad. He had the feeling that Winter himself was about to leave the rooftop, and Riad was horribly conscious of Gamal Tafak's last words to him.

'We need that Englishman, Ahmed – an Englishman can operate in the West without suspicion. Our own spies watching oil movements are shadowed everywhere by Western security services. And it is a British ship which must be involved. You must persuade him – if you have to negotiate for a week and in the end offer him the full amount . . .'

A week? They had been sitting on this rooftop for little more than half an hour and already Riad was trembling inwardly with fury and fear – fury at the way he was being treated, fear at the thought he might lose the Englishman.

'I can go up to seven hundred thousand,' he said.

'You can indeed . . .' Winter stubbed out his cigarette in the saucer. 'And you can catch the first plane back to Jeddah and tell them you have failed.'

'I control this negotiation . . .'

Winter glanced at him without speaking – to show how absurd he thought the idea was.

'I must consult a certain committee . . .'

Winter glanced at his watch, took out his wallet and put money on the table to pay for the coffee.

'You cannot expect this to be decided in an hour . . .'

Winter stood up, buttoned his jacket.

'A million. That was the top figure . . .'

The negotiation had lasted exactly thirty-five minutes.

*   *   *

Arrangements were concluded about payment into a Beirut bank; Winter was quite certain that no bank in the western world would be safe, once this operation was concluded. He was provided with one hundred thousand dollars for immediate expenses, given a Paris number where he could contact LeCat. He flew to Paris the next day.

On November 3 he spent an acrimonious morning with the ex-OAS terrorist in a Left Bank flat, tearing up all LeCat's plans and substituting his own. LeCat, a clever and resourceful man when working to a plan put before him, was not capable of originating the plan itself. 'You are playing at pirates,' Winter told him roughly when the Frenchman pushed his own plan for seizing a British cargo ship – plenty of them called at Victoria in Canada and sailed away again. 'This idea of yours of colliding with a vessel at sea is pure moonshine. In any case, the vessel we hi-jack must be an oil tanker. It has a compact crew, about thirty men, ample fuel supplies aboard, but above all it provides a platform we can land the helicopter on while the tanker is at sea . . .'

Winter checked over the terrorist team LeCat had assembled, which included a number of men he had known during the *Pêcheur*'s smuggling operation days. He didn't like some of them, vicious thugs who would have done better to die in Algeria, but it was too late to start switching things around: zero hour for the hi-jack was January. 'Just make sure you keep them under control,' he told the Frenchman. 'No harm must come to the hostages.'

'Riad has already told me that,' the Frenchman replied with his eyes half-closed.

Winter left Paris the following day and flew to London. First he checked the transfer of twenty-five thousand dollars from a Paris bank to a City bank which he had arranged before leaving Paris. The money had arrived, he collected a cheque book, and armed with this he took a taxi to Mount Street where the Mayfair estate agents live. He found the property he was looking for in an agent's window, a glossy photograph advertised as 'Fine Old Manor House, East Anglia. Six Months' Lease'. After a brief discussion with the agent, he hired a car and drove to East Anglia where he put up for the night at King's Lynn.

Next day the local sub-agent showed him over the property. As he had hoped, it was exactly what he wanted. The house itself, Cosgrove Manor, was surrounded with parkland, and the twenty acres of isolated grounds concealed it completely from the road. He concluded the deal at once, explaining that his family would be coming over from Australia in the next few weeks. The six months' rent he paid in advance with a cheque drawn on the London bank in the name of George Bingham.

The following morning he drove back to London, reserved a room at Brown's Hotel in Albemarle Street, again in the name of George Bingham, and then took a cab to the world-famous shipping organisation, Lloyd's of London. Wearing a tweed suit and rimless glasses, he posed as a writer researching a book on the oil crisis.

After making certain enquiries about shipping movements, he consulted the *Shipping Register*, a remarkable publication produced daily which records the present positions of all vessels at sea. It took him several hours to check on ships moving up and down the West Coast of America, but when he left the building he was fairly sure he had found his target ship. The following day he flew by Polar Route direct to Los Angeles, and there he caught another plane on to San Francisco.

Joseph Walgren, the fifty-year old ex-accountant who had helped LeCat with the hi-jack of the armoured truck in Illinois eight months before, an incident Winter knew nothing about, was waiting for him. In response to a cable from LeCat, the American met Winter off the plane at the International airport. There was an immediate disagreement over the modest-priced hotel Walgren suggested for the Englishman.

'It's too cheap,' Winter said firmly as the American drove him into San Francisco. 'If you stay at a very expensive place the police in any country assume you are respectable. I'll take a room at the Huntingdon on California Street . . .'

For three days he ran Walgren, an energetic character, into the ground. Constantly on the move, Winter drove round the city familiarising himself with its layout, driving as far out as Oleum, the oil terminal, scouring Marin County north of the city and then, when Walgren thought he had finished, the Englishman hired a launch and explored the coastline of the Bay. Before he left the city – and a somewhat limp Walgren – Winter gave him certain instructions which included involving the American in a brief trip to Mexico. He also provided him with a large sum of money. On the fourth day Winter left for Canada.

He paid a brief visit to the trawler *Pêcheur*, still moored at a dock in the port of Victoria. Brief as it was, he took the time to make sure the Canadian Port Authority were happy about the vessel's continued presence, and he found that LeCat had handled the problem satisfactorily. Using the Frenchman as an agent, Arab money had not only purchased the *Pêcheur* from the French Syndicate of Marseilles businessmen – it had also formed the World Council of Marine Biological Research with headquarters on the rue St Honoré in Paris, a body nominally headed by a Frenchman, Bernard Oswald.

Marine research was the latest scientific fad, the progressive thing to engage in, so the Canadian authorities gave little thought to the arrival of the trawler and its continued stay in their port. And, as he had once assured an Italian Customs official in Naples about the Alouette helicopter on the *Pêcheur*'s deck – '. . . a new technique. We use it to spot fish shoals from the air . . .' – so he now set about reassuring a Canadian official.

'We shall have a Sikorsky helicopter arriving here before we leave for the Galapagos . . . Certain places we want to explore we can only reach by chopper . . .'

The Canadian port official found George Bingham, the British marine biologist, an amiable fellow, and now he understood fully why the *Pêcheur* was still in harbour – she was waiting for the arrival of the helicopter.

While in San Francisco Winter had found time to arrange with Walgren for the purchase and delivery of the Sikorsky, which would be flown to Canada by a pilot friend of Walgren – the man who can fly a Beechcraft cannot necessarily pilot a helicopter. Twenty-four hours after his arrival in Canada Winter was on his way to Alaska.

He spent three weeks in Anchorage, Alaska's largest city, which lies at the head of the Cook Inlet, the site of the state's first oil discovery. Today, people think of the great North Slope field when they think of Alaskan oil, but when Winter was in Anchorage the only oil which flowed from Alaska to California, two thousand miles south, came from Cook Inlet. A shuttle service of tankers – one of them British – was moving backwards and forwards, carrying the desperately needed oil to San Francisco.

During his long journey Winter had seen many signs of the way in which the fifty per cent oil cut controlled by Sheikh Gamal Tafak was crippling the West. Planes nearly always arrived late, due to fuel shortages; the street lights in California were turned off at ten o'clock at night; power blackouts were frequent, plunging whole cities into darkness without warning. And still, so far as Winter could see, there was no effective resistance to the sheikhs' blackmail. It was early December when he returned to Europe.

'Have there been any whispers about the operation?' was his first question to LeCat when he arrived in Paris.

'None so far,' LeCat replied, 'but I have set up listening posts in different countries . . .'

They talked in French, one of the four languages Winter was fluent in, and Winter's question was a key question. When you organise an operation on a large scale, sooner or later there are liable to be rumours of something going on. It was, in a way, a race against time – to get the operation moving before a hint of it reached the outside world. From Winter's point of view, the listening posts would provide a warning if rumours began to spread, but LeCat regarded them in a very different light. If someone began making enquiries and he heard about it, then drastic action might have to be taken. After all, it would probably only mean killing whoever looked like getting in the way.

5

Larry Sullivan, thirty-two years old, was in the same age range as Winter, and the similarity between the two men did not end there. Sullivan also was a lone wolf, which was one reason why his career in naval intelligence was brought to a rather abrupt conclusion; Sullivan, with the rank of lieutenant, did not suffer fools gladly – even when they held the rank of admiral. When it was indicated to him indirectly – he hated people who indicated things indirectly – that his route up the promotion ladder was blocked permanently unless he became more flexible, he indicated his own reaction quite directly. 'You can stuff the job,' he told his superior.

With his background and experience he had no trouble finding a job as an investigator with Lloyd's of London. Unlike the peace-time Navy, this unique organisation is anything but hide-bound in its methods; it has, in fact, a reputation for free-wheeling, for observing tradition in the face it presents to the public, while behind the scenes it breaks every rule in the book if that is the only way to get results. Only the British could have invented such an institution which, deservedly, has a world-wide reputation for integrity among all who deal with it. And Sullivan fitted in well.

A lean-faced, smiling man, lightly built and five feet nine tall, he had a thatch of dark hair which women found attractive; so much so he had postponed any idea of marriage yearly. His job was as unique as the organisation he worked for. Investigating suspect insurance claims which might amount to twenty million pounds for a single vessel, he carried no authority in the outside world. He lived by his wits.

He could lean on no one, give orders to no one, but this inhi-bition had its advantages. He was not too restricted in the methods he used – or persuaded others to use. He lived by his contacts and friendships, by getting to know people far outside the range of the shipping world. It was important to him to know police officials all over the globe, that he could phone certain Interpol officers and call them by their first names, that he attended Interpol con-ferences where he never stopped talking and listening. He was also one of the most persistent people who walked the face of the earth. 'Do it, get him off our backs', was a phrase often used behind his own back. Loaned by Lloyd's to their client, Harper Tankships, he started his enquiries about the whisper in January.

One January evening – his diary shows it was Sunday January 5 – Sullivan was in Bordeaux, checking the most efficient grapevine in the shipping world, the waterfront bars where seamen gather and gossip. His style of dress was hardly elegant: he wore a none-too-clean sweater and stained trousers under a shabby overcoat.

Not that this choice of clothing fooled the men he talked to, but it helped them to feel less embarrassed at being seen talking to him.

The Café Bleu was the normal, sleazy waterfront drink shop which is reproduced time and again all over the world; layers of blue smoke drifting at different levels like strato-cirrus at thirty thousand feet, lantern lights blurred by smoke, an unsavoury stench compounded of alcohol and smoke and human sweat.

It always amazed Sullivan that men cooped up together in ships for weeks should, the moment they came ashore, rush to coop themselves up again in an atmosphere where oxygen was the least of the chemical elements present. 'Cognac,' he told the barman, Henri, 'and for a little information I could lose a little money . . .'

'Yes?' Henri, a low-browed, fat man in a white jacket which was surprisingly clean, pushed the cognac towards him. 'For a long time we do not see you, M. Sullivan . . .'

'Harper Tankships – British outfit. They could be . . . looking forward to a little trouble, the whisper tells me.'

'This whisper I do not know . . .' Henri leaned forward to polish the counter close to Sullivan's elbow and dropped his voice. 'You ask Georges – with the beret at the far end of the bar . . .'

'You ask him.'

Henri shrugged, finished his polishing, took the cloth down to the far end of the crowded bar where a small man wearing a black beret sat. He talked with him briefly and then came back, shrugging. 'Georges does not know your whisper either . . .'

'Then why is he leaving so suddenly?'

'Maybe his ship sails, maybe his woman waits. Who knows about other men's problems?'

Henri waited until Sullivan had left the bar, then he used the phone. He couldn't be sure, but he knew a man who occasionally paid to hear who was snooping round the waterfront . . .

Sullivan watched Henri making the call from the almost-closed door of the lavatory. He left the bar by the second exit. It probably meant nothing, but outside he walked close to the shutdown shop-fronts, so he was walking as far away as possible from the harbour edge on the other side of the street. On a foggy evening it really is too easy to ram a knife into a man's back – when there

38

is a ten-foot drop into fog-concealed, scummy water so conveniently at hand to dispose of the body. He visited nine more bars that night.

It went on, day after day as Sullivan worked his way north up the west Atlantic coast, driving from port to port, prowling the bars and the brothels night after night, asking the same questions, getting the same negative answers. But not always. There were several occasions when seamen said they might know something, said it in low tones as they glanced carefully round.

A meeting would be arranged, usually in daylight on the following morning, and for a quite different rendezvous. This suggestion was quite routine for Sullivan – informants did not like to tell him things which other ears might register. What was not routine was the outcome. No one ever kept the appointment.

Bordeaux ... La Rochelle ... Brest ... Le Havre ... Ostend ... Antwerp.

They followed his progress all the way up the coast, tracked it on a map of western Europe torn from a school atlas which they had pinned to the wall of the Left Bank apartment in Paris. A phone call came in. Bordeaux. 'An Anglais ... Sullivan. Asking about Harper Tankships ...'

The forty-four year old André Dupont, the man who had helped Winter disable the Italian Syndicate motor-cruiser by throwing a thermite bomb, relayed the message to the older man who was short and wide-shouldered, whose cruel, moustached face was only a shadow in the dimly lit room – Paris was enduring yet another voltage reduction. LeCat took the phone.

'Next time, do not mention the firm's name – you do not wish to end up in an alley with a red half-moon where your throat should be? Follow him ...'

La Rochelle ... Brest ... Le Havre ...

The names were circled on the atlas map and the dates of Sullivan's visits to each port were carefully recorded. 'He will go home from Belgium,' LeCat predicted. 'He will give up and catch the Ostend ferry. He has found out nothing.'

'Who is this man, Sullivan?'

'An agent from Lloyd's of London. He has heard a whisper, no more. Winter said it was inevitable. Why do you think we are paying out all this money to keep loose mouths shut? I would handle it more cheaply – with a knife. But you know Winter . . .'

Ostend . . . Antwerp . . .

'He is not going home,' André said. 'For a man who has had no answers to his questions he is very persistent. What if he goes to Hamburg?'

Hamburg . . .

On January 9 Sullivan arrived in Ostend. On January 9 Ross arrived in Hamburg.

Mr Arnold Ross, managing director of Ross Tankers Ltd, registered in Bermuda, was an impressive figure. Over six feet tall, thin, bowler-hatted, he was faultlessly dressed in a dark business suit which looked as though it had just been collected from Savile Row. His black shoes positively glowed, his gold cuff links showed discreetly as he shot his cuffs after taking off an overcoat which could not have cost less than three hundred guineas. Certainly he impressed Mr Paul Hahnemann, construction director of the Hamburg shipbuilding firm of Wilhelm Voss.

'A fifty thousand ton tanker we would be interested to build in our yard,' he assured Mr Ross.

'Cost, time of delivery – the key factors as usual,' Ross replied, staring out of a large picture window overlooking the yard. 'You do understand that this enquiry is very tentative; also that it is quite secret at this stage?'

'Of course, Mr Ross. We shall use our discretion. You can give us some details of the vessel you have in mind?'

'Something very like a ship you built for Harper Tankships – the *Chieftain* . . .'

Everyone at Wilhelm Voss was impressed by Arnold Ross, the most typical of Englishmen when he spoke in his clipped voice, when he absent-mindedly pulled at his neat, dark moustache. The *Chieftain*, it appeared, was very similar indeed to the ship Ross had in mind. Blueprints of the tanker were produced, spread out on a drawing table, and Ross spent a lot of time studying them, asking questions about *Chieftain*'s design and structure.

Hahnemann, a giant of a man who started work at seven each

morning and was lucky to drive home to Altona by nine in the evening, understood the reason for secrecy. Ross had implied the reason. 'For ten years we have built in Japan. The chairman thinks we should continue this policy. I want a complete scheme worked out before I tell him what I have in mind . . .'

Ross thawed a little over lunch, talked about his home in Yorkshire, about the place he kept in Belgravia for weekdays, his love of shooting. It all fitted in with Hahnemann's conception of how a certain sort of wealthy Englishman lived.

During the afternoon a call came through from London, from the headquarters of Ross Tankers. Again discretion was preserved: the caller merely gave her name as Miss Sharpe. Hahnemann handed the receiver to Ross who was bent over yet another blueprint of the *Chieftain*. Ross took the phone, listened, said yes and no several times, then goodbye. 'Always a crisis while I'm away,' he remarked, and went back to his blueprint.

He left the yard at six in the evening to go back to the Hotel Atlantic, the most expensive hostelry in Hamburg. 'I want to think about what you have told me alone,' he told Hahnemann when the director suggested a night on the town. 'Make a few notes. I'm not a great night-clubber . . .' It all fitted in with the image Hahnemann was filing away of a rather austere Englishman who travelled the world but was only really at home on his Yorkshire estate.

'And no estimates yet,' Ross repeated as they shook hands. 'I don't want any communication from you until I see my way ahead. When I'm ready, I'll need estimates fast . . .'

'You give us the time limit.' Hahnemann grinned. 'Lots of night work and strong black coffee. Incidentally, we did build a twin ship to the *Chieftain* for Harper, a tanker called the *Challenger* . . .'

'You may hear from me – inside two or three months.' Ross was stepping into his waiting car. He did not wave or look back, and the last view Hahnemann had of the elegant Englishman was of the back of his head as the car swept away through the gates.

Paul Hahnemann was not a gullible man. He had been intrigued when Ross first phoned him from London, warning him that on no account must Hahnemann try and get in touch with him: the matter was highly confidential. It was not too unusual, the discreet enquiry, but Hahnemann was a careful man. He checked just before Ross's arrival at his office.

He put in a call to Ross Tankers in London and asked to speak to Mr Arnold Ross. Miss Sharpe, Ross's personal assistant, took the call. Mr Ross was away abroad, she explained. Could she help? Who was speaking? Hahnemann said no, the call was personal, and put down the phone. Of course Mr Ross was abroad – he was in Hamburg, just leaving the Hotel Atlantic on his way to the Wilhelm Voss shipyard.

'Money for old rope...'

Judy Brown replaced the phone after making the Hamburg call and studied her nail varnish critically. She would have to make another application before she went out with Des this evening. She looked round the Maida Vale flat critically; what a dull creep this man Ross was; everything ordinary, dull. The furniture, the decoration. Soulless. She even wondered whether it was one of those flats you could hire by the week for fun with the girl friend while the wife was away. And who the hell was Miss Sharpe?

The job was a bit odd, but Judy Brown had her own ideas about that. As a temporary secretary she was used to funny jobs, funny people, and this was definitely one of the funnier ones. She looked again at the typed sheet of questions she had relayed over the phone, questions Ross had dictated to her. Something to do with a ship called the *Mimosa* proceeding from Latakia and bound for Milford Haven, wherever that might be.

She'd had to ask the questions when she phoned Hamburg, wait for Ross to answer, then ask the next question. And call herself Miss Sharpe. Daft. A kid could have done it. But the pay was good.

Ross had hired her from an agency and then promised her an extra twenty pounds if she did exactly as he asked. The money would arrive by post tomorrow, Friday, if she did the job properly.

'You come here each day at 9.30 and leave at 4.30 for the whole week,' Ross had told her. 'There may be some phone calls – make a note of them and leave it on the table. If my wife comes she may have some dictation for you.'

'Nothing else?' Judy had asked.

Ross, tall and thin, stooped and wearing thick pebble spectacles, had hesitated. 'Don't let my wife know about my trip to Hamburg. She doesn't know I'll be there.' He had snickered. 'Business. You know?'

Judy knew. More like having it off with a foreign bit. But she still didn't see how the Hamburg call fitted in. That was on Thursday. She came each day and there were no phone calls, no sign of Mrs Ross. On Friday, the day after the Hamburg call, Ross phoned her. 'That extra money – look inside Burke's Peerage . . .' He broke the connection before she could say anything, rude bugger. She found the big red book, opened it, and tucked inside the front cover was a brand new twenty-pound note.

Evening came and still no phone calls, no Mrs Ross, thank God. A right old bag, Judy guessed. She collected her wages from the agency and bought a new shade of nail varnish. Money for old rope.

Antwerp . . . Rotterdam . . . Bremen . . . Hamburg.

'He has reached Hamburg,' André Dupont said as he replaced the phone in the Left Bank flat in Paris. 'He is staying at the Hotel Berlin. I have the number, the address. He has crossed half western Europe – all the way from the Spanish border to the Baltic, almost . . .'

'You are theatrical,' LeCat said. 'The map speaks for itself. He is in Hamburg. So, now you make another phone call to Gaston whom I sent ahead – just in case. Sullivan must be killed.'

'Winter won't like that . . .'

André stopped speaking as the other man stared up at him with his lips pressed together. André felt frightened, cursed himself for opening his mouth. It was not even comfortable staying in the same room with this man and they had been together for almost a week, tracking Sullivan's progress.

'Sullivan must be killed,' the other man repeated. 'He is in Hamburg. And – like so many things – Winter will know nothing about it. The killing will be an accident, of course. A seamen's brawl in a bar – the Anglais likes to visit bars. Arrange it . . .'

LeCat spoke as though he were arranging for the weekend's meat to be delivered. Which in a way he was. It was Saturday evening.

43

It was Saturday evening January 11. At the Hotel Berlin Sullivan felt better after a bath. He felt better still after a drink in the bar which contained not a single seaman, very little smoke, and certainly no stench of human sweat that he could detect. For the first time in a week he felt relaxed. He felt even better after eating in the circular dining-room where the service was excellent and the food superb. And the tender fillet steak was from north Germany. It melted in his mouth while he listened to the two businessmen at an adjoining table talking in German about the oil crisis.

'These swines of Arabs . . . twisting the screw again . . .'

'No, turning off the tap again. It's that bastard, Tafak. I think they're going to have another crack at Israel . . .'

After dinner he felt so refreshed that he decided to get on with it, to continue the search which so far had yielded him nothing positive. But was that correct? Because he had learned something – that somewhere there was something to learn. You cannot go all the way up the Atlantic coast from Bordeaux to Le Havre, and then go on through Belgium and Holland into Germany, offering to pay for information – not without someone trying to con you, offering you some imaginary piece of information in the hope that you'll pay out good money. You can't do it – but Sullivan had just done this.

As he finished his coffee he went over the past week in his mind. No one had tried to con him, no one had even tried to take advantage of his offer and – more significant still – not one person had asked him the kind of money he was offering. To Sullivan, who knew his seamen, there was only one explanation. Fear.

Because of the new fifty per cent cut in oil supplies, which was strangling Europe, Sullivan had to wait an hour before a cab arrived at the Hotel Berlin to take him to the Reeperbahn. He arrived in the night club district soon after midnight. On his last visit he had seen the neon glow from a long way off, but now the glow had gone – the energy crisis had seen to that.

The Reeperbahn is the Soho of Hamburg; night clubs line both sides of the street, their windows filled with photographs of provocative girls. The seamen's haunts are down the narrow side streets, little more than darkened alleys now the street lights had been switched off. Sullivan paused outside the *New Yorker*, took a deep breath. Here we go again: smoke, sweat, the lot.

The smoke inside the tiny bar off the Reeperbahn was thick at midnight, so thick the seamen customers were only silhouettes. Tobacco from a dozen nations polluted the air, the background was a babble of foreign tongues. Max Dorf, the barman, had never heard of Harper Tankships. 'I don't hear so much these days, Mr Sullivan,' he explained. 'People don't talk so much any more . . .'

'Not for five hundred dollars?'

'That's a lot of money, Mr Sullivan. You wouldn't be carrying it on you?'

'Do I look stupid?'

The burly seaman with the French beret sitting on the stool next to Sullivan lurched sideways, speaking German with a thick foreign accent. 'You look as stupid as they come, brother – and you just tipped my drink over . . .' He had almost knocked Sullivan from his stool but the Englishman regained his balance, stepped back, bumping into people as he cleared a space. 'So, you buy me another one,' the seaman went on as he faced Sullivan, 'before I smash your teeth down your throat . . .'

A short, thick-necked man, he was swaying on his short, thick legs as he shouted the words and behind Sullivan the babble of voices stopped. Without looking round he knew everyone was looking at him, sensing trouble. A little entertainment was about to be provided: someone was going to get hurt.

'You want a fight?' the seaman demanded.

'Don't make a meal of it, Frenchie,' Sullivan said sharply.

The Frenchman's hand blurred and then he was holding a short, wide-bladed knife. People moved back, getting out of the way. The drunken seaman stopped swaying, sobered up in seconds, then lunged forward. Someone grunted, anticipating the penetration of the knife. There was a blur of movement, this time Sullivan's movement. Kicking the seaman's right kneecap, he jumped to one side, grabbed the Frenchman's wrist, twisted it, smashed it down on the edge of the wooden counter. The knife fell from the broken fingers and the seaman moaned.

Normally a placid man, Sullivan went berserk. The seaman was still plucking feebly at the bartop with his maimed fingers when Sullivan kicked his legs from under him, waited until he collapsed on the floor, then grabbed him by the ankles and hauled him round the end of the bar. 'Get out of the bloody way!' he yelled. They got out of his way as he swept the prone, struggling body along the floor. He opened the half-closed door at the end of the bar with a heave of his back and hauled the seaman inside Max Dorf's office.

The office was empty, furnished with filing cabinet, chairs, a table covered with a mess of papers. Sullivan dropped the assassin's ankles, then heaved the Frenchman up on the table and grabbed a handful of long hair. Max Dorf came inside the office and then stopped as Sullivan shouted at him. 'Get the police – or get out . . .' Dorf disappeared, pulling the door shut behind him. Sullivan twisted the Frenchman's hair.

'I want information,' he said grimly, 'and you're going to provide it – unless you want me to break the fingers of your other hand.'

'I know nothing . . .'

'Then you're not going to be using either hand for six months.' Sullivan jerked and half the hair nearly left the scalp. 'Now you bloody listen to me. I've been coming up the Atlantic coast for a week, asking questions, as well you know. You're giving me the answers . . .'

'I know nothing . . .'

The seaman screamed as Sullivan jerked a handful of hair loose, then grabbed another handful. 'Who is after one of Harper's tankers? Who is behind this business? Someone big – the money they must be spending to stop people talking doesn't grow on trees. Whose money is it?'

'Arab money . . .' The seaman's face had turned a grey pallor, he was gasping for breath. 'That's what I heard,' he croaked. 'Barrels of money for this operation . . .'

'What operation? Which tanker?'

'Don't know . . .' The seaman was close to collapse. 'So help me, God, I don't know. Some Englishman, Winter, is running the thing . . .'

'Who is Winter?'

'Don't know. Never met him. Just a name . . .' A cunning look came into his eyes. He was getting his nerve back. 'Can I have a drink?'

'Certainly . . .' Sullivan reached across to a side shelf and grasped a half-full bottle of wine by the neck. Smashing it on the edge of the table he thrust the jagged end towards the seaman who stared at it in horror. 'You're not telling me everything,' Sullivan informed the Frenchman in a strangely quiet voice. 'If you don't want me to use this you'll keep on talking. You tried to kill me . . .'

'I was drunk . . .'

'Sober as a hanging judge,' Sullivan said softly, 'the way you came at me with that knife. Who hired you to put me to sleep permanently?' He shoved the jagged bottle forward. The seaman raised his left hand, the undamaged hand, to ward off the bottle.

'For God's sake . . . I was phoned from Paris – by a man called Dupont. I do jobs for him, this and that . . .' The Frenchman tried to gesture with his right hand and groaned. 'My hand is broken,' he whimpered.

'They would have carried me out of here on a stretcher on my way to the morgue. Who is controlling this operation?'

'Paris . . . so I heard.' The Frenchman's face twisted with pain as he stared piteously at his limp fingers. 'I don't know who. Just Paris . . .' He fainted, keeling over heavily until he lay sideways on the table, his head cushioned on a pile of papers.

On the morning of Sunday, January 12, Sullivan phoned the home number of Pierre Voisin of Interpol. The French policeman, who had a private income and was therefore quite incorruptible financially as well as by inclination, lived in the rue de Bac; as it happened only a stone's throw from the flat where LeCat and Dupont had tracked Sullivan's progress through the ports of France.

'How are you, my friend?' Voisin enquired.

'I nearly got killed last night.'

A pause, then, 'You ask too many leading questions.'

Sullivan gripped the receiver a little tighter. With Voisin you could never be sure; sometimes he hinted at things. 'And what does that mean?' he asked.

'It is your profession – to go round asking questions, sometimes, dangerous questions. You are all right?'

'Yes, I'm all right.' Sullivan was still unsure. 'Sorry to bother you at home, but this is urgent – to me. Have you ever heard of an Englishman called Winter? Like the season . . .'

'No, never.' This time there was no pause. 'But I could check for you – this morning, as a matter of fact. We have a bit of a flap on, as your countrymen say, so I have to go into the office. The records people will be there too.' Voisin chuckled. 'It is an outrage, is it not – Frenchmen working at the weekend? These are difficult days, with our Arab friends, and so forth . . .'

Sullivan gave him the number of the Hotel Berlin and put down the receiver with a frown. Really, you could never tell whether or not Voisin was hinting at something. That reference to 'our Arab friends'. The hired French assassin had referred to 'Arab money . . .'

It was less than a straw in the wind, but a faint theme was beginning to recur – the Arabs . . . Paris. He felt relieved that his oldest friend, François Messmer of French counter-intelligence, would be arriving in Hamburg tomorrow. And that was a strange incident. He had called Messmer at his Paris flat before phoning Voisin, and to his surprise Messmer had cut the call short, saying only that he would be at the Hotel Berlin on Monday morning. It was after the mention of the name Winter. So Messmer, at least, had heard something about him. Voisin phoned back just before lunchtime.

'We have no record on the name of the English criminal you mentioned . . .' Voisin sounded crisper, more businesslike, as though he had adopted his official manner. 'Nothing official at all,' he added.

'Anything unofficial?'

'I mentioned it to one or two non-political friends . . .' His voice had a cynical tinge now. He was referring to men he knew who were without political ambition and who could, therefore, be relied on to tell the truth. 'No one has ever heard of this man. I am sorry.'

'Thanks for calling back . . .'

'Be careful, Larry. You are always going about asking these questions some people do not wish you to ask. *Au revoir!*'

Later in the afternoon of Sunday, January 12, while Sullivan was waiting in Hamburg for the arrival of François Messmer, while Winter had arrived at Cosgrove Manor in East Anglia, Sheikh Gamal Tafak was holding a secret meeting at the edge of the Syrian desert, two thousand miles away from Hamburg.

'I can now reveal the plan,' he said quietly, 'the plan to deliver a terrible shock to the western nations . . .'

Tafak paused as he looked down the long trestle table inside the tent. Five serious-faced men in Arab dress sat round the table, the five leaders of the most extremist terrorist groups in the Middle East. Outside the wind blew off Mount Hermon, shivering the canvas like the flap-flap of a vulture's wings.

They did not look so dangerous, these five men. Three of them had a studious air and wore glasses; they could have been professors planning the curriculum for some new university. But all the men inside the tent – including Gamal Tafak – were on a secret Israeli list of men who must be eliminated before there could be any hope of lasting peace in the Middle East.

'Before our armies engage Israel in the final war,' Tafak continued, 'we must first immobilise the West so no fresh arms can be sent to Israel as they were in 1973. To do that we need an excuse to cut off all oil from the West – all oil,' he repeated. 'That will immobilise them. But I foresee difficulty in persuading all Arab states to agree, so we must create the atmosphere in which they will have to agree. We must make the western countries scream at us, call us again Golden Apes. Then all Arab states will agree to cut off the oil.'

'But how are you going to do this?' the serious-faced man on Tafak's right enquired.

'By creating a terrible incident. If that does not make everyone fall into line – if, say, Kuwait, will not cooperate, then the sabotage teams you have organised will fly there and blow up the oil wells when I give the order . . .'

Gamal Tafak was, in his own way, a sincere man. He could not stand the thought that in Jerusalem Arab holy places were in the grip of the detested Israelis, but he was also ruthless, a man who was prepared to bring down the world if necessary to achieve his ends. He did not like these five men he was meeting. He even fore-

49

saw the day when they would have to be eliminated if the new rulers in Saudi Arabia and Egypt were to keep their power. This is always the dilemma of the extremist; he looks over his shoulder at men even more extremist than himself. Terror is an escalating movement.

'And how,' the same serious-faced man enquired, 'are you going to outrage the West when this British tanker has been seized. You have given us no details – we do not even know where the incident will take place.'

'I will give you all the details when we next meet,' Tafak replied. 'But I will tell you now that it concerns a very large bomb which will destroy a city.' Tafak indulged in his liking for a theatrical departure. He stood up. 'I am talking about San Francisco.'

6

'When Sheikh Gamal Tafak came to Paris one year ago he demanded the release of a criminal, Jules LeCat, from the Santé prison. I think it all began then, Larry . . .'

François Messmer, a member of the Direction de la Surveillance du Territoire – French counter-intelligence – stopped at the edge of the lake to light another Gauloise. The Aussen-Alster in Hamburg is the larger of two lakes in the centre of the city and here, in green parkland, you can talk without risk of being overheard.

On Monday January 13 it was cold in Hamburg. The savage winter, worse even than in the previous year – even nature seemed to be on the side of the sheikhs – had frozen the river Elbe and the lake they walked beside was a sheet of ice. Both men huddled in heavy overcoats and the wind from the north froze their faces.

'Surely that was going beyond the limit – even for a sheikh,' Sullivan suggested. 'We have to stand up somewhere . . .'

'You think so?' Messmer, a small, compact man in his fifties with a face like a monkey's, smiled cynically. 'I think this is a lesson the British still have to learn – that there is no limit where these golden apes are concerned. They have western civilisation by the throat and they intend to squeeze our throat until we are gasping for air – for oil. When total power is available the extremists move in for the kill – they have literally killed the King of Saudi Arabia and the President of Egypt. Tafak is a fanatic – he may well be replaced by an even greater fanatic. So, when he threatened to cut off more oil, our government gave way . . .'

'Released a criminal?'

'Not officially. Officially LeCat, who was arrested in Marseilles for illegal activities, is still in the Santé – in solitary confinement. Which means no one ever sees him.' Messmer grinned sourly. 'It is rather like Dumas' man in the iron mask. Some poor devil is in solitary who is called LeCat – but from what I hear . . .' He shrugged.

'What has this to do with the Englishman called Winter?'

'Winter is an associate of LeCat's . . .'

They walked slowly across the snow along the lake shore. A seagull landed on the ice-bound lake and beyond the far shore the apartment blocks and hotels kept their distance. A few cyclists rode along the nearby highway. No cars – not with the fifty per cent oil cut in force.

'Tell me something about this man, Winter,' Sullivan said.

'I know nothing – he is only a name. No record, so no pictures, no fingerprints. He is like a ghost . . .'

'Tell me about LeCat then. And any reference you have heard to Harper Tankships.'

'I do not know that name. As to LeCat, there are rumours – that he has recruited a team of terrorists from his old OAS associates – the secret army organisation which revolted in Algeria, which was beaten. He had many men to choose from, of course – men in need of money who still dream of the old days when life was an adventure.' Messmer became caustic. 'He chose only from the élite – a special team of absolute bastards for this operation.'

'Any idea what kind of operation?'

'None. No one knows anything. The word has gone out – LeCat is in the Santé. Forget him.' Messmer screwed up his monkey-like face to keep smoke out of his eyes. 'You see, my friend, everyone is embarrassed about what happened to LeCat, so they hope it will soon all be over. I have heard that the operation is vast and very expensive, that it is taking a huge sum of money to finance – who knows, maybe Arab money. They are the ones who can do these things now, not us.'

'You're not saying that Paris – the French government – is behind this operation?' Sullivan asked carefully.

'I don't think they know what's going to happen – I heard they put a shadow on LeCat and he shook it off. He would, of course. But they have not interfered with his efforts to recruit a team of terrible men. You know why I insisted on coming here to talk when you phoned me yesterday?'

'No. I was surprised.'

'My phone is tapped.' Messmer gave his wry smile again. 'In France it will soon be a distinction not to have your phone tapped. We are becoming a police state – and I am a policeman. I think they will make me retire soon. I was foolish enough to protest over the Tafak affair – I have been watched ever since. And that is why I came to Hamburg, Larry – I thought that someone ought to know what is happening, however little information I have given you.'

'Thanks.' Sullivan looked round the view of the city. 'You know, François, I came all the way up the Atlantic coast asking questions and no one tried to warn me off – until I got here. I think there is something somewhere in Hamburg, but where, for God's sake?'

'That is your problem. Tell your government we cannot all go on giving in to Arab power for ever. Although I fear they will, they will . . .'

'It is not only the Arab allocation of oil, it is the money. We face a situation without precedent in history – and when an unprecedented situation arises which threatens to ruin the West financially, then we must consider unprecedented action . . .'
Minute of Prime Minister's comments at British Cabinet meeting the previous November.

On Monday January 13, Sullivan was walking along the shore of the Aussen-Alster as he talked with François Messmer. On the same morning Winter was at Cosgrove Manor, the house he had leased two months earlier during his flying visit to London. Twelve miles from King's Lynn, isolated inside its twenty acres of grounds, it suited his purpose perfectly. LeCat and the fifteen-man OAS terrorist team were with him. The final stage of the operation prior to action – training – was almost completed.

The plan of attack on the British oil tanker *Challenger* had been meticulously organised. From memory Winter had reproduced sketches of the blueprints he had seen in Paul Hahnemann's office of the *Challenger*'s twin tanker *Chieftain*. Each of the terrorists had to study these sketches until he was thoroughly familiar with the tanker's layout. And Winter cross-examined each member of the team personally when they had studied the sketches, determined to make every man walk mentally over the vessel as though he were already on board.

'The entrance to the coffer dam is through the hatch on the starboard side of the ship,' he pointed out to André Dupont during one of his briefing sessions.

'No! It is on the port side! The helicopter landing point is on the starboard side . . .'

'Which means you have just transposed everything on the main deck.' Winter unfolded his sketch and showed it to the Frenchman. 'Take the drawing away, start all over again, and make your own sketch . . .'

Winter had the main living-room, which was thirty-five feet long – roughly one-twentieth of the total length of the 50,000-ton tanker – cleared of all furniture and carpets. He had it well scrubbed and then with coloured chalks he reproduced a plan of the main deck. Again Winter trained each man individually, walking round the room with his student, drilling into him the position of the main features – catwalk, foremast, pipes, breakwater, helicopter landing point, loading derricks. It was the main deck he spent most time over – because this was where the helicopter would land.

Inevitably, men not accustomed to this kind of study became restless, so each evening he let them have a party with plenty to drink. Winter himself drank very little and he left LeCat, who consumed enormous quantities and still stayed on his feet, to look after the drinking sessions. And LeCat himself grew restless. 'Is all this necessary?' he demanded truculently one morning as they waited for the team to return from a daily run through the estate grounds. 'In the Mediterranean we just did a job . . .'

'Not a job like this,' Winter said coldly. 'When they land on that tanker's deck they must feel they have been there before. Within five minutes of the helicopter landing we must control the ship – or we have failed. Tomorrow we must help them grasp the scale of the ship . . .'

Oil drums – symbolically enough – which had been brought to the house by truck, were placed at intervals across a vast lawn which ran away from the front of the house into the fields beyond. They were placed at intervals in two rows at right-angles to the house, each row one hundred and ten feet apart – the width of the *Challenger*. Earlier, Winter had paced out seven hundred and fifty feet from the steps of the house and he ended up with the tanker's bow in a field close to an old oak tree. Already several men were muttering about the size of the thing.

From the steps of the house a double row of posts was erected right out to the distant oak tree, and this marked out the catwalk. Other poles represented the derricks and the foremast; a circle of rope on the port bow located the helicopter landing point. Then Winter took the team to the roof of the house which was fifty feet above the ground. They were now standing on the bridge of the *Challenger*, staring towards the distant oak which was the bow of the ship.

'It's bigger than I thought,' LeCat admitted, staring at the distant oak.

'It is a steep drop to the main deck,' Armand Bazin, a younger member of the team commented with surprise as he gazed down over the edge of the parapet.

'Steeper than you think,' Winter warned. 'We are fifty feet up and it's a sixty-foot drop from the island bridge of the *Challenger*. All of you go down now on to the lawn, walk along the main deck, get some idea of what it will be like. And look up at this roof – which is the bridge. It will be like looking up a cliff . . .'

They got ready to leave, but first Winter insisted on a huge cleaning-up operation. The oil drums were hidden inside a wood in the grounds. The sticks and poles which had represented cat-walk and derricks and foremast were broken up and burned. Winter personally supervised a thorough scrubbing of the living-room floor to make sure that no traces were left of the chalk marks which had outlined the main deck. Furniture and carpets were put back as they had found them there.

The debris of meals and drinking sessions – cans and bottles – were buried in a deep hole inside the wood, and French cigarette butts also went into the hole. No one had been allowed to smoke outside the house. These precautions LeCat appreciated – he re-membered the care he himself had insisted on when the house on Dusquesne Street in Vancouver had been abandoned, when all the rooms had been Hoovered. And this, of course, was something Winter knew nothing about, just as he never dreamt there was a nuclear device hidden aboard the *Pêcheur*.

Late on the afternoon of Tuesday January 14, Winter counted the sketches of the tanker prior to burning them. Tomorrow they would fly to Alaska.

Because Harper was out of town, Sullivan had to wait until Tues-day before he could phone the chairman of Harper Tankships at his London office in Leadenhall Street. Which meant that while Winter was packing up at Cosgrove Manor, Sullivan was still in Hamburg.

'In a way I've got nothing,' Sullivan told Victor Harper, 'only the fact that a hired thug tried to kill me in a bar when I went round asking about your company. But it happened in Hamburg – as though there's something here they don't want me to find out. What connection has your firm got with Hamburg?'

'Nothing that I can see might have any bearing on this situation.' Harper's precise voice sounded irritated. 'Is this whole business becoming rather a wild goose chase? And who is this friend you refer to so mysteriously – the one who told you this yarn about French terrorists?'

'Can't even hint – certainly not on the phone.'

'I'm inclined to drop the whole thing . . .'

'You've never had any connection with Hamburg at all?' Sul-livan persisted.

'Built a couple of ships there, that's all . . .'

'Which ships?'

'Couple of 50,000-tonners – the *Challenger* first, then its twin, the *Chieftain*. Both of them at the Wilhelm Voss yard. Paul Hahnemann is the boss – good chap, typically German; he drives the place like a steam engine. Both delivered bang on time, of course. I don't see how he could help . . .'

'Frankly, neither do I. Where are those ships now? In the Middle East?'

'Neither of them. *Chieftain* is in dry-dock for repairs at Genoa, *Challenger* is on the Alaska-San Francisco run. Better come home, Larry. Call it a day . . .'

'I may see you late this afternoon . . .'

Sullivan put down the phone and yawned. He had made a night of it with Messmer before the Frenchman caught the morning train back to Paris. Paul Hahnemann wasn't going to tell him anything, so why hang about? Yawning again, he began packing his bag.

The telephone message travelled a devious route before it reached Gamal Tafak at the Saudi Arabian embassy in Damascus. Originating from Paris, the call was taken by a man in Athens who then phoned a number in Beirut. From there Ahmed Riad phoned the message to Damascus. Tafak was just about to have lunch when Riad called him from the Lebanese capital.

'Excellency, KLM Flight 401 from Amsterdam to Paris has just been hi-jacked by terrorists. There is going to be trouble about this . . .'

'Why?'

'The plane is carrying three senior Royal-Dutch Shell executives, including a managing director. . .'

'Keep me in touch with developments.'

Tafak replaced the receiver. If anyone had been listening in to the call, which was unlikely but not impossible the way the American intelligence services were tapping phones all over the world these days, the conversation would have seemed innocent enough.

But the call told Tafak that the diversionary operation was under way. This had been Winter's idea, as was the timing. While LeCat set up listening posts to check on any loose security Winter

56

had come up with a more imaginative plan. To mask the hi-jack of the ship, he had suggested a plane should be seized a few days before the real event, something to keep the newspapers busy, to divert anyone who might have heard a whisper of what was really going to happen.

The hi-jack had been organised by the serious-faced man sitting on Tafak's right at the recent secret meeting in the Syrian desert. The KLM plane would now be kept hopping about from airport to airport while the main operation was under way. It still seemed easy enough to hi-jack a plane; Tafak hoped it would prove equally easy to hi-jack a 50,000-ton oil tanker.

'It did strike me that if someone wanted to sabotage one of Harper's tankers they might try and check the layout and structure of the tanker they were after. Can you tell me, Mr Hahnemann, has anyone asked to see blueprints of a Harper tanker recently?'

At the last moment before leaving Hamburg, Sullivan's natural obstinacy had made him stay. He had made an appointment to see Paul Hahnemann very late in the afternoon, so late that it was dark outside, too dark to see the falling snow. A letter of introduction from Victor Harper – 'to whom it may concern' – had got him inside the Wilhelm Voss shipyard. His Lloyd's of London identification had convinced the German he ought to see the Englishman. Hahnemann was a discreet man.

'I find that a strange question,' the German said woodenly. 'You say you have heard vague rumours – about Harper. The shipping world lives on rumours. Surely you know that by now?'

'I withdraw the question.' Sullivan smiled amiably. 'I've told you what I've been doing for the past week – coming up the Atlantic coast. Two nights ago someone tried to kill me in a Hamburg bar. That makes me think there is something – something in Hamburg I'm getting too close to.'

'I don't see how I can help you,' the German replied. 'We have no one suspect here. We are very careful who we let inside this yard – you yourself had to produce proof of identity before you were allowed in.'

Sullivan was in a difficult position. He realised that Hahnemann was too shrewd by half, that he wanted some evidence, that there was no evidence to show him. Sullivan wasn't even sure what he was looking for himself.

'There may be an Englishman in this business somewhere,' he suggested.

'Can you give me a name?' Hahnemann enquired.

'Winter.'

'I have never heard of or met anyone with that name.' The German clasped his hands across his stomach and looked up at the ceiling. 'Perhaps if you could give me a description?'

'I've no idea what he looks like . . .'

Sullivan heard himself saying this. God, how vague can you get? In another minute or two the German would start shuffling papers on his desk, maybe even look pointedly at his watch. It was hopeless.

'Would you like some coffee?' Hahnemann ordered coffee over the intercom and then excused himself. He was gone for thirty minutes by Sullivan's watch and the Englishman wondered whether he was calling the police. When he came back into the office he was followed by an attractive girl carrying a tray with the coffee. 'I will pour it,' Hahnemann said. He waited until they were alone. 'I apologise for being so long, but I decided to phone Mr Harper in London. I hope you don't mind – documents can so easily be faked these days.'

'A wise precaution.' Sullivan was puzzled. Why would Hahnemann take this trouble if he had nothing to say to him? The German took out a photograph which he placed face down on the desk, then he poured the coffee.

'Mr Sullivan, I imagine you know most of the top shipping people in London?'

'Most of them, yes – it's my job.' Sullivan carefully did not look at the concealed photograph as Hahnemann went back and sat down behind his desk.

'Charles Manders?'

'He's an old friend . . .'

'Willie Smethwick?'

'Another friend...'

'Arnold Ross?'

'Had lunch with him a couple of months ago.'

Hahnemann turned up the photograph and pushed it over the desk. 'Is that man familiar? Specifically, is he Manders, Smethwick or Ross?'

'No, he isn't . . .'

'He isn't Arnold Ross?'

'Quite definitely not. Ross is a small, well-built man with a face like an amiable gargoyle. This time of the year, he's usually off on a cruise to the West Indies.'

'That man called on me five days ago and passed himself off as Arnold Ross of Ross Tankers.'

Sullivan stared at the picture with fascination, the first picture which had ever been taken of Winter, except for passport purposes when the likeness changed as rapidly as the names. It showed a distinguished-looking man wearing a bowler hat and an expensive overcoat striding up a staircase. He appeared to be staring at the camera without seeing it.

Like a Guards officer, Sullivan thought. Trim moustache, erect bearing, a clipped look about the face. All the clichés. God, he even carried a tightly-rolled umbrella on his arm. The absolute personification of a European's idea of the City Englishman. And he existed – you could see him walking past the Bank of England each morning at 9.30. With nothing to go on, Sullivan had the strongest of hunches: this man was Winter.

'How did you take the photograph?' Sullivan asked.

Hahnemann looked embarrassed, then laughed. 'I am giving away my trade secrets. I have a fetish for security, I admit it. But we live in a dangerous world and one day someone who does not like my customers may try to sabotage a ship I am building. So everyone who comes into the building is secretly photographed. We have your own picture, Mr Sullivan. I hope I have not shocked you – Watergate and all that . . .'

'Thank God you do use a hidden camera. You take just one shot?'

'No, several . . .' Hahnemann took an envelope out of his breast pocket and spilled glossy prints on to the desk. 'I showed you the best, although this is more of a closeup.'

Winter was nearer the camera, probably just turning on to the staircase landing – his head was turned and showed in profile. He had a cold, very alert look. 'Who is this man?' Hahnemann asked.

'Probably a dangerous terrorist.'

'I find it hard to believe – he was in my office, sitting where you are sitting.'

'That's probably his secret,' Sullivan commented drily. 'He doesn't look the part. Before I leave Hamburg could I have three copies of the profile shot and the one you showed me first?'

'No problem, as the Americans say.' He used the phone and told Sullivan they would be ready in thirty minutes. 'He spent the whole day poring over blueprints of the *Chieftain*, asking questions about her. He pretended he wanted a ship built to a similar specification.'

'The *Chieftain*? He didn't take any interest in the twin ship you built for Harper, the *Challenger*?'

'None at all. I think I mentioned that vessel once and he wasn't interested.'

So now we know, Sullivan thought. The target ship was the *Chieftain*, lying up in dry-dock in Genoa, a perfect place for an act of sabotage, while the ship was immobile and helpless. He would fly back to London tomorrow and get Harper to have the security stepped up in Italy.

Heathrow Airport, London, Wednesday January 15.
12.15pm Flight BA 601 took off for Montreal, Canada. Aboard the Boeing 707 travelled thirteen of the fifteen ex-OAS terrorists. Such a large group of Frenchmen was hardly likely to excite any interest since they were flying to a city where French is spoken on every street. When they reached Montreal in charge of André Dupont, they would stay there overnight; the following day they would catch another flight on to Vancouver, the Canadian city close to the port of Victoria where the trawler *Pêcheur* was moored. Dupont would take them straight on board and there they would wait, confined to the ship until Winter arrived from Alaska.

Winter himself had watched them go into the final departure lounge at Terminal One, then he hurried to report for his own flight with LeCat and two other terrorists, Armand Bazin and Pierre Goússin.

12.45pm Flight BA 850 took off for Anchorage, Alaska.

Aboard the Boeing 707 travelled Winter and LeCat and the two Frenchmen. Ahead of them was a nine-hour flight by the polar route non-stop. They travelled separately, Winter and LeCat occupying separate seats as though they had no connection with each other, while in another part of the plane Bazin and Goussin travelled together, sitting side by side. They all held economy class tickets, although with the huge sums of money at his disposal Winter could easily have afforded first-class seats. Here he was reversing his normal procedure when staying at a hotel – stay at the best and the police will assume you are respectable. On a plane the passenger who is not noticed is the economy class man. While the other three men stayed awake eating, trying to read magazines, then eating again, Winter slept through most of the flight, only waking up when he was within half an hour of his destination.

1.15pm Flight BE 613 arrived from Hamburg. Among the first passengers to alight from the Trident was Sullivan.

Arriving at Heathrow airport, Sullivan phoned his flat in Battersea, and then wished he hadn't bothered. His charlady, Mrs Morrison, gave him a number to ring urgently, and he knew immediately it was Admiral George Lindsay Worth, RN, the man who had been responsible for his leaving naval intelligence. Worth was now with the Ministry of Defence. To get it over with, he phoned at once and Worth's secretary made an appointment for them to meet at the RAC Club in Pall Mall. At 3pm.

'You can't mean today,' Sullivan protested.

'He said it was very urgent. You are to ask for Mr Worth. No mention of rank . . .'

Sullivan went straight to Pall Mall from the airport, swearing at himself all the way inside the cab; he was still being treated like a naval lieutenant. Why the hell hadn't he said no?

Worth, a crisp, compact man of sixty, was waiting for him in the members' lounge, a vast, empty-feeling room with tall windows at either end. It was cold; there seemed to be no heating at all in the place. Not that this was likely to worry an admiral who had faced hurricane-force winds in the north Atlantic as a matter of course. Worth was sitting against the wall in a dead man's chair, a huge, low arm-chair often occupied by members whose appearance suggested the immediate calling of an undertaker.

'Prefer to sit over there?' Worth enquired, pointing to one of the tables. 'Thought you might . . .' He heaved himself up. 'How's Peggy? She's the latest girl friend, I take it?'

'She is.' Sullivan wondered how Worth managed to throw him off balance each time they met. 'What's all this about? I just came in from Europe and I could do with some kip . . .'

Worth stared across the table, registering the note of independence. 'I know,' he said quietly. 'Asking a lot of questions, stirring things up all down the French coast.'

'How do you know that?'

'Coffee? No? Perhaps just as well – it's lukewarm, anyway. As to your question, it's my job to know things. I asked you here to request you to stop stirring things up.'

'Why?'

Admiral Worth smiled, at least his mouth performed a bleak grimace which Sullivan took to be his version of a smile. 'I can't answer questions, you should know that by now. All this is off the record, of course. Official Secrets Act and all that . . .'

'You should have said that when I came in here, I think I'm going . . .'

'Bear with me a few minutes longer,' Worth suggested. 'You haven't changed, I see. Harper Tankships, isn't it?'

'You said it was your business to know things.' Sullivan was becoming angry, but his expression remained blank. 'If you'll give me a good reason I might consider it – dropping the whole thing. I said consider it.'

'We heard the whisper too – about a hi-jack, or sabotage. It was a smokescreen – to cover something else our Arab friends had in mind. Buy the 4pm edition.'

'Could I ask what you're talking about?' Sullivan enquired.

'Not a ship – another plane. KLM Flight 401 from Amsterdam to Paris. Beggars got on board at Schiphol. Something special about this job – there are three senior Royal-Dutch Shell chaps aboard, including a managing director.'

'That makes it special?'

'I think so. There's already been a demand by radio. Some nonsense about Royal-Dutch must do this, not do that – or their directors get the chop.' Worth stared bleakly at Sullivan. 'So the whisper you were chasing was pure camouflage – it was this plane hi-jack they were covering. It's really another demonstration of Arab power, of course . . .'

'And again, we give in?'

'It's become a way of life.' Worth reverted to his salty, commander-on-the-bridge language. 'They have us by the balls and they enjoy squeezing them. Can't do anything about it – the British government is resigned to an Arab condominium over the West for as far ahead as we can see.' He stared as Sullivan stood up. 'Can we rely on you?'

'You didn't think you could when we last met. I'll have to think about it. Please excuse me, but as I told you, I'm straight off the aircraft . . .'

Sullivan was fuming as he left the club. Prior to meeting Worth he had decided to drop the whole thing – after warning Harper to tighten up on security round the *Chieftain* in Genoa, although at the back of his mind he still wasn't sure. Now, if he did drop it, it would look as though he were falling in with Worth's odd request. He was still fuming when he went on to see Victor Harper.

Admiral Worth's view of the British government's attitude was not entirely correct at the highest levels. In the previous September there had been an unexpected change of premiership when the previous prime minister resigned due to ill health.

The new man, who had risen to the rank of brigadier during the Second World War, immediately took a decision which went unreported in the British press. A large area of the west coast of Scotland was declared a prohibited military zone. It was rumoured locally that a new artillery range was being set up. The curious thing was that crofters on an offshore island heard no thump of artillery shells; instead they saw frequent practice parachute landings, some of the airdrops taking place from helicopters.

Another event which was also not reported was the prime minister's secret meeting with General Lance Villiers, Chief of General Staff. Villiers, reputed to be the most efficient and ruthless Chief of Staff for three decades, had only one eye – his left eye had been left behind in Korea in 1952. He wore a black eyepatch and moved in a curiously stiff manner, but he possessed one of the quickest brains in the United Kingdom. His earlier career had been spent with the airborne forces.

Sullivan met Harper in his office at five o'clock and they talked by candlelight while snow piled up in the street outside. The chairman of Harper Tankships, a restless, energetic man of fifty with thinning hair, immediately decided he would fly to Italy the following day to sort out the security of the tanker *Chieftain*.

'Of course,' Sullivan remarked at one stage, 'it just might not be the *Chieftain* . . .'

'How do you make that out?' Harper snapped.

'Winter – if it was Winter in Hahnemann's office – made it a bit obvious the way he examined *Chieftain*'s blueprints. And I have an idea this chap is clever – don't ask me why.'

'Why?'

'Well, for one thing he's some kind of criminal – maybe adventurer would be the better word. And yet no one has any record on him. On my way here I phoned a chap I know at Scotland Yard and he'd never heard of him.' Sullivan leaned across the desk. 'No one's got him on record, for Pete's sake. You have to be clever to keep the slate as clean as that.'

It was agreed that Harper would still go to Genoa. It was also agreed that if Sullivan came up with something else while Harper was away, he could collect a cheque for more funds from Vivian Herries, Harper's secretary. At the end of a long day Sullivan went home.

It was probably his dislike of seeming to fall in with Admiral Worth's request to drop it which kept Sullivan going the following day. Refreshed by a good night's sleep, he checked every known source he could think of. Somewhere, someone must have heard of Winter.

He first tried a contact in Special Branch. The contact phoned him back later in the day. 'We've never heard of your chap, Winter. Doesn't ring any bells at all. Sorry . . .' He went back to Scotland Yard and his friend there, Chief Inspector Pemberton, told him he had been intrigued by Sullivan's enquiry. 'So, I checked further. Not a dicky bird. Drew a complete and total blank ...'

Exasperated, Sullivan extended the net, began phoning outside the country. His call to the FBI in Washington was answered within an hour. 'Nothing in the States. In view of what's happening everywhere, I checked with one of the intelligence services. Nothing on a man called Winter. Have you tried Interpol?' Yes, Sullivan had tried Interpol. He phoned his good friend, Peter van der Byll of the South African police. The answer was negative. In the late afternoon he went back to see the one man he had missed when he visited Lloyd's of London before he had set out for Bordeaux.

'It looks as though I'll be off this job for Harper Tankships,' he told MacGillivray. 'Bloody blank wall everywhere. It's beginning to annoy me.'

Jock MacGillivray was one of the backroom men concerned with the general administration of Lloyd's. When asked what he did, he was liable to reply, 'Help to keep the place going – or maybe it helps to keep me going. Never sure which.' He leaned back in his swivel chair and tossed a cigarette to Sullivan. 'So what's the problem?'

'I missed you when I came here at the beginning of the year. As to the problem, no problem as far as I can see. I've checked with just about everybody and come up with sweet nothing.'

'You haven't talked to me.' MacGillivray, freckled-faced and forty, grinned. 'The founthead of all wisdom.'

'I need any scrap of gossip you've heard about Harper Tankships during the past six to eight weeks – however trivial.'

'No gossip ...'

'There you are.'

'Nothing really . . .' MacGillivray was consulting his diary. 'Except for the chap who came in last Friday. He was doing a series of articles on the oil crisis for an American paper. He came in a couple of months ago, apparently, working on a previous series. He was asking about Harper's ship *Chieftain* – she's in dry dock at Genoa. Said he might go and have a look at her.'

'Was this him?' Sullivan put the photograph of Winter on

Hahnemann's staircase in front of MacGillivray who peered at it uncertainly.

'Wonder what he looks like without that moustache?'

'Like this . . .' Sullivan showed him a profile print he had worked on the previous evening in his flat, eliminating Winter's moustache with white paint. 'I doubt if he'd be wearing the bowler this time . . .'

'He wasn't,' MacGillivray said promptly. 'He had a tweedy thing on. That's him. Who is he?'

'Mr X. Did he mention any other Harper ship?'

'Yes. The *Challenger*. Was she exactly like the *Chieftain* – or was there any difference between the two vessels? I said they were twins and that was it, as far as I knew. Come to think of it, he asked quite a lot about that ship.'

'What's quite a lot?'

'How many crew she carried, whether she sailed with one or two wireless operators. What sort of man was the captain? I know Mackay, so I gave him a thumbnail portrait. I got the funny idea he knew most of these things already and he was just checking. That ship is on the milk run, you know – from Alaska to San Francisco and back.'

'And that's a piece of history – a British tanker taking oil from one American port to another . . .'

'Well, they did repeal the Jones Act of 1920 which said only Yank vessels could move cargo from one American port to another. They found they had a terrible shortage of tankers on the West Coast. What's the matter with Mr X?'

'Probably everything.' Sullivan stood up, collected his two prints of Winter off the desk. 'I've got a lot to do in the next hour – collect some money, check with the airlines . . .'

'Going on holiday?'

'That's right. To Alaska.'

Somewhere about this time Sheikh Gamal Tafak had his second secret meeting with the terrorist chiefs in the Syrian desert. Again he arrived in a motorcade of three cars, riding in the rear vehicle alongside his driver. The two cars in front, both of them black Mercedes like his own, also carried a driver and one passenger in the front seat. The waiting terrorist chiefs thought they understood the reason for this precaution: anyone lying in ambush and waiting to throw a bomb at Tafak could never be sure which car he was riding in. The real reason for the motorcade was more sinister.

Tafak detested dealing with these people, but these were the men he feared, whom he was anxious for the moment to keep on his side. One day it might be necessary to lose them; on that day the motorcade of three cars would contain other passengers, men with automatic weapons who would eliminate the terrorist chiefs. Meantime, let them get used to the arrival of the motorcade.

Anxious to get away, he explained what was going to happen in as few words as possible. He had told them before the plan was to create an outrage that would so appal the West that its press, radio stations and TV networks would scream with furious indignation at the Arabs. This, in its turn, would create an atmosphere in which Tafak could pressure all the Arab oil-producing states to stop the oil flow completely. Then they could launch the final attack against Israel while the West was immobilised. Everything depended on what happened aboard the British oil tanker once it had been seized.

'Winter, who knows nothing about the final outcome,' Tafak explained, 'is necessary for the hi-jack of the tanker. He is a better planner than LeCat – and being British he will know how to handle the British crew. Later, he will be withdrawn from the operation. LeCat will control the last stage.'

'And then?' the serious-faced man on his right asked.

'The negotiations between LeCat and the American authorities will break down. There will be a fàtal misunderstanding – it will be reported that American marines attempted to storm the ship.'

'And then?'

Tafak stood up, ready to go. 'It has happened so many times in history. For the sake of the multitude – our brethren who yearn to return to Palestine – the few must die. The hostages – the British crew – will all be killed.'

Part two The hi-jack

7

In the United States, as in Europe, the energy crisis was beginning to take on the character of a war – with oil in all forms as the ammunition dumps the enemy sought to destroy. The lights were starting to go out all over the continental mainland – in Texas where oil was moving away from the state to the hard-pressed north-east, so there was not enough oil left for home needs. The recent large-scale sabotage of the Venezuelan oilfields at Lake Maracaibo was turning a tense situation into near-disaster.

No one was sure who the saboteurs were – who had placed and detonated the charges at Maracaibo, who had blown up a section of the Alaskan North Slope pipeline being constructed to Valdez, who had blown up key refineries at Delaware and in Texas – in Britain and Germany and Italy. Arab terrorists were the obvious suspects; extremists employed by remote control by the sheikhs who wished to make their products even more valuable because it was daily becoming a scarcer commodity, already selling at fifty dollars a barrel, free on board Gulf ports.

Inside the States, the FBI worked on a theory that revived dissident groups like The Weathermen were behind the sabotage. Pamphlets were being distributed by the underground press – 'Bring the Capitalist Colossus to its Knees! Burn Oil!' It was not a slogan appreciated by motorists searching for an extra two gallons to get them home. But whoever was responsible, the situation was becoming desperate. Europe – and America – were close to their knees.

The sabotage of the Maracaibo wells meant that, added to the other damage, the States needed ten per cent more oil from outside sources just to keep the machine turning over. The ten per cent was not available – except from Arab sources. As Sheikh Gamal Tafak well knew.

Oil became more valuable than gold – and was guarded with more security than gold. The Mafia was continuing to hi-jack tankers on highways and freeways. To counter this, Washington organised a convoy system not dissimilar to the Allied shipping convoys during the Second World War. It became normal to see huge fleets of petrol and oil tankers moving through the night with armed guards in the front and rear trucks. Freight trains transporting oil carried machine-gunners mounted on their roofs with searchlights playing over the surrounding countryside whenever a train was halted in the middle of nowhere. Like Europe, where similar precautions had to be taken, the United States was moving into siege conditions.

Refineries and pipelines became strategic points to be guarded night and day against the bombers. Bulldozers urgently scooped out tracks alongside pipelines – tracks along which jeeps carrying armed men could patrol. And still America was slowly grinding to a halt as the winter grew in severity, as blizzards swept down into the Middle West and as far south as northern Florida. 'Unprecedented temperatures in the north-east,' the US Weather Bureau reported.

In a locked file inside the White House rested a detailed forecast of the estimated gap between fuel requirements and fuel deliveries – assuming the Siberian weather continued. It was calculated the nation might just squeeze through to spring – with a lot of hardship–providing the Arabs maintained their oil cut at the savage fifty per cent. In the event of a fresh cut the forecast for the United States and Europe was summed up in one graphic word. Catastrophe.

Six thousand miles away in the Middle East terrorist teams waited for further instructions from Sheikh Gamal Tafak – to destroy the oil-wells if certain other sheikhs refused to cut their oil flow to zero when the moment came.

It was snowing when Winter arrived in Anchorage, Alaska, on board Flight BA 850. Because of the wide difference in time zones, although he had left London at 12.45pm he arrived in Anchorage at 11.45am, and it was still Wednesday January 15. In London it was 8.45pm on the evening of the same day and Sullivan had returned to his Battersea flat. He spent part of the evening packing, ready for his departure for Anchorage the following day.

At Anchorage International Airport, Winter presented his passport in the name of Robert Forrest. His profession was shown as geologist, but the Immigration official guessed he had something

71

to do with North Slope oil before he even glanced at the false document Winter casually handed him.

There was the obvious clue: the folded copy of a British Petroleum house journal in the Englishman's sheepskin pocket. The passenger was also carrying looped over his shoulder a device which registers seismic shocks after explosives dropped into a hole have been detonated, a tool of the geologist's profession.

'North Slope?' the Immigration man enquired with a grin. 'We need you guys to checkmate those A-rab bastards.'

'Take more than North Slope to do that,' Winter replied noncommittally. 'Is there a cab outside?'

'If you run – after you get through Customs. Cabs are in short supply these days – you'll have to share ...'

Winter was passed through Customs with equal good humour and speed. His case was chalked without anyone checking it, as though they were unwilling to hold him up a moment longer than was necessary. He shared a cab with LeCat and two other people, and the Frenchman gave no sign that he had ever met Winter before. Behind them the other two Frenchmen followed in a separate cab.

The Westward was a typical American hotel; tall, shaped like an upended shoe-box, it had a rooftop restaurant. Only half the lights were on in the lobby even though outside it was almost dark; a heavy cloud bank hung over the city whose streets were ankle-deep in slush. Nor, in this state which would one day be knee-deep in oil, was it very warm inside the lobby. Obeying government regulations, the manager had the thermostat turned down to sixty-two degrees.

Winter booked accommodation in the name of Forrest, dumped his bag in his sixth-floor room, and by the time he walked out of the hotel a hired Chevrolet was waiting for him at the kerb. Behind the wheel sat Joseph Walgren, the American Winter had last met in San Francisco two months earlier. In the back was LeCat, whom Walgren had picked up from another hotel.

'Drive me to the Swan home,' Winter said abruptly. 'I want to check the timing ...'

'I checked it,' the fifty-year-old Walgren objected. 'You got the timing in the letter I sent to Cosgrove Manor ...'

'Drive to the Swan home,' Winter repeated. 'I'm checking it myself.'

The first stage of the operation was the most difficult, the most likely to go wrong. The key man aboard any ship is the wireless operator, the man who communicates with the shore, however distant; Charlie Swan, the radio operator aboard the *Challenger*, had to be kidnapped so Winter could put his own man, Kinnaird, in his place before the tanker made its next trip to San Francisco.

'The *Challenger* docks at the Nikisiki oil terminal at six this evening,' Walgren said as he drove out of the city, 'like I told you in the coded letter. Captain Mackay will come and stay overnight at your hotel, the Westward. Swan, the radio guy, drives home and stays there overnight. He'll drive back to the airport tomorrow, leaving home at 3.30 in the afternoon. He links up there with Mackay – who takes a cab from the hotel to the airport. Then they both get flown back to the oil terminal in the Cessna piloted by Mackay's buddy.'

'Do either of them ever vary that routine?' Winter asked.

'I've been up here a month watching them.' Walgren switched off the windscreen wipers: it had stopped snowing. 'That makes three trips for the *Challenger* – in and out. Those two have schedules like a railroad timetable – never varies. They get so little time ashore they do the same thing. It's become a habit. Kinnaird is shacked up at the Madison downtown – this piece of paper gives you the phone number, and the Swan number.' Walgren gripped the wheel a little tighter. 'I'm glad the hanging around is over. So we make the Swan snatch tomorrow and we're in business . . .'

He stopped talking when he saw Winter's expression. Jesus, the Britisher was an iceberg, unlike the Frenchie behind who would sit and drink brandy with a guy like any other normal human being. Walgren tightened his thick lips and concentrated on his driving. For thirty grand he could put up even with Winter . . .

Heavy grey clouds hung over the Matanuska valley as they sped north-east along the highway and there was snow on the hills. More snow up in those clouds too, Walgren thought. 'You're exceeding the speed limit,' Winter said icily. Swearing inwardly, Walgren dropped down to fifty-five. Everybody exceeded the speed limit if they thought there was no patrol car ahead. It began to rain, a steady, depressing drizzle which blotted out the surrounding countryside. Walgren switched on the wipers, hunched over the wheel, hating the silence inside the car. He drove for almost an hour.

'That's the Swan home coming up,' Walgren told Winter.

'You're almost ten minutes out on your timing,' the Englishman snapped.

'So, I beat the limit a couple of times. Swan keeps the needle on fifty-five the whole way. At least he did the three times I followed him out here from the airport.'

Winter said nothing, hiding his annoyance. British, American or French, it seemed impossible to find people who were precise. He had the same trouble with LeCat. So he had to check every damned thing himself.

Walgren turned off the lonely highway down a track leading through a copse of snow-covered fir trees. Inside the copse he backed the car in a half-circle until it faced the way they had come. Through a gap in the snow-hung trees the Swan home was clearly visible, an isolated two-storey homestead three or four hundred yards back from the highway with a drive leading up to it. Behind the house stood an old Alaskan barn and a red Ford was parked at the front. In the bleak, snowbound landscape there was only one other house to be seen.

'Won't that car freeze up?' Winter asked as he lowered the window and focused a pair of field glasses.

'They got it plugged into a power cable,' Walgren replied. 'That keeps the immersion heater under the hood going. You forget to plug in your cable and inside two hours you got a block of ice instead of a motor...'

It was already getting cold inside Walgren's car; to save gas he had switched off the motor while he parked. From a chimney in the Swan household blue smoke drifted, spiralling up in a vertical column. The rain had stopped and the leaden overcast was like a plague cloud covering the Matanuska valley.

'That house in the distance beyond the Swan place – know anything about it?' Winter enquired.

74

'Belongs to some people called Thompson, friends of the Swans.' Walgren lit a cigarette. 'Sometimes when Charlie Swan is home the two couples get together – they did on the last trip.'

'Go out, you mean?' Winter asked sharply.

'No, visit each other's homes. The Swans went over to the Thompson's. When you're home only once in ten days like Charlie Swan is you don't drive into town. You meet up with the folks next door.'

'How did you find out all this?' Winter asked curiously.

'Used to be a private dick. There are ways. And,' Walgren said aggressively, 'I can't see why we came out here – the snatch is set up for tomorrow . . .'

'Trial run,' Winter said brusquely. There was no point in explaining that this was another rehearsal, just as Cosgrove Manor had been a rehearsal for the ship hi-jack. He studied the house for a minute or two longer, then told Walgren, 'Drive back into town.'

On January 15 it was dark in Anchorage at three in the afternoon. Walgren dropped Winter near the Westward and the Englishman had a late lunch at a coffee shop. So that he was remembered as little as possible he would eat only one meal in the hotel restaurant. Walgren, who ate very little – he was badly overweight and had been reading the health ads – dropped LeCat at his own hotel. Next, he picked up Armand Bazin and started the long drive to Nikisiki oil terminal on the Kenai peninsula.

It was six o'clock in the evening when Walgren collected Winter again from the Westward after returning Bazin to his hotel. He drove the Englishman out of the city to an isolated spot where an old barn stood amid a clearing surrounded by evergreens. 'Everything is OK,' he told Winter as they pulled up in front of the building. 'You didn't really have to make the trip . . .'

'I like to see things for myself.'

Winter inspected the barn where Swan and his wife would be kept prisoner for a week. Everything, as Walgren had said, seemed OK. The place was secure, new padlocks had been put on all the windows and doors, and there was a Primus stove for cooking and an adequate supply of canned food, milk and fruit juices. The Swans should be as comfortable as it was possible to make them –

including the provision of five oil-heaters and enough fuel to last them a month. Winter didn't bother to ask the American whether he had stolen the oil or brought it on the black market. 'Satisfied?' Walgren enquired drily when they were leaving.

'It will do. Get me back to the hotel fast, Mackay should be arriving soon. But keep inside the speed limit . . .'

Which was a bloody contradiction in terms Walgren thought sourly as he gunned the motor and headed back for the highway. And this was one hell of a long day, the American reminded himself, a day which was by no means over. As soon as he had left Winter at his hotel he had to drive out to the airport, wait for the Cessna bringing Mackay and Swan, the radio operator, from the *Challenger*'s berth at Nikisiki, then follow Swan all the way out to his home in the Matanuska valley.

'Is that really necessary?' he had complained.

'Swan is the key to this part of the operation – we must be sure he has arrived home safely,' Winter had replied.

Winter got out of Walgren's car a short distance from the Westward and walked the rest of the way to the hotel. He had kept the key of his room in his pocket to avoid appearing too often at the reception desk and went straight up in the elevator. Once inside his room he checked his watch and then went over in his mind the present whereabouts of everyone involved.

7pm. Captain Mackay would be landing at the airport in the Cessna in fifteen minutes; Walgren would be waiting there to follow Swan home. As he stripped off to take a shower Winter went on checking in his mind. LeCat would be at his own hotel, ten blocks away, probably in his room nursing a bottle of cognac. Armand Bazin and Pierre Goussin, who would guard the Swans while they were held in the barn, would be at their own hotel, eating dinner provided by room service while they pretended to pore over a pile of papers. No one would leave their hotel tonight – Winter was not risking someone falling on the icy sidewalks and breaking a leg – and Winter would be the only man eating in a restaurant. He turned on the shower. Finally, Kinnaird, the substitute wireless operator, would be keeping under cover at the Madison.

•　　　•　　　•

Ten thousand pounds. Every man has an amount at the back of his mind which he feels would give him freedom from the cares and worries of the world. For 'Shep' Kinnaird it was ten thousand pounds. Pulling back the curtain of his bedroom at the Madison he peered through the gap. It looked reassuring: a deserted, snow-bound street dimly lit by street lamps which would be turned off at ten o'clock, and no car parked where someone might be keeping an eye on the hotel.

Kinnaird, thirty-seven years old, twice divorced – neither woman had been able to endure his gambling habits – was the wireless operator Winter had hired for the *Pêcheur*'s radio cabin during the smuggling days in the Mediterranean. Prior to that, Kinnaird had been with the Marconi pool of radio operators, working on the Persian Gulf-West Coast run. Now the ten thousand pounds was within his grasp – it was the payment for substituting himself for Swan, the *Challenger*'s regular wireless op.

Less than a mile away inside the Westward Hotel, Captain James Mackay, fifty-five year old master of the *Challenger*, was sitting down to a late dinner in the rooftop restaurant. A heavily-built, florid-faced man who was surprisingly quick on his feet, Mackay had been on the shuttle run between Alaska and San Francisco for five months. It was a shade too straightforward for his liking: Nikisiki is approximately two thousand miles from San Francisco and the *Challenger*, travelling at an average speed of seventeen knots, made the trip to the oil terminal of Oleum on the east side of San Francisco Bay in a little over four days.

She discharged her precious Alaskan oil in twelve hours and then headed back for Nikisiki. It took a day and a quarter to take on more oil at Cook Inlet – the time in dock could have been shortened but Mackay, mindful of hurricanes in these waters, insisted on meticulous maintenance – and then she started south again for Oleum. So one trip occupied ten days. And it never stopped, the shuttle run. And this, Mackay thought as he studied the menu, was oil from the little known Cook Inlet field. What the hell would it be like when they opened up North Slope?

'T-bone steak and French fries and a glass of beer,' Mackay ordered. He always studied the menu and then always ordered the same food. A widower for ten years, Mackay was a creature of habit, always coming to this same hotel to sleep overnight, always leaving it at 4pm the following day to return to his ship. The vessel then sailed for California at midnight. 'Follow a routine,' Mackay was fond of telling his crew, 'then you'll never forget anything important . . .'

He looked round the almost empty restaurant while he waited for his steak. Four tables away, a tall, thin man wearing horn-rim glasses sat absorbed in his newspaper. When his meal came Mackay ate it quickly – a shipboard habit – and he hardly noticed the man in horn-rim glasses leaving the restaurant just before he finished his own dinner.

In the lobby below Winter was studying some brochures when Mackay stepped out of the elevator and went into the bar. Again, part of the routine Walgren had described: after dinner Mackay always had a second beer in the bar before going up to his room early. The photograph of Mackay sent by Walgren to Cosgrove Manor had been a good likeness.

Winter wondered how Walgren had taken the picture without being seen, then he strolled over to the entrance to the bar, taking off his horn-rims and tucking them inside his pocket. Mackay was sitting with his back to him, reading a magazine. The barman behind the counter looked straight at Winter, who glanced away as though he had changed his mind and went across to a telephone booth.

Phoning Bazin's hotel at the number Walgren had given him, Winter waited to be put through. It was the last thing he had to attend to tonight. Bazin came on the line, confirmed cautiously that he was ready, which meant he was familiar with the Nikisiki oil terminal Walgren had driven him to in the afternoon, that Walgren had handed over to him what he would use – a thermite bomb.

8

At 3pm on Thursday January 16 Winter turned into the drive leading to the Swan homestead and drove slowly through the darkness toward the house; no rush, nothing to disturb the Swans if they noticed the car coming. Snow crust crackled under the wheels.

LeCat sat beside him, Pierre Goussin rode in the back, and when he reached the house he drove round the side where the parked vehicle would be hidden from the Thompson home in the distance. His headlights swept over a blue Rambler standing in front of the house with the power cable plugged into it; Walgren had told Winter that Swan drove a Rambler.

Winter left the car quickly, walked round to the front door, his right hand inside his sheepskin, gripping the Skorpion pistol in its holster. The unexpected happened immediately. The porch light came on and Swan, due to leave at 3.30pm, opened the front door before Winter could press the bell. He was wearing a British Gannex raincoat and carrying a bag.

'Mr Swan?' Winter enquired.

'Yes...'

'Don't get excited and no one will get hurt.' Winter pointed the pistol at Swan's chest. 'We just want to use your phone and then we'll leave you in a locked room...' He was speaking rapidly, weighing up the slim, thirty-year-old who faced him, guessing his reactions, warning him with the gun, reassuring him with the reference to a phone call.

'Where's he going?' Swan demanded.

LeCat had pushed behind him, disappearing into the house as Winter went on talking, holding his attention. 'Let's go inside and find out ... No! Don't hurry – no need for a nasty accident ...' Winter followed him across a hall and into a large, L-shaped living-room. A dark-haired woman in her thirties had her hand up to her throat, her eyes wide with fear as LeCat held one arm round her back and a knife close to her breast. He pressed the knife tip to her throat as Swan started across the room and then stopped. 'Keep away or she's dead,' LeCat warned.

'Take the knife away from her throat. That's better . . .' Winter could have knocked the Frenchman down. The stupid cretin! He could have caused a bloodbath. There was an atmosphere of shock, disbelief in the living-room which Winter had foreseen and was determined to exploit. To counter LeCat's blunder the Englishman became crisp, businesslike. Placing a hand on Swan's shoulder, he pressed him down into a chair; a man sitting down feels less aggressive, is less likely to do something violent. 'Let Mrs Swan sit down,' he told LeCat, 'and stop manhandling her . . .'

'We're expecting friends any minute,' Swan warned. 'They could walk through that front door . . .'

'Which is why you're dressed to go out,' Winter interjected coldly. 'You were leaving to go back to your ship, the *Challenger*, so stop making up fairy tales . . .' He had Swan's measure now: a quick-witted, determined man, he would try to outwit them, given half a chance. At the moment he was in a state of deep shock; pale-faced, he couldn't keep his eyes off his wife who was sitting down, hands clasped in her lap.

'What do you want?' Mrs Swan asked quietly. She had, Winter realised, recovered her self-possession. Even quicker than her husband, she had asked the key question. What do you want?

'Your husband's job for a week.' To create a calmer atmosphere Winter himself sat down in one of the Scandinavian-style chairs as Goussin came in from the rear of the house. 'All clear at the back? Good. Now, Swan, you mean nothing to us dead or alive – and heroes make widows in this awful world we live in. I want you to phone Captain Mackay at the Westward Hotel in Anchorage. Tell him you're sick – that you've caught a bad dose of flu. Tell him you have found a replacement wireless operator from the Marconi pool who is on holiday in Palmer. He's visiting his sister who is married to an American. Kinnaird is the replacement's name – he's taking your place on the next trip the *Challenger* makes to San Francisco.'

'What happens to us?' Swan asked. He was still pale but his voice was steady.

'You'll be kept in a place about fifty miles from here under guard for a week. By that time the *Challenger* will have reached San Francisco. Then you will be freed.'

'It won't work. Mackay won't agree...'

'Yes, he will,' Winter interrupted sharply. 'Within sixty minutes he'll be leaving the Westward to go back to his ship. When he hears you're sick he'll be appalled – when you tell him you've found a replacement he'll be relieved, more than ready to accept Kinnaird on your say-so. Do you want me to repeat what you have to say to him?'

'No,' Swan looked anxious and uncertain. 'What happens if I...' He glanced at his wife and stopped. He looked at LeCat who was standing behind his wife's chair. He had been going to say what happens if I refuse, then he decided he didn't want his wife to hear the answer.

'What about my wife – Julie?'

'She'll be with you all the time. I give you my word...'

'Fat lot of use that is...'

'Charlie...' Julie leaned forward, her clasped hands bloodless with tension. 'Do as he says.' She looked at Winter. 'The man behind me won't be staying with us, will he?'

'No,' said Winter, his face expressionless. 'I do have some feelings...'

'Then tell him to stop staring at her,' Swan burst out.

'Go over by the window,' Winter told LeCat. He pointed his pistol at Swan while he spoke to Julie. 'Tell him, Mrs Swan, not to try and warn Mackay about what is happening – for the sake of everyone...'

'Do exactly as he says, please, Charlie,' Julie Swan said. 'For my sake,' she added. She meant for her husband's sake.

Swan looked at the phone. 'Mackay will ask questions...'

'You're sick,' Winter repeated, 'so you'll want to get off the phone. You've got to convince Mackay in as few words as possible that Kinnaird is all right, that you've known him in the past, that he'll find his papers in order – because he will...'

'This man is a good wireless op.?' Swan asked unhappily. 'A ship's survival can depend on the wireless operator...'

'He's absolutely competent and he did once work for the Marconi pool. Mackay will be in a spot,' Winter repeated. 'He sails at midnight and he'll be ready to be convinced.' Part of the problem, Winter had realised beforehand, would be to convince Swan that he could get away with the deception. He repeated his earlier warning. 'In case you've thought of some clever little phrasing to help Mackay catch on, remember we'll have both yourself and your wife for one week after you make that call.'

'What ships has this Kinnaird been on? He's bound to ask me that . . .'

'Ellesmere-Luckman Line,' Winter said promptly. 'He spent three years on the tanker *Maltese Cross*, two years aboard the *White Cross* before that. That was a few years ago but make it sound recent. They're on the Persian Gulf to West Coast run.'

'I know.' Swan stared directly at Winter. 'What is Kinnaird going to do?'

'Charlie! For God's sake do as he asks,' Julie burst out.

'A reasonable question,' Winter replied. 'We have to get a man into the States, a man already known to the American police. The safest way is to put him on a ship as a crewman and let him walk off at the other end. Kinnaird is not his real name, of course . . .'

'It's going to be difficult . . .'

'Get on with it!' Winter checked his watch. 'Dial the Westward now. And make it work – for Julie's sake.'

It was less than five minutes since they had entered the house when Swan made the phone call: enough time for Winter to persuade Swan, not enough time for Swan to think too much. Winter wanted the call made while the wireless operator was still in a state of shock.

Swan handled the call to Mackay well. He even talked through his nose to fake an impression of flu. The call lasted less than three minutes. Swan put the phone down and turned to Winter. 'He swallowed it – hook, line and sinker . . .'

'Excuse me . . .' Winter carried the phone across the room to a sideboard, stood with his back to Swan and dialled a number. 'Forrest here. Make the call. Now!' He broke the connection, dialled a fresh number. Again the phone at the other end was answered immediately. 'Forrest here. Get moving – it's all right . . .'

The timing of these calls was crucial. The first call had been to Walgren, waiting in a phone booth outside the Westward Hotel. Already Walgren would be phoning Armand Bazin, who was waiting at the Nikisiki oil terminal with the thermite bomb. Walgren would then wait for five minutes before he put in a call to Captain Mackay at the Westward. The second call had been to Kinnaird, already outside Anchorage and well on his way to Nikisiki. Winter put down the phone and saw that Swan was standing up with LeCat close to him, his pistol aimed at the wireless operator's heart. The Frenchman was showing sense: with the gun aimed at her husband there was no need to watch Julie Swan.

'Leave my wife here,' Swan pleaded with Winter. 'She won't say anything to anyone – not if I come with you . . .'

'Not possible.' Winter shook his head. 'It would be too much of a strain on her – wondering what was happening to you.'

'I'd sooner go with him.' Julie Swan was standing up now, a plucky woman Winter had come to admire during the short time he had been with her. 'Can I get a few things – for my face and . . .'

'Jesus Christ!' LeCat stormed.

'You'll never meet him,' Winter observed. 'Go with her and check what she takes – no nail files. Take Swan with you, too.' He waited until he was alone with Pierre Goussin, who had remained silent at the back of the room. He didn't like either Goussin or Bazin, the two men who would stay with the Swans, but both had lived in Quebec after the Algerian débâcle and had the advantage of speaking good English. He stared at the Frenchman, a grim-looking man of the same age as LeCat. 'Let me remind you, with LeCat you will take them to the barn in Swan's Rambler outside . . .'

'I've heard all this . . .'

'You're going to hear it again. You use the Rambler – it would look funny if it was found here by some nosey neighbour when Swan is supposed to have driven back to the airport. One week from today you leave them locked up inside the barn. You fly to Canada and phone the police here telling them where to find the Swans. If anything happens to them I'll come and find you myself . . .'

'What could happen to them . . .' Goussin couldn't hold Winter's gaze and the Englishman was troubled by a flicker of doubt, then LeCat returned with the Swans and Winter was distracted by the next thing to do.

'One more phone call,' he told Julie Swan, 'and this time you make it. You're in a rush – Charlie has just told you Mackay has softened on his rule that no women must travel aboard his ship. So you're travelling aboard the *Challenger* on her next trip to San Francisco. That will explain your absence from the house. I'm referring to your neighbours, the Thompsons . . .'

'I was going to see Madge – Mrs Thompson – this evening . . .'

'So now you're phoning to say you won't be able to make it.' Winter looked at LeCat. 'Take Swan out to the car – we'll be with you.' He waited until they had gone. 'Mrs Swan,' he said quietly, 'you just have to get this right – for your husband's sake.'

'I'll get it right . . .'

He watched her dialling the number with a steady finger. She had nerve, this American girl. Why was it that so often women grasped a spine-chilling situation faster than men, realised that the only way to survive was to cooperate?

Julie Swan handled the call perfectly; she even managed to get a hint of excitement into her voice as she talked about the prospect of her trip aboard the tanker with her husband. So far as Winter could see, Mrs Thompson suspected nothing. 'That was fine,' he assured her as she put down the phone. 'If you carry on like that everything will be all right.'

'Will it?' She looked at him over her shoulder as she put on her heavy coat. 'You're British, aren't you? Or shouldn't I ask?'

'You shouldn't ask.' He took her by the shoulders as she prepared to leave and saw her mouth tighten. 'It's going to be all right – just so long as your husband does nothing stupid. Another guard will arrive later today and replace the man you dislike. But remember, the men who stay with you will be armed.'

'My husband thinks too much of me to do anything stupid as you put it,' she snapped. Her voice wavered. 'It's no good – I'm scared . . .'

'One week from now you'll be free.'

'I'm praying for the eighth day.'

Captain James Mackay, wearing a parka he had hurriedly put on, carrying the overnight bag he had thrown his few things inside, left the Westward Hotel and went out into the night at 3.30pm.

The street lamps were blurred with mist as he ran to where his car was parked by a meter.

Within less than five minutes of receiving the phone call from his wireless operator, Swan, warning him that he was ill, telling Mackay that he had found a replacement called Kinnaird, the phone had rung again. This was in response to the first urgent call Winter had made from the Swans' home.

Walgren's American-sounding voice had complained of a bad connection, saying he could hardly hear Mackay, and the caller had been in one hell of a hurry. A fire had broken out at the oil terminal, close to the *Challenger*. 'You'd better get down here fast,' the man on the phone had warned Mackay, then he had rung off before the captain could ask any questions.

Mackay did not realise it, but he was being subjected to shock treatment by Winter to keep him off balance – to get him moving out of Anchorage, to stop him thinking too much about the substitute wireless operator who was also on his way to the terminal.

Mackay reached his parked car, then swore. 'Bloody kids . . .' The power cable from the meter he had plugged into the immersion heater under his bonnet had been hauled out from the socket, lay useless amid the frozen slush. Useless, quite useless. The radiator and sump would be frozen, the battery dead. Swearing again, he climbed out, locking the vehicle as a car cruised towards him. Walgren pulled up and stuck his head out of the window. 'Trouble?'

'Someone hauled out the cable.'

'It happens,' Walgren commented sympathetically. 'All part of the good neighbour policy. Where to?'

'Airport . . .'

'We're already there – fasten your seat-belt, we're about to take off . . .'

Mackay settled himself in the back seat as Walgren took him at speed through the city and the darkness, well above the regulation fifty-five. He had only one thought on his mind – to get back to his ship, to find out how bad the situation was. He was due to sail at midnight and he had to meet the tanker's deadline for arrival at San Francisco.

The 'cab driver' tried to talk to the British sea captain, and then gave up when all he got was one-word replies. It suited Walgren: he had no particular desire to talk to the passenger Winter had arranged for him to pick up when he found the car Walgren had immobilised was dead. From the moment Swan made his phone call to Mackay, it was important for Winter to keep the captain under his control. And it had worked – Mackay was thinking about nothing except his ship – and leaving Alaska.

The fire at the oil terminal was gushing out vast clouds of black smoke, the fire caused by the thermite bomb Armand Bazin had ignited close to the new refinery. He had put this act of sabotage into operation the moment Walgren's phone call came through to a nearby pay booth. The authorities were appalled but not surprised. For them it was simply another outrage in the pattern of bombings taking place all over Europe and America at this time.

During the last few hours before sailing, a ship's captain is absorbed in making sure he will get away on time. He is likely to be even more absorbed if a fire is raging within a quarter of a mile of where his ship is moored – far too absorbed to take much interest in a replacement wireless operator.

'I'm Kinnaird . . .'

As Mackay hurried along the jetty towards the gangway a thin-faced man in his late thirties, alert, competent-looking, neatly dressed – Mackay noted this swift impression in the few steps it took him to reach the gangway – walked up to him. The deckhand at the foot of the gangway had identified Mackay to Kinnaird, who carried a suitcase and wore a parka and a Russian-style fur hat.

'Come aboard,' Mackay replied briskly. 'Report to Second Officer Walsh. I'll see you later . . .'

In his day cabin, Mackay listened while First Officer Sandy Bennett gave him a brief report on the present position. 'The tanks should be full within seven hours. I estimate we'll be away by midnight . . .'

'We may be away earlier if we can manage it. Better warn the harbour master. I may leave with a couple of tanks empty if that thing spreads . . .' Mackay was looking out of the portside window across a maze of pipes and jetties to where a red glow was breaking through the pall of dark smoke drifting upwards. It was misleading, he hoped, but he had the impression the whole terminal was going up in flames. 'How did it start?' Mackay asked.

'Too early to say yet, sir. We were lucky to get this replacement for Swan so quickly.' Bennett paused. 'How was it we were so lucky, sir?'

'Chap Swan knows. He's just come aboard, by the way. He's from the Marconi pool – happened to be on leave visiting his sister in Anchorage . . .' Mackay sounded impatient, anxious to move on to other topics.

First Officer Sandy Bennett was twenty-eight years old; a man of medium height and medium build, his sand-coloured hair was cut short and reappeared again in his thick eyebrows; under the brows were a pair of shrewd, watchful eyes which rarely took anything or anyone at face value. Mackay thought he overdid things a bit with his habit of questioning everything.

'You saw Swan, sir?' Bennett enquired. 'He introduced you to this Kinnaird?'

'No, he didn't.' Mackay let go of the curtain and turned away from the disquieting view. 'He phoned me from his home out near Palmer while I was at the Westward. Is something bothering you?'

'Not really, sir. It's just such a happy coincidence – Swan falls ill and there's a replacement at hand, here in Alaska of all places. I'll check his papers before we sail . . .'

'Walsh is already doing that. Repeat the process, if you must. And now, Mr Bennett, maybe we can get on with the business of running a ship . . .'

It was still Thursday January 16 when Captain Mackay went aboard his ship in Alaska. On the previous day everything had gone smoothly at Heathrow Airport, London. Flights had arrived and taken off exactly as scheduled in the airline timetables. But this was a fluke; in the days of the Second Energy Crisis timetables were printed merely for propaganda purposes, bearing little or no relationship to what actually happened. For Sullivan things returned to normal.

There are no flights from London to Anchorage on Tuesdays and Thursdays, so on Thursday January 16 Sullivan had to head for Alaska by a different route. At 9.30am, London time, he left Heathrow aboard Flight BE 742 bound for Copenhagen. From the Danish capital Scandinavian Airlines Flight SK 989 was due to leave at 3.30pm. It would land at Anchorage at 1.15pm, Alaskan time.

This would mean Sullivan reaching Anchorage almost two hours before Swan was due to be kidnapped. He would undoubtedly have gone straight to see Mackay at the Westward; he would have been there when the phone call from Swan came through. Being Sullivan, his suspicions would certainly have been aroused. Unfortunately it was a normal day.

Due to shortage of aviation fuel, Flight SK 989 took off ten-and-a-half hours behind schedule. When Kinnaird arrived at the foot of the gangway leading on to the *Challenger*, Sullivan was still in mid-air, thirty thousand feet up, over seven hours flying time away from Anchorage.

'More trouble. This is not our day, Bennett . . .'

Mackay handed the message he had received from the radio cabin to his first officer and stood at the front of the wide bridge with his hands clasped behind his back, staring at the persistent red glow of the fire growing in the dark. Bennett read the signal which had just come in from London office.

Please extend all courtesies to Betty Cordell American journalist joining Challenger for voyage to Oleum commencing January 16. Cordell arriving Anchorage airport 1810 hours aboard North West Airlines flight from Seattle. Will make own way to ship. Harper.

'It's a woman,' Mackay said from the front of the bridge.

'I would assume so, sir,' Bennett replied, 'unless the Americans have gone in for some strange christening rites.'

'Are you trying to be funny?'

'Merely making an observation, sir,' Bennett replied respectfully. 'I'd better warn Wrigley to prepare a cabin . . .'

'No frills,' Mackay snapped. 'She'll have to live like the rest of us and like it. Aren't there enough men journalists in the world to go round? If she wants breakfast in bed, she can't have it. You'd better go and tell Wrigley . . .'

Bennett left the bridge before the captain thought of some other way of expressing his feelings. It is not so unusual for a woman to travel aboard an oil tanker; many companies permit officers to have their wives on board occasionally, but Mackay, a widower, would not allow the practice. 'If a man has spent the night in bed with his wife enjoying the normal marital opportunities he is not fit for duty in a hurricane,' he was fond of saying. And he had not overlooked the phrasing of the signal which left nothing to his discretion. Harper had ordered him to take the damned woman aboard. Brian Walsh, the Second Officer, made the mistake of coming on to the bridge as soon as Bennett had gone in search of the steward.

'We've got a woman with us on this trip,' Mackay snapped at his second officer.

'Really, sir?'

Perhaps Walsh, a professional bachelor, allowed a little too much enthusiasm to enter his reaction to this damning statement. Mackay swung round slowly and eyed Walsh with a distinct lack of enthusiasm.

'An American journalist. She will probably be bandy-legged, pigeon-chested and wear horn-rim glasses like twin gun barrels.'

'Yes, sir.' Walsh, twenty-six years old and boyishly good-looking, blinked at his captain's picture of the average woman journalist. 'Any special precautions, sir?'

'Precautions?' Mackay's voice went up an octave. 'What the devil do you mean?'

'Certain areas out of bounds?' Walsh's memory was going back to what his father had told him about life aboard a troopship which also carried WREN officers. 'Where will she eat, sir?'

'In the saloon with the rest of us. She might, of course, miss the sailing,' Mackay went on with a hint of hope. He had already issued orders that the *Challenger* would sail at 2200 hours – two hours before her normal departure. 'London office has asked us to extend all courtesies,' Mackay added grimly. 'She's probably writing some damnfool article on life at sea.'

'Ought I to warn the deckhands about her? Their language . . .'

'No! I'm not having my crew turned into a bunch of nancy boys just because a woman has come aboard. She'll have to take the ship as it is, warts and all.' Mackay checked the bridge clock. 'That is, if she gets here at all . . .'

'I think she's just arriving,' Walsh observed, staring out of the port-side window. 'And, respectfully, sir, I don't think she has bandy legs . . .'

To keep under the low cloud ceiling Winter flew the Cessna light aircraft at only a few hundred feet above the Cook Inlet. It was dark, the time on the control panel clock registered 10.30pm, and navigation was not easy under these conditions. In the seat beside Winter, LeCat was leaning side-ways, staring downwards. 'That will be the fire,' he said into his headset microphone.

It was a heavily overcast night, but there was more illumination below the machine than might be imagined, flying as they were over the area where Alaska ended and the Pacific began its long surge towards Japan and Siberia. Gas burn-offs from the oil rigs glowed like fireballs in the night, like great torches held aloft by giants, and ahead an even fiercer glow lit the darkness. The refinery fire which Bazin's thermite bomb had started earlier in the day was spreading in the terminal where firemen from Anchorage were fighting to get it under control.

'There's the *Challenger* . . .'

Even below them in the night it looked enormous; 51,332 dead-weight tons of ship, seven hundred and forty-three feet long, one hundred and two feet wide, a floating platform of steel with the island bridge close to the stern, the bridge which had been represented by Cosgrove Manor, over four thousand five hundred miles away.

Winter lost a little altitude and pointed the plane's nose so it would pass directly over the navigation lights moving down the main channel. Besides her navigation lights the tanker had her deck lights on and a cluster of lamps attached to the foremast spotlit the forepart of the ship – and it was the forepart Winter was interested in.

'On the left side – near the front?' LeCat queried.

'On the port side, yes,' Winter replied as he angled the plane downwards. 'You can just see the landing point – that white-painted circle with the dot in the middle . . .'

'It's a damned small target,' LeCat complained.

'Big enough, and next time it will be daylight.' Winter leaned forward, putting the Cessna into a shallow dive. The lozenge-shaped platform of steel hardly seemed to move as he went down towards the tanker like a pilot on a bombing run-in. 'That's the catwalk down her middle,' Winter observed. 'That's important – so don't forget it. That takes us straight from the landing point to the bridge . . .'

LeCat said nothing, leaning well forward, his eyes taking in every detail, photographing it on his mind. Someone on deck near the foremast was looking up as the plane came in, shielding his eyes against the glare of the lights. 'There's the foremast with the crow's nest platform,' Winter pointed out.

'I see . . \'

LeCat was totally concentrated on his observation of the 50,000-ton tanker, like a soldier on reconnaissance assessing a fortress he would later have to storm. Winter lifted the nose of the machine so he was well clear of the radar mast, then he waggled his wings as the vessel vanished under them. Above the roar of the engine a faint sound came, the sound of the ship's siren. Mackay, a curious character, so remote in some ways, always acknowledged a salute, however bizarre.

'Now we know what it will look like from the air,' Winter said. 'That was the dress rehearsal – next time it will be the real thing . . .'

Turning the plane in a wide arc over Cook Inlet, he headed back at speed for Anchorage. After they landed, he phoned the reopened United Arab Republic consulate in San Francisco from an airport booth, asking for Mr Talaal Ismail who was waiting for the call. Winter's message was simple: Case Orange has been delivered.

They left Alaska aboard a North West Airlines flight at 11.30 pm which would land them at Seattle in the United States. Walgren, sitting apart from them, travelled in the same plane; from Seattle he would proceed direct to San Francisco. At 11.45pm the much-delayed Scandinavian Airlines Flight SK 989 from Copenhagen arrived at Anchorage. Sullivan was the first passenger to alight from the aircraft.

9

The 50,000-ton *Challenger* was rolling gently as she proceeded through the night at seventeen knots. She was now clear of Cook Inlet, heading out into the Pacific Ocean on her way to distant San Francisco. It was six in the morning and most of the crew were asleep, except for those on duty in the engine-room, the officer of the watch and the helmsman.

Seen from the sixty-foot high island bridge at her stern, this huge vessel was all deck, a vast platform of steel extending seven hundred and forty-three feet from stem to stern with a breadth of over one hundred feet. From the island bridge, five decks high, her endless main deck below was a maze of piping and valves with a breakwater in front of the main distribution area close to the base of the bridge – the area where pipes would be attached to suck out her desperately-needed cargo of oil when she reached the terminal near San Francisco.

A raised catwalk ran down the centre of her main deck to the distant forepeak, a catwalk men could move along when the main deck was submerged under heavy seas, a not infrequent hazard at this time of the year. Two large loading derricks reared up to port and starboard on either side of the catwalk near the bridge; five hundred feet beyond them the foremast loomed up with its crow's nest circular platform close to its summit. And these three vertical structures were the only mast-forms raised above the main deck beyond the bridge.

The *Challenger*, like so many other ships of her kind, was designed as a floating storage tank of oil, a tank divided into eighteen smaller tanks – one row of centre tanks and two more rows of wing tanks to port and starboard. This sub-division of the cargo-carrying space was vital because it provided stability and safety in turbulent seas: carried in one single, vast compartment fifty thousand tons of oil could endanger the life of the ship had it been able to sway and slosh about as one huge liquid unit. The weight alone would have become an unmanageable menace. On the morning of Friday January 17 the meteorological report forecast a quiet and uneventful voyage for the *Challenger*.

Betty Cordell stirred in her bunk, switched on the light and saw that it was almost six in the morning. She hadn't been able to sleep for the past hour. First night on board, she assumed. Sitting up in her bunk, she yawned and stretched and then got up sleepily. It might be interesting to see what the ship was like at this hour. Might even make an interesting story angle: *While The Ship Slept*.

Twenty-seven years old, slim and fair-haired, her hair cut short and close to the neck, there was a severity and detachment about her expression as she gazed critically at the reflection in the mirror over the basin. She knew people found her disconcerting when they first met her, that they described her as attractive but cold, and the description pleased her: it made people less inclined to draw her into a crowd. Like Winter, like Sullivan, even like LeCat, Betty Cordell was a lone wolf who preferred to go her own way.

She dressed quickly and without fuss: slacks, sweater and fur-lined parka. As an afterthought she decided to clean her teeth, then she collected her camera and opened the cabin door quietly. The ship creaked, rolled a little, tilting the deserted alleyway. She closed the door and went silently along the alleyway.

There was a light under the door marked 'Radio Cabin', which struck her as odd at this early hour. She paused, listening to the irregular tapping of a Morse key beyond the closed door, a familiar sound when her father had been a ham radio operator at their home in the Californian desert. She walked on, past the next cabin door, which also had a light underneath it, climbing a companionway, holding on to the rail. Bennett met her at the top.

'Didn't expect to see you up at this hour, Miss Cordell . . .'

'Betty, please . . .' She liked Bennett: he had a quiet sureness of manner she found appealing. 'I thought it might be interesting to get the atmosphere of the ship when everyone was asleep,' she explained. 'This series of magazine articles I'm doing on the energy crisis – I want to get an unusual angle on it.' She smiled. 'In any case, I'm not the only one up – the radio operator is working.'

'Working?' Bennett frowned. 'You must be mistaken . . .'

'I'm not!' Her natural combativeness surfaced. 'There's a light under his door.'

'Maybe he can't sleep. He's new to the ship.'

93

'He's working,' Betty insisted. 'I heard the Morse key tapping.'

'There's no message to send at this hour ...'

'He's sending one. Is something wrong?'

Bennett was frowning again, as though he couldn't understand why she was going on about it. 'Are you on your way up to the bridge?'

'If I may ...'

'It's all right – tell them I said you could come up. I'll be there myself in a few minutes. You'll find Walsh up there – he has this watch.'

'Then what are you doing up at this hour, Mr Bennett?'

'Couldn't sleep.' He grinned, then went quietly down the companionway and along the alleyway. And she was right, he thought. There was a light not only under Kinnaird's cabin door but also under the radio cabin door. He stopped at the second door, listening, hearing nothing but the creak of the woodwork and the faint hum of the engines. He opened the door.

The lean-faced wireless operator jumped, swivelled round in his chair and stared blankly at the first officer. An open handbook lay in front of the transmitter, a notepad with a pencil by its side. 'You should be catching up on sleep, Kinnaird,' Bennett said.

'I didn't know it was your watch,' the wireless operator observed.

'I didn't know you were up,' Bennett countered. 'The bell rings in your cabin if our call-sign comes through.'

'I know. I was memorising what has to be done. The sooner I know all Swan does the better for all of us.'

'You're an old friend of Swan's?' Bennett leaned against the bulkhead, watching the new man. He offered him a cigarette, but Kinnaird shook his head and said he didn't smoke. He waited while the wireless operator yawned before replying.

'I've known him for years. I hope the flu gets better soon. It can lead to complications ...'

'Kinnaird, what was the message you sent?'

Bennett shot the question quickly and unexpectedly, following his previous domestic enquiry, and he studied the reaction closely. Kinnaird looked bewildered. 'I haven't sent any message ...'

94

'The message Miss Cordell heard you sending,' Bennett explained patiently. 'She can't sleep either and she heard the key when she passed this cabin door a few minutes ago.'

'She must have heard this.' Kinnaird picked up the pencil and beat an irregular tattoo on the table. 'I do it when I'm concentrating. Some people have music on – I tap a pencil.'

'Doesn't sound much like a Morse key tapping.'

'How would she know the difference?' Kinnaird shut the handbook. 'I think I will go back to bed. The met. report looks good.'

'It always looks good just before hell breaks loose.'

Because Victoria, Canada, is two hours ahead of Anchorage time, it was eight in the morning when André Dupont came on to the bridge of the *Pêcheur* with a piece of paper in his hand. 'The first position signal has just come through from *Challenger*,' he told the French captain of the trawler.

The captain marked the position and the time carefully on the chart he had already. From now on they would receive a flow of signals as the *Challenger* moved hourly closer to an approximate position two hundred miles off the coast of British Columbia. By the time she reached that position the *Pêcheur* would also be there. This would be the interception point.

The North West Airlines flight carrying Winter and LeCat to Seattle landed at that American city close to the Canadian border at 4.25am, local time. Both men were tired now – they had missed a night's sleep – so they took a cab to the Greyhound bus terminal in Seattle. Waiting fifteen minutes inside the bus station – they had now effectively broken any link between themselves and their airport arrival – they took another cab to the most expensive hotel in Seattle, the Washington Plaza.

Booking their rooms independently, as though they didn't know each other, they slept through most of the day. After a quick meal in an outside coffee shop, they took a cab back to the bus station, waited there another fifteen minutes, then travelled in a different cab to the railroad station. Boarding the 5.20pm train to Canada, they arrived at Vancouver at ten o'clock at night. Dupont was waiting for them with a powerboat to take them to Victoria.

By the time they boarded the *Pêcheur*, Winter was in a hurry. It was close to midnight; soon it would be Saturday January 18 and zero hour was Sunday morning. 'I want this ship at sea by midnight,' he told LeCat. 'Tell your French crew to get off their backsides . . .'

'That may not be possible . . .'

'Make it possible.'

LeCat returned to Winter's tiny cabin after carrying the Englishman's order to the bridge. 'The captain says he may manage it – for you,' he added sourly. 'He has informed the port authority . . .'

'The weapons are aboard?'

'In the explosives magazine.'

Winter went up on deck to check for himself. The marine biological research the vessel was supposed to be engaged in was good cover for this purpose also – concealment of the weapons. Certain forms of research involve the use of explosives, and LeCat had organised the construction of a magazine on deck. A steel compartment was bolted to the deck; painted warning red, it carried the words 'Explosives Magazine' stencilled across two sides.

'Open it up,' Winter told LeCat.

'You want to check everything?'

'Everything. Open it up . . .'

A bank of fog had drifted in during the evening. On deck seamen were moving about in the gloom, preparing for the ship's midnight departure; at the foot of the gangway a fog-blurred silhouette stood on guard. Winter shone a torch inside the magazine LeCat had unlocked. The contents looked innocent and standard, considering their resting-place – until LeCat lifted up several sticks of explosive to expose the Skorpion pistols underneath.

'You remembered the stencils and spray-guns?' Winter asked.

'Under the pistols,' LeCat snapped irritably. 'Customs men don't like fooling around inside here . . .' Which was just as well, otherwise they might have wondered what was going on when they found stencils bearing the legend 'USCG' – United States Coastguard.

'What about the wet-suits?' Winter asked.

LeCat had to show him everything, including the escape apparatus for when the time came for them to leave the hi-jacked *Challenger*. On their way to the carpenter's store under the high forecastle, Winter climbed up into the S.58 Sikorsky now delivered by Walgren's pilot friend and sitting on the platform constructed over one of the fish-holds.

He kept LeCat waiting while he checked the fuel and oil gauges. As soon as dawn came on Saturday morning – when the *Pêcheur* would be well out in the Pacific – he would take off in the helicopter for a trial flight. LeCat would fly with him; also the thirteen-man terrorist team which had flown from London to Montreal half an hour before Winter himself had departed for Anchorage three days ago. These men were now aboard the trawler they had filtered on to in parties of two's and three's when they reached Victoria. Once again Winter had decided on a rehearsal for the next stage of the operation – the seizure of the *Challenger*.

Jumping back on to the main deck, he looked at the machine. It was painted pale grey, the standard colour of United States Coast Guard helicopters. During the night André Dupont would use the hidden stencils and spray-gun, painting on the necessary insignia; by morning the *Pêcheur* would carry on her platform a perfect reproduction of an American Coast Guard helicopter. Winter led LeCat through the fog to the carpenter's store on the forecastle.

LeCat was sweating as he raised the hatch cover, cursing the Englishman for his insistence on seeing everything for himself, sweating because inside the carpenter's store was hidden the one thing Winter must not find.

The Frenchman went down the ladder first into the cramped compartment where wood shavings littered the floor; the atmosphere was tinged with their odour. 'There,' LeCat said. 'Satisfied?' Winter looked round carefully. An inflatable Zodiac, a large rubber craft to which an outboard motor could be attached, was roped to a bulkhead; the motor inside its casing stood in a corner. Inside several large suitcases – each of which LeCat had to open for Winter – fifteen wet-suits were packed with masks and air bottles. Against another bulkhead a large, box-like seat, made of new wood, was bolted to the deck. 'That wasn't there before,' Winter said. 'What is it?'

97

'The captain decided the carpenter needed a seat – to keep him off the deck,' LeCat replied.

He held his breath, waiting for the Englishman's reaction. 'Good idea.' Winter went back up the ladder, followed by the Frenchman, who was sweating now with relief. As he closed the hatch LeCat glanced down at the carpenter's seat, a seat large enough to conceal a suitcase-like object made of steel, a case measuring sixty centimetres in length by thirty centimetres in width, an object weighing almost two hundred pounds, its canvas cover plastered with hotel labels from all over the world. Jean-Philippe Antoine's nuclear device.

A fresh signal from Kinnaird confirming the *Challenger*'s latest position came in soon after Winter had arrived aboard the *Pêcheur*. It was added to the chart showing the British tanker's southern progress from Alaska by André Dupont. Winter was studying the chart when the *Pêcheur* put to sea a few minutes after midnight, moving slowly through the fog, its siren sounding one long blast at the regulation two-minute intervals as it headed out past the southern tip of Vancouver Island. The Englishman pointed to a cross he had marked on the chart. 'My guess is we shall intercept *Challenger* somewhere about here – roughly about thirty-six hours from now. It will mean hanging about in mid-ocean, but that gives us a margin for error . . .'

Past midnight, it was already Saturday morning, January 18. The cross Winter had marked on the chart stood at latitude 47 10 N, longitude 132 10 W – approximately two hundred and fifty miles west of Vancouver Island.

10

'There is a limit. When a handful of men – primitive men with the minds and morals of bandits – lay their hands on the keys to a whole civilisation's survival, then we have reached that limit. Then is the time to act . . .'

Extract from minutes of British Cabinet meeting when Prime Minister spoke to Inner Cabinet on December 1.

US War Department report to National Security Council in Washington, January 17.
'Satellite surveillance of the Indian Ocean area shows two British supertankers, *York* and *Chester*, leaving the Mozambique Channel, heading north-east towards the Persian Gulf. Photoanalysis reveals canvas-covered cargoes on the decks of these 200,000-ton ships which could be arms (no confirmation of this). Believed Britain may be bartering arms for oil at Abu Dhabi.

Comment: No recently concluded British oil deals with Abu Dhabi have been reported.'

It was fifteen minutes away from Friday January 17 when Larry Sullivan's Boeing 707 landed at Anchorage International Airport ten and a half hours behind schedule. He phoned the Nikisiki oil terminal from the airport and heard that the *Challenger* was now at sea.

Sharing a cab with three American oil men, Sullivan was taken to the leading hotel in Anchorage, the Westward, where he booked a room and went to bed. He gave up the attempts to sleep at three in the morning, got up, shaved and dressed. He was suffering from an overdose of jet lag, the disorientation of mind and body which comes from flying long hours across the roof of the world. Physically exhausted, he was mentally alert, excited as his internal clocks struggled to adjust themselves to the time lag.

At three in the morning in southern Alaska it was noon in London – the States was on daylight saving time. He put through a call to Victor Harper and sat on the bed smoking while he waited. Seen from London, he had felt there was good reason to come to Alaska – Winter had been placed in Hahnemann's office in Hamburg where he had studied blueprints of the *Challenger*'s twin ship *Chieftain*; in MacGillivray's office he had been placed making specific enquiries about the *Challenger* herself. But that was seen from London.

Seen from Alaska at three in the morning, enduring the weird after-effects of jet lag, the reasons for making the trip seemed less weighty. For one thing the tanker had sailed safely; in about four days' time she would dock in San Francisco. The phone by his bedside rang.

'Larry, Mr Harper is out of the country,' Vivian Herries, Harper's personal assistant explained. 'He's still in Genoa, so he can't be reached . . .'

'Damn!' Sullivan said. 'Sorry, not you – I'm reeling from jet lag. Vivian, I just missed the *Challenger* by hours – she's on her way to San Francisco. As far as you know, is everything normal? Nothing out of pattern?'

'As normal as anything is in the shipping business these days – with the energy crisis. Just a minute, there was one thing out of pattern – she has a woman aboard on this trip.' She chuckled. 'Can you imagine that, knowing old Mackay thinks his ship should be run like a St James's club – strictly for men only. But he's got a real live woman prancing about on board this trip.'

'Who is she? Officer's wife?'

'She must be. Mr Harper just mentioned it in passing on his way out. I think it could be the chief engineer's wife – she's been longing to do the trip for months . . .'

Sullivan rubbed at his forehead; for a moment he had felt dizzy. 'Vivian, can you think of anyone here in Anchorage I can talk to about the *Challenger* – apart from the oil terminal people, that is . . .'

'Mrs Swan, the wireless operator's wife,' Vivian suggested promptly. 'She was in the office here about three months ago and she told me she lived outside Anchorage. Would you like the address?'

Sullivan noted down the address, said he might phone Harper tomorrow, said yes, he'd try and get some sleep, and put down the phone. Five hours later, having just eaten his second breakfast, he found Swan's number in the directory, phoned the number and couldn't get an answer. He decided to drive out to the Swan home.

The house had a shut-up look. There was snow on the mountains beyond the Matanuska valley, snow on a copse of fir trees on the far side of the highway. Sullivan rang the bell again and then

100

strolled round the back. A very shut-up look indeed. He peered into a window in the barn and saw a power cable plugged into a red Ford. Anti-freeze measure. It was a wasted trip – he could have been sleeping at the Westward. Sullivan felt he could sleep now.

He walked round the front of the house back to his hired car as a blue Chevrolet came down a distant drive and turned on to the highway. He stood there as the car slowed, then turned into the Swan's drive. A red-haired woman of about thirty who wore a skull-fitting, fur cap rolled down the window as she stopped. 'Are you looking for someone?'

'For Mrs Swan. Place seems to be shut up.'

'They've gone away – on Charlie's ship. Are you a friend?'

'My company insures the *Challenger*.' Sullivan grinned. 'I'm the best friend they've got. I thought the captain didn't like women aboard too much?' It was something to say. The whole thing was explained now, including Vivian Herries' reference to a woman aboard the *Challenger*. Mrs Swan had struck lucky; she was travelling with her husband on the trip.

'I'm Madge Thompson.' The red-haired woman extended her hand through the window. Sullivan gave her his name. 'Julie – that's Mrs Swan,' Madge Thompson explained, 'was in quite a rush. She phoned me about a quarter after three just before they left. The captain must have mellowed. I gather the whole thing was a last-minute arrangement. She sounded tense . . .'

'Tense?'

'Excited. She's wanted to do the trip for ages . . .'

They chatted for several minutes and then Mrs Thompson left for Anchorage. Sullivan had trouble starting his car – the engine was already starting to freeze up – and drove back to the city. He had come all the way to Alaska for nothing; no one was trying to sabotage the tanker. And he needed some sleep.

'What time did this fire at the oil terminal start?'

Sullivan asked the question as he sat at the bar of the Westward Hotel in Anchorage. It was 1pm, Friday January 17. Almost asleep behind the wheel during his drive back from the Swan home, he had freshened up the moment he had stepped into the hotel lobby;

still another reaction from jet lag. Now he felt strangely alert, hepped up as though he had taken drugs. It was the barman who had mentioned the fire at Nikisiki.

'About a quarter after three in the afternoon,' the barman said as he served Sullivan his second Scotch on the rocks. 'They think it was sabotage,' he went on with relish. 'I guess the A-rabs are behind it – like in Venezuela. They want us to freeze to death. And we could do it here . . .' He glanced behind the bar. 'Thermostat turned down to sixty-two – in this climate, in this state which is swimming in oil . . .'

'Not yet,' Sullivan reminded him, 'not until North Slope comes on tap . . .'

'You British?' the barman enquired. 'Lots of people think the British are Australian, but I can always tell.'

'I'm British . . .'

'You got a car?'

'I managed to hire one – cost me a fortune . . .'

'You remember to plug in the power cable? Guy was here yesterday who forgot to plug in the cable – though he reckoned someone pulled out his cable. He was British – a sea captain.'

'Not Captain Mackay?'

'You know him? That was his name.' The barman chattered on. 'Took a call here at the bar and gave his name. He left in a rush – ran back to his room, then I saw him leave with his bag, still running. About a quarter after three it was . . .'

'You say someone yanked the power cable out of his car?'

'So they say. Well-built guy, your Captain Mackay – with a red face and those blue eyes sailors is supposed to have and seldom do. I got a memory for faces. A guy comes into this bar once five years back, comes in again tomorrow and I'm going to remember him. If he only looks in this bar and I see him, I remember him . . .'

'That was Mackay,' Sullivan said absent-mindedly. Everything seemed to have happened at three-fifteen the previous day. The Swans had left home hurriedly at 3.15pm. Mackay had rushed out of the hotel about 3.15pm. The fire at the Nikisiki oil terminal had started at about 3.15pm. And the fire was sabotage.

He blinked, suddenly so tired he could have fallen over. He left the bar and went up to his room, trying to recall an idea which had passed through his head while the barman was chattering away. Something to do with remembering faces . . . Closing the door, he locked it, flopped on the bed and fell asleep.

When it was one o'clock in the afternoon, Anchorage time, as Sullivan listened to the barman at the Westward, it was midnight, Damascus time, as Sheikh Gamal Tafak savoured the cup of black coffee he was drinking.

It probably wasn't quite true to say that Tafak was savouring the taste of the black coffee, because it is difficult to relish two things at the same time. As he sat in his room in the Saudi Arabian embassy in the Syrian capital, Tafak was savouring the message he had received a few hours earlier. *Case Orange has been delivered*. Winter, he was thinking, was an ingenious man; anyone transmitting the message would assume that it was a mistake, that it meant cases of oranges had been delivered. To Tafak it meant that all was going well, that the British tanker *Challenger* had now left Alaska – with Winter's own wireless operator aboard.

He checked his watch. Soon the Mercedes would arrive, the car taking him to a secret headquarters where he would remain until the operation had been completed. He would stay there until the Frenchman, LeCat, had done the job, until all the British hostages aboard the ship had been killed, until San Francisco had been ruined by the catastrophic explosion. Then he would hurry back to Damascus for the next meeting of OAPEC, the Arab oil-producing countries' organisation. At that meeting he would persuade or compel all of them to cut off the oil flow to the West. If any country refused, the Arab terrorist dynamite teams would move in, destroying that country's oil-fields. Someone tapped nervously on the door. 'Come in,' Tafak called out.

'Your car has arrived, Excellency . . .'

It was 5.30pm on Friday evening when Sullivan walked back into the bar at the Westward. He ordered a Scotch on the rocks. 'Yes, sir!' The barman looked at Sullivan. 'You've changed your suit. Like I said, I notice things . . .'

'You said you remembered people,' Sullivan reminded him.

'Never forget a face . . .'

'Test the memory.' Sullivan laid the photo of Winter on the counter, the profile shot where he had painted out the moustache Winter had worn while visiting Paul Hahnemann. He picked up his drink and sipped it while the barman made a performance out of studying the print.

'He's never been in my bar. I'll stake my job on it. Not while I was on duty ...'

'I'll take your word for that ...'

'Disappointed?' The barman grinned at Sullivan who shrugged his shoulders. It had been a very long shot indeed. 'Not in my bar,' the American emphasised. 'But two nights ago he was standing in that entrance over there. He looked in, changed his mind and disappeared. Mackay was in here at the time, having a beer. Be about nine in the evening.'

Sullivan nearly choked on his drink. 'You're sure? Yes, of course you are,' he added hastily. 'Was he staying here?'

'No idea. He never came back. Wednesday night it was. You could enquire at reception ...'

Sullivan drank the rest of his large, neat Scotch in one gulp and didn't feel a thing. Winter was in Alaska.

Sleep was the last thing Sullivan thought of during the next few hours as he stirred up half Anchorage, asking questions, showing the photograph, checking, checking, checking ... The night clerk at the Westward recognised the picture, confirmed that Winter had stayed there one night, the same night Mackay had stayed at the hotel, that he had registered in the name of Robert Forrest, that meals had been sent up to his room – the duplicate copy of the bill was full of information. Winter had booked out the following day, Thursday January 16, the same day the *Challenger* had sailed from Nikisiki at ten in the evening.

Chief of Police Jo Mulligan of Anchorage took Sullivan's information very seriously when he saw the Lloyd's of London identification. Within one hour – close to midnight – an all points bulletin was circulating throughout the whole of Alaska with Robert Forrest's name and description and reproductions of the photograph Sullivan had supplied. And Sullivan himself was driven in a patrol car to the oil terminal at Nikisiki. He arrived there at two in the morning, hardly able to keep his eyes open.

It was something that Winter, believing there was no photo of himself on record, could never have foreseen – that a photograph taken secretly in a German shipbuilder's office in faraway Hamburg would be transported by a persistent British investigator to Alaska, that it would be identified by a barman whose conceit and hobby was his ability to remember people he saw for only a few seconds.

And Chief of Police Mulligan acted with vigour because he immediately linked Winter's record and presence in Alaska with the firebomb attack on the oil terminal. Who knew – Mulligan might be the first policeman in the world to get a lead on the international terrorist gang or gangs which were blowing up pipelines and oil refineries all the way from California to central Europe? He went to the International airport himself.

Sullivan found nothing at the oil terminal. No one had seen Winter in that sensitive area. The departure of the *Challenger* had been perfectly normal. 'Sure,' the terminal superintendent informed Sullivan, 'the ship left two hours ahead of schedule with two tanks unfilled. But Mackay registered his early departure in advance – he was worried about the fire spreading to the jetties. And no one gets aboard that ship without Mackay knowing about it – he's one hell of a careful guy. There's a seaman at the foot of the gangway until they haul it aboard.'

Dropping from lack of sleep, Sullivan was driven back in the patrol car to the Westward where he flopped into bed at six in the morning and slept through the day. He was consuming a large steak, washed down with a gallon of strong coffee, when the call came through from police headquarters at seven in the evening. Mulligan had found something.

'Thursday, close to midnight, Robert Forrest took the night flight for Seattle. He moved out just as you were moving in, Sullivan. The airport girl who recognised his picture came back on duty an hour ago; hence the delay. Want some more coffee?'

Jo Mulligan was a round-bodied man of fifty, hard-looking and with his still-dark hair cut short to the scalp. A smile rarely crossed his face and he talked quickly. Sullivan liked his businesslike approach to life.

'So, we've lost him,' he said as the chief of police poured more coffee. 'It's curious, you know – he spends twenty-four hours here and he's away.'

'Long enough to detonate that bomb inside the terminal. He could have organised that North Slope pipeline bust we had a couple of months back. My guess is he comes in at the critical moment, sees that the bombs detonate, then moves out. And my further guess is he's on his way now to another prime piece of oil property.' Mulligan leaned back in his swivel chair. 'Maybe Texas. There are some nice targets for him in Texas. We're extending the all points bulletin to cover the whole of the States – the FBI are in on this thing now.'

'So you don't think that tanker – the *Challenger* – is involved?'

'No!' Mulligan was emphatic. 'They're not hitting tankers. Yet. These bastards are going for gut – the refineries processing the oil we so desperately need, the pipelines which carry the juice through our industrial veins. Those A-rabs are out to bring western civilisation toppling – so long as Israel exists. The extremists have got the whole Middle East oil bowl in the palm of their hands.' Mulligan sighed. 'We should have seen it coming after 1973. We should have seen it coming . . .'

'Nothing for me here any more.' Sullivan pushed his empty coffee cup away. 'I'm catching a plane tomorrow.'

'You going back home. To London?'

'No. To Seattle . . .'

The machine landed with a heavy bump, roared forward, its engines filling the interior with vibration. It seemed to be going too fast, to be heading for disaster, and the view beyond the window was a blur. Sullivan pushed a magazine into the pocket of the seat in front of him and relaxed as the Boeing 707 slowed. For the first time in his life he was in Seattle.

It was just after two o'clock in the afternoon of Sunday January 19 when he alighted from the plane. FBI agents Peters and Carmady were waiting for the flight and took him into a private room. They listened to his story without too much enthusiasm when he talked about the *Challenger*, it seemed to the Englishman; perhaps it was because they were so polite.

'You can forget the tanker,' Peters advised. 'This man is sabotaging refineries. After he came off the plane last Friday he spent several hours at the Washington Plaza Hotel here. A reception clerk who booked him in recognised your photograph. And we found a cab driver who dropped him at the bus terminal later. Then he vanished.'

'My bet is we'll never find him again,' Sullivan replied. 'In Europe nobody knows a thing about him – that photo I got from the German shipbuilder is the only one in existence, I gather . . .'

'We'll go on trying,' Peters said reassuringly. 'Interpol have nothing on him – and our Washington records don't have him. But one day, somewhere, he has to surface . . .'

When they had gone Sullivan sat in the airport coffee shop drinking more coffee. The trail had gone dead, and now he was inclined to agree with Mulligan and the FBI agent that the tanker was not involved. When he had finished his coffee he would put in a phone call to Harper, telling him he was catching the Pan Am evening flight back to London.

Staring through the window he was looking north-west where the sun was filtering through a heavy overcast. Somewhere in that direction, about five hundred miles away, the *Challenger* was proceeding southwards on another uneventful voyage.

11

Lat. 47.50 N Lon. 132.45 W 1300 hours.
The US Coast Guard helicopter was coming in at no more than a hundred feet above the grey waves. On the starboard wing deck of *Challenger* Captain Mackay focused his glasses and the machine crisped into his vision, filling the lenses, showing the insignia on

its pale grey fuselage. *No. 5421. USCG.* First Officer Bennett ran out from the navigating bridge on to the wing deck.

'Emergency, sir. That chopper is in trouble. Message just came in from her – permission to land before she crashes . . .'

Inside Mackay's glasses the machine blurred as it passed through a patch of mist, then its silhouette was crisp again. It was impossible to see inside the control cabin. A puff of black smoke was rising from the silhouette now and Mackay thought the engine was coughing.

'Clear the main deck, Mr Bennett . . .' Mackay's expression tightened as the puff expanded into a billow of ominous smoke. 'Turn the ship into the wind. Reduce speed to fourteen knots.' Mackay walked quickly back on to the navigating bridge where Betty Cordell was keeping out of the way, staying close to the front of the bridge. Mackay stood beside her and she was careful to say nothing. The chopper was closer and smoke was pouring off her, plucked away by the wind.

'Fire precautions, Mr Bennett . . .'

Mackay looked grim: fire was something you could do without aboard a tanker carrying fifty thousand tons of oil. And he faced an impossible choice – either to let her land on deck or signal her to stand clear, in which case the chopper might sink before a boat could reach her.

Sixty feet below where he stood by the bridge window with the American girl, men were already evacuating the main deck. The engine throb was slower. The huge vessel was beginning her turn into the wind. Bennett issued more orders for fire stations to be manned. 'Shall I get off the bridge?' Betty Cordell suggested. Mackay shook his head. 'Might be a story in it for you – so long as it doesn't end in tragedy . . .'

The huge ship continued its turn as the helmsman gripped the wheel. Mackay checked the time by the bridge clock. It was exactly one in the afternoon of Sunday January 19. 'Get a message off to the mainland,' he ordered. 'I am picking up your helicopter Number 5421 . . .'

Bennett phoned the radio cabin, instructed Kinnaird to send the signal instantly, then returned to the front of the bridge. 'I wonder where she comes from, sir? We're over two hundred miles from the Canadian coast . . .'

'Must be off some weather cutter.'

'There isn't one stationed on the chart within five hundred miles. I'm afraid I don't quite understand this . . .'

'Thank God for small mercies,' Mackay growled. The smoke was disappearing; no more was emitting from the machine which was now turning in a circle to fly towards the bow of the ship. Mackay wasn't too happy about what might happen in the next few minutes. Landing a helicopter aboard a moving ship in mid-ocean calls for a certain skill.

They waited and it was very quiet on the bridge. All the necessary orders had been given. The tanker, originally proceeding at seventeen knots through a gentle swell, had reduced speed to fourteen knots, had turned into the wind. A skilled pilot should have no trouble landing his machine under these conditions – providing his engine kept functioning. Inside three minutes she should have landed.

'Signal final permission to land?' Bennett asked.

Mackay looked down along the main deck. It had been cleared of all personnel except for three fire-fighting seamen on the fore-castle – close to the landing point. Visibility was good: the white-painted circle on the port bow where the helicopter should alight showed up clearly. 'Permission to land,' Mackay said. Bennett relayed the message to the radio cabin.

The machine was hovering now, letting the 50,000-ton tanker steam towards it. 'Seems to have his machine under perfect control now,' the sceptical Bennett commented. 'Wonder what's wrong with it?'

Winter maintained his hover, letting the lozenge-shaped steel platform cruising over the ocean come towards him. He had turned off the tap which had fed heavy oil into the exhaust – creating the ominous smoke Mackay had seen from the starboard wing deck.

The psychological timing was important. First he had emitted smoke as they were approaching the *Challenger* to worry the captain, to persuade him to give permission to land. Then he had later turned it off in case Mackay became too worried and decided to refuse permission. The radio cracked and Kinnaird's signal came through. 'Permission to land . . .'

'We're going in . . .'

The *Pêcheur* Winter had flown off was forty miles away, too far away for Mackay to see her even from his high bridge. It had been an anxious time, searching for the tanker even while Kinnaird wirelessed *Challenger*'s position at frequent intervals, a reasonably safe action since this was the time of day when he sent a routine report to the London office. But they had found her.

Seated beside Winter, staring at the ocean, LeCat had heard the final words through his headset. 'We're going in . . .' His stomach muscles tightened. It was always like this just before an attack – the physical and mental shock to the system when you realised it was really going to happen. Just like Algeria . . .

'Remember what I told you,' Winter warned. 'I go out first. You wait until I'm on the catwalk and almost under the bridge. The others stay inside – the sight of a dozen men piling out on deck will alarm them. We must seize control before the penny drops . . .'

LeCat took out his Skorpion pistol, balancing the weapon in his hand. A quite unnecessary gesture, it put a finer edge on his nerves. When they got moving it would be all right: it was the last few seconds before the landing which were unpleasant.

It was Winter who had chosen the Czech Skorpion .32 pistol for arming the terrorists. LeCat would have preferred a heavier-calibre gun. The version which slipped inside a shoulder holster carried ten rounds; another version which would not fit inside holsters carried twenty rounds. It was, up to a point, like a small sub-machine gun. Winter had issued the strictest instructions that there should be no shooting, but in case something did happen a heavier-calibre weapon would have been more dangerous; after all, they were landing on a floating oil tank.

'Going down . . .'

The ocean came up to them hungrily, a grey, white-capped ocean, cold and forbidding. Winter was descending towards the water as the tanker came on at fourteen knots, and it looked as though they could be submerged – with the massive steel bow riding over them. LeCat leant sideways, saw the unstable water coming up.

He disliked the sensation because he was wholly at the mercy of another man's skill. Slipping the Skorpion back inside its shoulder holster, he pulled his parka front together to hide it. Behind him another thirteen men crouched together nervously, not enjoying the experience, not looking at each other for fear their nervousness showed. There was André Dupont, who had flown with Winter the day they had attacked the Italian Syndicate motor cruiser in the Mediterranean, who had phoned through LeCat's order to Hamburg that Sullivan must now be killed. There was Alain Blancard, a veteran of Algeria and a skilled sniper. And there were eleven others.

LeCat, ignoring the intense vibration, the thumping beat of the rotor overhead, pressed his cheek hard against the window. Where was the bloody tanker? They were almost in the sea. Had Winter, despite his pilot's skill, mistimed it? LeCat's stomach ached with the strain and his hands were sweating. Where the hell was the ship? Grey steel slid past below them, so close he felt he could reach out and touch it. There was a bump. They were landing.

'Text book landing,' Bennett observed as the US Coast Guard helicopter hit the deck.

The pilot cut the motor, the rotor-whizz faded, the blades appeared, spinning fast, then more slowly before they stopped moving. The three seamen on the forecastle with fire-fighting apparatus ran down on to the main deck as the machine's door opened and a tall man jumped out, landed in a crouch, straightened up and headed along the catwalk for the bridge.

'Doesn't waste much time, does he?' Bennett remarked. 'Big chap, must be six feet tall . . .'

The pilot was still wearing his helmet and face shield over his eyes and this gave him a sinister appearance as he half-ran along the catwalk, glanced up at the bridge, saluted and disappeared. In the distance Bennett saw two more men jump out of the machine and then start talking to the three seamen. It all seemed very normal, a routine rescue operation. Mackay turned to face the entrance to the bridge where he expected the pilot to appear.

'Five more men have come out of that machine,' Bennett said sharply. 'How many is the damned thing carrying?'

Mackay strode to the front of the bridge and stared along the main deck. He counted five more men coming out of the helicopter while he watched, but they were all staying close to the landing point, chatting with the three seamen as far as he could see. 'Send the bosun down there,' he said. 'Send him with a walkie-talkie...'

'Stay exactly where you are, gentlemen. If anyone moves the captain dies from a bullet – instead of from old age...'

Mackay spun round. The pilot stood in the wrong place – he was standing at the entrance from the starboard wing deck. He must have dodged along under the bridge when he was out of sight. He held a pistol in his right hand and the muzzle was aimed at Mackay's stomach. The gun, with only one-and-a-half inches of the barrel protruding from the body of the weapon, had a highly lethal look.

'This is a hi-jack,' the pilot warned. 'We shan't hesitate to shoot...'

'Who the hell are you?' Mackay demanded.

'The Weathermen. Stop asking questions. You...' The pilot gestured towards Bennett. 'Go and stand at the front of the bridge where my men can see you. Then wave to them – swing your arms round like a windmill.'

The helmsman, a man called Harris from Newcastle-upon-Tyne, gripped his wheel and kept the vessel on course. He had received no fresh orders from the captain. By the window Betty Cordell froze. 'Do as he tells you,' Mackay said quietly to Bennett.

'Move!' The pilot elevated his pistol, aiming it point blank at Mackay's chest. 'Do you want to get your captain killed?'

Bennett moved, went over to the window and swivelled his arms in a windmill motion. A group of men came running down the catwalk at a fast trot, leaving two men behind with the seamen at the landing point. Bennett counted twelve men running down the catwalk, all of them armed, the man in front very nimble in spite of his short height and wide shoulders. They vanished under the bridge.

The pilot waited, holding the pistol very steady, and twice he glanced at the bridge clock as though checking the elapse of a specific number of minutes. The helmsman, a short, dark-haired man with quick eyes, stayed frozen behind his wheel. Betty Cordell stood stiffly, her hands clenched as she stared at the eyes behind the shield. They were stunned, all of them except perhaps Bennett whom Mackay had ordered to obey the pilot, sensing that he might have done something dangerous; so easy to make a quick gesture of resistance, and so easy to get shot when the other man has the gun.

There was a clatter of feet and two armed men appeared from the same direction the pilot had come – from the starboard wing deck. They took up positions on either side of the bridge, aiming their pistols so they had the prisoners in a potential crossfire. The pilot spoke to one of them in French, which Mackay understood. 'Has LeCat gone straight to the engine-room? Good. When I leave the bridge these people are to stay exactly where they are – including the woman.' He looked at Betty Cordell, speaking in English. 'Why are you on board?'

'I'm Betty Cordell, a reporter. I came for a story. It looks as though I've got one . . .'

The pilot smiled bleakly. 'You may wish you had stayed at home. You will remain here on the bridge until I decide where to put you. You are a problem I didn't anticipate.' He looked at Mackay. 'Get your ship back on course, Captain.'

'On course?'

'Yes, for San Francisco. And be very careful what instructions you give. I have a man who can shoot a sextant and plot a course as well as your first officer.'

Mackay grunted. 'You know the penalty for piracy on the high seas?'

The pilot walked towards the captain, stopping when he was a few feet away, leaving a clear field of fire for the guards at either side of the bridge. Stripping off his helmet, he looked down at Mackay who was five feet eight tall, inches shorter than the thin, bony-faced Englishman. 'My name is Winter. I seem to remember I asked you to issue a certain order.' His voice was soft and menacing and Mackay stiffened. 'You do value the lives of your crew, I take it?'

'Mr Bennett,' Mackay said crisply. 'Put the ship back on course for San Francisco. Increase speed to seventeen knots.'

Bennett issued the order to Harris, the helmsman, and then the bridge phone rang. 'That may be the engine-room chief, Brady,' Winter told Mackay. 'At this moment there are four armed men in that part of the ship. Warn Brady that he is to carry out any instruction they give him – and that he will continue to receive all navigational orders from you.' He smiled bleakly. 'Engine-room chiefs are notoriously men with minds of their own . . .'

Mackay said nothing as he lifted the phone, then personally gave the order to increase speed. He added his own warning: 'These men who have come aboard are armed and dangerous – do nothing that could affect the welfare of the crew, Chief . . .'

'Very good.' Winter turned to Betty Cordell who had been watching him for several minutes as though trying to assess what kind of man this was. 'I say it again, Miss Cordell – you will not leave this bridge without my personal permission. You are a problem I shall have to work out . . .'

'She is an innocent passenger,' Mackay broke in with a rasp in his voice. 'She is also an American citizen and I would advise you . . .'

'When I require your advice I will request it. If you had let me finish what I was saying I would have said I am concerned for her safety.' Winter glanced at the French guards who did not understand what he was saying. 'Some of these men are not the best of company for women, so you must not do anything foolish. Later, I will decide whether you should be confined to your cabin for the rest of the trip . . .'

Winter left the bridge abruptly and Mackay stared at his first officer. 'I don't understand that man, Winter, at all. And who the hell are The Weathermen?'

'A particularly savage bunch of American underground terrorists. They blew up a lot of banks in the States a few years ago. I thought they were all dead . . .'

'Someone resurrected them,' Mackay muttered. 'And keep your voice down. I'm not convinced these two thugs with us on the bridge don't understand English. I also don't understand why

Winter has Frenchmen with him when you say The Weathermen were Americans...'

'The same thought had crossed my mind.'

Mackay looked across at the swarthy, tanned ruffian who was leaning against the starboard bulkhead, one ankle crossed over the other, his pistol barrel resting on his left forearm. The barrel was aimed at Bennett but it was the amused, insolent way the Frenchman was studying Betty Cordell's figure Mackay found most disturbing. 'One thing puzzles me, Bennett,' he said softly. 'Winter said this was a hi-jack – and yet he still wants us to continue on course for San Francisco. Doesn't make sense.'

'It shouldn't be long before they tumble to the fact that something's wrong here, sir – I mean the people on the mainland,' Bennett murmured. 'Kinnaird got that signal off before these swine came aboard – reporting that we'd picked up a Coast Guard chopper. If Winter hi-jacked the machine as well, the Coast Guard will know where to look for it now.'

'So maybe in a few hours we can look forward to a US cruiser looming over the horizon. In which case we shall have a lot to thank Mr Kinnaird for...'

Within fifteen minutes of landing aboard the *Challenger* – as soon as he left the bridge – Winter proceeded rapidly with certain precautions. He called Bennett down from the bridge to accompany him on his swift tour of the ship. His first trip was to the dispensary next to the galley. The poisons cupboard, containing drugs – including sleeping pills – was locked up and Winter pocketed the key. 'I wouldn't like the cook to start mixing something with our food,' he told Bennett. 'Most unprofessional...'

He then demanded that Bennett hand over the pass-key which opened every cabin door on the ship. Escorted by a guard, the first officer fetched the key from his cabin. Winter pocketed this key and then made his way to the boat-deck with Bennett and a guard. He waited while the guard climbed up into each of the two large boats and heaved the hand-cranked radio transmitters, part of the standard equipment of a lifeboat, overboard.

'For God's sake,' Bennett protested, 'if something happens to this ship...'

'Something has happened to it,' Winter reminded him. 'And I don't want spare transmitters hanging about where some quick-witted seaman can send out an SOS. Now, I want all the walkie-talkies you use when you communicate with each other while the ship's docking . . .'

Winter also reserved the captain's day cabin for those of the ship's crew not on duty to be kept inside. This reduced the limited manpower at his disposal which had to be employed on guard duty. As Winter had foreseen two months ago when he met Ahmed Riad in Tangier, the most suitable ship for a hi-jack was a large oil tanker – with no passengers, a compact crew of twenty-eight men, and the living and working quarters concentrated in one part of the ship, in the island bridge, a fact which gradually dawned on Bennett. 'You've been planning this for a long time, I see,' he commented grimly as the walkie-talkies were locked away in the cabin Winter had reserved for his headquarters.

'I worked the whole thing out in three days,' Winter told him. 'You must admit we're reasonably well-organised now. You can't poison us, you can't unlock a single cabin on the ship, you can't communicate with the outside world. Have I forgotten anything?'

'If I think of something,' Bennett replied grimly, 'I won't let you know.'

'I'm speaking from Seattle,' Sullivan told Victor Harper when the chairman of Harper Tankships came on the line. 'I tried to call you from Anchorage . . .'

'Miss Herries told me. Have you talked to Mackay?'

'No. The ship left early . . .'

'I know,' Harper interjected irritably. 'There was a fire at the oil terminal so Mackay cleared out – with two tanks empty . . . Oh, bugger it. Wait a minute . . .' There was a pause. 'Just knocked over the damned candle. You wouldn't believe it but we're out of oil for the lamps – and I'm in the oil business. Power cut here, of course . . .' At 3.30pm in Seattle it was 10.30pm at Harper's home in Sunningdale. 'What's all this about the *Challenger*?' Harper demanded.

'I had an idea she could be the target, as you know. I've tracked a man half way across the world almost – from Hamburg to Lon-

116

don and then on to Anchorage and Seattle. Now I've lost him. And one or two things I came across made me wonder, but they were dead ends. Like that business about the wireless operator, Swan. It turned out to be nothing more than he'd taken his wife with him on the *Challenger* . . .'

'Taken his wife with him?' Harper's voice had an edge to it. 'Bad enough for Mackay having one woman aboard – and a journalist at that.'

'What are you talking about?' Sullivan asked. 'Who is the woman who went?'

'An American journalist I know called Betty Cordell.'

'And you say Swan's wife isn't on the ship? I think you're wrong . . .'

'I'm not wrong! Swan isn't aboard either – although you seem to think he is. He missed the ship. He's ill.'

'Ill at home, you mean?' Sullivan asked gently.

'Where else would he be?'

'That's what I'm beginning to wonder. Because he's not at home – neither is his wife. I've been out there. They both left for the ship at three-fifteen last Thursday . . .'

'You saw them leave?'

'No, I didn't,' Sullivan said slowly. 'Come to think of it, no one saw them leave – but they're gone . . .'

'Look, Sullivan . . .' Harper's growing impatience came clearly over the line. 'There's a replacement wireless operator aboard. Chap called Kinnaird. So Swan must be at home – unless he's in hospital.'

'Any idea when all this happened? And how did Mackay come up with this Kinnaird so conveniently? In Alaska, for God's sake?'

'Swan knew him, recommended him. He just happened to be there. Short of a job, I suppose. As to the timing, I'll read you Mackay's cable. *1518 hours. Wireless operator Swan taken ill. Recommended replacement George Kinnaird. Kinnaird sailing with us this trip. Mackay.* Straightforward enough . . .'

'No, it isn't. At three-fifteen Mrs Swan phoned a neighbour from home saying she was just leaving to sail with her husband. At three-eighteen – according to that cable – Swan is ill and has found someone else to replace him. All inside three minutes?'

117

'Does sound peculiar,' Harper admitted.

'It's more than peculiar, it's bloody sinister. Is there anything unusual about this latest trip of the *Challenger*? Anything at all?'

'Not according to Ephraim – nor from the routine reports coming in from Kinnaird . . .'

'Who the hell is Ephraim?' Sullivan enquired.

'Sorry, I think you were away when I added him to the insurance cover. Ephraim is an automatic monitor I've had installed in the engine-room – one of those mechanical brain things which independently check the engine performance of the ship. And it is quite independent of the ship. It flashes radio signals to a computer at the Marine Centre in The Hague. The computer decodes the signals and the report comes to me by telex. Whole operation takes less than thirty minutes – seconds for the radio signals to get to The Hague, the rest of the time getting the data back here.'

'And how is the world according to Ephraim?'

'Normal. The *Challenger* is moving through a gentle swell at seventeen knots. She should reach the oil terminal at Oleum – that's near San Francisco – on schedule.'

'And according to Kinnaird?'

'Again normal. Routine messages come through on time. It's fascinating to compare notes – to see how Kinnaird's weather reports exactly match Ephraim's . . .'

Latest toy, Sullivan thought. He'll soon get tired of it. 'I'll keep in touch,' he said. 'I may call you from San Francisco – because that's where I'm going . . .'

'I thought you were coming home. Why San Francisco?'

'That's the end of the line for the *Challenger* – and I want to be there when she reaches it . . .'

Sullivan put in another call, this time to Mulligan, chief of police at Anchorage. He told him about the Swans, that they weren't aboard the *Challenger*, that maybe it would be a good idea if a patrol car went out to the Swan home and if someone talked to Madge Thompson, the next-door neighbour.

Mulligan reacted with his usual vigour. 'I think maybe we'll go further – we'll send out an all-points bulletin for the Swans. And I'll send patrol cars to take a good look at the whole Matanuska valley area. Of course, Swan could be faking the whole disappearance himself . . .'

118

'Why?'

'Supposing the guy reckons he's short on leave, wants to take his wife for some ski-ing up in the mountains? So he fixes up with a pal to take his place, phones Mackay to tell him he's ill, and then takes off for some ski-ing. How does that grab you?'

'It doesn't . . .'

'Me too neither. We'll check everywhere . . .'

Sullivan broke the connection, then made a fresh call to get information on the next flight to San Francisco. He could have had no way of knowing – at that time – that the call he had made to Mulligan would have enormous repercussions which would reach half way round the world. Within a few days.

Winter had the whole ship sewn up tightly, absolutely under his control as he supposed. Two guards were mounted permanently on the bridge where Betty Cordell was spending most of her time. Three more guards were stationed in the engine-room, the heart of the ship. A sixth guard was on duty outside the locked day cabin where the crew not on duty were kept, and a seventh man kept an eye on the galley where Wrigley, the steward, and Bates, the cook, presided over the mysterious rites of their culinary arts. Yet another armed guard was on duty outside the radio cabin. Including Winter himself and LeCat, this left a reserve of seven men who could rest, in readiness to relieve other men at intervals.

'He's a bloody good organiser, I regret to say,' Bennett whispered to Mackay on the bridge. 'And I have more bad news.'

Mackay grunted. 'Just like listening to the news bulletins at home. What is it now?'

'Lanky Miller told me he saw Kinnaird going inside the radio cabin.'

'Which is where I would expect Kinnaird to be . . .'

'Not while the armed guard stays outside the cabin – with the door closed in his face.'

'Are you sure?'

'Miller is very sure. You see what that means? They would never leave Kinnaird alone in there – with the transmitter – unless he's working with them.'

119

Mackay sighed heavily. 'So you were right – there was something funny about him.'

'There had to be. I should have realised it at the moment the terrorists came on board. How else could they find us in the middle of the Pacific – unless Kinnaird was sending them regular signals reporting our position? Betty Cordell was right – she did hear him transmitting the other night.'

'At least Winter has let her go back to her cabin.' Mackay glanced at one of the guards. 'I didn't like the way that thug over there was eyeing her. I think we're going to have to get accustomed to bad news on this trip, Mr Bennett.'

'I have more for you already . . .'

'I rather thought you might have.'

'Since Kinnaird is working for them, that means he never sent your last signal – the one reporting to the Coast Guard that we were picking up their chopper. So forget the hope about a US cruiser looming over the horizon.'

'I grasped that a moment ago,' Mackay said sourly. He dropped his voice to a shade of a whisper. 'Winter seems to have thought of everything, doesn't he? But luckily no one is perfect. The one thing he hasn't thought of is the crew member who isn't on the list – Ephraim. Which is ironical, Mr Bennett – that our lives may depend on Harper's bloody mechanical toy locked away in the engine-room – the only crew member who still has freedom of action aboard this ship.'

Ephraim.

Engine Performance Remote Control Monitor – nick-named Ephraim. Quite independent of all other engine-room operations, the mechanical brain installed inside the control panel was relaying radio signals over many thousands of miles to the master computer in The Hague, reporting constantly on the tanker's performance for the duration of the voyage.

Ephraim reported many things – monitoring fuel consumption, boiler pressures, boiler temperatures, which boilers were fired up, which were not. He reported the speed of the engines and the speed of the ship – not always the same thing if an engine was

120

functioning incorrectly. And he reported the degree of the tanker's pitching and rolling – which meant he was sending his own weather report.

In his London office, Victor Harper was never sure whether he had installed an expensive toy, or whether Ephraim might help to make voyages more profitable. And Ephraim was expensive. The signals he was constantly transmitting were received and decoded by the master computer at the International Marine Centre in The Hague; then the information obtained from the *Challenger* had to be re-transmitted to London by telex.

And Kinnaird was cooperating with Ephraim – without having the least idea he was doing so. Part of the ship's routine which had to continue if conditions aboard were to seem normal to the outside world, was for Kinnaird to transmit a radio message to London at regular intervals. This message confirmed the position of the ship – and included a weather report.

All would be well for Winter so long as Kinnaird continued 'cooperating' with Ephraim. But if for some reason Kinnaird was ordered to fake a weather report, to send to London a message pretending they were passing through quite different weather from what they were experiencing, then deep down in the guts of the ship Ephraim would become a mechanical spy, the only member of the crew who could tell London what was really happening.

The Armalite .22 collapsible rifle with its 4 × 18 telescopic sight, three spare magazines and a yellow package of fifty spare rounds, lay beneath the underclothes almost at the bottom of Betty Cordell's suitcase. Not that it immediately looked like a rifle since the main object on view was a tortoiseshell-coloured stock which concealed inside it the dismantled elements of the weapon. The stock was fashioned of plastic foam: dropped into a pool or lake it would float.

Alone in her cabin, Betty Cordell picked up the package of .22 hollow point ammunition and weighed it in her hand. It gave her a comfortable feeling, submerged for a few moments the state of terror she was adjusting to slowly. Then she replaced the package, took one last look at the stock and re-packed her case, filling it up with neat piles of underclothing until once again it had the innocent look of a woman's travelling bag.

Since late childhood she had owned her own gun. At her home near Pear Blossom in the southern Californian desert her father, a strange and independent character like his daughter, had trained the girl to use a weapon. 'It's a violent world we live in, pet,' he used to say. 'Look how your mother died in San Diego – and all that murdering thief got was her billfold. Twenty-five lousy dollars...'

From the age of eight she was brought up by her father, a farmer, and as the years went by Betty Cordell became skilled to the point of marksmanship with a rifle. She never hunted with it, never went in for competitions, but at twenty-seven she still carried it with her everywhere away from home. Sometimes, driving in the desert, she would stop, set up a line of tin cans as targets and blaze away, working off frustration. Every can was always punctured.

She lit a rare cigarette and stood in the middle of the cabin smoking. The huge tanker was swaying gently as it went on through the swell towards San Francisco, now less than thirty-six hours away. She was thinking that with the mags and the package of spare rounds she had enough ammunition to kill every terrorist on board. The trouble was Betty Cordell had never even shot a bird. She hated the thought of killing live things. Hearing the door open, she turned. LeCat stood in the doorway.

LeCat stood in the doorway holding a full bottle of red wine and behind him the armed guard was leering. LeCat shut the door in his face by leaning against it. Betty Cordell remained standing in the middle of the cabin, staring back at the terrorist with a cold expression which verged on arrogance. She had a constricted feeling in her throat. She was scared and furious with herself at the same time – furious because her heart was thumping and her legs felt weak.

'There is nothing to fear,' LeCat said roughly. 'We did not expect to find a woman on board. But it will only be for a few days, so you might as well make the best of it. The best of it,' he repeated, looking at her closely.

122

'I don't want to talk. Would you please leave my cabin.'

At least her voice sounded steady, almost insolent. Hearing herself speak, she was surprised that her voice sounded so normal, thank God. I've got to deal with this, she told herself, get rid of him. Quickly. He put the bottle down on a table near the door and walked towards her. There were blobs of moisture on his upper lip below the curved moustache.

'I am a bachelor,' he remarked as he stood close to her. 'My name is LeCat. I have known a lot of women – many beautiful women . . .'

His approach was so ridiculous, so ham-handed, that for one wild moment she wanted to laugh in his face. Waterfront whores, she thought cynically, that's about his taste and experience. With me he doesn't quite know how to go about it, but his bashfulness won't last for long. Then she caught a whiff of his breath. My God, he's drunk . . .

Even though he had consumed a third of a bottle of cognac, LeCat was not drunk. It was simply that his movements were a shade more deliberate than usual. Cognac he could take in generous quantities; he was still capable of hitting a moving target at a hundred yards. She moved casually sideways and stood with her back to the steward's bell. 'I was thinking of taking a bath,' she said. 'Could you please leave the cabin. Now!'

'A bath?' He looked towards the adjoining bathroom. 'Take your bath – then afterwards we can have a drink together . . .'

'Get out of this cabin, LeCat. Get out now or I'll ask the guard to fetch Winter . . .'

'Like myself, the guard is French. He takes his orders from me,' LeCat replied equably.

The longer-term significance of this remark did not strike Betty Cordell – her mind was fixed on only one objective. Survival. She lifted her head and clasped her hands behind her back, assuming a most arrogant posture. The animal likes that, she noted: a peculiar gleam came into LeCat's eyes and he wiped his lip dry with a finger. While he was distracted her own index finger moved towards the bell-push on the wall. 'I think Winter will probably kill you,' she said.

'If you mention Winter again I will hit you . . .' There was a

123

look of fury in his eyes, an undertone in his voice not far from hatred. Shaken by his ferocity, she felt her control going. She took a step away from him and pressed the bell hard. 'Go and get your bath,' he told her viciously. 'Do not bother to dress when you have had it . . .'

He was still standing close to her so she couldn't move towards the bathroom when the cabin door opened and Wrigley, the steward, came bustling in. A tall, stooped, middle-aged man with brisk movements, he carried a tray with a pot of coffee, cream, a cup and saucer. He stopped for a moment and frowned as LeCat glared at him over his shoulder, then, apparently noticing nothing wrong, he began chattering.

'Fresh-made coffee, Miss Cordell – nice and strong the way you Americans drink it . . .' He began laying the things on the table. 'Better come and get it now while it's hot. Helps to keep up your strength under trying circumstances . . .' He glanced at LeCat. 'You may have a visitor any minute, Miss Cordell – Mr Winter was in the galley and said he'd be coming along here to see how you are getting along. Funny chap . . .'

Wrigley paused as LeCat turned his back and left the cabin. The steward glowered and made a forked, two-fingered gesture towards the empty doorway. 'Sorry about that, Miss,' he apologised, 'sometimes my feelings run away with me . . .'

'Thank you, Wrigley,' she murmured as she picked up the pot. 'You were just in time . . .'

Winter heard about the incident within five minutes of its happening. Wrigley met him in the alleyway while he was returning to his galley, escorted by an armed guard, and had no hesitation in telling him about the near-rape. Winter reacted instantly. He summoned LeCat to his cabin.

'I told you to leave that American girl alone . . .'

'You want her for yourself . . .'

Winter took three strides across the cabin and LeCat, seeing his expression, grabbed for the pistol in his shoulder holster. Winter's hand closed on the wrist, digging into the nerve centre. LeCat's hand, still holding the pistol butt he had no time to extract, felt paralysed. His limp fingers released the butt as Winter

124

twisted the hand violently and spun the Frenchman round by the shoulder hinge until he was half-crouched with his back to the Englishman. The pain in his shoulder was acute and he dared not move for fear of breaking his arm.

'You will break the arm . . .' LeCat gasped.

'I will break the neck . . .'

Winter trundled the bent man forward until he was close to the edge of the bunk. Releasing his grip a little, he allowed LeCat to lift his head a few inches, then he used his other hand to press the Frenchman's head down over the bunk with his throat rested on the hard wooden edge. The hard edge of the bunk rasped his victim's Adam's apple. 'One sharp movement and your neck is broken, LeCat,' Winter said softly. 'You know that, don't you?'

'Mercy of God . . . Winter, please . . .'

LeCat was terrified. He knew exactly what could happen, what he had done to a man in a similar position in Algeria once. A movement, one horrendous jerk, and his neck would snap. He was almost sick with terror.

'If you even go near that woman again for the rest of the trip, I'll kill you.' Winter's tone was detached, almost conversational.

Grasping a handful of hair, he lifted LeCat's head clear of the bunk, swung his body round and shoved him forward. Off-balance, the Frenchman cannoned hard against a bulkhead and fell on the floor. Getting up slowly, dazed by the impact, LeCat left the cabin. It hadn't made him love Winter any the more, but he felt the cause of his humiliation was the American girl. Added to his crude desire for her was a bitter hatred.

Less than an hour before night fell on the Pacific, the helicopter was flown away from the *Challenger* by the only terrorist – other than Winter – who could fly the machine. Guided by continuous radio signals from the *Pêcheur*, he reached the trawler which was sailing a hundred miles south of the *Challenger*. The moment the plane landed its insignia were covered with canvas flaps specially prepared for the purpose. It didn't matter if a ship or a plane saw the machine sitting on the deck of the trawler, but it would have seemed very strange had it been spotted aboard the 50,000-ton tanker.

Before it flew off, the machine had been unloaded by LeCat and

André Dupont. The escape apparatus – the Zodiac inflatable boat, the outboard motor, and the wet-suits – were all stored away in the carpenter's store under the forecastle. And during this work, carried out many hundreds of feet away from the distant island bridge, there was also unloaded a steel case weighing almost two hundred pounds which was transported with some difficulty and carried down the ladder into the cramped compartment.

12

When Sheikh Gamal Tafak moved to his secret headquarters on the first floor of a building on the outskirts of Baalbek in the Lebanon, it was partly considerations of policy which decided the Saudi Arabian oil minister to go to ground – he wanted to isolate himself until the San Francisco operation had been completed. A man who cannot be found cannot answer any questions, and there were certain statesmen in the Middle East who were already very worried by Tafak's extremist views.

But that was only part of the reason. The other part was more simple and human – Tafak was frightened that he might be assassinated. There had been too many rumours that Israeli gunmen were on the move; there had even been a whisper that British and American secret service men were cooperating with the Israeli intelligence service. In Baalbek, a place he had never visited before, he felt safe.

The first message he received at his new headquarters was from Winter. Within thirty minutes of seizing the *Challenger* a brief radio signal was transmitted anonymously to the United Arab Republic consulate in San Francisco. *Avocado consignment has been delivered*. Inside a locked room in the consulate Talaal Ismail reached for the phone and put in a call to a Paris number. From here the message was transmitted to Athens and on to Beirut. The man Ahmed Riad had placed in a flat in Beirut made one bad slip when he phoned Tafak. He referred to him as 'Excellency' while he was reporting the message confirming the tanker's seizure. 'No titles,' Tafak snapped and slammed down the phone as soon as he had heard the message. Not that he really believed the phone would be tapped.

The girl who worked as switchboard operator in the block of flats on Lafayette Street in Beirut waited until both receivers had been replaced before she turned down the switch. Then she started attending to the incoming calls she had kept waiting.

She was nervous. It was the first time she had listened in to calls for money. To pass the time of day, to listen to a woman making a furtive and erotic call to her lover while her husband was out; that was another thing. Most switchboard operators did that, or so Lucille Fahmy consoled herself. But this, she suspected, could be dangerous. And who was 'Excellency'?

She went off duty half an hour afterwards, saying very little to the young man who took over her night shift. Then, clasping her handbag tight, she walked to the Café Léon. The mournful-faced man arrived less than a minute after she had sat down at a corner table.

'Good evening, Lucille . . .' He greeted her like an old friend, leaning close to make himself heard above the racket of the juke box which was playing the latest Tom Jones record. At six in the evening the place was filling up with Lebanese teenagers. Despite the chill in the air outside it was hot and stuffy in the Café Léon. Plenty of oil for heating here; oil coming out of their ears. The mournful-faced man ordered coffee and cakes.

'He made a call . . .' Lucille had to repeat what she'd said as she lit a cigarette with a shaking hand. 'The first in five days. When do I get some money?' she asked.

He patted his breast pocket. 'I have the fifty dollars with me. Was it a local call?'

'No. To a Baalbek number. I have it in my bag.'

'Give it to me.'

She hesitated, then opened her bag and took out a folded bank-note with the number written inside which she handed to him. Anyone watching would have assumed he was short of cash, that his girl friend was paying tonight. He slipped the folded note into his wallet, next to another note he had folded earlier. He would pay with that note – just in case someone was watching him.

'Can you trace the telephone number?' she asked.

Again it showed nervousness – she was talking for the sake of talking. Of course he could trace any number in the Lebanon, and find the address – because it was the address which interested him. She waited until the waiter had brought the coffee and cakes and then leaned towards him. 'It was about some avocados – he just said the avocado consignment has been delivered. Oh, and he called the man at the other end Excellency . . .'

'He might . . .' The man who had told her his name was Albert appeared to know all about it – or this was the impression he deliberately gave her – and now he understood her nervousness. Like so many people in the Middle East she was frightened of the powerful. He went on sipping his coffee, hiding his shock, his hope. It looked as though they had found Tafak.

One Fleet Street newspaper in London caught a hint of a whisper of a rumour – and had a 'D' notice served on it – an edict it could not ignore, so the story went unpublished. As it happened, the story was true.

The British Prime Minister had driven secretly to Lyneham air base in Wiltshire, one of Britain's remoter airfields in the Salisbury Plain area. His timing was good: as his car sped towards the airfield buildings a Trident dropped out of the grey overcast and cruised along a nearby runway.

When the machine had stopped, the Prime Minister was driven close up to the aircraft, so close that it pulled up at the foot of the mobile staircase which had been hastily rushed into position. He waited inside the car as a man appeared at the top of the mobile staircase, ran briskly down the steps and climbed inside the rear of the waiting car.

Had a photograph been taken of the man who stepped out of the plane he might well have been mistaken for Gen. Villiers; he was bearing a black eye-patch. But at that moment Gen. Villiers was many thousands of miles away from Britain. The secret visitor, therefore, had to be someone else. He did, in fact, look very like another general whose picture had often appeared in the pages of the world's press, a certain Israeli general.

It was the afternoon of Sunday January 19, the day when Winter seized control of the *Challenger*.

Winter took his decision to let Betty Cordell move freely round the ship immediately after the incident with LeCat. He had been appalled to find a woman on board, knowing the character of some of the ex-OAS terrorists, and now it struck him she might be safer wandering round the ship rather than locked away in her cabin. He came to the cabin to tell her his decision. 'You can roam round the ship as much as you like, but you are to report to the officer of the watch on the bridge every hour. Understood?'

She stood quite still, studying his unusual face, the boniness of his hooked nose, the wide, firm mouth, the steady brown eyes which were so remote and disconcerting. 'Why are you doing this?' she asked quietly.

'Because it appears you may be safer not hidden away in a cabin.'

'I meant why are you taking part in this horrible hi-jack?'

'Money.'

He left her abruptly and a few minutes later she started moving about the ship which was still proceeding through a gentle swell. It was a nerve-wracking experience which she never got used to – walking down an alleyway while a terrorist in the distance watched the fair-haired girl coming with a pistol in his hand; turning a corner into what she imagined was a deserted passageway beyond, only to find another terrorist guard just around the corner; being followed down another alleyway by a man with a gun, who, it turned out, was merely checking to see where she was going.

Her mind was working at two levels – noting everything that might be copy for the story she hoped to write one day – *Eye-Witness Account of Terrorists' Hi-Jack* – and noting the precise position of all the guards, information she intended to pass to Bennett at the first available opportunity. There were no signs that the British crew were planning any resistance; outwardly they seemed still stunned by what had happened. But she detected

129

an odd atmosphere, particularly in the engine-room.

A guard with a blank expression stood aside to let her go inside the engine-room – Winter, with his usual efficiency, had passed the word to the entire terrorist team that she was allowed to move round the ship freely. Stepping over the coaming she stood on the high platform, already sweating a little in the steamy atmosphere as she gazed into the bowels of the ship. The noise was appalling, like the thunder of steam-hammers, and everywhere things moved; pistons chomping, machinery which meant nothing to her. She went down the vertical ladder.

The steep, thirty-foot drop behind her as she descended didn't worry her – she had climbed near-precipices in the Sierras – and then she was threading her way among the machinery, seeing men she had earlier met and chatted with before the seizure of the tanker. Monk, a burly, thirty-four year old engine-room artificer, a very tough-looking character indeed, his dark hair plastered down over his large skull, nodded to her as he wiped his hands on an oily rag but he seemed abstracted, as though his mind was on something important.

Bert Foley, a small, bald-headed man of forty, another artificer, did speak to her after glancing up to make sure the guard on the high platform couldn't see him. 'Things might turn out better than you imagine, Miss. Have patience . . .' Feeling better in the presence of the British seamen, she explored further. There was something here she couldn't put her finger on, a smell of conspiracy in the air. It didn't seem possible: Winter had severed all communication between one part of the ship and another. Then she saw Wrigley, the steward, coming down the ladder into the engine-room.

The steward, carrying a tray with one hand while he used the other to support himself, reached the floor, hurried to the control platform where Brady, the chief engineer, was directing operations. Brady, a stocky, grey-haired man in his early fifties, took a mug of tea from the tray, helped himself slowly to a ham sandwich. Nothing strange there that she could see. She checked her watch; soon it would be time to report to the officer of the watch, to tell him the present position of every terrorist guard aboard the ship. She still couldn't rid herself of the feeling that something was going on under the surface. She climbed up on to the platform beside Brady, then pointed to a black box embedded into the control panel. 'What does that do – or do you keep your sandwiches inside it?' She was smiling; it was something to say. A man in trousers and spotless white vest standing close to the chief swung round with a startled expression.

'Get on with your work, Wilkins,' the chief said calmly. He grinned at Betty. 'Just a standard piece of equipment, Miss.' He patted his ample stomach. 'I store my sandwiches in here.'

It was unfortunate. The black box she had pointed to was the only outward evidence that Ephraim existed, and by now the chief had realised that the mechanical man was their only outside contact with the world – even if the communication was purely one-way.

'It's like being back in my old prisoner-of-war camp,' Mackay murmured to Bennett in the chart-room. 'My own ship has become the cage. At least we've set up a communications system – the first thing to do when you're inside the cage . . .'

The system of communication between Mackay and his crew hinged on Wrigley, the steward, who was being kept constantly on the move supplying food and coffee to both the British crew and their terrorist guards. Winter had foreseen this nutriment problem; he had placed a permanent guard outside the galley to escort Wrigley as he trotted all over the ship.

What Winter had not foreseen was that Bennett would exploit Wrigley as a means of passing messages to anyone Mackay wished to communicate with. The messages were scribbled on small pieces of paper which Wrigley concealed under plates of sandwiches, under pots of coffee, under anything he happened to be carrying on his tray. Another development Winter neither foresaw nor noticed was the increase in the thirst of the man on the bridge; drinking far more coffee than ever before, they provided Wrigley with more opportunities to pass messages.

Another change in the ship's routine which went unnoticed was the frequent discussions on navigation Mackay and Bennett felt compelled to indulge in during visits to the chart-room behind the bridge. The first time this happened the guard was suspicious.

'We are going to the chart-room,' Mackay informed the guard, a man called Dupont, who understood English. 'We have to check our future course . . .'

He walked off the bridge with Bennett and Dupont followed them into the chart-room. Mackay stood by the chart-table and stared at the Frenchman. 'Look, plotting a ship's course is a complex business – it calls for concentration. I can't work while you stand there pointing that gun at me. If you want us to get this ship to San Francisco you'll have to wait outside . . .'

'You've searched this place,' Bennett pointed out, 'and you've locked the other door. Our only way out is back on to the bridge. If you don't leave us alone we're not taking this ship anywhere.'

Dupont, who had been with Winter on the *Pêcheur* in the Mediterranean, who had been with LeCat in Paris when they tracked Sullivan up the French coast, hesitated as Mackay picked up a pair of dividers while Bennett concentrated on studying a chart. It was intimidating: both men were acting as though he were no longer there. He went back on to the bridge and took up a position where he could watch the open doorway.

'Mr Bennett,' Mackay said quietly, 'the system of communication is working well. I'm not so sure about your idea of arranging for a man to go missing.'

'We can't just stand around and let them get away with it,' the first officer murmured. 'Ultimately I want to organise a mass break-out. Subtracting the man who flew off in the chopper, there are fourteen terrorists and twenty-eight crew – we outnumber them two-to-one . . .'

'But they have the guns . . .'

'So we need to cut down the odds – by getting rid of one or two key terrorists. I don't think we'll aim to tackle Winter yet – he's the only one you can talk to, and I don't think he'd be an easy man to catch off guard. My plan is to go for LeCat – he's a very nasty piece of work and seems to be second-in-command.' Bennett unrolled a fresh chart as Dupont peered inside the chart-room, then disappeared. 'I had a word with the chief down in the engine-room while the guard was boozing wine. Brady says Monk would be more than happy to go after LeCat – if Monk can go missing and stay missing without Winter knowing . . .'

'I don't like it,' Mackay objected. 'Violence begets violence . . .'

'The ship was seized with violence,' Bennett argued. 'LeCat was close to assaulting the American girl when Wrigley turned up in time. Some of these men are killers, LeCat certainly, I'm sure. And men do go overboard frequently at sea . . .'

'I'll think about it.'

'Dirty weather would help – and I think dirty weather is on the way.'

'That typhoon should miss us . . .'

'My bet is it won't, sir. Typhoons have a nasty habit of changing direction. I think we ought to be prepared – which means we must organise Monk's disappearance if we can.'

'You could be right . . .' The captain stared down at the chart, weighing pro's and con's. If something happened to Winter and LeCat assumed control, he wouldn't give twopence for the lives of his crew. 'All right,' Mackay said, 'we'll give it a try – but warn Monk to be very careful . . .'

'It will look like an accident,' Bennett said.

At ten o'clock at night the *Challenger* was still proceeding through calm seas. Within two hours it would be Monday January 20.

Typhoon Tara came out of the spawning ground of the most hellish and violent weather in the world – out of the north Pacific. A US weather satellite first spotted her menacing growth; a US weather plane confirmed that something enormous was building up north-east of Hawaii.

Winter was the first man on board to receive all weather reports coming in from the mainland; receiving them from Kinnaird, he read them and promptly passed them to Mackay. After all, Mackay had to get the tanker to San Francisco. When the captain had absorbed this new signal reporting on Typhoon Tara, Winter took it back to the radio cabin where Kinnaird, increasingly nervous about the job he had undertaken to lay his hands on his dream bonanza – ten thousand pounds – sat in front of the transmitter. It was five o'clock on the morning of Monday January 20.

'When does the next routine report go off to Harper in London?' Winter demanded.

'Within the next hour . . .'

'Submit this weather report . . .' Winter was writing out the report in a quick, neat hand. 'Alter it to conform to technical jargon, but this is the gist of it.'

Kinnaird stared at the message. 'I don't understand . . .'

'Because you can't think ahead – like so many people. Our great problem may be to persuade the authorities at San Francisco to let this ship enter the Bay as soon as we reach the entrance. There could be a delay for any number of reasons – a lot of shipping in the channel, fog . . . The port authority is far more likely to let us steam straight in if they think we're in trouble – if we have men aboard injured while we were fighting the typhoon.'

'You could be right . . .'

'I have to be right – ninety per cent of the time – if we are to survive.'

The signal Winter had written out was simple and graphic. *Moving through typhoon conditions. Two seamen injured and out of commission. Main deck awash. Speed reduced to eight knots effective. Wind strength one hundred and ten miles per hour. Mackay.*

Deep down in the engine-room, not one hundred feet from where Winter stood as he handed the signal to Kinnaird, the mechanical man, Ephraim, went on flashing out radio signals to the master computer a third of the way across the world in The Hague, diligently reporting on present conditions. *Speed seventeen knots . . .*

Just as the similarity with a prisoner-of-war camp had occurred to Mackay, so it occurred to Winter to reinforce security on the ship by checking the numbers of the British crew at frequent intervals. He had put this idea into operation within thirty minutes of coming aboard, and it was the engine-room which most concerned him. While at sea, and including the chief, Brady, there were seven men on duty inside the vast and cavernous engine-room. So easy for a man to go missing.

It was six in the morning – the tanker was less than twenty-four hours' sailing time away from San Francisco – when Brady made a gesture to Monk, the engine-room artificer, and Monk disappeared behind a steel maintenance door flush with the wall. On his platform Brady wore his normal grim expression: he was taking a calculated gamble. This time it was LeCat who was going to check the seven men.

The gamble lay in the fact that the Frenchman had spent little time in the engine-room; he was quite unfamiliar with the crew who worked there. The risk lay in the fact that it was LeCat himself who would personally count the crew. Brady watched him descending the vertical ladder backwards, hopeful that the terrorist might slip and plunge down to land crushed on the steel grilles below. It was an empty hope: LeCat descended swiftly and agilely, then gestured to one of the armed guards to come with him.

'We will count the crew,' LeCat announced as he reached the control platform and stood looking up at the chief. 'Everyone will stay exactly where he is . . .' He had his Skorpion pistol in his hand and it amused him to point it at the chief's large stomach. 'If anyone moves, he will be shot.'

Brady exploded, shouting to make himself heard above the din of the machinery. 'If you want this ship to reach San Francisco you will get your bloody count over with and get to hell out of my engine-room.'

'So?' LeCat climbed very deliberately up on to the platform and beside Brady his assistant Wilkins was sweating. Not that it showed particularly; in the engine-room everyone sweats. LeCat himself was sweating enjoyably with the heat – it reminded him of summer in Algeria. He touched the chief's stomach with the tip of his Skorpion. 'One twitch of my finger and you are meat for the sharks . . .'

Brady stood quite still, looking down at the pistol. 'One twitch of your finger and you'll never reach the mainland. I keep this ship moving – not even the captain can do that.'

LeCat smiled unpleasantly, withdrew his weapon. 'You are right, of course,' he agreed. 'But when we do reach California we shall no longer need you, shall we?' Leaving Brady with this unsettling thought, he began counting the crew.

They were scattered round the engine-room and LeCat had to thread his way among the machinery to find them. He didn't mind; he was convinced that his threat to shoot any man who

135

moved would keep the British motionless. He counted three men and then found Foley round a corner, bent over a machine-guard, wearing vest and trousers, his bald head gleaming with sweat as he stood with his back to the Frenchman. 'Four . . .'

LeCat moved on with the guard, went round another corner, and Foley moved. Hauling off his vest so he was naked to the waist, he grabbed a soiled cap from behind the machine, jammed it on his head, then he crawled on his hands and knees along the gratings until he was under the control panel. On the platform Brady, who was watching the catwalk guard above, made a signal. Foley stood up, walked five paces to stand beside Lanky Miller. Pulling a pair of large horn-rimmed spectacles out of his pocket, he put them on.

Thirty seconds later LeCat came round a corner and stopped to look at the two men carefully. 'Six . . . seven.' The full complement of engine-room staff. Lighting a cigarette, LeCat continued studying the two seamen. Lanky Miller was the tallest member of the crew, six foot two inches tall. Beside him Foley's height seemed to have shrunk. LeCat stared at him, frowning.

Up on the control platform Brady's hand moved so swiftly no one saw the slight movement. Above the pounding of the machinery hammering at LeCat's ear-drums the Frenchman heard a sudden, hissing shriek. Steam billowed into the engine-room. 'Emergency!' Brady roared. 'Boiler overheating!' There was a clatter of feet across the gratings as the crew dispersed all over the engine-room. Miller and Foley rushed past LeCat and disappeared. The Frenchman looked round irritably, shrugged, went to the ladder and climbed up out of the hideous bedlam.

The chief, a resourceful and determined man, noticing that LeCat had left the engine-room, that the guard above was still on the catwalk, increased the volume of steam until soon the entire engine-room was filled with a gaseous white mist which blotted out everything. He sent Wilkins to the storage compartment where Monk, who had missed the count, was hiding.

Looking down from the catwalk above the guard could see nothing and it worried him. Anything could be happening below inside that seething white cauldron. Were they on the edge of disaster? Was the ship about to blow up? Should he warn Winter immediately? Then he heard a horrible scream just underneath him, a scream so penetrating it travelled up to him above the hammering of the machinery and the hissing of the escaping steam.

He went down the ladder quickly, found himself at the bottom, enveloped in steam, but he was also resourceful. A seaman loomed up out of the mist and the guard grabbed him, forced the man to walk ahead of him with the Skorpion pistol pressed into his back. If anyone attempted to attack him as they moved through the steam clouds the seaman would be shot. He guided the man to the control platform and yelled up at Brady. 'What is this that happens?'

'Just getting it under control,' Brady roared. 'Boiler got badly overheated . . . Nothing to worry about.'

And it seemed that Brady knew what he was doing. The steam was beginning to thin out, the sinister hissing sound had stopped. The guard made his way back to the ladder and climbed up to the catwalk he had left unguarded.

On the platform Brady wiped his mouth with the back of his hand as he watched the guard leaving with grim satisfaction. The trial run had worked: they could fool the terrorists when the next man-count came. They had to fool them, in fact. Because next time there would only be six men in the engine-room. While the ladder was smothered in steam Monk had gone up it and was now hiding in a storage cupboard well clear of the engine-room.

On the mainland some people took a swim each day even in January. Les Cord, a student at Stamford University near San Francisco, parked his car and went down on to Ocean Beach. The Pacific was grey, the heavy overcast hanging close above it was grey, and the combers coming in were large. It was the morning of Monday January 20.

Cord was sitting on the beach, taking off his shoes, when he first noticed it, a disturbing sensation as though some massive force were approaching. Slipping his shoes back on again, he stood up and stared at the sky. It had a stormy look, but he had seen stormy skies before. A few yards away the giant combers coming in hit the beach. He looked out to sea.

There was a storm swell now. Far out to where the grey horizon almost lost itself in the ocean he saw an enormous swell building up, great windrows of endless width sweeping towards him. They had come in over vast distances, these windrows, and now he became more aware of the power of these combers crashing down on the beach. He felt their vibration through the soles of his shoes and the whole beach almost shuddered under the impact. Vaguely, he realised that this was what had first disturbed him, the massive thump of these great waves as they hammered down on the beach.

He changed his mind, still unsure of what precisely was so disturbing, went back to his car and drove away to the city. He had broken his record of a swim a day, but it didn't worry him – he was just glad to get away from that beach, from that unnerving sensation.

Les Cord didn't realise it, but what had shaken him was the rhythm of the incoming combers – they were advancing onshore at the rate of four waves to the minute instead of the normal seven. Nor did he know that at that moment seismographs as far away as Alaska were registering the massive shock of these waves, recording them as they would have recorded earth tremors. Typhoon Tara was coming, reaching out her fingers to tap a warning on the beaches of mainland America.

At about the same time as Les Cord decided not to take his daily swim from Ocean Beach, a few miles away on the other side of the peninsula Sullivan was putting in a call to the chairman of Harper Tankships.

Sullivan had arrived in San Francisco from Seattle late on Sunday afternoon, had waited one hour at the International airport for a yellow cab – owing to the gas shortage – and had been driven to the St Francis Hotel on Union Square. As the phone rang he was looking down from his bedroom window on the roof of a cable car heading up towards California Street.

'Sullivan speaking. I'm at the St Francis in San Francisco . . .' He gave Harper the phone number. 'When does the *Challenger* get here?'

'Estimated time of arrival at the moment is eight o'clock tomorrow morning – your time. Frankly, I wouldn't bet on it.'

'Something's happened?'

'I don't know, Sullivan . . .' Harper sounded perplexed. 'It probably doesn't mean anything, but Ephraim seems to have gone off his head . . .'

'What does that mean?'

'We have the usual bulletin from Kinnaird on the ship's position, etc. – plus the weather report. According to Kinnaird Typhoon Tara has got them – just a minute, you probably don't know but there's a typhoon coming in from the north Pacific . . .'

'I do know – I picked up a weather bulletin in Seattle. I don't get the point . . .'

'You would, if you listened to me. According to Kinnaird the *Challenger* at this minute is riding out this typhoon – there's been some damage and a couple of men injured . . .'

'And according to Ephraim?'

'Ship is still proceeding at seventeen knots through a gentle swell. I just don't understand it. Kinnaird, by the way, reported speed reduced to eight knots.'

'Have you wirelessed Mackay?'

'I was just going to do so when your call came through . . .'

'Don't! Don't send any signal to the ship referring to Ephraim.'

'Why on earth not?' Impatience was creeping into Harper's voice.

'I'm not sure why not – but don't, at least not yet. It's just a feeling,' Sullivan replied. 'How long ago was your mechanical friend put on board?'

'Six months ago.'

'During those six months has there been any other instance of conflict between a wireless operator and Ephraim?'

'None at all. These computerised systems do snarl up though.'

'What time lapse would there be between Ephraim's report and Kinnaird's?'

'Hardly any – I checked that point . . .'

'So the two reports are damned near synchronised? Harper, have you a number where I could call the International Marine Centre people at The Hague?'

'Wait a minute.' Harper read out a number. 'You could get someone there now – or later. They run a twenty-four hour service. Typical Dutch efficiency. You'd really rather I held off contacting Mackay?'

'Yes, I want to find out if there's a chance Ephraim has gone on the blink . . .'

'He must have. There's no other explanation . . .'

'Yes, there is. Ephraim hasn't got hiccups and the ship is still moving through nothing fiercer than a gentle swell. In which case Kinnaird is sitting in his tight little radio cabin drunk as a lord – but he thinks it's the ship that's drunk . . .'

'Is that some kind of a joke?' Harper asked waspishly.

'It could be a very grim joke.'

A Miss Van der Ploeg, very precise and crisp, knew all about the master computer and Ephraim. No, there was no possibility of Ephraim transmitting misleading data. He might send a nonsense report, but it would be a nonsense report – a jumbled mess.

Yes. Mr Sullivan, she had made a check while she kept him waiting on the line. The system was functioning perfectly. If Ephraim said the ship was proceeding at seventeen knots through a gentle swell, then that was what the ship was doing. Sullivan got the impression that she was slightly incredulous that he might think a mere human wireless operator could be superior to Ephraim . . .

Sullivan thanked Miss Van der Ploeg, put down the phone and lit a cigarette. It was the first time he had been on the West Coast and he had no contacts out here. He'd better phone Bill Berridge of the New York Port Authority to get some local names. Alone in a strange city, Sullivan was in his element now he had one tiny indication suggesting that something weird was happening aboard the *Challenger*. The trouble would be to convince other people.

By three o'clock in the afternoon Sullivan had tried everything he could think of. Using the introduction from Bill Berridge of the New York Port Authority had got him in to see Chandler of the San Francisco Port Authority, and that was all it had got him. Chandler, a large, friendly man, had listened to his story and had then pointed out that he hadn't one solid piece of evidence that anything was wrong aboard the incoming British oil tanker.

'Except that the wireless operator aboard reported they were caught up inside a typhoon while the monitor, Ephraim, said the ship was in a gentle swell . . .'

'There is a typhoon and it's just changed course. These mechanical devices can go wrong, Mr Sullivan,' Chandler pointed out politely as he lit his pipe. 'Now, my bank has a computer . . .'

'I told you, I checked with the Dutch people at The Hague,' Sullivan said obstinately.

'Naturally they'd have faith in their own system . . .'

After all, Holland was a long way from San Francisco. And Chandler wanted more to go on before he pressed any panic buttons. 'Give me a real emergency and I'll report it fast enough,' he explained. 'In a real emergency I could escalate.'

'How high?'

Chandler counted it off on his fingers. 'First, O'Hara, my boss. The next step would be the mayor. He might contact the FBI. The Coast Guard would come in early, of course. If it was very big we might contact the Governor – of California. That's Alex Mac-Gowan. He's due back from vacation in Switzerland soon . . .'

The next step Sullivan took was to call the FBI. Rather to his surprise two men called to see him at the St Francis within half an hour. Special Agent Foster – Sullivan didn't catch the other man's name – was very polite and listened without interruption. Then he used almost the same words Chandler had used. 'If you could provide us with any real evidence . . .'

It was four o'clock in the afternoon when the FBI men left the St Francis and Sullivan knew he still hadn't lit a fire under anyone. And the *Challenger* was due to arrive in sixteen hours' time.

'Intelligence reports from Beirut indicate that the Gulf states are on the verge of drastically reducing oil output below the present fifty per cent cut. The reports, emanating from a source close to Sheikh Gamal Tafak, say this decision will be put into effect one week from today . . .'

The report was delivered to the British Inner Cabinet on Monday January 20. 'We need four more days,' the Minister of Defence commented. 'So long as they don't advance their decision we may be just in time. I think there is a danger they will not only shut down the oil wells – they may dynamite them. The other report is highly worrying . . .'

The 'other report' was a message received from the British military attaché in Ankara. 'New attack on Israel appears imminent. Syrian tank forces have moved up overnight close to the Golan Heights. There is intense radio activity behind the Egyptian lines in Sinai . . .'

In Israel at this time the population was depressed. In the streets of Tel Aviv and Haifa and Jerusalem men and women openly wondered how much longer they had left to live. And in the higher echelons of Israeli leadership there were bitter recriminations. *We should never have withdrawn from the December 1973 frontiers.*

Because now – yielding to pressure from the western nations – the Israeli army was well east of the Suez Canal. And the Egyptian army commanded by the fanatical General (self-promoted) Sherif was closer to Tel Aviv.

As Tafak had said during a secret meeting with Gen. Sherif and the president of Syria in Damascus, 'Diplomacy squeezed the Israelis far enough back for the last strike to be launched. But first the stage must be set to guarantee that this time no reinforcements reach Israel at the final moment of truth. This is the operation I have already set in motion. The Israeli state will be destroyed on the West Coast of America – in San Francisco . . .'

13

At ten o'clock on Monday evening the outriders of Typhoon Tara closed round the *Challenger*, great waves which rolled towards the ship at regular intervals. It was this irregularity which bothered Mackay. If the giant combers grew in size they could be very dangerous indeed.

The British crew's counter-attack against the terrorists was due to be launched at the height of the typhoon. Hoping that sooner or later Mackay would remove his veto on the plan, Bennett had worked out the details meticulously, almost as meticulously as Winter had planned the seizure of the tanker.

The total crew numbered twenty-eight men. Of this complement six men were on duty in the engine-room – excluding Monk – three more on the bridge (Mackay, the officer of the watch and the helmsman), and the cook and steward were on almost permanent duty in the galley. So eleven men were on duty while the remaining sixteen – again excluding Monk – were under guard in the captain's day cabin. It was this reserve of sixteen men cooped up in the day cabin which Bennett had his eye on.

'First we get rid of LeCat,' he had suggested to Mackay during one of their frequent trips to the chart-room, 'then Monk helps me deal with my own escort guard when I go back to the day cabin – before I get there. The two of us then set about dealing with the armed guard on the day cabin . . .'

It was a planned escalation of release. And Bennett had also considered the problem of weapons. One pistol would become available when his own escort had been disposed of; a second pistol would be in their hands when the day cabin guard was eliminated. And other weapons could be improvised from the storage cupboard where Monk was still hiding. Ropes, for example could quickly be converted into nooses for strangulation. In his own way, Bennett could be as ruthless as LeCat.

But everything depended on the elimination of LeCat. If a fierce struggle developed for control of the ship and Winter died, LeCat must not be alive to assume control. With LeCat taking over command, the reprisals would be atrocious, both Mackay and Bennett agreed. LeCat must go first.

The captain had listened to his first officer's proposal with some misgiving; he disliked violence and he mistrusted the odds against them – with the terrorists holding the guns. For the moment he had given approval for Monk to try and get rid of LeCat, but he had reserved judgement on the rest of Bennett's plan. This was the state of Mackay's thinking when Typhoon Tara began to close in on the *Challenger*.

And already another part of Bennett's plan was taking shape – the guards were beginning to feel the effects of sea-sickness. This was why he had planned the break-out for when the typhoon was at its height; he could expect maximum disorganisation of Winter's carefully-planned security system.

The wind began to rise. LeCat, who had come on to the bridge where Bennett stood with Mackay, disliked the wind – it was so unpredictable. He stood at the front of the bridge as the wind rose, heaping up the seas in moving mountains which rolled all round the tanker. In the darkness there was a feeling of endless movement – the tanker pitching and tossing, the bridge tilting so LeCat had to spread his feet to counter the movement.

Beyond the bridge window as LeCat peered out, wavetops loomed, their crests wobbling unsteadily, the waves bearing down on the ship like a roller-coaster collapsing. Everywhere – movement. Great sliding seas, high crests dimly seen, which made them even more terrifying. Mackay raised his voice loud enough for the French terrorist to hear him. 'It hasn't really reached us yet. Inside an hour we'll see this 50,000-ton ship shifting about like a rowing boat . . .'

'You'll cope with it though . . .' It was Winter's voice. He had come quietly on to the bridge, had heard the remark, had seen that it was directed at LeCat. Mackay swung round and stared at the tall Englishman.

'Winter, have you any conception of the power of a Pacific typhoon? Have you ever experienced one before?'

'No, but I have sailed in the Aegean.'

'The Aegean can be choppy, I grant you,' Mackay said grimly, 'but this is the big ocean. Out here nature has elbow room to marshal her power – and all the power man has harnessed in the atom bomb is like a match-flame compared with what we may see tonight . . .'

The 'rowing boat' remark had frightened LeCat; now the inadvertent reference to a nuclear device reinforced his fears. The Frenchman was staring towards the distant forecastle which contained below decks the carpenter's store. Inside that tiny compartment he had stored away something which might have only the fraction of the power of a typhoon, but the thought that he might not have stowed it safely, that it might already be shifting about the bulkheads, cannoning against them under the impact of the rising storm, was making his hands sweat so profusely that they were running with moisture. And Mackay had said far worse was on the way.

'Inside twenty-four hours we shall have left this ship,' Winter warned Mackay. 'We shall be no more than an unpleasant memory – so I advise you to nip in the bud any mad ideas Bennett may have about organising resistance. It's not worth it.'

To hide his astonishment Mackay walked to the front of the bridge, walking upwards as the ship tilted. Winter's intuition was diabolical, as though he had guessed the first officer's plan, which was impossible. Quite apart from the growing fury of the typhoon as it came up to midnight, the atmosphere on the bridge was strained.

Once again he had asked Winter what was going to happen when the ship reached San Francisco and once again the Englishman had refused to tell him anything. And there had been a violent argument about turning out all the lights – including navigation lights. It was criminal, Mackay had said bitingly, to sail in mid-ocean without navigation lights.

But Winter had insisted; the lights had been turned out. The trouble was they were within only a few miles of the US weather cutter *Champlain* which was on two weeks' station in this part of the Pacific. Winter wanted no communication between the *Challenger* and this vessel, and if they sailed without lights the chances were they would pass her by unseen. Unless they collided with her in the dark . . .

Storm, collision, explosion, shipwreck – these were the four hazards the master of a seagoing tanker feared. And two of them now faced the *Challenger* Mackay thought grimly as he stared down at the main deck. They were caught up in Typhoon Tara, and as if that were not enough to worry about, this madman, Winter, had seen to it that they might face collision with the weather cutter *Champlain* somewhere out there in the heaving ocean. Bennett was right Mackay told himself: we have to make some effort to rid ourselves of these gangsters before they destroy us.

With no lights on except the one over the wheel and the illumination from the binnacle, Mackay's night sight was exceptionally good. He almost stiffened, but held himself motionless when he saw a shadowy figure moving along the catwalk sixty feet below on the main deck. He immediately recognised the short, wide-shouldered figure from the agile way he moved. LeCat. Why the hell was he heading for the forecastle in conditions like these?

For most of the day Monk, the seaman who had escaped from the engine-room when Brady filled the place with clouds of steam, had survived undetected inside a large storage cupboard for cleaning materials on the deck below the bridge. It was close to midnight when Monk opened the door cautiously, no wider than a crack. He saw LeCat walking away from him down the alleyway.

Monk had just finished consuming the iron rations he had taken with him inside the roomy cupboard; two bottles of beer and sandwiches provided by Wrigley before he left the engine-room. Hemmed in by the large collection of brushes and buckets inside the storage cupboard, Monk was stiff from staying in the same cramped position for so many hours. He would have to watch that if it came to a hand-to-hand grapple with LeCat. Air supply had been no problem; ventilator holes had been drilled in the door to prevent a musty atmosphere building up, and the manic pitching and tossing of the ship was nothing new to Monk. He opened the door wider.

The alleyway was deserted except for the diminishing figure of LeCat walking away from him. Monk waited until LeCat vanished round a corner and then left the cupboard, closing the door behind him. The alleyway tilted at a surrealist angle as Monk moved along it, splaying his legs to counter the motion. Somewhere, not far away, LeCat was moving ahead of him and Monk approached the corner with caution.

In his right hand he held a marlinspike, as vicious a weapon as can be found aboard a ship. And he was dressed to merge with darkness; a thick, dirty grey pullover, a scarf of much the same colour, and heavy trousers. His boots were rubber-soled. Close to the corner he paused, listening. The overhead lamps in the alleyway were dim, the shadows moved with the tilt of the ship, moved sometimes like a hunched, waiting man crouched behind a corner. The ship creaked and shuddered with the impact of the ocean. As he went round the corner a door began slamming.

Thud-thud-thud . . . The slamming door was caused by the ship's movement, by the wind blasting into the alleyway Monk was looking along. Only seconds earlier LeCat must have stood in this alleyway, seconds before he went outside and down the ladder on to the main deck. Monk was surprised. Where could the French terrorist be going on a night like this?

A bleak smile crossed his severe face. Couldn't be better: LeCat had gone down on to the open deck. In a typhoon a man could get washed overboard just by being in the wrong place at the wrong time. He crept towards the slamming door, held it open only a few inches. The wind pushed at the door, screamed through the gap in his face. He had to press his shoulder hard against it to hold it.

He waited for his night vision to develop. Sharp-eyed from watching the quiver of gauge needles, the engine-room artificer watched the blurred shape below him on the main deck where sea was washing over it. In the darkness he caught movement rather than the outline of a man, the movement of the Frenchman climbing up on the catwalk. For some crazy reason LeCat was going away from the bridge, heading along the catwalk towards the distant forecastle. Monk took a firmer grip on the marlinspike. Couldn't be better.

Monk waited until LeCat had disappeared along the catwalk, then he went out, closed the door and shinned rapidly down the swaying ladder. He reached the bottom as an inundation of sea swept inboard, swirling round his knees. Ignoring it, he held on to the ladder, staring up at the bridge. No glow of light, the whole vessel was in darkness. The bridge didn't worry him – he guessed that the guards were sea-sick and that the last place they would look was out over the ocean. If Mackay saw him it didn't matter. Monk was puzzled about the lack of navigation lights, but he assumed there must have been some temporary power failure. He headed for the catwalk as the water subsided over the rail.

Instead of following LeCat up on to the catwalk, Monk moved along its outer edge on the port side, staying down on the main deck, hanging on to the lower rail. It was very dark and Monk, soaked to the waist, was creeping forward with extreme caution, relying entirely on his eyesight to locate the Frenchman. It would be impossible to hear him – the slam of the waves, the surge of the water and the howl of the wind muffled any sound LeCat might make. It worried Monk that the Frenchman had vanished. If he were waiting inside one of the curved, open-ended shelters spread along the catwalk at intervals it would be impossible to see him.

He continued moving forward with the wind in his face, sucking the breath out of him, drenched to the skin, his hair plastered to his skull, his hands and feet growing numb with the penetrating chill, his marlinspike tucked in his belt so he could use both hands to cling to the rail as the vessel pitched and tossed with increasing violence. Still no sign of LeCat. He had just passed a shelter when he heard something behind him. He swung round, holding the rail with one hand, grabbing for the marlinspike with the other, and heard the same sound – the slam of the water against the break-water which protected the distribution area for'ard of the bridge.

Monk waited a moment, swearing under his breath, his heart thumping. He was still determined to find LeCat without having any idea how much was at stake. He had volunteered to finish off the Frenchman, but it was only later in the day – long after Monk had hidden himself inside the cupboard – that Bennett had developed his plan for a mass break-out. And the key to this plan was the elimination of LeCat. Monk moved on towards the forecastle.

The bloody ship seemed to have stretched out, all seven hundred and fifty feet of her, and it took him an age before he passed the last shelter, and then he was under the forecastle, staring up as the bow climbed a huge comber, the whole deck heaving up as though some huge underwater creature was lifting the tanker out of the ocean. It was a freak wave. Monk's stomach warned him that the trough beyond would be one hell of a drop.

Monk went on staring up at the forecastle as the wind tore at him, trying to wrench his hand off the rail, as spume struck him in the face with a stinging slap like the cut of a whip, as the deck went on climbing like a lift going up non-stop. One bloody hell of a drop beyond this . . . Then he saw LeCat.

Monk stared up, stunned. The Frenchman must be mad, clear out of his mind, couldn't possibly know anything about the sea. He had just come up out of the hatch leading down into the carpenter's store and was perched on the forecastle. The Pacific was going to do the job for him.

LeCat was a courageous man – if courage is defined as doing something which scares the guts out of you. Sometimes one fear submerges another – and scared as LeCat was of Typhoon Tara, he was even more scared by his dread of the nuclear device coming adrift, cannoning from side to side against the bulkheads of the carpenter's store.

Reaching the forecastle, he clawed his way up the ladder, drenched in spray, the wind screaming in his ears, threatening to tear him off the ladder and hurl him overboard. Here, up on the forecastle, he was even more exposed to the wind than he had been below on the main deck. Getting the hatch open was an ordeal of strength, and he chose a moment when the tanker was climbing out of a trough, mounting the glassy wall of another huge wave. Opening the hatch, he went down the ladder inside, closing the hatch cover above him. The smell of wood shavings filled his nostrils. He switched on his heavy torch.

He was inside a large cell, a working cell. A carpenter's table was clamped to the deck, some shavings were neatly stored in a wooden box, the Zodiac inflatable boat was roped to a bulkhead ring alongside the outboard motor. The large suitcases containing the wet-suits and air bottles were wedged in between table and bulkhead, roped to each other and then to the table legs clamped to the deck. Underneath the pile was another suitcase-like object, the nuclear device.

There had been no movement, everything was as he had left it. He heaved a sigh of relief. God he was earning his two hundred thousand dollars. Time to get back on deck, to get back to the bridge. The sense of instability was worst at the bow of the tanker, quite terrifying. LeCat went back up the ladder and out on deck.

Buffeted by the blinding wind and spume, LeCat closed the hatch and hung on to the starboard rail. The ship was climbing steeply, going up and up at so acute an angle he had trouble staying on his feet. His experience at sea warned him that this was a very big wave indeed. He lifted his head and saw beyond the bow a cliff of water sliding down above him, a grey, massive wobble which seemed about to collapse on top of him. LeCat froze.

This was the sight Monk saw as he looked up, the sight of LeCat holding on to the starboard rail and staring for'ard with his back turned to the main deck. Monk hesitated, saw that he had a unique opportunity and hauled himself up the ladder on to the fo'c'sle as the ship reached the crest of the giant wave.

LeCat heard nothing. He reacted to instinct as it struck him how vulnerable he was. Monk was almost on top of him, his marlinspike raised, when LeCat swung round. LeCat's right hand flashed out, the fingers stiffened. His left hand held on to the rail. Monk was too close to dodge and his other hand was grasping the rail. The nails of LeCat's stiffened fingers slashed across Monk's eyes and he was blinded as the Frenchman grabbed for the flailing marlinspike. Twisting his wrist, the Frenchman forced Monk's body backwards against the rail. The marlinspike dropped, going over the side as the tanker hovered on the wave crest and then fell into the green chasm below.

They were both holding on to the rail with one hand, knowing that if they let go they were overboard. LeCat let go of Monk's sprained wrist and his clawed hand flew upward, grasping Monk by the throat, squeezing, pushing the seaman over backwards as the ship went on dropping. With his sprained hand Monk tried to locate LeCat's eyes, crawling upwards over the powerful chest. LeCat dropped his head, bit the exploring hand savagely. As Monk began to choke LeCat released the grip on his throat, grabbed a handful of clothes and heaved the seaman upwards and outwards. Hoisting his feet clear off the deck, he bent him over the rail, gave one fierce heave – and Monk was gone.

LeCat knew how he had been fooled now. Returning along the

catwalk after killing Monk, he had gone to his cabin where he changed into dry clothes, then he had gone straight to the engine room where he spent some time. After studying each member of the crew, he made a fresh head-count. This time Foley had not tricked him with his quick-change act; LeCat spotted the disguise, the seaman naked to the waist with the greasy cap and horn-rimmed spectacles. But he had not appeared to notice. 'Six . . . seven.' Then he left the engine-room, much to Brady's relief.

LeCat had no intention of reporting to Winter what had happened; he would not even let him know that one of the British seamen was missing. LeCat disagreed violently with Winter's methods of controlling the prisoners: terror was the only effective method of controlling men, of keeping them under. And chance had given him such a weapon. From now on the British crew would be wondering what had happened to that seaman; uncertainty, the unknown plays havoc with men's nerves. He would fray their nerves to shreds so they were pliant when he took over command.

Inside her locked cabin – Winter kept the key in his pocket – Betty Cordell had no sleep. She lay awake in her bunk, fully dressed in slacks and sweater, listening to the ominous creaking of the woodwork, the horrifying smash as the ocean shuddered the bulkhead, the endless howl of the wind outside the porthole where at times it seemed it was about to burst the glass.

Earlier she had made her final report to Mackay – who made one of his frequent visits to the chart-room – on the exact position of every guard on board. She had the impression that they were checking her information against data supplied by Wrigley, that for some reason the information was valuable to them, but they had thanked her and told her nothing.

She checked her watch. 4am. The typhoon seemed to be getting worse – her cabin was being tilted at angles she never imagined it could assume while the ship remained afloat. The noise was terrible – the wind, the ocean – almost deafening as though she were outside on the main deck. She comforted herself with the thought that maybe this often happened, that on the bridge Mackay regarded it as almost routine for this part of the Pacific in January . . .

She was wrong. On the bridge at 4am Mackay regarded what was happening as anything but routine. They were moving close to the eye of the typhoon, but they had not reached it – and Mackay was beginning to fear for the survival of the 50,000-ton vessel.

At 4am the watches changed and Bennett, who had overstayed his watch at midnight, was urgently recalled to the bridge, relieving Second Officer Brian Walsh. Mackay had taken an unprecedented decision. 'Sorry to bring you up again,' the captain remarked, 'but the situation makes me thoughtful.'

The situation makes me thoughtful . . . For Mackay this was the equivalent of ordering panic stations. Bennett, who trusted his master's judgement, also began to wonder whether they would survive the night.

From the bridge window the view was horrific. The *Challenger* was labouring amid a world of violence which never stopped moving, so the mind could never adjust as the ship wallowed amid waves ninety feet high – as high as a nine-storey building – from crest to trough. There was no moon, no sky, only the massive cauldron of seething ocean as the ninety-foot waves bore down on the vessel from all quarters. Mackay was standing close to the window when the wave struck.

The wind strength was now one hundred and ten miles an hour, the strength Winter had noted down in the signal he had earlier handed to Kinnaird for his imaginary typhoon. As a prophet Winter was being vindicated with a vengeance. The wind's scream was now so ferocious that it had drowned out the thump of the labouring engine beat, a manic scream which chilled the guards as they stared at each other across the width of the bridge. Then the scream was momentarily lost as another sound penetrated the bridge, a tremendous whoomph as a giant wave struck the port side.

A great column of surf and spume climbed for'ard of the port side of the bridge, then a white shadow broke full against the bridge, blinding all vision as the vessel shook under the impact. The thought flashed through Mackay's tired mind that they were caught between two powerful and competing wave systems, then there was a second whoomph as a second wave exploded, far too close to its predecessor. The wave rhythm had gone, the ocean had gone wild, the wind strength climbed to one hundred and twenty-five miles an hour as the bridge plunged and toppled like a building collapsing floor by floor.

The quartermaster damned near lost his grip on the wheel, the stocky guard on the port side let go of his grip on the rail and was thrown clear across the bridge, vomiting all over the deck as his pistol slid ahead of him. The other guard retrieved the weapon as it slid over and touched his boots. A head-breaking crack like a gun going off resounded inside the bridge. But it wasn't the head of the guard which had cracked – as the spray ran off the armoured glass of the window the captain stared at a zigzag fracture which disfigured the window. Carried forward at the speed of a projectile, the sea had struck the glass like lead shot. Walsh, who had lingered on the bridge, wanting to stay near his captain, winced.

'My God, sir,' Walsh gasped. 'I've never seen that happen before . . .'

'Calm yourself, Mr Walsh, this is going to be quite a night . . .'

Winter came on to the bridge as he was speaking, as the stocky guard hauled himself to his feet, reaching out for his pistol with a trembling hand. 'I'll take that,' Winter said crisply, 'go get yourself cleaned up . . .' He waited until the tilting deck was momentarily level, then went across to join Mackay by the bridge window.

Winter had not been expected back on the bridge, for the simple reason that no one knew when to expect him. Tireless, he roamed all over the bridge structure from one level to another, checking, checking, always surprising people by his arrival – both the terrorists and the British crew. He deliberately followed no set routine because it kept them off balance, and never more than this night of the typhoon which he foresaw could be the time of maximum danger. If the crew – spearheaded by Bennett, of course – attempted a break-out it would be at the height of the storm, while the guards were disabled all over the ship with sea-sickness.

'What is the position?' Winter demanded.

'It will get worse,' Mackay said in a monotone.

Wind speed rose to one hundred and thirty miles an hour – almost without precedent. Winter clung to a rail, watching Mackay, knowing that this man was the real barometer of the extent of their danger. Sixty feet below the bridge there was a surge of sea – the main deck vanished under the teeming ocean, was below water level. Catwalk, breakwater, pipes and valves – all had disappeared. Only the two derricks and the distant fore-mast showed above the raging surface. It was as though the ship had gone down except for the island bridge which floated like a remnant of a submerged ship. For two more hours Tara battered the *Challenger*, and then she turned away, heading south-west into the vast reaches of the Pacific.

As dawn came at 7.12am, it was a time of relief and bitterness for Bennett; relief that they had survived, and bitterness that they had lost their last chance to take back their ship. Monk had never reappeared after Mackay had seen him moving along the main deck after LeCat. The French terrorist had reappeared later in the engine-room when he had sprung his surprise head-count. There would, Bennett felt sure, never be another chance. If they hadn't managed it at the height of the typhoon when half the guards were seasick, they were unlikely to pull if off in broad daylight. And the *Challenger*, though much delayed and thrown off course by Tara, was now little more than twelve hours' sailing time from San Francisco. Winter had won the game.

14

'Challenger (t), British, Nikisiki, Harper Tankships, Oleum.'
Shipping notice under heading 'Arriving Today'.
From San Francisco Chronicle, *January 21.*

The idea came to Sullivan when he was returning from breakfast at a coffee shop on Geary Street. He was going up inside the glass elevator at the St Francis Hotel, an elevator which moves up an open shaft attached to the outside of the building, so he had an unobstructed and dizzy view of Union Square far below. Turning the idea over, he hardly noticed the view.

He hurried to his room, took off his coat and threw it on the bed. He was going to do something he had urged Harper not to do; he was going to communicate with the *Challenger* while she was still at sea. It might be illuminating to see what reply he received – whether, in fact, he received any reply at all.

It took him a few minutes to work out a message on a scribble pad, a message which could do no harm if there was something seriously wrong aboard the tanker, and the message would have to pass through the replacement wireless operator, Kinnaird. When he had composed the message to his satisfaction he picked up the phone and spoke to the operator who relayed messages to ships at sea. The message was quite short but it compelled a reply – if everything aboard the *Challenger* was normal.

Suspect contraband was taken aboard at Cook Inlet. Possibly drugs. Please confirm immediately whether new personnel joined ship at Nikisiki for present voyage. Will expect immediate reply to Sullivan, St Francis Hotel, San Francisco. Repeat expect immediate reply. Sullivan.

When the *Challenger* was within twelve hours' sailing time of San Francisco it was almost a year to the day since the Gulf states, led by Sheikh Gamal Tafak, had cut the flow of oil to the West by fifty per cent. The reaction to this event inside Soviet Russia was strangely muted.

The Soviet government, which in the past had urged the Arabs to use their oil weapon, was appalled by the revelation of what it involved, by the sheer immensity of Arab power. It suddenly dawned on the Russians that they had spawned a monster. A Golden Ape was now stalking across the face of the earth, an ape which could destroy the great industrial machines of the West on which Russia depended for aid to develop her own industrial machine.

So, the Soviet government absorbed the shock, recognised the potential danger of the situation, and waited. While Sheikh Gamal Tafak remained convinced that he held all the trump cards, to the north of the Arab oil bowls the Russian colossus loomed like a giant shadow, patient, watchful, waiting.

*   *   *

Moving ever closer to San Francisco, the *Challenger* limped out of the embrace of Typhoon Tara. On the morning of Tuesday January 21, as the sun broke through a heavy overcast, the British tanker was a grim sight.

Her funnel was bent at a weird angle, although still functioning. The port derrick was twisted into a bizarre shape. Hatch covers had been blown away in the night. The port-side lifeboat had been wrenched clear of its davits and lost in the ocean. Three port-side portholes with inch-thick glass had been smashed in. The bridge window which Mackay had heard crack was gone, blasted into the bridge interior by a later wave, and it was only by a miracle that the men on the bridge at that moment hadn't been cut to pieces by flying glass. The bridge structure itself had a lop-sided tilt. The *Challenger* looked a wreck but she was still steaming for California at a speed of seventeen knots.

From the main deck Winter looked up at the ruination with quiet satisfaction. In this state he had no doubt the port authority at San Francisco would permit *Challenger* immediate entrance into the Bay beyond. It was a sentiment he was careful not to share with Captain Mackay. He looked up as LeCat called down to him from the battered bridge. 'A signal from the mainland has just arrived...'

Winter went up on to the bridge quickly and LeCat handed him the signal Kinnaird had just received. Reading it with an expressionless face, Winter stared critically at Mackay. The captain was grey with fatigue. He had been on the bridge all night, guiding his ship through the worst Pacific typhoon in thirty years.

'Ever heard of someone called Sullivan?' Winter asked.

Mackay stared back at Winter with an equal lack of expression. The only Sullivan he could think of was Larry Sullivan, the man from Lloyd's he had once invited aboard the *Challenger*. Something told him to be careful.

'Yes,' he said.

'He's connected with Harper Tankships?'

'Yes.'

'What's his job? And don't be so monosyllabic...'

Mackay blew his top. 'Damn you!' he roared. 'I've taken my ship through one hell of a typhoon. I've done that with you bastards aboard, standing around with your popguns in your hands, getting in the bloody way when my whole attention should have been concentrated on saving my ship . . .'

'Take it easy . . .'

'Jump over the bloody side! I've just about reached the end of my tether with you swine. If you talk to me like that again on my bridge I'll order the engine-room to stop the ship and you can do what you like . . .'

'You will shut up . . .' LeCat began, raising his pistol.

'No, you shut up!' Mackay roared. 'You can shoot every man jack aboard and where will that leave you? Floating around out here in the bloody Pacific not able to sail one mile closer to San Francisco . . .'

Winter pushed down LeCat's pistol arm, told him to shove off the bridge. Mackay, driven too far, was on the verge of calling his bluff. Shoot us all . . . Winter wasn't prepared to shoot anyone. 'I withdraw the remark,' he said quietly. 'I think you ought to get a few hours' sleep in a minute. But first, could you tell me who this Sullivan is?'

'Senior man on their staff.'

Tired out as he was, Mackay had had time to think while he raved on at Winter. He wished to God he knew what was in that signal. He sensed that there could just be a chance to warn the mainland of the terrible situation aboard his ship. If only he could get a look at that signal – before he replied to Winter's questions.

'Does Sullivan travel about much?' Winter asked.

'Most shipping people do – from time to time . . .'

'So it wouldn't surprise you to hear that Sullivan was at this moment in San Francisco?'

'Not particularly,' replied Mackay, who was astonished.

Winter handed the signal to him. 'What do you make of that?' Mackay took his time absorbing it while Bennett read it over his shoulder. *Suspect contraband was taken aboard at Cook Inlet. Possibly drugs. Please confirm immediately whether new personnel joined ship at Nikisiki for present voyage. Will expect immediate reply to Sullivan, St Francis Hotel, San Francisco. Repeat expect immediate reply. Sullivan.*

Mackay's expression remained unchanged but his mind jumped

157

backwards and forwards. Contraband? New personnel? Was it even barely possible that Sullivan, who had turned up in California, had even an inkling that something was wrong? In a turmoil, Mackay felt he was treading through a minefield.

'Well?' Winter demanded.

'Well what?' Mackay growled.

'Why doesn't he know Kinnaird is a replacement wireless operator? Why the question about new personnel being taken on board? Isn't he in touch with head office? Didn't you tell Harper about Kinnaird?'

'I sent a message to London about Kinnaird before we sailed,' Mackay said shortly.

'Then why doesn't Sullivan know about that? Isn't he in constant touch with head office?'

'How would I know? Sullivan roams about a lot . . .'

'What about the reference to drugs?' Winter asked.

'No idea – except for smuggling. There are too many places aboard a vessel this size where you can hide a small package . . .'

'It's happened aboard the *Challenger* before?' Winter asked casually. He gave no sign that this was a trick question. If Mackay said yes, all he had to do was to question another member of the crew to check the captain's story.

'Not while I've been in command,' Mackay replied.

'I don't think I'm going to reply to this,' Winter said.

'Do what the hell you like.' Mackay stretched his weary shoulders. 'Mr Bennett, take over command on the bridge – I'm going to get a few hours' sleep. Call me if there's trouble of any kind,' he added.

'No, wait here a minute,' Winter said sharply.

He was in a dilemma. If he didn't reply to this Sullivan they might think something was wrong on the mainland, but he was suspicious. It seemed such a strange coincidence – that on this particular voyage there should be trouble of an entirely different nature. On the other hand, Mackay didn't seem to care whether he replied or not, which was exactly the impression the captain had struggled to convey. But if he didn't reply to this urgent request . . .

'I've changed my mind,' he told them suddenly. 'We will reply . . .'

He watched the two officers closely as he made the remark. Mackay looked out of the bridge window, bored. Bennett took out a packet of cigarettes and lit one. 'I'll word the reply myself,' Winter went on, 'telling him a search is being made of the ship and that you'll report the result when we dock at Oleum . . .' Mackay, who had hoped to word the reply himself, managed to hide his bitter disappointment. He started walking off the bridge.

'Just a minute,' Winter called out. 'Sullivan is a pretty common name – and I want this message to reach him at the St Francis. What's his Christian name?'

'Ephraim,' Mackay said promptly. 'Ephraim Sullivan.'

The signal signed Mackay reached Sullivan at the St Francis at eleven in the morning of Tuesday – eleven hours before the *Challenger* was due to dock at Oleum. *Message received and understood. Am instituting general search of ship. Will report result on arrival at Oleum.* Sullivan stared at the signal he had taken down over the phone on a scribble pad, stared at the address. *Ephraim Sullivan, St Francis Hotel . . .* He stood up, feeling almost light-headed, as though the jet lag had come back. I was bloody right, he said to himself, bloody right all the way from Bordeaux, and now I'm going to get some action.

After a lot of persuasive talking on the phone he was put through to the Mayor's secretary. Sullivan soon realised that she was well-chosen for her job of protecting the Mayor from crank callers. He went on talking and she was like a Berlin Wall. Taking a deep breath, he went overboard.

'I'm trying to warn him about a threat to the whole city of San Francisco, an imminent threat – as from about ten o'clock tonight . . .'

Mayor Aldo Peretti was a handsome-looking man of forty who smiled easily and frequently. Dark-haired, smooth-skinned, he had propelled himself upwards in the world from lower than zero as he was fond of putting it. Which was quite true; his father had been a fruit-picker from Salinas in the Salinas valley. Because of this background, Peretti was a man deeply interested in all forms

159

of modern technology, in anything which could take the muscle-power out of work. He was especially interested in computers.

'Let's go over it again, Mr Sullivan,' he said with a pleasant smile from behind his desk. 'You checked with the Marine Centre people in The Hague and they were sure the signals had to be accurate – that if Ephraim had crossed his circuits the result would be a mess, not a clear message?'

'That's right . . .'

'Which is my understanding of the way computers work – we're installing them this year in several more departments in the city. Frankly, what convinces me we ought to check is Ephraim – and the use of his name in this signal you got back from the ship. It almost suggests that someone, maybe the captain, was trying to tell us something is wrong.' He smiled again. 'You won't mind if I check myself with the Marine Centre at The Hague? Before I start raising hell I'd better make sure I have some kind of launch pad under me . . .'

It was one o'clock in the afternoon in San Francisco, nine hours before the *Challenger* was due to dock at Oleum.

As the *Challenger* steamed steadily towards San Francisco at seventeen knots, a battered, bruised, mis-shapen ship, but still with her engine power unaffected, an edgy tension grew on board. Which was strange because it might have been expected that morale would rise as they neared their ultimate destination which should see the end of their ordeal. Quite the reverse was happening.

The British crew and officers were badly affected by the un-explained disappearance of Monk, the missing engine-room arti-ficer. Brady, the engine-room chief, tried to keep up the morale of his men by suggesting that Monk was hiding somewhere. 'It would take more than one of these froggie terrorists to put paid to a man like Monk,' he assured Lanky Miller. 'He just didn't get his chance to sort out LeCat, so he's gone to ground somewhere . . .'

Mackay and Bennett had taken a more realistic view in the chart-room when they discussed it early in the morning before dawn. 'I think the cat got him,' Bennett said. They had taken to referring to the French terrorist they most feared as 'the cat'.

'I think you're probably right,' Mackay had replied. 'What I don't understand is why Winter has made no reference to it.'

'And we can hardly ask him. How would we go about it? "Mr Winter, we sent one of our men to kill your second-in-command and he's gone missing. Any news?" It's getting on the men's nerves, too. You know what seamen are – a man dying at sea rouses superstition, but a man disappearing, that's enough to send them round the bend . . .'

So LeCat's method was working, which was ironical. Winter had kept the crew under control earlier by being forceful but not brutal. He had, in fact, more than justified Sheikh Gamal Tafak's judgement that it would take an Englishman to control a British crew. Now, without anyone being aware of it – least of all Winter – LeCat's use of the terror weapon was also working, grinding away at the morale of the crew only a few hours' sailing time from San Francisco. LeCat observed what was happening through habitually half-closed eyes without apparently noticing anything. Soon Winter would leave the ship and he would assume control; meantime the crew was slowly losing its guts.

The tension on board was not confined to the prisoners; the ex-OAS guards themselves showed signs of mounting tension as they came closer and closer to the American mainland, and this showed itself in a stricter, more irritable, trigger-fingered attitude. Nor was Winter, cold and detached as he was, free from tension. It was not the approach to California which plucked at his nerves; the closer he came to the climax the more icy he became. It was the unexplained incidents which warned his sixth sense that something was going wrong. First, there was the second signal from the mainland which arrived at 2pm.

Please confirm urgently that all is well aboard your ship. I require a fully worded signal in reply. Certain of your signals have not conformed to normal practice. O'Hara. San Francisco Port Authority.

Winter immediately showed this signal to Mackay who had just come back on to the bridge after sleeping for four hours. 'I want to know what this means,' Winter demanded. 'You'll agree you wouldn't normally receive this kind of signal? What has aroused O'Hara's suspicions?'

'You have, I expect,' Mackay replied bluntly.

'What does that mean?'

'Since you seized control of my ship you have sent all the radio messages. Somewhere, it seems, you blundered...'

'So what answer would you send?'

'I'm not dictating a reply,' Mackay said firmly. He turned his back on Winter and stared through the smashed bridge window. Betty Cordell stood beside him, noting all that was going on. Because there were always two British officers present, she was now spending most of her time on the bridge; there was an atmosphere of rising tension on the ship which worried her. Beyond the window the ocean was incredibly calm, a grey, placid plain under a grey, placid sky. Typhoon Tara was now ripping her way south, causing havoc on the sea lanes to Australia, while *Challenger* approached San Francisco from the south-west. This route – normally the tanker would have come in from the north-west – was being followed under pressure from Winter who planned to arrive unexpectedly at the entrance to Golden Gate channel.

'You must work out your own reply,' Mackay repeated when he was asked a second time.

Winter let it go, decided not to make an issue of it with Mackay. Within a few hours' sailing time of his objective he was going to be very careful not to stir up more trouble. He wrote out the reply himself and then took it to Kinnaird.

'Does this mean that they know something?' Kinnaird asked nervously as he read the message. 'Are we in trouble?'

'Send the message,' Winter ordered him. 'Did you think getting into San Francisco was going to be a cake walk?'

He left the radio cabin, locking the door behind him and handing the key to the armed guard outside. Kinnaird began transmitting. *All is not well aboard my ship. Between 0100 and 0500 hours we passed through the eye of Typhoon Tara. Bridge structure extensively damaged but vessel seaworthy. Engine room unaffected. Proceeding on course for Oleum through calm waters at seventeen knots. Cannot understand your reference to my signals which have been transmitted as usual at regular intervals. Estimated time of arrival at Oleum still 2200 hours. Mackay.*

Winter, who had catnapped for short periods later in the night when the typhoon subsided, became more active than ever, turn-

162

ing up unexpectedly all over the ship. He noted the edginess of the guards, but that was to be expected – as they came very close to the Californian coast they were bound to be apprehensive, and most of them were recovering from sea-sickness.

What puzzled him was the sullenness of the British crew. Hostility he could have understood – expected – but there was something furtive in the way they looked at him when he went down into the engine-room, some mood he didn't understand. He checked to make sure that no man had been injured by LeCat. He questioned LeCat himself.

'Have you been threatening them?' he demanded when he was alone with the French terrorist inside the cabin he had taken over for his own use. 'There's a feeling growing on this ship I don't understand . . .'

'What kind of feeling?' LeCat enquired.

'A feeling of murderous resentment. If we're not careful there'll be an explosion just when I don't want it . . .'

'I'll warn the guards . . .'

'I'll warn them. You'd better get back on the bridge.'

Edgy as he was inwardly, Winter still remembered to send a guard to escort Betty Cordell off the bridge and back to her cabin; with LeCat now stationed on the bridge it was better to keep the American girl out of the way. At three o'clock in the afternoon there was a third incident, when the tanker was only forty miles off the Californian coast, something far more disturbing than the arrival of a fresh signal.

The US Coast Guard helicopter arrived at exactly 1500 hours, cruising in towards the tanker so close to the ocean that only a man with LeCat's sharp eyes would have seen it so quickly. He used the phone to call Winter to the bridge. Winter reacted instantly, ordering three seamen to be brought up from the day cabin.

'You will go out on to the main deck,' he told them. 'Take those cleaning materials the guard has brought and pretend to be working. If you make any attempt to signal for help to this chopper three men in the day cabin will be shot. Their lives are in your hands . . .'

163

At the front of the bridge Mackay was looking sour; Winter was the devil incarnate. He thought of everything. At the moment the deserted deck had an abnormal, naked look. By the time the helicopter arrived it would look as though nothing were wrong.

'Now let's all be quite clear about what's going to happen,' Winter said grimly as the three seamen were escorted off the bridge. 'Mr Mackay will stay where he is. You, Bennett, will go forward beside him. If the chopper flies alongside us you will wave to it. I shall be out of sight at the rear of the bridge, watching you . . .'

Mackay, still tired, tried desperately to think of some way he could indicate to the chopper pilot what was happening, but the problem defeated him. He watched this representative of the outside, sane world, the first representative he had seen since the terrorists came aboard, flying towards him. It was an anxious moment. For Winter also, as he stood well out of sight with LeCat beside him. The armed guards couldn't possibly be seen no matter how close the machine came.

It was heading straight for the bow of the ship, and through the open window they could now hear, above the throb of the *Challenger*'s engines, the lighter, faster beat of the helicopter's engine. There was no doubt about it: the machine was coming to take a look at them, maybe even attempt a landing where, two days earlier, Winter himself had landed a Sikorsky which in appearance was the twin of the one approaching them.

Inside her cabin Betty Cordell had her porthole wide open. With her acute sense of hearing, sharpened by a childhood spent in the desert, she had heard it coming a long way off. At first she thought it might be the terrorists' helicopter returning, but when she poked her head out of the open porthole she saw the tiny blip just above the sea, flying in from the east, from the direction of the mainland. She decided to take a chance.

Grabbing one of the white towels from out of the bathroom, she used her felt-tip pen to inscribe the three letters large-size on the towel. SOS. She went back to the porthole and waited. It was much closer now, she could tell from the engine sound, although the bow of the ship concealed how close it was. If only it would fly along the port side, along her side of the ship. The engine beat became a sharp drumming staccato. She leaned out of the port-hole again and still she couldn't see it. She licked her dry lips and waited with the towel in her hands.

The air coming in through the porthole was almost warm; the tanker was now moving through far more southerly latitudes than when it had sailed from Alaska. The engine beat of the incoming Sikorsky was rising to a roar when the cabin door behind Betty Cordell opened and the armed guard came inside. He ran across to the porthole, slammed it shut, pulled the curtain over it and dragged the towel out of her hand. 'You sit over the bed,' he said in halting English. She sat down on the edge of the bunk and clasped her trembling hands in front of her.

'You are bad,' he said, looking at the marked towel. 'LeCat will not like . . .'

'Tell Winter,' she said in a weary voice. 'He won't like it either . . .'

Inside the day cabin the seamen not on duty were lying face down on their stomachs while three guards stood close to the walls pointing pistols at them. The curtains were drawn over the port-holes. The same scene was taking place inside the galley where Wrigley had joined Bates, the cook, on the floor. It was a further order Winter had issued on the bridge when he saw the Sikorsky coming – that the prisoners above engine-room level must be put in a position where it would be impossible for them to signal to the US Coast Guard plane.

The Sikorsky reached the bow, flew at fifty feet above the ocean along the port side of the tanker. 'Wave!' Winter shouted from the rear of the bridge. 'Do you want your helmsman to get a bullet in the back?' Bennett waved without enthusiasm, and then Mackay noticed something – the helmeted pilot inside his dome was not waving back. Which was damned odd.

The machine flew past the stern and Winter watched it going through the rear window. 'Doesn't the pilot normally acknow-ledge your wave?' he asked. 'I didn't see him wave back . . .'

'They don't always,' Mackay lied. 'If they're near the end of a patrol they're only interested in getting back home . . .'

'He's coming back!' LeCat shouted.

Half a mile beyond the tanker's stern the Sikorsky was circling; then, squat-nosed and small, it headed straight back towards the tanker steaming away from it. As it came closer Winter gave a fresh order. 'Don't wave at it this time. Just watch it go. Do they ever communicate with you by radio when they're as close as this?'

'Not often,' Mackay said neutrally. He wasn't at all sure what was happening. The machine flew past them again, this time along the starboard side, still only fifty feet above the waves, which meant it passed below bridge deck level. On the main deck one seaman was hosing down the open areas while the other two seamen swabbed with brushes. They had decided to use the hose on their own initiative, to make it look good. As one of them said, 'Even if it lands and has Marines aboard those buggers will shoot our lads before they can get to them . . .' Mackay, as he watched, had never seen them work harder. He thought he understood why. Kinnaird, pale-faced, came running on to the bridge a moment later. He handed a message to Winter.

'I decided to bring it up . . .' Because you were scared, Winter thought, because you had to see what was happening. 'They've requested permission to land . . .'

Mackay swung round, his face grim and alert. And how are you going to cope with that, you bastard? Winter stood quite still for only a few seconds, watching the distant Sikorsky as it circled a mile ahead of the tanker which was now steaming towards it. He caught Mackay's expression and smiled bleakly, then gave the order to Kinnaird. 'Refuse permission to land. Tell them the deck-plates under the landing point were weakened by the typhoon, that we have two injured seamen aboard – not seriously – but they will need to go to hospital for a check-up when we reach Oleum . . .'

The Sikorsky flew over them once more, making this last run directly over the tanker at a height of one hundred feet, then it turned away and headed on a due east course until it was out of sight. 'Where would it have come from?' Winter asked.

'Off some weather cutter, I suppose,' Mackay lied. 'How the devil would I know?'

But he did know. There was no chance of a weather cutter being stationed so close to the Californian coast. And the machine had flown off due east, heading straight for the United States mainland.

* * *

The helicopter was coming back.

At 4.30pm on Tuesday, half an hour before dusk, Winter leaned out of the smashed window on the bridge and watched the blip coming in from the south on the starboard side, the Sikorsky returning from the trawler *Pêcheur*.

During the height of the typhoon Kinnaird had exchanged frequent position messages with the *Pêcheur*, so they each knew where the other vessel was. And because the *Pêcheur* had steamed through the night over a hundred miles south of the tanker she had escaped the typhoon. Which was just as well, Winter reflected: had the trawler endured only a quarter of the tanker's ordeal the Sikorsky would undoubtedly have been ripped from her deck and hurled into the ocean.

Winter had deliberately left it as late as possible before summoning the Sikorsky to return. A helicopter sitting on the *Challenger*'s port quarter would hardly have heightened an impression of normality if they had been seen and reported on by a passing ship – let alone by the genuine US Coast Guard machine which had circled them three times. Winter was still worried about that incident, as he was about the unprecedented signal from the San Francisco Port Authority. He turned round as Betty Cordell came on the bridge.

'How long before we reach San Francisco?' she asked Mackay.

'We'll be standing off the Californian coast in less than an hour,' he told her soberly. 'We are scheduled to dock at Oleum at twenty-two hundred hours. Don't count on it,' he warned her.

'What's going to happen?'

'Ask him . . .'

'What's going to happen to us?' she asked Winter coldly.

'Within forty-eight hours you are likely to be ashore – in San Francisco – with the story of your life,' he told her cynically.

'Why is your chopper coming?'

'Part of the operation . . .'

Winter went down off the bridge to meet the machine when it landed. The sky had changed during the past few minutes, and now an overcast from the north was spreading itself above the tanker as it continued heading direct for San Francisco. Winter, secretive by nature, had not felt inclined to answer Betty Cordell's

167

last question. In less than an hour he had to fly away from the tanker, leaving LeCat in sole command.

'So we stop her where she is now – about ten miles off the coast,' Mayor Peretti said. 'We order her to stay in her present position and send out a vessel with Marines aboard. Is that agreed, gentlemen?'

The table in the mayor's office was large and there was just room for everyone. Seated on Peretti's right, Sullivan looked round the table and marvelled. God, what a change in only a few hours. Gathered round the table was a representative of almost every law-enforcement agency in the States. Karpis of the FBI was there. Next to him sat Vince Bolan, police commissioner. Col Liam Cassidy of the US Marine Corps sat beyond him, and beyond him was Garfield of the Coast Guard and O'Hara of the Port Authority. Several other men whose functions Sullivan hadn't grasped made up the balance.

The Coast Guard helicopter which had circled the *Challenger* three times, which had flown past her twice at lower than bridge level, had no sooner landed when its cameras had been rushed to the processing laboratory where technicians waited. It was the enlarged prints taken from these films, infra-red films which had penetrated into the shadows on the bridge of the tanker, which had brought these men rushing to the mayor's office from all over the city, from the Presidio itself. The prints clearly showed men with guns standing at the rear of the bridge, guns pointed in the direction of the officers at the front of the bridge.

Sullivan had tracked a whisper all the way from Bordeaux to Hamburg, had then crossed to London, finding nothing concrete, nothing he could put his finger on, but he had gone on – all the way to Alaska, then down to Seattle and on to San Francisco. 'If only you could provide some real evidence . . .' the FBI agent had said to Sullivan at the St Francis Hotel. Sullivan looked at the blown-up prints scattered across the table.

The three men with guns had come out with remarkable clarity, although the face of the tall, thin man was blurred. Was this Winter, Sullivan wondered? The face was too blurred to make any real comparison with the prints Paul Hahnemann had given to him in Hamburg of his very English visitor, Mr Arnold Ross. The pistols the men held were clear enough, so clear that Col Cassidy had guessed they could be Czech Skorpions. 'That's only a guess,' he had added, 'but goddamnit, they're pistols, that's for sure...'

The signal was drafted for immediate transmission, the signal ordering the *Challenger* to cease steaming ahead, to stay where she was. The signal ended on an ominous note. *Any further progress towards the Californian coast will be interpreted as a hostile act.*

Dusk was gathering over the Pacific as the *Challenger* continued steaming for the coast of California at seventeen knots. The signal from the mainland had been received and Winter had shown it to Mackay, who gave no sign of elation as he read it carefully, then handed it back.

'What are you going to do now? You've been rumbled...'

'As I expected to be, sooner or later,' Winter replied coldly. 'Our great achievement has been to get so far undetected – right under the eyebrows of America. You will maintain present course and speed, Captain Mackay...'

'You must be mad. Get it through your head, Winter – the whole operation is over, finished. Any minute now I expect to see a US destroyer on my starboard bow...'

'That is highly unlikely. As I have just said, we have done better than I expected. Do you really think I did not foresee this contingency?'

Mackay felt a pricking of doubt. The supreme self-confidence this strange man had displayed from the moment he came on board was still there. At the front of the bridge, Betty Cordell, who had gathered the contents of the signal from their conversation, was studying Winter's cold expression to see how he took this overwhelming defeat. She couldn't understand his calmness, his detached aloofness. You might almost have thought he was seeing his plan working out...

Making a gesture to LeCat, Winter walked out on to the port wing deck where the two men could be alone. He started scribbling a reply for Kinnaird who was waiting, pale-faced, inside the bridge. 'That should do it,' Winter said, showing the reply to LeCat.

'Also no underwater surveillance,' LeCat suggested. 'They may try and track us with a submarine . . .'

Winter completed the message, handed it to LeCat to take to Kinnaird, then looked along the main deck in the fading light where the helicopter was waiting for him. The signal should be clear enough to the men waiting on the mainland. They'll get the bloody message, Winter thought.

We have had complete armed control of the Challenger for two days. We are proceeding for San Francisco Bay at a speed of seventeen knots. The British crew are hostages. Ransom of twenty million dollars is demanded for their safe release. In the event of any attempt to board this ship the twenty-eight hostages will instantly be shot. No surface ship, no aircraft, no underwater craft must approach this vessel. Any non-cooperation will be treated as a hostile act. The Weathermen.

Mackay was a very frightened man as he left the bridge and went down to the main deck as quickly as he could. Then he was running along the raised catwalk with the armed guard chasing him behind, shouting to him to stop. Mackay hoped he wouldn't get a bullet in the back, but he was even more scared of Winter leaving the ship. Ahead he saw Winter, close to the helicopter, turn and roar out an order in French to the guard running behind him. Had the terrorist aimed his gun? Had Winter shouted a command not to fire? Mackay kept on running.

Winter waited for him on the main deck under the dropped helicopter blades. It was getting dark now. A misty dusk which foreshadowed the onset of night was closing round the tanker. Someone turned on the lights at the head of the foremast ready for the take-off. Mackay, breathing heavily, was startled by the sudden illumination as he reached the machine.

'You are not leaving?'

'That was a damned silly thing to do – you could have got shot,' Winter snapped.

'You are not leaving the ship?'

It was very strange. There was no hostility in Mackay's voice, only an undisguised concern and anxiety, as though he were seeing a friend leave for ever. Winter caught the note in the captain's voice and smiled. 'I should have thought you'd be glad to see me go, maybe even pray a little that my engine failed over the Pacific . . .'

'Tell him to get away from us.' Mackay glanced back at the guard. Winter spoke briefly in French and the guard went back along the catwalk. 'You are not leaving us with LeCat?' Mackay demanded. 'Not with that animal . . .'

'We have a plan which must be carried out. Part of that plan means I must leave the ship . . .'

'You are British,' Mackay persisted. 'All right, you have taken my ship, the one thing no master can forgive. But you are British and I have a British crew to protect. If you stay, I shall remember it if things go wrong for you – I give you my word I shall speak up . . .'

Winter looked hesitant, the first time Mackay had ever seen even a hint of indecision in that cold, severe face. Mackay pressed home his plea. 'And there is the American girl – you know there has been one incident in her cabin already. I warn you, Winter, if you leave this ship there will be multiple rape . . .'

'LeCat will have his work cut out to cope with what's coming. In any case, I have spoken to him. He knows he needs the co-operation of your crew to get the tanker into San Francisco . . .'

'We are still going into the Bay?'

'Yes.' Winter was studying Mackay's drawn face. 'Look, it will turn out all right. There will be negotiations with the authorities to secure your crew's safe release . . .'

'You sound very confident.'

'I'm a confident chap.' Winter grinned. 'Always have been.' He swung round as he heard a boot scrape behind him. LeCat was standing near the nose of the machine, his pistol dangling from his hand. He had come quietly down from the fo'c'sle, creeping round the far side of the machine, and now he stood watching.

Mackay was appalled. Had the Frenchman heard all they had

171

said? Winter climbed up inside the machine, slammed the door shut, and the slam sounded like a death sentence to Mackay.

LeCat sent Mackay back to the distant bridge with an armed guard. The foremast lights were switched off as soon as Winter's machine had taken off. So it was almost dark when LeCat descended alone into the carpenter's store, beaming his torch over the stacked suitcases wedged behind the table. He was sweating several minutes later when he went back up the ladder, carrying the two hundred pound case by its reinforced handle, then he transported it down on to the main deck.

Opening up the hatch cover of one of the empty tanks which had remained unfilled since the ship left Nikisiki, he went carefully down the almost vertical ladder leading to the depths of the tank. He rested for a moment on a steel platform, then went down the next ladder. Once, he caught the case a glancing blow on the ladder. Its hollow echo reverberated inside the immense metal tomb. LeCat was sweating horribly as he continued his descent. He had almost dropped his burden, dropped it from a height of twenty feet to the floor of the tank below.

His expert knowledge of mechanisms told him that nothing would have happened, the hellish thing could not possibly have detonated – the timer device wasn't activated, the miniature receiver was useless until the radio signals reached it, but LeCat was still sweating horribly. Reaching the bottom, he lifted the case, activated the magnetic clamps, and the case was attached to the hull of the ship.

He spent more time down in the bowels of the tank, fixing up the boobytrap – the anti-lift devices – he had earlier left at the bottom of the tank. And before he climbed the ladder he once again wiped sweat off his hands. When he returned to the main deck he closed the hatch and looked towards the bridge. No one could possibly have seen him in the darkness. Now there was only one other man on board who knew his secret; André Dupont, the man who had helped him bring the atomic physicist, Antoine, to Canada; the man who had watched over Antoine while he worked in the house on Dusquesne Street in Vancouver. And the nuclear device was in position, ready to be activated when the time came.

Part three
The San Francisco experience

15

No one notices the postman.

Everyone along the Californian coast is familiar with the sight of a US Coast Guard helicopter – these machines make daily patrols up and down the foreshore, often flying low over the beaches. So who would think the appearance of Winter's Sikorsky strange?

It was deep dusk when Winter came in sight of the coast close to Carmel-by-the-Sea. From the chart spread out over his knees he identified Point Lobos, then he turned due north. There were lights down in Carmel, in Pacific Grove on the Monterey peninsula, and in Monterey itself. All the lights disppeared suddenly. Another power failure. Sheikh Gamal Tafak's oil weapon was biting deep.

The helicopter flew on over a dark and quiet ocean, flew on until vague clouds blotted out the sea. Fog. The moon rose and shone down on greyness, a shifting greyness of thick fog banks which made Winter feel he might be thirty thousand feet up in a Jumbo jet, speeding at five hundred miles an hour from Heathrow to Anchorage. That was only six days ago; to Winter it seemed a whole lifetime. Ahead he saw the twitch of a flashing light exploding through the fog.

One million dollars . . . Time to retire, to get out like a racing driver before the world caught up with you, detonated in your face with a blinding flash and billowing clouds of black smoke. He checked his chart. The twitching flash would be Mile Rocks lighthouse at the entrance to Golden Gate.

He flew past the lighthouse on his right as the moon shone on slow-rolling fog which revolved like steam in a cauldron, on coils of fog which filled the entrance channel. Soon the *Challenger* would have to move through that cauldron. For a few seconds the distant fog lifted; a chain of lights crawled over the fog, barely moving it seemed, then the blanket closed down and his glimpse of traffic crossing Golden Gate bridge vanished.

He turned inland, away from the ocean, over Stinson Beach, still flying at a thousand feet with the fog three hundred feet below. Over Marin County – north across the bridge from San Francisco – the fog thinned, and now he was moving at minimum speed, staring down into the night, searching. He circled the area north of Novato once and then he spotted lights – alternatered and white flashes. He lost altitude and the lights came up to him amid a blur of dark trees and scrubby hill slopes. Walgren, the American who had shadowed Swan, the wireless operator in Anchorage, had not let him down.

Descending vertically towards the slope, he saw the lights were inside a tree-enclosed oval clearing, saw a small shadow which could be a parked car. The machine landed on hard earth inside a tangle of undergrowth, landed with a bump and then he cut the engine and the rotors slowed, stopped. It was 6.30pm. Walgren was waiting when he opened the door and dropped down on to the hill slope. 'Welcome to California,' Walgren said. Winter had arrived inside the United States.

They left the helicopter where he had landed it, concealed inside the copse of trees. And Winter had prepared for the possibility that it might be discovered within a few hours. Inside one of the seat pockets was a paid bill from a cheap hotel in Tijuana and a pack of Mexican cigarettes, some of the items Winter had instructed Walgren to obtain while he was in San Francisco the previous November. There was a thriving smuggling trade between Mexico and California, so when the FBI examined it they would conclude that this machine had come in from Mexico, probably with a haul of drugs.

Walgren, who had earlier obtained both hotel bill and the cigarettes, had also spilled a minute quantity of heroin on the floor of the pilot's cabin. The Drug Squad's Hoover would pick up these traces; their laboratory would analyse them. And these were extreme precautions Winter had suggested: the helicopter might well not be discovered for days.

At Winter's insistence, Walgren drove him first to Richardson Bay, where, under the treed lea of a headland, a small seaplane rode on the water. This was the escape vehicle. Later the terrorists would leave the ship under the cover of darkness or fog, speeding across the Bay inside the inflatable Zodiac, equipped with the

175

outboard motor. The choice of this craft by Winter was deliberate. Made of rubber, it would not register on a radar screen, and he had foreseen the possibility that while the tanker was stationary in the Bay the harbour police might establish radar lookout posts onshore.

When the time came the terrorists inside the Zodiac would make for the seaplane and this machine would fly them either to the *Pêcheur*, waiting out at sea, or across the border to Canada. And even if the seaplane was noticed in this remote spot there was little danger it would cause comment. Only a few miles further up Richardson Bay there was a seaplane base near Marin City. The wet-suits taken aboard the *Challenger* were for an emergency, so the terrorists could drop off the Zodiac close to the shore and swim the rest of the way. Winter hoped it wouldn't come to that – the currents out in the Bay can drown the strongest swimmer.

'Now drive me to San Francisco,' Winter told Walgren as he came ashore from examining the seaplane. His main concern had been the fuel tanks, and these were full. 'No trouble getting gas for this car?' he asked Walgren as they approached Golden Gate bridge. 'Every trouble,' the American replied. 'Cost me two dollars fifty a gallon on the black market. Mafia premium grade . . .' Winter made him stop at the far end of Golden Gate bridge while he went back alone along the sidewalk.

He studied the bridge where within a few hours the *Challenger* would pass under the huge span, leaning over the rail to stare down into the fog. The highway span seemed to be floating on the fog, as did the seven-hundred foot high towers which, in the moonlight, looked like temples in a Chinese painting.

Carrying out Winter's instructions, Walgren dropped him at the Trans-Bay bus terminal in the city. Taking the bag which Walgren had brought for him off the back seat, Winter said goodnight, and walked inside the terminal. He spent only ten minutes there, then he ran out and grabbed a yellow cab which had just delivered passengers, and told the driver to take him to the Clift Hotel on Geary Street.

Precautions, precautions . . . Winter never stopped taking them. Hotel doormen have retentive memories and it would look just a shade more normal if he arrived in a cab. Giving the cab driver

the usual fifteen per cent tip, he walked past the coloured door-
man and followed the bell-boy across the lobby to reception.
Keeping to his normal routine, he was booking in at one of the
most exclusive hotels in San Francisco; the police always assume
such visitors must be respectable.

'You have a room reserved for me for one week. Mr Stanley
Grant – from Australia...'

He would be staying for only three days, when he would pay
the bill for one week, saying he had been called back urgently to
Los Angeles. But if the hotel register were checked by the police
there is a certain unhurriedness, a respectability about a one-week
reservation. He followed the bell-boy into the elevator and went
up to his room on the tenth floor. Alone in his room he felt a
certain surprise. He was in California.

*... Any non-cooperation will be treated as a hostile act. The
Weathermen.*

Mayor Aldo Peretti was not smiling as he looked round the
table in his office at the men gathered there. Again, Sullivan was
on his right and beyond him were the same men who had attended
his previous meeting. No one was smiling. For over an hour they
had been arguing about the threatening signal which had come in
from the *Challenger*. It was 6.30pm.

'I don't believe it,' Sullivan said. 'That reference to The
Weathermen, I mean. This isn't a gang from the American underground. For some reason they just wish to hide their real identity
from us. It's too much of a coincidence,' he went on. 'I traced
Winter to Hamburg. Someone high up in France told me he was
involved with LeCat, who had recruited a team of ex-OAS terrorists. I then traced Winter to Alaska just before the *Challenger*
sailed again. I think that French terrorist team is aboard – and
they were financed by Arab money according to my French contact...'

'It sounds like a simple ransom demand,' Peretti pointed out.
'And in any case, what is at stake are the lives of twenty-eight
British seamen – and one American girl. I'm not prepared to risk
the lives of those innocent people.'

'We're not going to let that terrorist ship into the Bay, I hope,' Col Cassidy protested.

'We could negotiate with them in the Bay,' Peretti said firmly. 'Once they pass under Golden Gate bridge we have them at a disadvantage. They can't get out of the Bay again if we don't want them to – they're trapped . . .'

'I don't like it,' Cassidy snapped.

'I don't too much like it either,' Karpis of the FBI agreed.

'And I don't like risking twenty-nine people – including one American girl – getting shot,' Peretti replied forcefully. Aldo Peretti was a very humane man; something of his humanity had undoubtedly impressed enough voters at the previous election to make him mayor of San Francisco. He was, a lot of people agreed, a pleasant change from the tough and ruthless Governor of California, Alex MacGowan. The recent Grove Park scandal, involving corruption at a high level, had hammered the final nail into Alex MacGowan's political coffin.

The argument swayed backwards and forward for another hour; whether or not to let the terrorist ship inside the Bay. If he put it to the vote, Peretti calculated, they would split evenly down the middle, the humanitarians against the rest, as he privately put it to himself. He was on the verge of taking a decision when the phone rang. He listened, asked a few questions, then replaced the receiver, his face grave.

'I don't understand what's happening, gentlemen, but it just became a political matter. A fresh signal has come in from the *Challenger* – and for some reason I also don't understand, the people aboard her seem to want maximum publicity. They radioed the signal to the United Press wire service. The news will race round the world within hours. Now they are demanding two hundred million dollars – yes, Col Cassidy, I did say two hundred million – to be paid into the account of a bank in Beirut. The signal was signed the Free Palestine Movement. Sullivan was right – we are dealing with the Arabs, maybe by remote control with the Golden Apes themselves . . .'

At ten o'clock at night inside the Clift Hotel Winter sat in front of the colour TV set holding a glass of Scotch. He was reading the newspaper, not listening to the FBI thriller, not looking at it. His role now was to remain inside the city as a one-man Trojan horse, checking on the authorities' reactions to the terrorists' demands, then warning LeCat if he considered a change of tactics was called for.

His means of communicating with the tanker had been organised by Walgren; a mobile transmitter had been set up inside a truck which at the moment was hidden inside a nearby garage. The moment Winter wished to get in touch with LeCat, he only had to phone Walgren at the number the American had given him. The truck would then be driven to a remote part of Marin County across Golden Gate bridge, Winter would transmit his instructions, and the truck would be driven away before it could be located by any radio-detection equipment the Americans might be operating.

The news flash came through at 10.5pm. 'Terrorists have seized a British oil tanker off San Francisco . . . demand two hundred million dollars for the lives of the twenty-nine hostages aboard, one of them an American girl . . .'

Winter drank some more Scotch and waited for the comment. LeCat was working exactly to the plan he had devised – to keep the Americans off balance with a series of alarming and confusing messages. The real demand would come later – after the next subterfuge, after the Americans had let the tanker enter the Bay…

It was ten o'clock at night in San Francisco when Winter heard the news flash. In Baalbek, seven thousand miles away, a fresh day was dawning where it was seven in the morning. Sheikh Gamal Tafak lit another American cigarette and switched off the radio, then walked over to the lattice-work window which looked out over the anti-Lebanon mountains. In January there was snow along the crests.

It was the news item which had rattled him: the Americans were still discussing whether to let the tanker inside the Bay. It was time LeCat played his next card. He had to get the timing right, to hit them before they took a final decision. With his eyes half-closed, Tafak recalled the personal briefing Ahmed Riad – who would shortly land in San Francisco – had given LeCat.

'They will not decide to let you in at once. There is bound to be a delay while they think about it. But they are a sentimental people, the Americans. So, choose your moment, then play the big card . . .'

By now Tafak had completely forgotten that it was Winter who had fashioned the big card, the incident which would persuade the Americans to let the ship pass through the Golden Gate narrows. Taking his cigarette out of his mouth, Tafak looked at his hand. He was sweating. He would go out and get a breath of fresh morning air. It was not the atmosphere which was making him sweat. To bring about the final catastrophe it was vital that the Americans let the tanker inside the Bay.

As Sheikh Gamal Tafak stood in the front doorway, breathing in the morning air, his head and shoulders filled the telescopic sight, the vertical crosshair split him down the middle, the horizontal crosshair guillotined his neck. The target was in view, thirty metres from where the Israeli marksman lay sprawled out on a table inside a first floor room.

The rifle was propped on a sack filled with sand and the muzzle pointed through an open window. The room was in shadow because the sun was aimed in the same direction as the rifle barrel. The marksman, Chaim Borgheim, took the first pressure. A second squeeze and Tafak was dead.

Albert Meyer, the man who had quietly intimidated Lucille Fahmy, the switchboard operator who had provided a telephone number in Beirut, sat at the back of the room with an automatic weapon across his lap. He jumped when the phone rang, jumped because it could have disturbed his colleague's aim. He moved very quickly, scooping up the phone by his side. 'Albert here . . .' His eyes widened as he listened, then he said 'understood,' put down the receiver and moved swiftly and quietly across the room. Albert was sweating.

'No, Chaim . . .' He extended one finger carefully across the top of the rifle barrel, being very careful indeed not to touch the weapon. He could feel sweat dribbling down his back. 'Jesus Christ . . .' Chaim released the first pressure, looked up with a blank expression.

'I had him . . . what's wrong? You look terrible.'

'I thought I was too late. They just phoned through – not yet. Not yet, they said.'

'They bloody near had it – so did he.'

'Some crisis – in another part of the world. They cannot yet assess its implications. We must wait.'

'So, the world is normal – some crisis, somewhere . . .'

Through the fog the men on Mile Rocks lighthouse at the entrance to Golden Gate channel saw the *Challenger* burning.

It was dark, it was foggy, but the glare of the flames broke through both darkness and fog, a hideous half-seen conflagration which chilled them even more than the night air round the exposed lighthouse. They immediately signalled the Port Authority, which transmitted their signal to the mayor's office, and this signal arrived at almost the same moment as a message from the tanker.

The meeting in the mayor's office, which had gone on for hours, with a brief break for refreshments, was breaking up. Peretti listened on the phone, said wait a minute, then called out to the men leaving the room. 'Hold it! Something else is just coming through . . .'

They waited while he went on listening, scribbling notes on his desk pad. They were tired, worn out with arguing, and Cassidy, by sheer force of character, had persuaded the mayor to wait until morning before he finally decided – whether or not to let the terrorist ship inside the Bay. There had been more threats from the ship, now signed by LeCat, and Peretti was wracked with anxiety that he might be responsible for the violent deaths of twenty-nine innocent human beings, one of them a woman. Reluctantly, he had given way to Cassidy.

In his shirtsleeves despite the low room temperature – to save fuel the thermostat was turned down to sixty-two degrees – Peretti felt soiled and rumpled and badly in need of a shower. That was, before the phone rang. Now he had become alert again,

staring at Cassidy while he listened on the phone. He put down
the receiver, glanced at his notes. 'Get back to your seats, gentlemen, this thing isn't finished for tonight. It's only just beginning.'

'What's happened?' Cassidy demanded crisply.

'Two more signals – one from Mile Rocks lighthouse, one from
the *Challenger* herself. There's been a serious explosion aboard
the tanker, then a bad fire. Nine people have been very seriously
hurt – five of them hostages, and one of them is Miss Codrell.
They're asking for immediate permission to steam into the Bay so
the casualties can be taken off. Four of them are terrorists . . .'

'That's the signal from the *Challenger*?' Cassidy asked.

'Yes.'

'It could easily be a trick. I don't believe it . . .'

Peretti exploded. How like the goddamn military . . . 'You may
not believe it – or want to believe it – but I have a message here
from Mile Rocks lighthouse confirming that they have seen the
tanker ablaze,' he rasped. 'The fire has gone out now, thank God.
And I'm giving permission for that ship to enter the Bay . . .'

'We could lift the casualties off the tanker by chopper maybe,'
Garfield, the Coast Guard chief suggested.

'The message repeats the earlier threat – if any aircraft, surface
or underwater vessel approaches the tanker all the hostages will
immediately be killed . . .'

'I still don't like it,' Cassidy said.

'Colonel, no one is asking you to like it,' Peretti snapped. 'You
just haven't thought this thing through. One wrong move on my
part and those people on that tanker may die. I have to think of
the British crew, helpless men with guns pointing at them. When
we take off the casualties we shall have four terrorists in our hands
for questioning. Some human contact even with terrorists is better
than . . .'

Even while Peretti was speaking they were hauling up the side of
the hull of the *Challenger* the remnants of the two Carley floats
which had been attached to her with cables. The floats, crammed
with petrol-soaked rags, had earlier been lowered over the side,
each with a tiny thermite bomb and a timer device aboard, so

when they drifted with the current they were well clear of the tanker as they exploded and ignited the floats, creating the two separate blazes which had been seen from Mile Rocks lighthouse.

'. . . human contact even with terrorists is better than trying to communicate across a void through the medium of radio signals,' Peretti continued. 'These misguided men are not necessarily all wild beasts . . .'

'You could have fooled me,' Cassidy said, then regretted the remark. It had sounded damned rude.

Peretti sat up straight at the head of the table and spoke without rancour. 'You are a soldier, Colonel Cassidy. You have been trained to shoot at the enemy. Sometimes that is necessary, but here we have hostages from another country – from Britain – to think of. I am not putting this to the vote, I am taking the decision myself. The tanker *Challenger* will be given permission to enter the Bay . . .'

It was close to midnight when Governor Alex MacGowan's Boeing 707 approached the runway at San Francisco International airport, his flight much delayed owing to a petrol shortage which had kept him waiting for seven hours at Heathrow Airport, London.

16

'From the point of view of the Red Army, if the western nations attempted to break the Arab stranglehold on their economies, then a favourable situation might arise whereby the Soviet Union could secure for itself certain oil reserves essential in the event of a future confrontation with the People's Republic of China . . .'

Extract from photostat of confidential report from Marshal Simoniev to First Secretary of Union of Soviet Socialist Republics handed to Ken Chapin of CIA by Soviet defector, Col Grigorienko.

*　　*　　*

'After a night in bed with his wife, Peretti is the kind of guy who has to be helped out of it in the morning . . .'

'No need to be coarse, Alex,' Miriam MacGowan said quietly.

'Before this thing is finished I'm going to get a whole lot coarser,' the Governor assured his wife. He peered out of the window into the dark. 'Where the hell is the airport?'

The Boeing 707 was losing altitude rapidly, coming in to the San Francisco runway from the north-east – all planes had been routed away from their normal entry over the Pacific so they wouldn't pass over the tanker *Challenger*. It was the flying moment Miriam MacGowan hated most – the downward drop at speed towards a solid concrete avenue somewhere out of sight. Mac-Gowan's attitude was more brutally fatalistic – either we hit the deck and cruise along it – or we burn. He was careful not to express the sentiment.

MacGowan was fuming. Half an hour ago, while the plane was flying over San Luis Obispo, he had received a radio message from an aide Col Cassidy had spoken to. Occasionally, in the States, when a military man does not agree with a decision, he has been known to leak the decision to a political friend whose views equate more closely with his own. MacGowan now knew that the terrorist ship he had heard about while changing planes at Los Angeles was going to be allowed inside the Bay. It was, of course, a typical Peretti decision. Milk in his spine and jello in his guts. MacGowan couldn't stomach the bloody matinée idol.

The wheels touched down, bumped. Miriam swallowed, waiting for the hideous thing to slow down. It always seemed it was going straight through the airport buildings. MacGowan undid his seat belt before the green light came on. A stewardess leaned over to reprove him, but he forestalled her. ' *You* are supposed to be seated while we're landing – and don't forget I'm the first off this air-craft . . .'

'Yes, Governor.'

He was on his feet as the machine taxied to a halt, a short, heavily-built man with a large head, thick hair and thick eye-brows and a wide, grim-looking mouth. In build he was not dis-similar to LeCat. He ran down the mobile staircase and past a group of reporters. Inside Miriam apologised to the stewardess.

'He's terribly worried about what's happening...'

MacGowan used one of the phones in TWA's back office – the reporters had run after him, intrigued by his haste. His first call was to Peretti. 'I want that ship stopped. It's not coming into the Bay with an army of terrorists aboard ... Don't argue, Peretti – if I have to, I'll call out the National Guard ...'

He called in rapid succession General Lepke at the Presidio, the US Coast Guard, the Harbor Police, and finally, Police Commissioner Bolan. Nobody had a chance to express an opinion; nobody really tried. But he did explain to Bolan what he was doing, telling him to phone Peretti the moment the call was over. This was simply to bring more pressure to bear on the mayor.

'I want this thing put on ice till I get a grip on it. So the ship stays where it is for the moment. I've told Peretti to signal those bastards that there's been a collision – that no ship can enter or leave Golden Gate till the channel is cleared. They may not believe it but they won't be sure. And it will throw them off balance – first they get permission, then a temporary refusal. I'm coming in now ...'

It was typical of MacGowan to be in a fury but still to be thinking clearly – to freeze the situation and throw his opponent off balance at the same time. 'I've stuck my head in a political noose,' he told his wife during the drive into the city, 'but I don't care. I know I'm doing the right thing.'

'Peretti will pull the skids from under you, give him half a chance,' she warned.

'You've forgotten something – politically I'm finished anyway after the Grove Park business. Now I'm thinking of the hostages' problem.'

'Peretti probably feels he's thinking of them, too ...'

'In the wrong way, in the Peretti way – let's all sit down over a cup of coffee and talk things out. I've got a hunch about this thing ...' They were passing through Brisbane and he saw her looking at him. 'I mean we may have to kill every terrorist aboard that tanker ...'

Ten miles ahead of them a yellow cab was moving into San Francisco with four strangers sharing the vehicle. On the back seat was a passenger off the same flight as MacGowan, but whereas MacGowan had travelled first class this passenger – to avoid being conspicuous – had travelled economy. Ahmed Riad sat upright, very tense on his first visit to the United States.

When he arrived in the lobby of the Hotel St Francis on Union Square, he reserved a room in the name of Seebohm and was taken up in the glass elevator which crawled up the outside of the building. The experience terrified Riad as he gazed down at the tiny rooftop of a car turning into the car park under the square. Riad had a pathological fear of heights. Still, he would only be in this place one night. In the morning he would inform the Englishman of the change of plan, telling him to catch the first plane back to Europe.

Aboard the *Challenger* LeCat had waited confidently for Mackay to receive permission to enter the Bay when the burnt embers of the Carley floats had been hauled up on the main deck. The signal granting permission had arrived later; the captain had prepared to sail into the channel; the next signal – refusing permission – had arrived just after midnight. It had been a thunderbolt for the Frenchman. His face working with fury, he waited on the bridge while Mackay absorbed the message.

'You will take the ship into the Bay at once,' the terrorist ordered.

'Impossible.' Mackay handed back the signal to LeCat. 'I cannot steam inside Golden Gate until they have cleared the channel. You've read it yourself – there's been a collision.'

'I do not believe it! This is a trick the Americans are playing on me. First they say yes, then they say no. They cannot do this to LeCat . . .'

Mackay glanced at him, careful to conceal his growing anxiety. The Frenchman's personality seemed to be changing – these constant references to 'me', to 'LeCat', as though a power complex which had remained submerged was surfacing now Winter's restraining hand was gone. He tried quiet reason.

'Listen to me. The moment they give permission I will take the ship in through Golden Gate. If I take it in now – without permission – we may well collide with those damaged ships somewhere in the channel . . .'

LeCat raised his Skorpion, aimed it point blank at Bennett. 'If you do not immediately sail this ship to San Francisco I will shoot three of your men . . .'

'If I sail this ship in now and there is another collision – which there will be in this fog, for God's sake – *Challenger* may go down, taking you and all your men with you. We would go down as well. So, shoot every hostage on this ship if you like, but I will not sail my ship through fog under these conditions.'

Mackay turned his back on the terrorist and went to the bridge window. For the second time in only a few hours he felt his back muscles brace themselves for a bullet. Behind him LeCat's eyes flickered. If there was a collision the whole operation was finished. He left the bridge and went to his cabin. To soothe his fury he began drinking cognac.

LeCat stood in the open doorway of Betty Cordell's cabin. He had opened the door quietly and she was lying full length on her bunk, exhausted, half asleep. When she saw him she whipped her long legs over the edge quickly. 'Well, what is it?'

He closed the door, locked it, came swiftly over to the bunk and looked down at her. She tried to stand up but he placed a spread hand over her chest and pushed her hard. She fell back into the bunk, caught her head on the woodwork and was dazed. 'If Winter finds you here . . .' Then she remembered that Winter had gone, flown away. She tried to keep calm but the blow on the head had addled her, she was having trouble focusing on the heavily-built figure which loomed over her.

'Winter isn't here,' LeCat reminded her.

'Oh, my God . . .'

'Scream – and I'll cut you . . .'

The knife point tickled her cheek and the full horror of what was coming hit her. The blurred figure came closer, lowered itself, then his hand ripped her blouse down the front. She clawed for his eyes but he moved his head and again the knife pressed against her cheek. 'Ruin your good looks for life,' he whispered. She sank back and he came on top of her.

She tried to think of something else – anything – to think that she was at home, that this was only a nightmare, to switch her mind to anything except what was happening. It didn't work, she knew where she was, what was happening. The bloody gun . . . far too far away. 'Scream and I'll cut you . . .' One day she would forget it, pretend to herself it had never happened, that it had all been a nightmare . . . Oh, Daddy, you made it sound so easy – looking after yourself. It went on for eternity.

LeCat climbed off the bunk. She lay with her eyes shut, trying to control her breathing. She pulled a handful of sheet and blanket over herself, her eyes still tightly shut. He was moving about the cabin. She heard the clink of the water carafe, a loathsome swallow. She kept her eyes shut very tight indeed.

'You tell Mackay . . .' LeCat paused, still whispering, somewhere close to her. 'You tell Mackay and I will kill little Foley. I will shoot him low down and he will die slowly – if you tell Mackay . . .'

The knife tip touched her cheek. 'Answer me, you cold bitch. You heard what I said?'

'Go away.' She swallowed, her eyes still closed. Anything to be alone again. 'I heard you. Now go away . . .'

The cabin door closed. She had not even heard him unlock it. She opened her eyes only a fraction, frightened he was still there. The cabin was empty. Very faintly she heard the slap of the ocean against the hull, a strangely peaceful sound.

She lay in her bunk a long time before she got up and went under the cold shower. Then she peeled off her sodden clothes, screwed them into a tight bundle and dropped them out of the porthole. She went back again to the shower until the cold water made her tremble. Drying herself automatically, she carefully selected new clothes and put them on. Fresh underclothes, slacks, two sweaters.

She wouldn't tell Mackay, wouldn't tell anyone – she decided that while she was under the shower. And not entirely because of poor Foley. Going to the door, she tried the handle carefully and the door was locked. She pressed her ear to the door and listened. No sound of a guard stirring restlessly. She went to her suitcase, opened it, extracted the rifle under the spare clothes.

She stood with it in her hands for a long time, resisting the temptation to assemble it. In this suddenly confined world where the past no longer seemed to mean anything the weapon was her only friend. Life had closed in, had become only the ship – and the men on board. She had no feeling of panic or hysteria, only a dead sensation, and she had come to a decision.

No one, however clever, was perfect – because you couldn't be sure of what would happen next, however much you planned things. At some unguarded moment LeCat would make a slip, a slip which might last for no longer than a minute, but he would make that slip, she felt sure of it. So she would have to wait and watch and use any feminine skill she had to deceive them, to make them forget her, to think that, being a woman, she was of no account at all. She would live for that moment, then she would kill as many of them as she could.

At nine o'clock on Wednesday morning January 22, Winter picked up the *San Francisco Chronicle* which had been delivered to his bedroom with his breakfast and started reading. The *Challenger* was headline news. TERRORISTS SEIZE BRITISH TANKER OFF SAN FRANCISCO. The detailed story which followed was garbled, mostly inaccurate, but that was to be expected at this early stage. Winter read with interest that Governor Alex Mac-Gowan had arrived dramatically in the city at midnight, that he had countermanded the mayor's permission to let the tanker into the Bay, that he had now established a headquarters in his offices in the Transamerica Pyramid building. The fact that the ship was still outside the Bay didn't worry him; he was prepared for setbacks and it might soon be necessary to radio LeCat fresh instructions.

Half an hour earlier Winter had received a phone call from the Hotel St Francis, from a Mr Seebohm. He was expecting the call because two months earlier it had been agreed that Ahmed Riad would come to San Francisco at this stage of the operation – to receive an on-the-spot report of progress which he would then fly back with to Beirut. Winter suspected that Riad might try to linger, to jog his elbow, and had already decided that if this happened he would have to persuade Mr Seebohm to catch an early plane back home. He went on drinking his coffee, turning to the nside pages.

The news item which made him freeze with his cup half-way to his mouth was tucked away at the bottom of an inside page. His reflection in the dressing table mirror showed a man whose features might have turned to stone, the bones sharp in the morning light coming through the window, the jaw rigid. He sat perfectly still, re-reading the news item, then he put the coffee cup down carefully on the table without drinking.

He sat there for some time, staring into space, then he got up and looked out of the window. The window carried a security device allowing it to be opened only a few inches – to discourage suicide cases – but Winter, who liked a lot of fresh air, had used a certain tool he always carried to neutralise the device, so now it was wide open. Geary Street yawned ten storeys below. Winter went on staring at the strange, mosaic-like panorama of San Francisco stepped up in a series of terraces towards Nob Hill, an intricate collection of buildings of varying heights so close together they resembled some bizarre jigsaw. Then he went back for the *Chronicle* and read the news item for the third time.

Charles Swan, British radio operator, and his wife Julie were found murdered late today in a remote barn on the outskirts of the city. Both victims were discovered by the police with their throats cut. – Anchorage, Alaska.

He sat down again, lit a cigarette, checked his watch. Ahmed Riad, travelling under the name Seebohm, would be arriving in a few minutes. Winter waited, sat in the chair for a quarter of an hour, smoking, his eyes cold, showing nothing of the terrible fury inside him. Then the phone rang. A Mr Seebohm was waiting in the lobby. Winter asked them to send up Mr Seebohm.

The Englishman closed the door, locked it as Riad, a careful man, walked into the bathroom, checked behind the door, then came out again and walked over to the window. Glancing down at the sheer, ten-storey drop into Geary, he shuddered and turned away. 'These American buildings are too tall. They have a megalomania for height. Perhaps it is something sexual . . .'

Winter stared at the Arab. 'Are you feeling all right?'

Riad assumed an air of command. He had arrived to give the Englishman his final instructions. 'We have no time to waste. Is everything correct on board the ship? Is LeCat reacting correctly? I would have expected the ship to be in the Bay by now.' The Arab, always nervous in Winter's presence, was wearing sharp-pointed, highly polished shoes and they squeaked when he moved.

'Everything is the way you want it, the way you planned it,' Winter said slowly.

Riad thrust both hands inside his raincoat pockets, hands which had been fluttering as though unsure who they belonged to. Standing stiffly, he spoke in what he imagined was a voice of authority. The feet also, Winter observed, seemed unsure where to put themselves.

'There has been a change of plan, Winter. You are no longer needed in San Francisco. You are to take the first available flight to Los Angeles. There you will board a plane for Paris.'

'Just like that?'

Winter sat down, sprawling out his legs and looking up at Riad with a cigarette in his mouth. 'Why?'

'You do not question me...'

'I'll break those shiny teeth of yours and poke them down your throat – if I feel like it. Actually, I feel just like that.'

Winter spoke so mildly that for a moment Riad could not believe he had understood. He moved forward and Winter lifted his foot. The movement was so quick Riad had no time to dodge. The heel of Winter's right foot smashed down on the shiny shoe and Riad squealed. 'I like people who keep still,' Winter remarked. 'Seen today's newspaper?' He folded the paper to the Anchorage news item and shoved it at the Arab. 'Read it! That bit at the bottom.'

Riad read it and the newspaper rustled as he tried to hold it steady. Then he dropped the paper on the table, took out an airline folder and handed it towards Winter. 'These are your tickets – in the name of Stanley Grant...'

'You haven't commented on the news item.' Winter stayed flopped in his chair, making no attempt to take the folder Riad was holding.

'They must have tried to escape,' Riad muttered. 'I do not wish to discuss this thing...'

'What you wish doesn't matter any more . . .' Winter stood up, walking towards Riad who backed away and then realised he was moving towards the open window. 'No one in Anchorage tried to escape,' Winter told him. 'Swan wouldn't have risked it – not with his wife being there. So, what happened?'

'I was not there . . .' Riad was trembling, trying not to catch Winter's blank gaze as he backed into an alcove which contained a writing desk. 'I have to leave at once . . .'

'For the United Arab Republic consulate?'

'I did not say that . . .'

'And you didn't say you knew this filthy thing in Anchorage was going to happen – but you did know. You weren't surprised or appalled when you read that paper – you were just worried that I had found out about it.'

'I know nothing about Anchorage . . .' Riad's arrogance had dissolved. Backed into the alcove by the cold-eyed Englishman, his nerve was going rapidly. He pulled at his collar which felt like a noose round his neck, his legs were trembling, there was a sharp pain of tension in his chest. Behind him he felt the wall; there was nowhere else to go and Winter kept coming towards him. 'I know nothing about Anchorage,' the Arab repeated. 'Nothing . . .'

'What is going to happen aboard that ship?'

'They will make the demand, the Americans will accept . . .' He choked on his own words as Winter grasped him by the throat, dragged him towards the open window. Riad, quick-witted, immediately understood. 'No! No! Please! I beg you . . .' Winter had both hands round his throat now, ignoring the frantic beat of Riad's fists, dragging him closer and closer to the wide-open window. The Arab obviously had a horror of heights. Winter stood Riad with his back to the window and bent him at the waist over and outwards, his own legs pressed hard against Riad's which were supported by the lower wall. Riad's upper half went further and further outwards over the ten-storey drop until his head was upside down and above the thump of blood pounding in his ears he heard the blare of traffic horns over a hundred feet below. He saw the sky, the drunken slant of buildings and felt Winter's hand on his throat pushing him down and down. Bile came into his mouth, the pain in his chest was appalling, the pounding in his ear-drums was like a drum-beat, then he felt Winter's other hand grasping his belt, lifting his feet off the bedroom floor and he knew he was going down into the chasm – hurtling through space – until his skull met the sidewalk and was crushed and he was dead for ever and ever.

Winter hauled him back inside, shook him like a child's doll while the doll drooled with terror, hardly sane at this moment as he saw Winter's bony face through a shimmering mist of near-faintness. 'What is going to happen aboard the ship?' the English-man hissed through his teeth. He shook him with cold intensity. 'What is going to happen aboard the *Challenger* that I don't know about?'

Riad was now choking for breath like a drowning man as his heart pounded so fast and heavily it felt it would burst out of his rib cage. He tried to speak, tried to tell Winter to stop shaking and he would speak . . . He gasped, started taking in such violent, wheezing gasps of air that Winter was alarmed that he would faint so he held him still. The Arab looked up at him with a pathetic look of a child. They were both human beings, caught up in a plot of unimaginable violence planned by a man a third of the way across the world who thought nothing mattered but the freeing of sacred Jerusalem from the grip of the intruder.

'They are . . . going to kill . . . all the hostages . . .'

'Whatever happens?'

'They are going to . . . kill . . .'

Riad collapsed, went limp in Winter's grip, sagging while the Englishman still held him up, more of a weight than Winter would have imagined, but a dead man is always heavy.

Ahmed Riad had not been well when he alighted from the plane at Los Angeles after his eleven-hour flight from London. The tension in the United States did nothing to improve his condition. The ordeal of hanging out of the window brought on the final, massive coronary which killed him – before he had a chance to say a word about the nuclear device which LeCat had smuggled aboard the tanker now waiting to enter the Bay.

Believing that Riad had only fainted, in a great hurry to make a phone call, Winter left the unfortunate Arab lying on the carpet while he lifted the receiver. The operator came on the line at once and Winter was mopping his forehead with a handkerchief when he spoke.

'Get me the Transamerica building, please. I want to speak personally to the Governor of California . . .'

17

It was 9.30am when Ahmed Riad died. Winter had been very brief on the phone. 'I'm not waiting here while you trace this call,' he told MacGowan's assistant. 'You have exactly forty-five seconds to get the Governor on the line and then I'm breaking the connection. I can tell him the complete structure of the terrorist team aboard that tanker outside the Bay . . .' Mac-Gowan's growling voice had come on the line within thirty seconds – Winter had timed it by his watch.

His call to MacGowan had been brief: Winter knew that if he was to carry any weight at all he had to get to the Governor as a free man, going to see him voluntarily. If they were able to arrest him first, they would never believe him.

Realising now that Riad was dead, Winter hung a 'Do Not Disturb' notice on the outside door handle before he left his bedroom. Riad's diplomatic passport – trade representative of some obscure Persian Gulf sheikhdom – was in his pocket as he hurried along Geary and found a cab just emptying itself of its passengers in Union Square. Arriving at the Transamerica building, the strange, pyramid-shaped edifice overlooking the Bay – if your floor was high enough – he went straight up to the Governor's floor. It was high enough for a view of the Bay, and plain-clothes detectives were waiting for him.

He had gambled on MacGowan's character, on the little he had heard about him, gambled on the independent-minded American wanting to see him. MacGowan came into the room while they were still searching him for weapons. They found nothing on him;

Winter had dropped the Skorpion pistol and holster from the Golden Gate bridge while Walgren had waited with the car. You don't, if you are staying at a good hotel in a city, arrive with guns. MacGowan, who had been watching Winter while they searched him, ushered the Englishman into his private office and shooed the police away. 'Hell, you searched him. I can take care of myself...'

The interview between MacGowan and Winter behind closed doors went on for one hour – a long time for both men who were quick-witted and incisive, who went to the guts of a problem immediately. Part of that time was taken up by MacGowan, once a trial lawyer, grilling the Englishman. At the end of the hour MacGowan was convinced Winter was telling the truth. Others – when he held a full meeting of his action committee – were less easy to convince. Peretti, backed by Col Cassidy, was particularly sceptical. 'We have to be sure there are no explosives aboard that vessel,' he insisted. 'Winter should be subjected to a lie-detector test...'

'Bloody waste of time,' MacGowan snapped. 'A scientist's toy for the enjoyment of idiots. Twenty years of criminal practice taught me to assess a man face to face. Anything that whirrs and flashes, Peretti, and you think it's God's answer to the human problem...'

They subjected Winter to the lie-detector and they were all there, firing questions at him. Karpis of the FBI, Police Commissioner Bolan, Garfield of Coast Guard, Col Cassidy... It was while he sat in the chair, with the electrodes on his arms, answering questions, that his almost hypnotic personality began to have an effect on the Americans. Sullivan, who had talked with him earlier at MacGowan's request, who had then agreed that Winter was telling the truth, watched the inquisition with growing fascination.

'Your name?'

'Winter...'

The machine registered 'lie'.

'You need something to check your box of tricks,' Winter observed.

'How many terrorists aboard the ship?'

'Thirteen – now I'm here!'

Truth.

'Did you intend to give yourself up when you arrived in San Francisco?'

'Certainly not...'

Truth.

'Did Ahmed Riad tell you before he died that all the hostages will be shot whatever happens?'

'Yes...'

Truth.

After fifteen minutes Cassidy asked the question which was worrying them all. 'Winter, you led the hi-jack of this ship and now LeCat is in control. Are there any explosives aboard that vessel?'

'No...'

Truth.

Which, although no one knew it, exposed the limitations of a lie-detector. It may be able to tell when a man is telling the truth or lies – but it cannot tell when a man gives a reply which is a lie although he believes it to be the truth. It was not apparent at that moment, but the holding of this test probably made it inevitable – in view of what happened later – that the *Challenger* would be permitted to enter the Bay, bringing with it twenty-nine doomed hostages, thirteen ex-OAS terrorists, and one nuclear device.

By three in the afternoon they had still found no even half-safe way of storming the oil tanker. They considered every possible approach but each time they were defeated by the conditions LeCat had imposed if the hostages were not to be shot – that no aircraft, surface or underwater vessel must come near the oil tanker. And, as MacGowan pointed out, they were running out of time. So far he had managed to keep LeCat at arm's length with a series of delaying messages. 'This can't go on much longer,' the Governor warned. 'From what Winter has told me LeCat is going to lose patience – he is going to start shooting hostages to prove he means business...'

MacGowan was secretly planning his intervention very carefully. They had to have enough time to realise there was no apparent way of tackling the terrorist ship – because what he was going to propose was so outrageous they would reject it out of hand – unless they had reached the stage where they would grasp at any straw. Even Winter's straw.

The Governor was now convinced that Winter was genuine. He had said as much privately to Cassidy. 'You mean he's undergone some kind of recantation – that he's sorry for what he's done?' the Marine colonel asked sceptically.

'No! He's out for blood. First, he's been double-crossed, and that kind of man you don't cross with impunity. Second, he's not a killer. The death of that couple in Alaska has hit him hard, I think, but he doesn't say much about it.'

And there were certain hard facts which reinforced Mac-Gowan's conviction. Winter had handed over Riad's diplomatic passport to the Governor, warning him there could be one hell of an international incident over the obscure death of an Arab diplomat. Winter's solution to this problem was simple: lose the passport. It was still locked away in MacGowan's drawer and he had not yet informed Washington of its existence.

More than that, an emergency autopsy had been rushed through on the body of Ahmed Riad. The bruises on the neck and the condition of the corpse had confirmed Winter's story of the incident at the Clift. Riad had died of a massive coronary. It was five in the afternoon when MacGowan decided to take the plunge.

'We're not getting anywhere,' he announced, 'and I can't hold LeCat off much longer. I think it's time we took a look at a plan for getting aboard that ship – Winter's plan.'

Waiting until the protests had subsided, MacGowan began talking forcefully, making no concessions to anyone, staring at them grimly from under his thick eyebrows as he pointed out that after hours of discussion they hadn't come up with even the ghost of a plan to tackle the situation. 'The one man who knows the real position aboard that ship is Winter, the one man who knows how the terrorists are liable to react is Winter, and . . .' he lifted his voice, 'the one man who might just get an assault team aboard the *Challenger* is Winter, whether you like it or not. In fact, I don't give a damn what you like – I want results . . .'

'Having talked to him,' Sullivan intervened, 'I think the Governor is right. Winter managed to seize that ship, to get it right under the coast of California. Now, because he was tricked, he's ready to put the same energy and brain power into reverse – into getting the ship back.' Looking round the table where twenty men sat in a state of indecision, he smiled bleakly. 'You know, gentlemen, there is no more dedicated man than the convert to the opposing side. Winter, as an anti-terrorist, could be very formidable indeed . . .'

Winter was brought into the meeting, escorted by the police lieutenant who had become his permanent shadow. There was no humility in his manner, Cassidy noted as the Englishman sat down on MacGowan's left. His face was as cold and distant as when he had been subjected to the lie-detector test. He looked critically round the table, as though assessing each man, wondering whether he was any good. He's a cool bastard, this one, Cassidy was thinking; maybe a good man to go into the jungle with. But, as yet, the Marine colonel wasn't sure. The mayor immediately expressed his disapproval of the whole idea.

'I propose he's sent out of here under armed guard,' Peretti snapped. Sitting on MacGowan's right, he faced Winter who studied him with interest. 'You are the guy who sicked this thing on to us,' Peretti went on. 'I don't agree with your even being in the same room with us . . .'

'You want the hostages – including one American girl – to die ?' Winter enquired. 'Because I'm sure now that LeCat will kill every hostage aboard that ship . . .'

'You knew that when you started this thing ?' Col Cassidy demanded, testing his reaction. 'Because if you did my vote is we put you in a cell and throw away the key . . .'

'Belt up,' Winter told him.

'You said what ?'

'Belt up – and listen. I know these terrorists – which is more than you do. When I was flying in over Marin County I saw a way to get men on to the ship – I was trying to look at it the other way round, to see how we might be stopped. You have to drop on to the tanker from the air . . .'

'Hopeless.' Cassidy sounded disappointed. 'We've thought of that – and rejected it. The chopper would have to land on the main deck. It would get shot to pieces from the island bridge – and so would anyone coming out of the machine . . .'

'We don't use a chopper,' Winter explained. 'A small team of heavily armed men waits on Golden Gate bridge. We give LeCat permission to enter the Bay – to pass under the bridge at night. As the tanker sails under Golden Gate the assault team drops on to her in the dark. If the fog lasts, the chance of success is that much greater.'

'The fog thinned this morning,' MacGowan interjected, 'but it could come back again tonight.'

'That's a crazy idea,' Commissioner Bolan objected, 'that tanker will be moving . . .'

'Very slowly, if we box clever,' Winter said. 'I understand the tide will be flowing out to sea strongly in the early hours. Can someone tell me what its flow-rate will be?'

'Seven-and-a-half knots until ten in the morning,' Garfield, the Coast Guard chief, said promptly.

'So, we radio Mackay to come in at eight knots – which means moving against the tide, his actual speed will be only half a knot.'

'That's a thought,' Cassidy said slowly. 'Go on, I'm listening . . .'

'The main problem is dropping three or four heavily armed men off the bridge span – off the highway level – down on to the ship as it passes under the bridge. We have to lower them ahead of the tanker coming in . . .'

'Some kind of mechanical cradle?' Sullivan suggested.

'No, a scramble net,' interjected Cassidy.

'Exactly,' Winter agreed. 'Or a cargo net – whatever we can grab hold of. Something men can cling on to during the long drop.' He looked round the table. 'How long a drop is it from the highway span?'

'Two hundred feet . . .' O'Hara, the Port Authority chief sounded dubious.

'It can be done,' Winter said emphatically. 'For lowering the net we need a mobile crane – with a foot counter . . .'

'A what?' someone asked.

'Foot counter,' Cassidy repeated. He had been whispering to an aide by his side who was making notes. 'The guy operating the crane has to know how far he's dropped them – so he holds them just above deck level as the tanker comes in . . .'

'And a weight indicator,' Winter added.

'So he knows when the men have dropped off,' Cassidy explained. 'Three men in the net weighing a hundred and sixty pounds apiece – makes four hundred and eighty pounds of manload. The indicator loses that amount, the crane operator knows they're down, he whips the net back up out of sight. That way, if they get aboard unseen in the fog, they have time to assemble on the fo'c'sle and reconnoitre the ground before they go in to the attack.'

MacGowan, who was unusually silent, sat with his chin in his hand, carefully saying nothing as the technical side of the plan was worked out. Earlier, Winter had privately outlined this plan to the Governor, who found it possible – just possible if the fog was thick enough. It was a wild, audacious plan, but so had been Winter's previous plan to hi-jack the *Challenger* – a plan which succeeded because it had been so totally unexpected. And it was unlikely that LeCat and the other terrorists would foresee men dropping down on top of them like spiders suspended from threads.

Its greatest virtue, as MacGowan saw it, was that it got round LeCat's insistence that no aircraft, no surface or underwater craft must approach the tanker, on pain of shooting the hostages. The tanker itself would sail up to the airdrop point. And there was no other possible plan – God knows they had chewed that over long enough.

MacGowan found it fascinating as the discussion of the plan continued – the way Winter was gradually dominating the meeting. Personality, he decided, of a rare order. A man who was so sure of himself, so compelling, that they were all, reluctantly, falling under his spell. MacGowan had once known another man like this in his early days as state prosecutor, a man he had known as guilty of the charge brought against him. MacGowan had lost this case, the defendant had gone free – because of his cold, clinical personality, the way he had swayed the jury.

'How will you know where to place that mobile crane?' the Governor asked ultimately. 'It has to be positioned exactly over the tanker's deck *before* she reaches the bridge?'

'Radar,' Winter said. 'We need mobile radar positioned on the bridge to track the *Challenger*'s approach. When Mackay sets a course he keeps it – and he won't start weaving about inside that channel ...'

MacGowan leaned forward, his hairy hands clenched on the table. 'As we work it out, we should start setting it up. We can't keep LeCat outside for ever.'

... Golden Gate channel will be clear within a few hours. Await next signal which may well authorise your entry into San Francisco Bay. Arrangements have been made to take off your wounded.

It was the fifth signal LeCat had received which was signed MacGowan, Governor of the State of California. This did something to soothe his irritation at the constant delay in permitting the tanker to proceed. And when daylight had come earlier on the morning of Wednesday January 22, when the sun had dissolved the fog in the channel, LeCat had reluctantly accepted the idea that there had been a collision.

About three miles from where the tanker stood off the coast, close to the distant Golden Gate bridge, two cargo ships were apparently locked together in mid-channel while another ship with a crane was close by. MacGowan had arranged for this tableau to be set up before dawn and O'Hara of the Port Authority had organised the 'collision'. Any doubts LeCat might have had about the genuineness of this scene were dispelled when he asked Kinnaird to tune him in to mainland news bulletins.

Peretti had issued a statement, reporting the 'collision', and this had been broadcast across the world as an adjunct to the reports of the hi-jack. For LeCat it was a satisfying day, receiving signals from the Governor of California, listening to bulletins from as far away as London, England, where always the main and lengthy news item was the terrorists' hi-jack. For the first time in his life, Jean Jules LeCat was world news.

'I think they are now taking me seriously,' he told Mackay, after showing him the fifth signal late in the day. 'If, however, we do not start moving soon, I will shoot two of your crew and throw them overboard. You understand?'

'I only understand that there has been a collision which you can see with your own eyes . . .' Mackay stared out of the smashed bridge window. It looked as though the fog wouldn't be coming back this evening, which was just as well if he had to take his ship through Golden Gate tonight.

It was dark in San Francisco at six o'clock, it was chilly inside MacGowan's office where the thermostat was fixed at the obligatory sixty-two degrees. And it had been decided that a three-man assault team would be dropped from Golden Gate bridge, a figure both Winter and Cassidy agreed on. 'Send down more men on to a fogbound deck and they'll end up shooting each other,' Cassidy warned.

They had been meticulous about the weapons the three men would carry. 'A gun with great stopping power,' Winter had insisted, 'the terrorists on board have to be picked off one by one as they are found. And a silent weapon, too. The DeLisle carbine would be ideal, but you don't have it over here . . .' Karpis of the FBI had found three DeLisles – by checking with the Alcohol and Tax Division which had registered four of these guns in Hollywood, of all places. A firm supplying the film and TV industry with weapons had the guns in stock. MacGowan had phoned a police chief in Los Angeles, a patrol car had sped to the firm on Hollywood Boulevard, and within one hour the carbines were aboard a plane for San Francisco.

Over at Fort Baker on the far side of Golden Gate bridge, a mobile crane was already on the move – in response to a call from Cassidy's aide. The Coast Guard people were bringing in radar, two scramble nets were already stored near the bridge, Commissioner Bolan had warned a number of patrol car drivers they would be needed that night, and a detachment of Marines were engaged in last-minute firing practice. At six-fifteen Cassidy looked round the table and asked the big question.

'Who goes on the one-way trip?'

There was silence for a moment and then Cassidy spoke again. 'I'm making the trip. I need two more people who know that ship – I don't.'

'You'll be taking me,' Sullivan said quietly. 'I've come all the way from Bordeaux to sit in on this meeting. But I'd like a little practice with the DeLisle gun when it arrives.'

'Ex-naval intelligence,' Cassidy said. 'You qualify. That leaves one more volunteer . . .'

Winter for once said nothing, feeling he would be excluded if he pushed himself forward. He lit a cigarette and stared at the Marine colonel with a blank expression. Cassidy smiled unpleasantly. 'You started this thing, so it's up to you to help finish it . . .'

'That I won't sanction,' Peretti protested violently. 'He could still be tricking us . . .'

'How, for God's sake?' MacGowan burst out. 'Or do you want him to have another session with your bloody lie-detector? This is a job for somebody who knows that ship well – for Christ's sake, Peretti, we're not going down the rope into the fog . . .'

'There isn't any fog,' the mayor pointed out. 'Do they go down it if it's a clear night – with the moon shining down on them like a spotlight?'

'We've already decided,' Cassidy snapped. 'If there's no fog we can't make it. But we have to send the signal bringing the tanker in soon – it will take it hours to get there, moving at only half a knot.' He looked back at Winter. 'As I was saying, it's up to you to help us finish this thing. Have you any objections?'

'Yes,' Winter said, 'we're wasting time. I want to get out to Golden Gate to take a closer look at that bridge . . .'

The fog came at 8pm.

It came in a great solid bank, sliding down the channel towards Golden Gate bridge like a siege train, sending out long fingers of grey vapour across the silent ocean surface. Rolling in from the Pacific, the fingers wrapped themselves round Mile Rocks lighthouse, enveloped it, then stretched themselves towards the bridge. Standing on the sidewalk of the six-lane highway span Winter saw it coming by the light of the moon. It reached the bridge, rolled underneath Winter, spread north along the Marin County shore, south towards the city. It was a very heavy fog indeed.

For the first time since the great bridge had been opened in 1937 no traffic flowed across it – it had been closed at both ends. A huge mobile crane was positioned close to where Winter stood near the centre of the span. He could see the radar operator a few feet away. A telephone link had been set up between the radar operator and the crane driver, and the crane, normally bright orange, had been converted to a neutral grey with quick-drying paint.

'Satisfied?' MacGowan asked from behind Winter.

'You've got the dummy traffic organised?'

'Waiting – at either end of the bridge.'

Because there had to be traffic moving across the highway span as the tanker approached Golden Gate bridge – a deserted bridge might strike LeCat as abnormal, and if he saw it above the fog there must be nothing to attract his attention to the span. Winter walked over to the crane and leaned over the sidewalk rail. Suspended from the crane a large scramble net hung over the invisible drop – invisible because there was nothing below but fog. This was the transport which would carry them one hundred and eighty feet down into the depths until they were suspended just above *Challenger*'s deck height.

'The way that tanker will be crawling in towards us,' Mac-Gowan said, 'she should pass under this point at about one in the morning.'

'You realise, don't you,' Winter warned, 'that when we land on the fo'c'sle we may have to hide for some time – to wait for the right moment to attack the bridge?'

'I just pray it won't be too long,' the Governor commented. 'The longer it is, the more time for something to go wrong.'

Wearing the same grey combat fatigues as Winter and Cassidy Sullivan came back from the Marin County end of the bridge at a brisk trot. Limbering up, stiff with sitting in on so many meetings, he had plenty of space for his exercise – the bridge is over a mile-and-a-half long from shore to shore. Leaning over the rail, he peered down where he was going. 'Like pea soup,' he remarked. 'Let's hope to God it stays that way.'

For over half an hour Winter moved restlessly about with

Cassidy, checking everything, asking questions, repeating the performance he had carried out when he had gone on board the *Pêcheur* in Victoria, Canada. The *Pêcheur*, waiting out in the Pacific, would soon be under observation from a submarine which had been despatched from San Diego. The seaplane moored in Richardson Bay was also under observation by a concealed detachment of Marines and a small artillery piece was trained on the aircraft. All escape hatches which LeCat and the others might use had now been closed.

'Something will go wrong, of course,' Winter remarked at one stage to Cassidy. 'There's always something you didn't foresee no matter how carefully you plan an operation ...'

'So, we change our minds fast – maybe while we're hanging in mid-air.'

And they had planned it carefully. Two cars without lights were parked close to the crane and inside were six Marines, marksmen with their rifles who had been hand-picked by Cassidy. Mac-Gowan had insisted on the precaution: if the fog cleared suddenly as the tanker came up to the bridge the men inside the scramble net – suspended in mid-air – would be sitting ducks for any armed terrorists on the main deck. If this happened the Marines would dive out of their cars, hang over the rail and pick off as many terrorists as they could.

At either end of the bridge a man waited with a cine-camera equipped with a telephoto lens. If the fog cleared even for a moment they would take as much film as they could of the tanker – they might just photograph something vital. Other men had gone up inside the elevators which ran up the towers and now they were perched five hundred feet up above the highway span, just below the airway beacons, men with powerful night-glasses and walkie-talkies through which they could communicate with O'Brien, the bridge superintendent. They had, Winter decided at the end of his inspection tour, done everything possible. Until one o'clock ...

'The whole thing could blow up in our faces unless *York* and *Chester* reach the Persian Gulf in time ... And I'm not happy about that British tanker *Challenger* at San Francisco. Our military analysts think there could be a connection – between the massing of Syrian and Egyptian troops and the outrageous demands of the terrorists aboard that tanker . . .'

Extract from Minister of Defence's comments to British Inner Cabinet, Wednesday January 22.

Nine hours away across the world from where Winter and Cassidy had just completed their inspection of the bridge, Sheikh Gamal Tafak was pacing about restlessly inside the room he was beginning to regard as his prison. Baggy-eyed, he had stayed up all night, listening to the news bulletins, waiting for the report which would tell him the Americans had allowed the tanker inside the Bay.

Instead, they had cancelled the permission – something about a collision, which Tafak did not for a moment believe. Nor had he received a message from Ahmed Riad confirming that Winter was flying back to Paris, from where someone else would instruct him to fly on to Beirut. Patience, he told himself, there will be good news soon . . .

The news of the hi-jack of the British tanker had captured the world headlines. It was the main item in all news bulletins from Washington to Tokyo. 'First major ship hi-jack . . .' And in Israel it had not gone unnoticed, where secretly the military chiefs suspected some link between this event and the disappearance from public view of Sheikh Gamal Tafak. It was a time of waiting – everywhere.

They were engulfed in damp, clammy fog, so dense they could hardly see one another as they clung to the large scramble net like men scaling a wall, their feet balanced on rope rungs, their hands gripping the net above them, their DeLisle carbines looped over their shoulders, their .45 Colt revolvers tucked inside shoulder holsters, their knives tucked inside their belts. Winter also had a smoke pistol attached to his belt. When they were lowered inside the fog the temperature dropped and the net began swaying. They could see nothing above them, below them, ahead – nothing but dense grey fog.

The net was in front of them, pressed against their chests, and behind them there was nothing but space and fog and the ocean far below. The crane driver dropped them at a rate of one foot per second, sixty feet per minute. He had to hold them in mid-air precisely twenty feet above the ocean, which should mean they would just clear the oncoming forepeak of the vessel they couldn't see, couldn't hear. It had been pointed out to the crane driver that if he miscalculated by only a few feet, held them, say, sixteen feet above the water, then the oncoming steel bow would hit them like an express train – not in speed but in impact. They would be battered, torn from the net and dropped into the water while the 50,000-ton ship cruised over them.

The drop went on. It would take three minutes precisely. Providing the crane driver dropped them accurately. Pinned against the net, his face running with moisture, Winter tried to see the illuminated second-hand on his watch. Two minutes to go.

They went on dropping through the grisly fog, clinging to the net with numbed fingers. They seemed to be dropping at an alarming rate, plunging towards the ocean as though the crane mechanism was out of control, dropping, dropping, dropping . . . And the sway of the net was bad, worse than Winter had anticipated. Above them, attached to the hook which held the net, was a lead weight, a weight which was supposed to minimise the sway factor. It was like being on a swing, swaying backwards and forwards slowly through nothing, with nothing under them.

Attached to the net, close to Winter's mouth, was a walkie-talkie linked direct with the crane driver now far above them in the clouds. If he saw something going wrong he might have time to shout a brief warning, which might reach the crane driver before it was too late. So many 'might's' he preferred not to think about them. At least they would be over the tanker when it passed below – the pinpoint accuracy of the radar set, Mackay's seamanship in keeping a steady course, and the one-hundred-foot width of the tanker practically guaranteed this. But when the hell was the descent going to stop? Winter peered at the watch on his wrist.

Ten seconds left and they were still going down like a lift. Had the footage counter – the instrument which told the driver how far he had lowered them gone wrong? They went on dropping.

LeCat had taken two precautions the men on Golden Gate bridge knew nothing about. He had placed one man – with a walkie-talkie – at the top of the foremast. A second armed guard stood at the forepeak of the tanker. Both men were peering into the fog as *Challenger* approached the bridge.

Inside the wheelhouse it was no warmer than at the top of the foremast – the window smashed in the typhoon was letting in the fog. LeCat stood near the window, holding a walkie-talkie, irritated by everything – by the regulation blast of the siren sounding its fog warning every two minutes, by the vessel's incredibly slow movement. Obeying MacGowan's signalled instruction – which he didn't understand – Mackay was taking his ship through the channel at eight knots, which meant they were moving 'over the ground' at half a knot. 'We can hardly be moving at all,' LeCat snapped. 'I still do not see why we have to move like a snail . . .'

'Fog.'

The reply did nothing to quieten LeCat's nerves. They were, he guessed, close to the point where the cargo ships had collided. He was even wondering whether the diabolical Americans had left the cargo ships in the channel – so the tanker would hit them, go down, and it could all be passed off as an accident, problem solved. LeCat need not have worried: at dusk the three 'collision' vessels had been withdrawn to the east side of the Bay.

Mackay turned his back on LeCat, went to stand by the helmsman. The steering was on manual, the engine beat was slow and regular, and for all they could see they might have been in mid-Pacific. Mackay went to the radar screen and stared down at the sweep as LeCat called up to the man at the foremast on his walkie-talkie.

'André, any sign of the bridge yet?'

'Nothing but fog.' The voice sounded sullen. 'Wait a minute – I can see something moving . . .'

High up to the left the fog was thinning, opening out a hole in the grey curtain. André pressed his glasses hard against his eyes. The fog swirled, the hole grew larger and his night-glasses picked it up, something moving – the blur of moving lights, car headlights. He adjusted the focus and saw the silhouette of a car.

'I can see the bridge!' André sounded excited. 'I can see the bridge! We are close ...'

'How close?' LeCat asked.

'Three hundred feet ...' It was Mackay who had answered as he came away from the radarscope. 'We shall pass under the bridge within a matter of minutes ...'

On the bridge thin traffic proceeded steadily in both directions, traffic composed of cars driven by police patrolmen in plain clothes. They were moving along an elongated ellipse, driving off the bridge at either end, turning round and coming back again. There was even a Greyhound bus appearing at intervals, a bus with a handful of passengers who were Marines out of uniform and with their rifles lying on the floor. They were proceeding along the four inner lanes, leaving the outer lanes clear for the cars parked close to the sidewalks without lights.

Mayor Peretti, muffled in a topcoat against the night chill, leaned over the rail, straining to catch a glimpse of the huge tanker somewhere below. The moonlight shone down on the rolling fog and he couldn't see anything – except the crane's cable dropping into the vapour.

A Marine threw open the door of his parked car and ran along the bridge to where MacGowan was standing close to the mobile crane. 'Guy on the Marin tower just came through on the radio. The fog broke and he thinks there's a lookout top of the foremast ...'

MacGowan climbed up to the crane driver's cab. 'Warn them,' he shouted. 'There's a lookout at the top of the foremast ...'

One hundred and seventy feet ... one hundred and seventy-five feet. The driver heard MacGowan without replying, his eyes fixed on the footage counter, the instrument which warned him how low the net had gone. One hundred and eighty feet. He stopped the descent, spoke into his walkie-talkie. 'Winter, you're twenty feet above the ocean. From now on I'll be listening for any instructions to drop you further. And Winter, I've just been informed they have a lookout top of the foremast . . .'

The driver switched his walkie-talkie to 'receive'. He had one more vital operation to perform. He sat in his cab, staring at the weight indicator gauge. When that lost about five hundred pounds, the approximate weight of the three men, he would whip the net back up through the fog. The assault team would have gone aboard. Or into the ocean.

'. . . a lookout top of the foremast.'

Which is what we didn't foresee Winter thought grimly. He was in the middle of the net with Cassidy on his right, Sullivan on his left, the three of them pressed together shoulder to shoulder, like men stretched on a multiple rack. The net was swaying gently, stopped in mid-air, enveloped in fog so like porridge that they couldn't see anything, let alone the ocean twenty feet or so below. They turned slowly below the invisible hook above them. The distant dirge of a foghorn was the only sound as they hung and twisted on the net. There was not a breath of wind, only the clammy feel of the all-pervading fog, the clammy sweat of fear.

'They have a lookout on the foremast,' Winter whispered to Cassidy. 'Which is too damned close to where we'll land for comfort . . .'

'Can't shoot him,' Cassidy said, 'that would alert them on the bridge before we could get anywhere near it . . .' Cassidy's voice sounded strained and unnatural in the fog. Winter was just about able to see him. How the hell was he ever going to see the ship's forepeak if it did pass below them?

'Carpenter's store,' Winter said. 'We may have to wait in there a bit – it's on the fo'c'sle. Did you hear that, Sullivan?'

'Too true I did,' Sullivan replied without enthusiasm.

Winter peered up at his watch. Bloody thing should arrive any second now, all 50,000 tons of it, gliding across the water like a moving wall of steel . . . He tensed, he couldn't help it. The fog warning, one prolonged blast, sounded to be in his ear, going on and on and on. He gazed down. Porridge, nothing but porridge. Any second now and they would feel the ship – as it slammed against them. It was close enough, dear God – the ship's fog warning blast was still deafening him. Where the hell was the bloody tanker –

'Jump! Now!'

The fog was not as dense as it had seemed. Less than six feet below a grey, blurred platform had started to glide past under them. Like a huge revolving platform. Winter thought he saw a man. Then he was gone. And Winter was gone. Dropping. With the others.

Two hundred feet above, the weight indicator needle flashed back over the gauge. Four hundred and ninety pounds. Gone! The driver pressed a lever. Full speed. The scramble net whipped upwards, out of sight. 'They've gone!' he shouted to MacGowan.

Winter hit the deck like a paratrooper, rolling, taking the impact on his shoulders as he slammed against the port rail. He came to his feet with a knife in his hand. A blurred figure came out of the fog, wearing a parka. Terrorist . . . The figure stopped, his head bent over backwards as Cassidy, behind him, clamped a hand over his mouth. Winter rammed in the knife, high up in the struggling man's chest. Still holding the knife handle, he felt the terrorist's last convulsive spasm, then the man slumped in Cassidy's arms. Sullivan helped the American carry the body to the rail where they heaved it over the side. They heard no splash, only the steady beat of the ship's engines as *Challenger* glided in towards the Bay under Golden Gate bridge. Winter left the Skorpion which had fallen from the Frenchman's hand close to the rail – it would help convey the impression the man had fallen overboard.

'Follow me,' he whispered, 'and keep close. The fog's thinner already . . .'

'Too thin to risk moving past that foremast yet,' Cassidy agreed, 'and that lookout may have walkie-talkie communication with the bridge . . .'

Winter found the hatch, began unfastening it while Cassidy looked aft, watching anxiously for the foremast. The fog was thinning – as it so often did east of Golden Gate. He swore under his breath as he saw the lower part of the foremast coming into view, but the top was still blotted out. What the hell was Winter playing at?

Winter was unfastening the hatch carefully, making sure he

made no noise. It was well-oiled, thank God, but this was a British tanker, not one of your Liberian efforts. He opened the hatch and let the others go down the ladder first, then he followed them, pausing when the hatch was almost closed, peering out through the inch-gap. The fog was still too thick to see the breakwater, let alone the bridge, but it was drifting away from the top of the foremast. Winter, peering through the narrow gap, saw the lookout clearly, staring south with night-glasses pressed to his eyes. Winter closed the hatch cover very slowly.

On the bridge of the *Challenger* Mackay was having a violent argument with LeCat as the ship moved towards Alcatraz Island which was already clear on the radarscope.

'LeCat, I will not take this ship near San Francisco. We're bound for Oleum – that's near Richmond on the east side of the Bay . . .'

'Then we will shoot Bennett in front of you on this bridge.' Second Officer Brian Walsh gulped as LeCat gave an order in French for one of the guards to fetch Bennett. Then LeCat told the guard to wait as the captain protested. 'You cannot murder a man just like that. It's inhuman . . .'

'You will be murdering Bennett – you have it in your power to save him. Come into the chart-room with me . . .' LeCat led the way and inside the chart-room he pointed to a chart on the table. 'You will take the ship to this position – where the cross is . . .' He was indicating the mark Winter had made on the chart before he left the ship.

'I must know what is going to happen before I agree,' Mackay said grimly.

'I want to be close in so I can use the ship-to-shore to conduct negotiations with the authorities. When they have agreed to my demands we shall go ashore to this pier. There we shall board a bus they will have supplied and drive to the airport where a plane will be waiting to fly us to Damascus.' I have, LeCat thought, as he watched Mackay's face, made it sound convincing. 'Now you know what will happen,' LeCat continued, 'get on with it. I have no desire to shoot anyone – it would complicate matters.'

'To this point ?' Mackay put his finger on the cross LeCat had indicated on the chart. 'That is barely half a mile from the San Francisco waterfront.'

'That is correct. Now, will you do what I say or do I have Bennett brought to the bridge? Time is not on my side so I have no patience left . . .'

Without a word Mackay went back on to the bridge and gave instructions to the helmsman personally. Then he went to the front of the bridge and stood there with his hands behind his back, looking down the full length of the main deck where the fog cleared until he could see the distant fo'c'sle. He went on staring in the same direction, never giving a thought to the fact that under the fo'c'sle lay the carpenter's store.

18

At 3am the *Challenger* – which had increased speed inside the Bay – was anchored half a mile from Pier 31 on the San Francisco waterfront. Ship-to-shore radio-telephone equipment had been set up in MacGowan's office in response to a signal from LeCat that he wished to establish direct contact with the Governor of California. Foreseeing long hours ahead of the action committee, MacGowan had brought in beds which now occupied adjoining rooms. It appeared that the three-man assault team had gone to ground – as Winter had warned might happen.

Watchers along the waterfront and high up on the Bay bridge linking San Francisco with Oakland across the Bay had scanned the stationary vessel through powerful night-glasses. There were no lights aboard the vessel, no sign of movement anywhere. 'It must be the thinning of the fog which stopped them,' MacGowan told General Matthew Lepke of the Presidio. 'They dare not try and storm the bridge until the fog provides cover – there's six hundred feet of exposed deck between the fo'c'sle and the bridge at the stern. All the hostages would be murdered before they got

213

there – and they would probably be shot down before they ever reached the bridge structure . . .'

Gen. Lepke, fifty-five years old and rumoured to be moving into the Pentagon over the heads of fifteen other generals, was a spare, wiry man with a bird-like face and restless eyes. 'Cassidy will know what he's doing,' he observed. 'Trouble is he may have to wait till tonight – another sixteen hours – before there's chance of more fog. You'll just have to spin out the negotiations with this terrorist chief, LeCat . . .'

'Except that we're pretty certain that at some stage he's going to shoot the hostages anyway,' MacGowan commented.

The first message came through on the ship-to-shore minutes later. The Frenchman sounded confident and decisive as his voice came through the speaker. He repeated his warning.

'All the twenty-nine hostages – including the American girl – will be shot instantly if the *Challenger* is approached by any aircraft, surface vessel or underwater craft . . .'

'What about the casualties?' MacGowan demanded. 'Your earlier signal said you had nine injured people aboard – including Miss Cordell . . .'

'There have been no casualties yet,' the Frenchman shouted. 'That was a mistake. Now, no more interruptions. I will only say it once . . .'

LeCat went on to say that his ultimate demand would be made in due course; in the meantime a Boeing 747 must be made ready to stand by at San Francisco International Airport with full fuel tanks; a Greyhound bus must be requisitioned, its windows painted over black, and then driven to Pier 31; finally, the sum of two hundred million dollars must be assembled at the Bank of America within five hours. 'You will be informed of where to take the money later,' LeCat ended.

MacGowan tried to protest, then realised LeCat had switched off the ship-to-shore. He had tried to intervene while LeCat was speaking, only to be talked down by the Frenchman. 'When I want you to speak I will tell you. Now, you will listen! If you interrupt again First Officer Bennett will be shot . . .'

A traumatic moment had followed. There was the sound of a

single shot being fired. MacGowan glanced at Lepke sitting alongside him. The general's mouth had tightened. LeCat came back on the ship-to-shore. 'That bullet went out of the window. The next one goes into Bennett . . .'

'He's a bastard,' MacGowan said when he had switched off the speaker. 'Is it possible that Winter got it wrong? Is he really going to negotiate? He made it sound damned convincing – the demand for a Jumbo, for the bus . . .'

'And what, I wonder,' Lepke said grimly, 'is the ultimate demand he's holding back on?'

MacGowan began using the phone at once, making arrangements about the bus, the Boeing 747, and enquiries about the money. It was important to appear to be cooperating at this stage – to keep LeCat in a state of suspension as long as he could, to buy time until the assault team aboard the ship could make a move. And still he was unsure about the genuineness of LeCat's demands, about whether Winter had been wrong.

Winter raised the hatch cover slowly, then held it open a few inches and peered along the main deck. The ship had stopped, his watch showed the time as 3am, a transparent trail of fog drifted across the fo'c'sle, but the main deck was clear. His night vision was good – he had switched off the light in the carpenter's store a few minutes earlier to get his eyes used to the dark. And the foremast was highly visible.

Something moved on the circular platform at the top of the foremast; a man was walking round it slowly, his back turned to Winter for a moment. The Englishman thought he recognised the man's movements, that it was probably André Dupont. He pressed the pair of miniature field-glasses he had brought with him to his eyes, adjusting the focus with one hand. The lookout was holding a box-like object in his right hand, probably a walkie-talkie. Cassidy had been right; there was communication between Dupont and the distant bridge.

He closed the hatch while the lookout was staring in the opposite direction, felt his way down the ladder in the dark, switched on the light. Sitting on the floor with their backs against a bulkhead, Sullivan and Cassidy looked up at him anxiously, a question in their eyes. 'No good,' Winter said. 'The deck is still practically free from fog – and the lookout is still on the foremast. He's carrying a walkie-talkie, I'm sure. He'd be reporting our presence before we even got off the fo'c'sle. Every hostage would be dead before we were half-way to the bridge . . .'

'Where are we?' Sullivan asked. 'Where have they stopped?'

'I can't be sure – there's a heavy belt of fog obscuring the shore, which means the people on the mainland won't be able to see the tanker. My guess is LeCat has stopped where I told him to – half a mile off Pier 31.'

'Jesus!' Cassidy stretched a leg which was stiffening up. 'Looks as though we could be here for hours.' He looked round their cramped quarters. 'You say the escape apparatus was in here?'

'Was . . .' The inflatable Zodiac was no longer in the store. The outboard motor had gone. The cases containing the wet-suits were no longer there. Everything pointed to LeCat opening up the planned escape route. It also destroyed Winter's first plan – to wait inside the carpenter's store until one or two of the terrorists arrived to collect the equipment. They could have eliminated the men quietly below deck, taken their outer clothes and then marched openly along the main deck in the dark. Now they would have to wait. It was an unnerving prospect and already tension was building up inside the carpenter's store.

On the bridge of the *Challenger* LeCat had let Mackay hear him talking to MacGowan over the ship-to-shore. Now he was in control, it seemed sensible to the Frenchman to keep the British crew quiet, especially its captain. As he ended his dictatorial monologue with the Governor and switched off, he thought he saw relief in Mackay's face at the reference to providing a bus, a plane. He checked his watch, noting when he must call up MacGowan again: the timing was important.

Earlier, as the tanker was passing Alcatraz Island, Dupont had reported to LeCat that the lookout on the forepeak was missing. LeCat had hurried to the fo'c'sle as the fog was thinning out. He had found the Skorpion pistol lying near the rail, and near that he had found an empty wine bottle. Cursing the lookout for drinking on duty, he had concluded the feeble-minded idiot must have toppled overboard. He had forgotten him as he went to his cabin to collect the miniature transmitter with an extendable aerial. From now on this instrument would accompany him everywhere he went.

Attached to the nuclear device now planted deep inside the empty oil tank was a timer mechanism – also a miniature receiver of the type used by aircraft model-makers. The receiver, which would set the timer mechanism going, could only be activated when a radio signal reached it. The radio signal would come from the miniature transmitter LeCat was now carrying with him. One turn of a switch and nothing on God's earth could stop the nuclear device detonating at the pre-set timing.

There was tension also in Paris, over five thousand miles away, where it was eleven in the morning, where an emergency meeting of the Cabinet had been called at the Elysée Palace. Earlier, Karpis of the FBI, after obtaining agreement from Washington, had phoned through direct to Paris, asking for information on a certain Jean Jules LeCat. The request – because of the world news bulletins – travelled like an electric shock through the upper echelons of the French government.

At first ministers considered telling Karpis that there must be some mistake, that LeCat was still in the Santé prison, that the San Francisco terrorist was clearly an impostor. French logic, however, prevailed – this was far too big an issue to risk any kind of deception. They argued about it for some time – the record shows that the meeting went on for over two hours – and then a realistic decision was taken.

The Sûreté Nationale transmitted to Inspector Karpis a detailed technical report on LeCat's known criminal activities – the political side was omitted. Reading this report in San Francisco, Karpis found it illuminating and not a little frightening. The man they faced was no common thug; he was a man of enormous experience in the more violent aspects of human activity, obviously had some skill as an organiser, and had at one time lived in the United States. The FBI man skipped some of the technical data, so he saw no particular significance at that moment in the reference at the end. 'Also expert in the remote control of explosives, that is, detonation by radio signals . . .'

The next communication from LeCat over the ship-to-shore came at 4am. Again, MacGowan was warned not to interrupt. 'You will warn the American ambassador to the United Nations that he should stand by to receive a message from you later. There will be a time limit for you to decide whether or not you will agree to my demand. If you do not agree, all the hostages will be shot at the expiry of the deadline . . .'

The entire action committee was assembled inside the Governor's office as LeCat began talking. They watched MacGowan as he sat grim-faced in front of the speaker, knowing that he just had to sit there and take it while the French terrorist lectured him, told him what he had to do, that he must not interrupt. MacGowan interrupted.

'If you shoot them now you won't have any cannon fodder left for the deadline,' he said brutally. 'I've listened to you – now you damn well listen to me. I'm providing a bus . . .'

Peretti winced, certain that this was not the way to handle it, that there was going to be a disaster, that MacGowan had the wrong approach altogether. LeCat's voice burst in, filled with venom.

'You will stop talking and listen to my demand . . .'

'As I was saying,' MacGowan interrupted, 'transport for you to escape is being provided. Whether we will ever let you use it is another matter – it depends entirely on what you propose, whether we agree. Now, get on with what you were saying . . .'

'I will shoot two of the hostages,' LeCat screamed.

'We will board the ship immediately. And I will not speak with you again unless you give me some proof that all the hostages are at this moment alive and well – alive *and* well. Put Captain Mackay on the air if you want me to speak to you again . . .'

MacGowan's voice was a growl, Peretti was pale-faced with apprehension, the other men inside the room were leaning forward in their chairs, their expressions tense. Gen. Lepke had his head on one side like a bird, listening, watching MacGowan. They were waiting for the sound of shots to come over the speaker.

There was a pause, some static crackle, confused noises at the other end on the bridge of the *Challenger* half a mile from Pier 31. MacGowan had his head down, staring fixedly at the speaker from under his thick eyebrows as though he could see his opponent, as though he were facing a hostile witness in the box. The seconds ticked by and the tension inside the room became almost unbearable. They were all still waiting for the sound of shots, their bodies tensed as though they might be the targets.

'Captain Mackay speaking . . .'

Firm, steady, unemotional, this was Mackay's first contact with the outside world since the terrorists had seized his ship four days earlier. It was, MacGowan thought, remarkable. 'Are all your crew still alive and well, Captain?' he asked. 'I want to know the position aboard that ship . . .'

'We are all alive, we are all well, at the moment. And that includes our American passenger, Miss Betty Cordell.'

'We will do everything we can to see you are released safely,' MacGowan said slowly and deliberately. 'We shall continue negotiating for that end,' he went on, knowing that LeCat was listening. 'But no one must be harmed or I shall immediately stop all negotiation . . .'

There was a flurry at the other end, a grunt of pain which every man inside the room felt, then LeCat repeated his instruction once more that no aircraft, no surface or underwater vessel must approach them and abruptly went off the air. Someone in the room let out a deep sigh and then everyone started stirring restlessly, getting up and walking about to ease the tension out of their muscles.

'I don't think you handled that too well,' Peretti said.

'Because unlike me, you never were a trial lawyer. That man out on the *Challenger*'s bridge is an egomaniac – I'm beginning to get to know him and I can hear it in his voice. For the first time in his life he has a huge audience – everything he says or does is reported across the face of the earth. He knows it, he likes it. His only trump card is he holds the lives of those hostages in his hands . . .' MacGowan leaned across his desk. 'He's not throwing that away – yet. And the main demand is yet to come – he'll not

219

shoot anyone until he's made that demand. My bet is we still have a few hours left . . .'

'Your bet is on the lives of twenty-nine people,' Peretti snapped. 'I'm not that much of a gambler.'

Gen. Lepke had been staring across the room with a faraway look, as though something had just struck him. 'Has he always made that reference to no underwater vessel approaching the tanker?' he asked. 'I'd like to see the transcripts of all the exchanges you've had with him so far – and the radio signals, too.'

'You've thought of something?'

'Yes, something curious – possibly even frightening . . .'

Gen. Lepke moved very quickly when he left the room. He knew he had little over an hour to act because soon after seven it would be sunrise. Alone in another office, he put through a call to the Marine base. The dolphins, which had been brought from San Diego for training in the Bay, were sent out within a few minutes of his making the call.

At 6.25am Mac the dolphin slipped away from a Marine launch anchored offshore and began swimming strongly into the Bay. Jo, the second dolphin, followed him almost immediately. They swam at a depth of ten feet under the surface, heading for the only ship within half a mile, the tanker *Challenger*, with Mac in the lead. He came to the surface for air at regular intervals, a graceful creature who had a great affection for his trainer, Marine Sergeant Grumann. It was dark, steamy and fogbound above the surface at that hour, and he went under again with a sense of relief, at home in his natural element as he came closer and closer to the motionless ship.

Attached to his nose was a sucker-like disc, rather like a compass set in a rubber base. He had got used to having this strange contraption fixed to him; for days recently Sergeant Grumann had taken him out into the Bay, had then released him and 'pointed' him in a certain direction. He knew exactly what he had to do and he enjoyed the work; even more he enjoyed returning to the launch when Grumann would reward him with a fish. He swam on, a menacing shape moving through the water with a power and sureness no Olympic swimmer could have emulated.

The hull of the tanker loomed ahead, an oscillating shape seen from under water.

Slowing down, he cruised towards the hull. He was hardly moving at all when he reached his objective and pressed his snout forward gently. The magnetic field inside the Geiger counter did the rest, hauling itself close against the steel hull. Plop! The sucker was attached to the hull. The dolphin paused, feeling the tug of the tide against his huge body. He paused for only a few seconds, then he bobbed his nose hard against the hull. The magnetic field was neutralised for thirty seconds.

Released from the hull, Mac turned in a great sweep, his tail swishing against the immovable steel. Then he was swimming hard again, leaving the tanker behind, moving like a projectile through the dark water, heading back for Grumann's launch moored close to the waterfront. Within a few minutes he was swallowing fish while Grumann checked the Geiger counter as the other dolphin reached him. Grumann's hand was unsteady as he picked up the field telephone which linked him to the shore.

It was close to sunrise when Gen. Lepke took the call in the outer office. He listened, said, 'Are you absolutely certain?' Replacing the receiver, Lepke walked unhurriedly into the Governor's office where early breakfast was being served to the action committee from a kitchen adjoining the main conference room. The mixed aroma of bacon and eggs and strong coffee did not make Lepke feel hungry. He spoke very quietly to MacGowan so no one else could hear him, and then the two men went into the office Lepke had just left and shut the door behind them. The Governor asked almost the same question Lepke himself had asked over the phone. 'You're sure?'

'The Geiger counter was positive. They have a nuclear device aboard that tanker.'

Thursday January 23 was a nightmare for MacGowan as he fought to keep control of the situation in his own hands. There were plenty of other groping hands trying to influence him, to turn him in another direction. Two State Department officials had come in from Washington, one of them George Stark, a lean-faced, precise man who urged the Governor to 'negotiate flexibly . . .' There were international implications – if there was a catastrophe, a wave of anti-Arab feeling might sweep across America. And there were already rumours that the Golden Apes were considering a further cut in the oil flow to the West . . . The Atomic Energy Commission experts arrived secretly in the city at ten in the morning – to assess the extent of the threat to the city posed by the nuclear device aboard the tanker.

Operation Apocalypse.

Dr Reisel of the Atomic Energy Commission flew in from Los Angeles where AEC experts had been attending a meeting on the future of nuclear power stations. He headed the team which would play the grim projection game, Operation Apocalypse. A room had been set aside on the floor below MacGowan's office in the Transamerica building and the team went into immediate session.

The team comprised experts from the US Air Force, from the US Weather Bureau, Coast Guard service, Planning Division of the Pentagon. US Navy and, above all, radiation specialists. Aboard the Boeing 707 from Los Angeles – they had started discussions while in mid-air – Dr Reisel had emphasised one point over and over again.

'Gentlemen, the thing we must not do is to underestimate the size of the catastrophe. On the basis of the report we draw up the authorities will take certain precautions . . .' He paused. '. . . which may include mass-evacuation. If we underestimate the area which could be affected we might all have to leave this country for ever – people would never forgive us. The hell of it is we have to make certain assumptions – as to the likely size of the nuclear device aboard that British tanker. I have made an assumption myself – based on a device manufactured from the five kilograms of plutonium hi-jacked from Morris, Illinois, ten months ago . . .'

It was Karpis of the FBI who had earlier pinpointed a possible source of the material used to make the device. At 7.30am he had phoned Washington; the reply had come back within thirty minutes. During the past year there had been only one reported case of a sizeable amount of plutonium going missing; the brutal hi-jacking of a GEC security truck in Illinois ten months ago when a canister containing five kilograms had been stolen.

The Apocalypse team was rushed from the airport by special

bus along Highway 101 with an escort of police outriders and a patrol car, its siren screaming non-stop. Peretti informed the Press that a team of anti-terrorist experts had arrived in the city. Arriving at the Transamerica building, they went up to the room set aside for them and started at once on their macabre exercise.

'Algiers . . .'

LeCat came back on the ship-to-shore at 10am while Apocalypse was in session, his voice full of confidence as he spoke to MacGowan who sat in his shirt-sleeves despite the morning chill.

'What about Algiers?' MacGowan demanded.

'The Jumbo jet waiting at the airport will have to fly us to Algiers. Inform the pilot so he can prepare his flight plan . . .'

Ask the bastard something, MacGowan reminded himself, make it sound like I believe him, for God's sake. He was beginning to feel the strain of being up all night and his face was lined with fatigue. He cleared his throat. 'We need to know what is going to happen to the hostages . . .'

LeCat sounded surprised, impatient. 'They come with us to the bus on Pier 31, of course . . .'

'After that?'

'They will be released at the airport when we are safely aboard the plane. All except one man – he flies with us to Algiers.'

'Which man?'

'You will be told later.' LeCat sounded very impatient. 'Inform the airport at once . . .'

He went off the air before MacGowan could reply. The Governor looked round the room. In a desperate attempt to keep secret the fact that there was a nuclear device aboard the ship the action committee had been slimmed down to six men – MacGowan, Peretti, Karpis, Commissioner Bolan, Gen. Lepke and Stark, from the State Department. 'Don't let's underestimate our opponent,' the Governor warned. 'That LeCat is clever – if I didn't know about the nuclear device I might almost believe him, the way he keeps on checking details.'

'He made no mention of the so-called ultimate demand,' Stark pointed out, 'And you didn't ask him about it . . .'

'Deliberately. He's holding that back to keep us on a high wire. Why should I jog his bloody elbow?'

The Apocalypse report was ready in two hours – a task which normally would have taken as many days – but as the men in the room below conferred more than one pair of eyes strayed to the window overlooking the Bay – because that was where it would come from when the nuclear device was detonated. The proximity concentrated their minds wonderfully. MacGowan went down to see them alone at noon.

'Nothing as definite as I would like,' Reisel warned, 'but I assumed a crash analysis is better than a detailed report after . . .'

'The thing has blown you to bits,' MacGowan completed for him. He knew it was bad the moment he entered the room; one look at the grave faces waiting for him told the Governor the worst. Or so he thought.

Reisel pointed to a map opened out on the table. 'That tells you better than I can – the circle . . .'

'Oh, my God . . .' MacGowan recovered quickly. 'You mean it's going to take out nearly every city in the Bay area – Oakland, Richmond, Vallejo, Berkeley – even San Mateo?'

'I'm afraid so . . .'

'This circle – it's your radiation limit?'

'God, no!' Reisel sounded shocked. 'That's just the area of total annihilation from blast . . .'

MacGowan sat down in the chair vacated by Reisel and looked round at the fatalistic expressions of the men gathered at the table. He didn't like the atmosphere. 'And San Francisco?' he asked quietly.

'Forget it – that's gone.' The man who replied was a gnome-like figure who sat opposite MacGowan, placidly puffing a pipe. MacGowan didn't like the look of him either: too detached and sure of himself.

'That's Francis Hooker,' Reisel whispered. 'He's putting in a minority report. Of one,' he added waspishly.

MacGowan stared at Hooker who was watching him through rimless glasses as though he found politicians inexpressibly comic. The Governor had heard of Hooker, a scientist with a unique

224

reputation, the only man who had warned Washington of the risk at the San Clemente nuclear power station just before the plant nearly ran wild.

'This minority report of yours, Hooker,' he said. 'You disagree with the majority assessment? You feel they overstated their case?'

'No. They've understated it – badly. I think the blast could easily destroy San José, which is many miles outside that circle...'

'And radiation?'

'Radiation depends on the wind, of course. I estimate that if an average wind for this time of the year comes along – and the device detonates – half California could be at risk.'

'So now we know...'

'Not yet ...' Hooker was holding the floor, building up a head of steam. 'The geography of central California is well adapted to maximise the catastrophe. You see, we have a long valley – the San Joaquin – with population centres scattered along it to Bakersfield. With the wind in the right direction the radiation would be funnelled straight down the valley, so we have to start thinking of Fresno and Bakersfield...'

'That's two hundred and fifty miles away...'

'Raise your sights. It might well reach Los Angeles in lethal quantities. On the other hand, if the wind comes off the Pacific we can assume Reno is in trouble,' Hooker went on. 'I'd assume Salt Lake City would be safe...'

'That's five hundred miles away...'

'It had better be,' Hooker replied. 'I'm only guessing at the size of the device, but I could tell you more if I knew who had made it. The degree of competence is a crucial factor.'

'I may be able to help you there,' MacGowan said slowly, 'even if it is a very long shot. Earlier this morning Karpis of the FBI phoned Paris for information on LeCat. He lit a fire under government circles over there, I gather. Half an hour ago he had a call from a François Messmer, a French counter-intelligence man. A couple of days ago, in some way, Messmer linked LeCat with a missing French nuclear physicist called Jean-Philippe Antoine...'

'I know Antoine's work,' Hooker said. 'I met him once at an AEC meeting in Vienna. I thought he was dead. He was an

225

innovator. If he designed the device we must be prepared for a very special kind of holocaust . . .'

At 1pm on Thursday January 23 MacGowan closed the Golden Gate bridge. At 1.30pm he closed the Bay bridge to Oakland. Half an hour later he shut down the BART – Bay Area Rapid Transport – subway. By two in the afternoon San Francisco, which stands on a peninsula, was isolated except for the roads going south through Palo Alto towards San José and along the coast.

The official reason for these unprecedented steps was that there were terrorists in the city connected with the men aboard the *Challenger*. To back up this explanation, all roads south had police road-blocks set up to check all traffic which might be transporting these fictitious men. For this measure, at least, there was unanimous approval from the Apocalypse men, including the maverick Hooker. 'When the device detonates,' Hooker said, 'both bridges will go, no doubt about it. And if it happened when they were carrying rush-hour traffic . . .'

They also agreed that the five other Bay bridges would be knocked out by the enormous shock-wave from the detonation. 'The blast will destroy all communications,' Hooker stated. 'Whatever is left of the Bay area after it happens will be isolated from the rest of the country . . .'

They had, these grim, spectacled men, MacGowan noted, begun talking about the catastrophe as a near-future inevitable event. This change had taken place after Karpis had referred to the French report on LeCat, a remark he made soon after yet another debate on whether the tanker should be stormed by a detachment of Marines.

'I can't back that,' Karpis said. 'This Paris report says LeCat is, I quote, expert in the remote control of explosives, that is, detonation by radio signals, unquote. My guess is that at this moment LeCat is on the bridge of that ship with some kind of radio mechanism that can flash a signal to the nuclear device. If I'm right, he only has to press a button and . . .'

So far, by restricting the knowledge to only a few people, MacGowan had managed to keep secret the terrifying news about the nuclear device. He knew that, sooner or later, this news must leak out. If it reached LeCat, whom they assumed was listening to radio bulletins, it might just cause him to detonate the device at once; it depended on the degree of his fanaticism, a completely unknown quantity. If it reached the city, God knew what would happen.

MacGowan, a very tough man physically and mentally, was slowly being worn down by the massive weight of his responsibility, although outwardly he showed no signs of this. There was constant debate about whether or not to try and storm the ship, and each time MacGowan vetoed any such suggestion. 'We already have a team aboard – even if they are still pinned down somewhere in the for'ard area. If fog comes tonight, they'll have their chance . . .'

'If San Francisco is still here tonight,' Peretti snapped.

There was constant debate about whether to start a mass-evacuation of the city. The Apocalypse men were again unanimous in their decision that people should start moving out at once. 'Do that,' MacGowan pointed out, 'and it will be screamer news in the radio bulletins, which LeCat must be checking on. He'll know then that we know – about what he has on board. He might press that button . . .'

More disturbing news had come in about LeCat's character. Winter had earlier told the action committee that the Frenchman had once lived in both Canada and the United States and a massive enquiry had been set in train. About the time MacGowan closed the Bay bridge a report came in from Quebec. A woman believed she had once rented a room to the terrorist; if it was the same man he had frequently expressed bitter anti-American views. Both decisions were postponed – about storming the vessel, about evacuating the city. At three in the afternoon LeCat came back on the ship-to-shore and made his ultimate demand.

Conditions inside the carpenter's store on the fo'c'sle of the *Challenger* were not good. The three men had now been confined below deck for fourteen hours, with only vitamin pills and a diminishing supply of water from one water-bottle to sustain them. They had foreseen that they might be there for several hours, but not for anything like this period. They already hated the sight of each other.

The fog had never completely left the Bay, the sun had never penetrated the heavy overcast which drifted above San Francisco for the whole of the day. But there had been no chance to leave the cell and approach the bridge. A fresh lookout had just climbed to the top of the foremast – there had been two changes since they came aboard. And each time Winter cautiously raised the hatch a few inches the view was always the same – an exposed, fog-free deck, a lookout with a walkie-talkie on the foremast.

'This is worse than a foxhole in Korea,' Cassidy remarked as Winter came back down the ladder, shaking his head. The Marine colonel was crouched on his haunches, exercising to ease the stiffness out of his limbs. 'Sooner or later we have to risk it – shoot the lookout on the foremast and head for the bridge...'

'Better wait for dark,' Sullivan advised wearily. 'That's only two hours away. Two more hours... Jesus Christ...'

They had used a bucket they found in a corner for performing natural functions. They had covered it with a piece of canvas, but a stale, urinal odour was seeping into the stuffy atmosphere. The only relief came during the few minutes when Winter had the hatch open. They agreed they must wait; the lookout could report their presence within seconds of their emerging from the hatch and all the hostages would be shot before they had covered half the distance to the bridge. They settled down to more waiting, until dark, until the fog came. If it did come.

'Unless the American ambassador to the United Nations makes a statement by six o'clock tomorrow morning that the American government will send no arms – not one single tank, gun or aircraft – to the State of Israel for the next six months, that is until July 23 this year, all the hostages aboard this ship will be executed...'

It was LeCat's ultimate demand. The time was exactly three o'clock. The Frenchman had spoken in a monotone, as though he were reading from a piece of paper. There was complete silence in MacGowan's office as the six men listened, knowing it was quite impossible to accept the ultimatum. Stark, the State Department official, scribbled a note and pushed it in front of the Governor, who brushed it aside without looking at it. As it happened, he asked the question Stark had written.

'What about the money – the two hundred million dollars?'

'We have dispensed with that demand. We are not interested in money. Is the Greyhound bus in position?'

'Waiting. On Pier 31 . . .'

'The Boeing 747?'

'At San Francisco International Airport . . .'

'With full fuel tanks?'

'LeCat, if one single hostage is shot we shall immediately board the tanker . . .'

A muffled 'Oh, God . . .' It was Peretti.

'If one single hostage is shot,' MacGowan repeated, 'I will not transmit your message . . .'

The sound of a shot came over the speaker. The men inside the room froze. MacGowan sat with fists clenched on the table. Gen. Lepke quietly picked up a phone which now had a direct line to the Presidio. Somewhere, a long way off, the sound of a foghorn came through the open office window. Karpis checked the exact time by his watch. The speaker crackled.

'Next time you threaten me,' LeCat shrieked, 'a man dies.'

The hysteria in his voice shook the men in the room. LeCat had played the same trick a second time. The impact had been just as shattering as on the previous occasion. MacGowan's voice was steady, aggressive, giving not an inch.

'Now I want to speak to Mackay again before I'll take any action at all – certainly before I think of transmitting the demand you just made . . .'

'The man who will be killed,' LeCat screamed, 'is Engine-Room Artificer Donald Foley who lives in Newcastle, England. Tell that to his parents, to his wife . . .'

MacGowan fought for self-control, his facial muscles tensed with cold fury, his wide mouth tight. He waited for a moment while the others watched him. He said – quite calmly – 'I'm waiting . . .'

'Mackay speaking . . .' The voice was crisp, firm. Had he slept for a few hours since they last communicated, MacGowan wondered. 'That shot went through the window. Miss Cordell is still alive and well . . .' The captain was talking fast, as though any second he expected to be dragged away from the ship-to-shore. 'All my crew are alive and well. We hope that . . .' They didn't get to hear what he hoped; they heard LeCat's voice say, 'No more . . .' The speaker went off the air.

The city had been in a turmoil since one o'clock when the first bridge was closed. Men who lived in Marin County knew they would not get home that night; it was too far to drive right round the Bay and they hadn't the gas. Then the Bay bridge was closed, then the BART system. Foreseeing what was coming, MacGowan installed a traffic controller, a man called Lipsky in one of his outer offices. Those who could, left early, driving to their homes, or the homes of friends, south of the city. By 2.30pm, as Lipsky relayed the traffic reports to MacGowan, it seemed as though the whole of San Francisco was on the move.

'I'd never have believed it,' he said to Lipsky.

'You wouldn't have believed they'd be coming in, too . . .'

'Coming in?'

'On Highway One and One-o-One. Steady build-up of traffic coming north – into the city. They must be using up the last of their gas . . .'

It went on growing through the afternoon. Soon it became clear that despite the exodus and the influx the majority of citizens were staying inside the city, were refusing to get caught up in the cauldron. Then a fresh movement began – towards the waterfront, to try and see the terrorist tanker.

Seeing what was happening, MacGowan reacted quickly with the mayor. A huge cordon of police was thrown round the waterfront, was extended across the top of Nob Hill, along the full length of California Street. Patrol cars formed barriers. The cable cars were stopped. Van Ness Avenue was closed. The bus station was open only for outgoing traffic, with orders that no bus must stop this side of Daly City.

The direction of the movement changed: people remembered the high-rise buildings. There was a concerted rush for any building higher than ten storeys which overlooked the waterfront. Men and women crammed inside elevators, headed for the top floors. The premium positions were the tallest buildings – with windows facing the Bay. MacGowan issued a fresh order which was phoned round the city by a corps of telephone operators, talking non-stop.

'Close the high-rises, put guards on the street doors . . . close off the high-rises . . .'

The ingenuity of human beings determined to get somewhere was endless. Those with money in their pockets decided to take a hotel room. 'Providing it faces the Bay . . . as high as you can go . . .' The great towers on Nob Hill sold out their accommodation within fifteen minutes. The desire to see the terror ship had increased when news of the latest demand became public. LeCat had radioed his ultimate demand to the UP wire service.

MacGowan became more and more grim-faced as the news poured in. He had hoped people would leave the city when he was compelled to close the bridges; now they were flooding into San Francisco. And he dare not make a broadcast, appealing for them to stay away – if LeCat picked up the broadcast when it was repeated in news bulletins he might guess the reason for it, he might press the button . . .

Eight thousand miles away from San Francisco the British super-tankers, *York* and *Chester*, were moving through the Strait of Hormuz, leaving behind the Gulf of Oman, steaming into the heart of the Persian Gulf, heading towards the Saudi Arabian coastline. The huge crates which had intrigued American photo-analysts were still on deck. There was one odd aspect about their apparently innocent passage. Against all regulations, they were proceeding at seventeen knots through the darkness without any navigation lights.

Within one hour of LeCat making his ultimate demand – that the United States should stop supplying arms to Israel, Sheikh Gamal Tafak heard the news in Baalbek where it was 1am. He immediately made a phone call, triggering off a series of messages summoning all Middle Eastern oil ministers to an emergency session of OAPEC (Organisation of Arab Petrol Exporting Countries). The climax was near.

At 5.10pm on Thursday January 23 dusk descended on San Francisco and then it was dark. At 5.10pm the cluster of lights near the top of the foremast on the *Challenger*'s main deck were switched on, illuminating the forepart of the ship. The information was relayed to MacGowan within a few minutes by observers with powerful night-glasses. He told Gen. Lepke.

'That means the assault team can't get from the fo'c'sle to the bridge along the main deck without being seen – unless we have very thick fog.'

The US Weather Bureau man gave them a qualified report. There might be fog; then again, the Bay area might remain clear all night. 'You don't bet on horses, do you?' MacGowan said savagely. 'I'm just glad Ike didn't have you on D-Day.'

MacGowan was in an evil mood. Stark, the State Department man who had taken up permanent residence over his shoulder, was in the other room on the line to Washington. He'd be back soon, with more urgent advice the Governor could do without. And MacGowan had just had his third session with Major Peter Russell, British military attaché in Washington, who had also taken up permanent residence in the Transamerica building. There was something odd about Russell's attitude.

Russell, who was acting as liaison with the British Ambassador in Washington because he happened to be on the West Coast when the *Challenger* entered the Bay, had probed MacGowan about his intentions. 'I suppose,' he said, 'your policy is to spin out the negotiations as long as possible in the hope that the situation will break your way?'

'We are doing everything we can to save the hostages' lives,' the Governor had replied.

'Deeply appreciate all you are doing.' Russell had paused, looking at Gen. Lepke. 'I imagine this will go on for days. No chance it will all blow up in our faces, say tonight?'

'It's impossible to forecast the outcome . . .'

Blow up in our faces? MacGowan had managed to retain a blank expression; Russell, of course, had no idea there was a nuclear device not one mile from where he was sitting. Mac-Gowan couldn't rid himself of the feeling that Russell, worried as he was about the lives of the twenty-eight Britishers on board, was even more anxious that the negotiations should drag on for a few more days. It was odd.

At seven o'clock in the evening MacGowan, whose ration of sleep during the past twenty-four hours had consisted of no more than a few catnaps, heard that his secret had leaked – it was spreading through the city that there was a nuclear device aboard the tanker lying half a mile from Pier 31.

It was a switchboard operator who passed the night hours listening in to calls who alerted MacGowan. Pretending she had someone on the line who could give vital information – 'He says he won't speak with anyone except the Governor . . .' – she found herself with MacGowan at the other end.

'It's not that I listen in to calls,' she explained, 'but I just caught . . .'

'Get on with it,' MacGowan snapped.

'I thought you ought to know there's a lot of unusual activity . . . more calls than I can remember at this hour . . .' She took a deep breath. 'They're all saying there's an atom bomb aboard that British ship out in the Bay . . .'

'All?'

'I listened in after I caught the first call . . .'

MacGowan thanked her, told her it was a ridiculous rumour, nothing more, then Police Commissioner Bolan came running in from another room. Reports were flooding in from all over the city, a mass exodus was under way; for the moment it was confined to certain districts, but it was spreading.

People began moving out of Telegraph Hill first, out of the packed rabbit warren below the hilltop where wealthy men paid a fortune for houses overlooking the Bay. It began to look as though the money had been badly spent – because Telegraph Hill now overlooked the British tanker anchored offshore. Here it was a quiet exodus. Taking any valuables they could grab, the inhabitants got into their cars and drove up Nob Hill to where the barricades had been erected along California Street. They were

233

allowed through – but no one was allowed to go back. One woman who had taken the wrong jewel case – the one with paste gems – had a hysterical scene with an Irish cop. 'Officer, I have to go back – I've left a fortune in my bedroom...'

'Lady, that tanker is half a mile from where we stand now – you see yourself wearing rubies – stretched out in the morgue?'

Some people with cooler heads exploited the situation. A gas truck, which had been parked in a garage before the barricades went up on California Street, prowled the lower slopes of Russian Hill. Three armed men sat in the cab as they watched for expensive cars parked by the kerb. They found a fresh victim standing by a Cadillac with an antique vase in his hands, loading up the car. The driver of the truck pulled up, lowered his window. 'Need any gas, buddy?'

'I'm down to one gallon. But you won't have a pipe...'

'We got the pipe that will stick it into your car,' the driver said coarsely. 'Top grade...'

'How much?'

'Fifty dollars a gallon. You heard about the atom bomb?'

'Why the hell do you think I'm leaving? I'll pay you twenty-five...'

The driver made a lot of noise loosening his brake and the man ran up to the cab, shouting hysterically. 'Fifty is OK, fifty is OK...'

If you have only a few hours left to live, what do you do with those hours? Arthur Snyder, insurance salesman, knew he'd never get out of the city: at this moment his car was stripped down in a repair shop a mile away. The nagging wife he'd come to hate over the years was upstairs in the bedroom, still screaming at him. 'Do something, you bum, do something . . .' He slammed the front door and made his way down the hill. It was convenient to have your mistress on the same street; it was a bloody life-saver now. Reaching the right door, he stuck his finger on the bell and kept it there until Linda, in pyjamas and robe – she had been going to bed early – opened the door on the chain. 'Who is it . . .'

'Me, Art. Let me in quick. Mildred's gone out to Letty's . . .'

He guessed she hadn't heard about the nuclear device – she'd have mentioned it by now, probably lost her fool head and phoned him. He went inside the dimly-lit hall and pressed the door shut behind him. 'Art . . . !' He practically raped her in the hallway while she gasped, first with alarm, then with pleasure as he shoved her hard against the wall. Snyder had thought it out while he hurried to her doorstep. She might go off the idea if she heard the news first. So, this was it. Fuck now, talk later . . .

Haight-Ashbury and the Western Addition were on the move. Haight-Ashbury is to San Francisco what the East End is to London, and here the panic was more brutal. But it was still the same instinct for self-survival which had infected Telegraph Hill; it simply took a different way out. A Greyhound bus, full of people, found itself blocked by a barrier of trucks – out of gas and dragged across the street.The driver got out of his seat,opened the door and stared at a man holding a Colt .45. 'Get out,' the man said. The driver protested. The man shot him in the stomach and jumped aside to let him fall to the sidewalk. He got back inside the bus and waved the Colt around.

'We need this bus to get clear. Get off this goddamn bus – all of you. Anyone stays on it gets a pill in the guts – like the driver . . .'

There was a scramble to leave the bus and the ordeal heightened as they reached the sidewalk. A huge crowd of evil-looking youths crowded round the exit, leaving only a narrow passage for the passengers to move through. As they left the bus hands grabbed for their bags, their wrist-watches. 'For Christ's sake . . .' one male passenger protested. An iron bar descended on his skull, his bag was grabbed, his body hauled out of sight. Someone spat on it.

The reports continued flooding into MacGowan's office as he presided over a meeting of the action committee, for once letting others do the talking while he turned the decision over in his mind. On the far side of the room Karpis was watching the TV set in case something came through they ought to know about. Once again the TV cameras played over the illuminated Boeing 747 waiting at San Francisco International. 'This is the escape plane . . .' They switched to the waterfront, showing the Greyhound bus with black-painted windows waiting on the deserted Pier 31. 'This is the escape bus waiting for the terrorists to board it . . .' Finally they showed the large police launch moored at the end of the pier in the darkness. To MacGowan it had the look of a funeral launch waiting to transport corpses.

He took his decision in a few minutes – because it was the only one to take. They had, in any case, reached the stage where San Francisco was in a state of siege. Many hours ago all shipping approaching the port from as far away as Australia had been diverted to other anchorages – to Canada, to Seattle, to Los Angeles. No planes at all were landing at San Francisco any more. Amtrak passenger and freight trains on the east side of the Bay had been stopped.

The problem was as simple as it was enormous. If word got through to LeCat that they knew about the nuclear device he might instantly press the button. Occasionally, the news media do not hear about a major development as soon as it happens, and MacGowan had already personally phoned local radio and TV stations asking them to clamp down on this item. But it would be broadcast soon – by someone – if they had the facilities. 'I've decided, gentlemen,' MacGowan said suddenly. 'It has to be done.'

'Could create a panic.' Peretti pointed out.

'We already have one. We have to buy every minute of time we can, hoping Cassidy's assault team can make it . . .' MacGowan gave the order. He blacked out the whole of central California, cutting all communications.

The Reuter news flash, dated January 23, came through just before the TV screens went blank.

It has just been reported that Russian airborne troops are boarding their transports all over Roumania . . .

'The negotiations between LeCat and the American authorities will break down . . . it will be reported that American Marines attempted to storm the ship . . . the hostages . . . will all be killed.'

Remarks made by Sheikh Gamal Tafak during meeting with Arab terrorist leaders, January 15.

'You will recall instantly the Marine boat coming towards this ship or all the hostages will be shot now! I tell you, MacGowan, I will shoot them all and throw the bodies down on to your men . . . You hear me? You hear me? You hear me?'

It was the voice of a man gone berserk, a raving, screaming voice coming out of the ship-to-shore speaker into the silent room. MacGowan felt chilled, stupefied. It had started like this the moment LeCat came back on the air. No preliminaries, no demands, just these ravings of a maniac . . .

At the first mention of a Marine boat, Gen. Lepke went into the next room, picked up the phone. There were Marine assault craft – full of Marines, too – hidden at strategic points behind Alcatraz Island and further back along the waterfront, well away from the tanker. But none of them could have been seen, none of them could have put out into the Bay. Lepke was appalled, intensely worried as he spoke to the Presidio, told them to check immediately while he waited.

He returned to the main office in less than two minutes to hear the sound of a shot coming over the speaker. LeCat was playing the same trick a third time, the sadistic bastard. MacGowan, shoulders hunched forward, sat staring at the speaker. He raised a hand to stop Lepke saying anything. A voice came over the speaker. Mackay's, very subdued, the voice of a man stunned with shock.

'They have just shot Foley . . .'

Lepke scribbled on a desk pad, pushed the note in front of MacGowan, who glanced at it, looked back at the speaker. *No Marine craft has left the shore. Positive. Impossible LeCat could have seen one.* Mackay was speaking again in the same disembodied voice.

'They are putting his body out of the bridge window . . . it just went down . . .' The voice changed, became something between a strangled roar and anguish. 'No! For God's sake, not again . . .', Sounds which might have been a scuffle, then LeCat's voice faintly . . . 'Stay where you are, Bennett – or we shoot Mackay . . .', Another shot, deafening, very close to the speaker, then another, strange, younger voice.

'They've shot Wrigley . . . the steward . . . the fuckers. For Christ's sake, MacGowan, storm the ship before it's too late . . .' The voice ended in a grunt, a groan, as though its owner had just been clubbed on the head. Then there was a terrible fusillade of shots, a whole magazine being emptied. Lepke scribbled another, shorter note. *Storm the ship!* MacGowan shook his head. He could count. Two men dead, but twenty-seven hostages still alive –unless that fusillade ... LeCat came back on the air.

'Those last shots went out of the window. Mackay!'

Mackay's voice came over the speaker again. 'They shot Foley and Wrigley ...' His voice was firmer. 'The other shots went out of the window. There are twenty-seven of us still alive. LeCat says he will not shoot any more ...'

'Not yet!' LeCat again. 'The Marine boat has turned away. If it does not come back the hostages are safe. I warned you, Mac-Gowan, I warned you again and again ...'

'No Marine boat has approached the *Challenger*,' MacGowan said in a steady monotone, keeping the fury out of his voice. It could be that LeCat's sanity was trembling in the balance. 'No boats at all are in the Bay. The Port Authority will not permit any craft to leave its berth ...'

'You are lying! You were testing me! Had I not shot those men your Marines would have stormed this ship! You have killed those men ...'

MacGowan sat quite still, his face blank as he listened to LeCat raving on. He didn't sound insane, he decided, just savage, a terrorist, a man from a world the public found hard to take in, so he had the advantage – the advantage of brutality. LeCat suddenly seemed to calm down. The unexpected switch to reason-ableness was in itself unnerving.

'Why have the lights gone out all round the Bay?'

'Massive power failure ...'

'Is the bus waiting for us on Pier 31?'

MacGowan clenched his fist, digging the nails into the palm. 'It has been there for many hours,' he said in the same monotone.

'And the plane? At the airport?'

'Like the bus ...'

'They are considering my demand in Washington?'

'The President is holding a special Cabinet meeting at this moment ...' Soothe him down, play up to his monstrous ego, keep his mind on something else – while twenty-seven hostages are still living. LeCat went off the air quietly, and even that was disturbing.

In the tension – made worse because none of it was seen, it was only heard, coming through the metallic, neutral speaker – no one noticed MacGowan's personal secretary, sworn to secrecy, slip inside the room and leave the met. report in a tray.

What everyone had hoped for, prayed for, was happening. The siege train was returning. It moved past Mile Rocks lighthouse – which sent the report – filled Golden Gate channel with dense fog, reached the bridge, surged under it to spread out into the vast Bay beyond, along the Marin shore to the north, then it advanced southwards and to the east, heading for Alcatraz – for the point where *Challenger* was at anchor half a mile from Pier 31. Judging by its progress, it would envelop the fo'c'sle first.

Winter, grimy with dirt, his jaw stubbled with beard, had the hatch open a few inches when he heard the first shot. With very little food in his aching stomach his hearing was exceptionally acute and he thought he heard a moment later a distant thud, like a body hitting the main deck, dropped from a height. He decided he had imagined it when he heard the second shot, then a fusillade, much louder than the previous muffled reports, so loud he instinctively ducked thinking they were firing at him. He waited, felt Cassidy's hand impatiently tugging at his thigh. He waited a little longer, then closed the hatch and went back down the ladder.

'Not yet . . .'

'What the hell is going on? Are they shooting hostages?' the American demanded. 'By God, we'd better make a move . . .'

'Not yet,' Winter repeated. 'The foremast lights are still on, the lookout is in his perch, there's no fog yet to cover us . . .'

'I agree with Cassidy,' Sullivan said. 'I don't like it . . .'

'You don't like it!' Winter exploded. 'You believe I like it? I think they just shot two hostages to show MacGowan they mean business. But I can count. That means twenty-seven people are still alive . . .'

'There was a fusillade,' Cassidy snapped.

'Which was a whole magazine being emptied out of the window, I'm sure. It was much louder than the first two shots. Look, there are only three of us. It doesn't matter what happens to any of us,

239

but we have to do the job first time or we're dead – and so are the hostages. We've been stuck in this stinking hole for over eighteen hours – we can stick it out a bit longer . . .'

The carpenter's store did stink by now. The stench of stale urine mingled with the stench of sour sweat. All three men were filthy, thirsty, bone-weary. Whatever awaited them, it would be a pleasure to get to hell out of this cesspit. Winter checked the hatch five minutes later, came back down the ladder, shaking his head, but Sullivan thought he saw a change of expression. 'Is something happening?'

'Give it a few more minutes . . .'

'Come back to the bridge immediately, André . . .'

Having recalled the foremast lookout, LeCat put the walkie-talkie down on to the table he had had brought on to the bridge. He was eating all his meals up here now, living in the wheelhouse. Since the *Challenger* entered the Bay the Frenchman had slept no more than MacGowan, and like the Governor his face was pouchy-eyed and strained, but his eyes were still alert.

They would be leaving the ship within an hour. LeCat looked at the miniature transmitter resting on the table beside the walkie-talkie. That would be his last job before they left, to turn the switch which would activate the timer mechanism. LeCat also had been waiting for heavy fog to obscure the ship; under its protecting cover they would leave in the Zodiac which was now waiting on the main deck with the outboard motor attached.

Most of his team, like LeCat himself, had now changed into wet-suits. Several of them stood around on the bridge, sinister figures in the gloom – only the binnacle light gave a faint glow, otherwise the bridge was in darkness. LeCat was confident his plan was working. Two hostages had been shot, which would deter MacGowan from launching any attack – he still had the remaining twenty-six hostages to think of. And it was twenty-six, not twenty-seven, but only LeCat knew that Monk, the man he had pushed over the side, was dead.

It would take fifteen minutes to reach the seaplane waiting in Richardson Bay. But first, the rest of the crew had to be taken to the day cabin. That was where it would be done. He looked round the bridge. Mackay was standing by the window, hands clasped behind his back as he watched the fog rolling in. Bennett, the man who had shouted into the speaker, warning MacGowan that Wrigley had been shot, was lying near the wheel, still unconscious. LeCat checked his watch as André Dupont, the lookout on the foremast, came on to the bridge.

Betty Cordell was ready. She had opened her shirt down the front, exposing her breasts. Get on with it, she told herself, don't think about it or you'll never do it. She walked to the cabin door, started rattling the handle. 'Come quickly! Please! Do come quickly! For God's sake open the door ...'

She was hysterical, terrified – so it sounded to the guard in the alleyway. He fumbled for the key, shouted back at her in French, words she didn't understand as she went on calling out, begging him to open the door. His first thought must have been that the cabin was on fire.

He pushed the door open, his pistol drooped in his hand. She was a woman, useful for cooking, for bed, so he had no fear of her at all. He came in and stopped, gaping at her open dress, then his mind churned. She threw the open pepper pot from her lunch tray full in his face and he took the powder in his eyes. He cried out, dropping his pistol, pressing both hands against his agonised, burning eyes, stumbling about. She grasped the wine bottle LeCat had left, the bottle she had never thought of opening, so it was a lethal weapon – she grasped it by the neck. Without even a hint of hesitation she smashed the bottle down with a terrible force on the back of the guard's head and the fury of her blow split his skull.

He collapsed on the cabin floor. There was wine like blood all over him, mingling with the blood of his smashed skull. She looked down at him coldly, watching only to make sure he didn't move. Then she dragged him further into the cabin like a sack of dirt, left him in the bathroom and ran back to close the cabin door. It was the fusillade of shots which had jerked her into action and she was in a hurry.

It took only a few seconds for her to button up the shirt, to slip on the coat, to grab the assembled rifle from under the bedclothes. She kicked the shattered bottle out of her way and opened the door again. The alleyway was empty, the key still in the outside of the door. Without knowing it, she had chosen the perfect time for her killing run – LeCat had called many of the guards to the bridge. She closed the door, locked it, pocketed the key and went slowly down the passage, listening, the Armalite rifle held in both hands at waist level. She was heading for the bridge, LeCat, she felt sure, would be on the bridge.

Winter stood clear of the hatch cover as the other two men came up behind him. The fog was thick now, pressing down on them like a smothering blanket. They went down off the forecastle cautiously, one man behind the other as Winter had suggested; Cassidy behind Winter, Sullivan behind the Marine colonel. Their DeLisle carbines were at the ready, Winter had the smoke pistol tucked inside his belt, they went down on to the main deck.

Winter avoided the catwalk, kept to the port side of the huge tanker where the deck was less cluttered with piping and valves, moving along close to the port rail. It was very silent in the misty darkness, the fog drifted in their faces, the only sound was the slap of water against the hull where the two dolphins, Mac and Jo, had earlier pressed their snouts up against the steel plates. Winter kept moving, creeping forward on his rubber-soled boots, alert for the slightest sound which might tell him something about the situation sixty feet above him at bridge level. Then something loomed up in the fog.

It was the port-side derrick, which told him he was close to the island bridge, still lost inside the swirling grey vapour. He waited for Cassidy to draw level with him, then looped the carbine over his shoulder and pulled the smoke pistol out of his belt. The fog was thinner, ebbing for a moment, and by now their faces and hands were chilled with the touch of the clammy moisture. The island bridge loomed above them as an insubstantial shadow.

They were within twenty feet of the five-deck bridge and these twenty feet were a death-trap. With the thinning fog any terrorist above, leaning out of the bridge window, could pick them off as they moved across the exposed space. And there would be more than one terrorist waiting up there. Possibly even LeCat himself. Then Cassidy plucked at his arm, pointed. A huddled corpse lay only a few feet away at the base of the bridge. Foley's.

Winter took his time, raised his left arm, using it as a rest to steady the smoke pistol, took careful aim, sighting the muzzle of the pistol at the centre of the bridge, away from the smashed window. The bridge was a blur, very high above him, and the angle of the shot was steep. He remembered looking up at the roof of Cosgrove Manor from the steps below, so many thousands of miles away, so many years away, so it seemed. He steadied his aim. He fired ...

The smoke shell spun upwards, out of sight, lost in a swirl of fog. He heard it strike the bridge. He took two steps forward. Black smoke billowed, spread a curtain of darkness masking the bridge windows. Cassidy had run into the open. He fired three times at the heads of two men which appeared over the edge of the port wing deck. One of them slumped forward, toppled, landed almost at the American's feet. He waited, carbine aimed upwards. The second man reappeared, as Cassidy knew he would, bloody idiot. Cassidy fired again and the man fell over backwards out of sight.

It was happening so quickly it was like a film being run at high speed. Blurred images. Sullivan flying up a ladder. The smoke obscuring three decks of the bridge. Cassidy going up a companionway, vanishing inside the smoke. Shots firing repeatedly, a steady drumfire of shooting, the ship coming horribly alive. Winter had long ago disappeared up another ladder. Entering an alleyway, Winter saw a guard who, seeing Winter, threw up his hands. Winter shot him twice through the chest. MacGowan's orders were explicit. 'No prisoners, no phoney trials with some gabby mouthpiece crying over them. Shoot the lot . . .' Winter ran down the alleyway, heading for a certain objective, the day cabin where so many seamen had been kept prisoner. He turned a corner, saw the entrance to the day cabin. A terrorist, Lomel he thought, had just kicked open the door and was standing back with his Skorpion aimed, ready to shoot the unarmed hostages inside. Winter shot him twice. When you are hit by a .45 bullet the sensation is like collision with a charging rhino. Lomel was hit by two .45's. He was carried over sideways, slammed against a bulkhead where he slid to the floor. Winter kept on running, trod over him, kept on running . . .

Betty Cordell moved very cautiously, like a hunter stalking a beast whose whereabouts are uncertain, straining her ears to catch the slightest sound as she moved up the companionway step by step. The ship seemed eerily silent, the alleyways oddly deserted, as though she were moving through an abandoned ship. She was going the long way round to get to the bridge, to approach it from the starboard wing deck.

The Armalite .22 survival rifle she had assembled was equipped with a ten-shot magazine. The ammunition was high-speed hollowpoint. The rifle was single-shot, with two trigger pressures. And she was carrying two spare ten-shot magazines in her coat pocket.

She reached the top of the companionway and another empty passage stretched ahead of her. Where had all the guards gone? She would walk into someone when she least expected it. She took a firmer grip on the rifle. Then she heard rifle shots, an irregular fusillade. She began running . . .

On the bridge LeCat grasped instantly what was happening when he saw black smoke – that an attack was coming. He shouted a warning. 'Shoot down through the smoke – to the base of the bridge . . .' He swore when nobody did anything. The guards at the window were choking, their eyes running, coughing and spitting black smoke, staggering like drunken marionettes. 'Fools!' LeCat screamed. 'Get to the window – shoot down . . .' The guards at the rear of the bridge rushed forward, leaned out, firing through the smoke at random, all of them, including LeCat, bunched together as a cannonade of shots and a reek of cordite filled the bridge and then LeCat remembered Mackay and swung round as the captain was moving towards him.

Betty Cordell came on to the bridge from the starboard wing. Her rifle was waist-high, held the way her father had taught her to hold it. 'In an emergency shoot from there – keep the barrel straight and shoot . . .' She came on to the bridge and saw half-a-dozen terrorists close together at the front. She saw LeCat. LeCat saw her.

The terrorist leader was stupefied. The woman. With a gun. His reflexes, faster than most men's, failed him for one fatal second. Betty Cordell held the rifle hard against her hip, her finger on the trigger. There was not a split-second's hesitation. She was firing, her trigger finger moving non-stop, bullet after bullet, killing live targets for the first time, a ten-shot magazine, moving the muzzle in a slight arc, right to left, firing – firing – firing . . . Three bullets struck LeCat. Four other terrorists died instantly. The barrel was angled slightly upwards. One man wasn't hit at all. Turning from the window, hauling up his pistol, he was thrown off-balance by a body falling against him. Betty Cordell rammed in a second magazine, began firing non-stop again. The uninjured terrorist, lifting his pistol, was struck by two bullets. She swivelled the rifle.

Mackay stared at her, astounded, frightened by her expression. No nerve, no fear, she stood as if not caring if she were killed, cold, ice-cold, her eyes narrowed against the smoke as LeCat staggered across the deck towards the table where the radio detonator lay. She fired twice at his back and he took two more bullets, then her rifle clicked, empty. LeCat fell over the table, reached out for the detonator.

LeCat, veteran soldier, veteran terrorist, now had five bullets inside him, but it is on record that men have moved carrying more bullets. His hand was clawing its way across the table like a crab walking because he could no longer use his shoulder hinge. There was smoke and confusion and screaming from a mortally wounded guard and the clatter of running feet. Winter came on to the bridge, saw what no one else had seen, saw the crab-like hand close over the radio-detonator. He guessed what it was, couldn't understand why it was there, raised his gun, fired twice. Two bullets struck the sprawled terrorist – .45's, not .22's – and his body jumped as though jerked by an electric charge. It could have been a reflex – his index finger pressed the switch down.

Winter grabbed hold of him by the back of his hair, lifted his head and stared down at LeCat. 'Why the detonator?' The

245

Frenchman's eyes were still open. Winter shook him roughly. 'Why the detonator? What have you done?' LeCat hardly seemed to recognise the Englishman whose face was stubbled and smeared and smoke-blackened. Winter shook him again. 'What the hell have you done?'

'Nuclear device ... ten minutes ... San Francisco goes.' LeCat's face twisted into what might have been a hideous grin and then the eyes rolled and the head flopped.

Ten minutes. The nuclear device was activated.

19

'The ship-to-shore?' Winter turned round and looked at Mackay. Under the bridge windows was a grisly sprawl of men and blood. One terrorist, André Dupont, was wheezing and panting, bent forward over his stomach. No one took any notice of him. Betty Cordell had gone limp and Sullivan was holding her up, taking the rifle away from her gently.

'Chart-room ...' Mackay led the way, turned on the ship-to-shore.

'MacGowan has a chopper standing by,' Winter said. 'Medics, Marines, the lot. Did you know about this nuclear device? Could he have been bluffing?'

The ship-to-shore crackled. A familiar voice, tired but still steady, rasped into the chart-room from the mainland. 'Mac-Gowan here ...'

'Winter speaking. We've taken the ship. LeCat is dead. Before he died he said something about a nuclear device ...'

'We know. We've known – lived with it – for hours ...'

'He activated it before he died – with a radio-detonator. We need a bomb squad ...'

'Bomb squad is aboard the chopper already on the way to you.' MacGowan paused. 'You're sure he activated it?'

'Certain. I saw him do it.' Winter paused as he heard the distant beat of a helicopter's rotors. 'He said we had ten minutes before it detonates. I don't believe him – he needed time to get well clear...'

'How much time?' MacGowan's voice was tense, abrupt.

'My guess – I warn you it can only be a guess – is maybe up to two hours. I told you we had a second escape plan in case the seaplane didn't work. Walgren would have driven LeCat to the coast near Stinson beach. He had to get there, radio the *Pêcheur*, wait for the chopper to pick him up. He wouldn't want to be on the mainland when the nuclear device detonated. I still say two hours...'

'You know where the device is?'

'No one does. The only chance is to try and get the tanker into the Pacific before she detonates...'

'Nothing in your way. We've been planning for this contingency.' MacGowan sounded calmer. 'There's a Captain Bronson aboard the chopper who can take over from Mackay. He'll get the ship out, if anyone can.' He paused. 'Assuming your guess on timing is correct...'

'I'm not issuing any guarantee,' Winter snapped. 'But they needed time to get away. On the other hand, LeCat was dying when he said ten minutes. What does a dying man say?'

'God be with you – with us all,' MacGowan said. 'I'm signing off – you'll be busy...'

Mackay had left the chart-room, was already on the phone to the engine-room. LeCat had kept the engine-room chief at his post, had ordered him to maintain boiler pressure in case, for some unforeseen reason, he had wanted the ship moved to another position in the Bay. Mackay replaced the phone as Winter came back on to the bridge. 'Brady will get her moving as soon as he can.'

'An American tanker master is aboard that chopper coming in,' Winter warned him. 'He's coming because MacGowan assumed you'd be exhausted...'

'MacGowan is not taking over this ship,' Mackay snapped. 'If this is her last voyage, I'm taking her out. Did you say something about a bomb squad?'

'They won't be able to do anything, I'm sure. LeCat was an

247

expert. He'll have boobytrapped the device.' Winter turned as he heard someone talking in French.

Cassidy was bent over the injured terrorist who was now sitting up and babbling. He looked at Winter. 'He's trying to tell us something, I guess – but I don't know the language . . .'

Winter crouched down beside Dupont, putting an arm round his shoulders and speaking quietly in French. 'Take it more slowly, Andre, and then we'll get you ashore into a comfortable hospital bed. What is it you are trying to say?'

He crouched close to André's face, telling him to repeat it, slowly, please, then he looked up at Mackay. 'The device is at the bottom of an empty oil tank, and LeCat did plant boobytraps – anti-lift mechanisms. I think the bomb squad will confirm they can't touch it.'

'Which means,' Cassidy said quietly, 'that we'll be steaming out on top of a floating volcano, but we have to get the ship clear of the city – if we can . . .'

The helicopter came aboard a couple of minutes later and Mackay led the bomb squad to the empty wing tanks. The dead terrorists were collected from different parts of the island bridge and put into the police launch which had arrived from Pier 31. At Winter's suggestion – there was no time to waste – the corpses on the bridge were heaved out of the window and dropped to the main deck. Dupont was carried aboard the helicopter on a stretcher, but he died on his way back to San Francisco.

The machine also flew away Betty Cordell who had gone into a state of shock, and the dead bodies of Foley and Wrigley. Kinnaird, the wireless operator, was the only terrorist who survived; hearing the shooting, he sensibly locked the door of the radio cabin and only came out when Winter ordered him to. He was taken off in the helicopter, guarded by a Marine. Within ten minutes of coming aboard, the leader of the bomb squad, a Captain Grisby, reported to Cassidy. 'It's as bad as can be. We daren't even breathe on it. The device is rectangular in shape, measures sixty centimetres long by thirty centimetres wide, and is attached to the hull at the bottom of the tank by magnetic clamps. It also has two separate anti-lift mechanisms linked to it which we can't neutralise. No way. So, while you get the ship moving, we'll plant our own explosives . . .'

'Your what?'

Grisby outlined the plan he had decided on before he came aboard. Some kind of immovable boobytrap had been foreseen by Grisby – after he read the report on LeCat's technical expertise which Karpis had obtained from Paris. If the device couldn't be moved the ship must be moved – as far out into the Pacific as they could make it. Every effort would then be made to ensure the device exploded underwater–so the tanker had to be sunk quickly. The only way was dangerous but MacGowan and Gen. Lepke had agreed it was worth trying – anything to try and minimise the radiation hazard to San Francisco and other communities. Grisby was going to lace the hull of the ship with jet-axe explosive charges of enormous power; he was going to try and blow the ship apart so the front section of the tanker – which contained the device – would sink first and fast.

'The charges will be set off by time mechanisms – timed to detonate after we've been lifted off. I brought in with us on the chopper enough explosive to blow up the Presidio. The trouble is,' Grisby explained with a humourless smile, 'the charges could just detonate the device – but since that's coming anyway, we figure we have nothing to lose . . .'

He left Cassidy to join his team who were already setting about their grisly task. Bronson, a tough-minded forty-year-old from San Diego, who had come aboard to take command of the ship, had changed his mind after talking to Mackay. 'He's haggard, tired, keyed up,' he informed MacGowan over the ship-to-shore, 'but he's still twice as capable as I am of taking out his own ship. And he'll get more out of the crew. I'm staying aboard – strictly as a passenger, courtesy Captain Mackay . . .'

The mainland was still blacked out when the *Challenger* began moving. In the late evening radio and TV stations all over the States were reporting on the massive blackout which extended from Yuba City in the north to Santa Barbara in the south, from San Francisco to the Nevada border. It was exceptional, the scale of the blackout, but by now the States was becoming used to power failures. This was simply a very big one, and the news of the nuclear device had not yet leaked.

The *Challenger* moved through the fog and the darkness, building up speed. And this too, as Grisby had pointed out, was a risk which was not calculable. It was unlikely, but not impossible, that the mounting vibrations of the engines might trigger off the device. Mackay's reply was that he would move through Golden Gate at maximum possible speed. Inside the steel tomb where the device lay, LeCat's clock mechanism was moving down towards zero.

They were heading through the night for Golden Gate bridge, which was still closed to traffic, and this was MacGowan's next nightmare as the ship began to move away from the city, the most scenic and beautiful city in America which Sheikh Gamal Tafak had chosen for devastation. As he waited in his office, lit by an emergency generator, MacGowan knew that it was highly possible the device would detonate as the tanker was passing under the great bridge. He was now waiting for radio reports from the American operator, Petersen, who had accompanied Bronson and replaced Kinnaird. The ship was within two minutes' sailing time of the bridge.

The siren sounded every two minutes, one prolonged blast which carried faintly through the fog. Before she had left, Mackay had spoken over the Tannoy, giving any member of the crew who wished to, permission to leave in the helicopter. No one had boarded the machine. Mackay's final comment before he switched off was characteristic. 'It's your funeral . . .' The fog thinned enough for them to see the huge span overhead as they came up to the bridge. 'And this,' Bronson thought to himself, 'would be just the moment for the device to detonate . . .' He stood two paces behind Mackay with his moist hands in his pockets.

Winter stood close to the bridge window between Sullivan and Bennett, whose head was bandaged; the first officer was still dazed from the blow he had received after he had rushed to the ship-to-shore when Wrigley was murdered. Winter was trying to locate the choppers. The *Challenger* sailed out of the Bay alone, but not alone in the air. A small fleet of American helicopters, ready to take off the crew, was escorting the ship, flying far too close to her in Mackay's opinion. If something happened now they would be liquidised. *Challenger* went under the bridge, headed down the channel.

Winter, always restless, always wanting to see for himself, started moving round the ship. It was a very strange atmosphere because the crew were unusually silent, attending to their duties. They glanced at him curiously – Mackay had told them briefly over the Tannoy what Winter had done – but he didn't think it was his presence which was keeping them so quiet. To every man on board on that last trip the engine beat sounded louder than it ever had before, as though it were pounding the hull only a few hundred feet away where there was a steel tomb containing a single object.

Mackay left it too late. Appalled that his ship, carrying this obscene thing, might be responsible for hideous casualties on the mainland, he insisted on taking her well out at speed. He took her ten miles out, close to the twenty-fathom line, before he gave the order to abandon ship. Petersen, the American radio operator, in constant touch with the helicopters, signalled them. There was a nervous, controlled rush to get down off the bridge, up out of the engine-room. Mackay remained on the bridge – with Winter. 'Join them Mr Winter,' he said stiffly. 'I shall be coming . . .'

'Since I am responsible for this,' Winter replied coldly, 'we shall leave the bridge together. I am in no hurry.'

The crew assembled at the emergency landing point on the port side of the main deck – the normal landing point was too close to the empty wing tank. A Sikorsky was coming down through thin fog with a roar, its rotor whizz a blur above the fuselage. Bennett checked his watch. 'How long have we got?' he asked Grisby, the bomb squad leader. 'Less time than I care to think about . . .'

The Sikorsky landed, bumped on the deck, a crewman opened the door, the waiting men piled aboard. Bennett counted them again with Cassidy and Sullivan, and the counts checked. They were waiting now only for Mackay and Winter who were expected any moment. The first jet-axe charge detonated prematurely – close to the bridge.

The charge detonated in a wing tank under the distribution area behind the breakwater on the starboard side. The thunder of the explosion was deafening, like an express train passing over the ship. The deck opened, a huge round jagged hole, and from the hole a stream of oil jetted upwards, curving through the fog in a shallow arc. The blast went away from the helicopter, but the machine shuddered. Inside it the men froze with fear; they thought the nuclear device had detonated.

On the bridge Mackay took the shock of the blast. It lifted him, threw him against the binnacle, and he stood up shakily with blood dripping from his forehead. He looked dazed, not sure what had happened. Winter, who had just missed the blast although he had stood not three feet from the captain, grabbed Mackay and took him off the bridge. He had to man-handle the half-conscious master down a companionway, using a fireman's lift, and when he reached the main deck everyone was aboard the Sikorsky. Bennett started to climb out of the machine. 'Get back inside the bloody machine! I've got him,' Winter yelled. He moved along the deck unsteadily.

Everything was confused. The fog was lifting, lifted perhaps by the detonation of the first charge. There was a stench of oil, oil lying on the deck, oil hissing weirdly as it poured out of the ruptured tank. Despite the explosion the choppers were still buzzing round overhead, searching for survivors. Cassidy was shouting, some warning about the oil lying on the deck. The pilot was shouting behind his controls, anxious to lift off. Winter heard nothing above the hammering beat of the rotors, the hissing of the escaping oil. He reached the machine.

He had wrenched his back, carrying Mackay, and now it was agony to straighten up a little, to hoist the captain up to the hands stretching out to take him. He took a deep breath, jerked himself up, felt as though his back had split in half, then the burden was removed from him as they hoisted Mackay inside the cabin. Winter relaxed into a stoop, bent over like a man playing leap-frog, his head twisted so he could see the machine. 'Next chopper!' The pilot didn't hear him but he saw the upwards gesture of Winter's finger, indicating the helicopter which had just flown over the ship. Cassidy was still protesting in barrack-room language as the pilot took off.

When Garfield, the Coast Guard chief directing operations, flew over the ship at a hundred feet, he could see Winter clearly on deck by the lights from the bridge which were still functioning on the port side. A tiny figure, he seemed to be hobbling about as another Sikorsky descended to take him off. Garfield adjusted his night-glasses, saw the helicopter's fuselage blot out Winter as it was within ten feet of the deck. The second jet-axe charge detonated. There was a flash in the lenses which nearly blinded him, a roar, his machine shuddered under the shock as the pilot fought for control. When he recovered his vision there was only a huge hole with oil pouring out where Winter had been standing. The rescue machine had gone too.

Garfield sent away every machine but his own, ordered them back to the mainland. Below him the stern of the *Challenger* was lost under a seething mass of black and oily smoke, but the bow projected from it. The forepart of the ship was still afloat, the nuclear device was still above the surface. He told the reluctant pilot to keep circling. Then three charges detonated simultaneously with a flash and a blasting roar which convinced Garfield the device had exploded. He told the pilot to get the hell out of it. As the machine was turning he saw the forepart of the ship going, the bow rising up like a shark's snout, hovering, then it was sucked under. Seismographs registered the nuclear device's underwater detonation ten minutes later.

The depth of the water, the direction of the blast – mainly south – and the fog, minimised the amount of radiation reaching the mainland, but the sea was polluted. The oil pouring out from the *Challenger* flooded ashore at Carmel-by-the-Sea where sand dunes link the town with the ocean. For six months the only people seen on Californian beaches from San Francisco to San Diego were white-uniformed, helmeted men with Geiger counters. The white whale, which heads south along this coast to its spawning ground off Lower California, was not seen again for five years.

Fifteen minutes before dawn on Thursday January 23 the two British supertankers, *York* and *Chester*, were steaming slowly just north of the Saudi Arabian coastline. The canvas coverings had been stripped from the huge crate-like structures, the skeletal frames which had faked the crate-like shapes had been removed. On board *York* the strike aircraft were lined up, the pilots in their cockpits. On board *Chester* the Sea King helicopters were in position, the airborne troops already inside them. Dummy pipes and catwalks had been removed from the decks, leaving natural runways.

On the bridge of *York* Gen. Villiers, Chief of General Staff, stood alongside Brigadier Harry Gatehouse, airborne commander. It was very dark, it was fifteen minutes to dawn . . .

Round the delta of the Danube in Roumania all military airfields had been closed to traffic. Soviet communication experts had taken over the telephone exchanges in nearby towns. Soviet airborne troops were already aboard their aircraft, had in fact been inside their cramped quarters for several hours. Each pilot had his flight routing which ended in Iraq, close to the Mosul and Kirkuk oilfields, close to Baghdad. The Soviet air commander was smoking cigarettes in an airfield building while he waited for the signal from Moscow . . .

The British Foreign Office believed it had calculated correctly. When an Anglo-French expedition had once landed at Suez, the Russians grasped their opportunity to take over Hungary. If it became necessary to occupy the Saudi Arabian oilfields as custodian for the West, the Russians would see their opportunity to take over Iraq, and Arab power would be broken. If it became necessary . . .

The news raced across the world. All the terrorists have been killed, the British tanker *Challenger* is steaming out of the Bay. It reached Baalbek, where Sheikh Gamal Tafak listened to two separate radio bulletins before he believed it. It also reached Tel Aviv.

At nine o'clock in the morning in Baalbek a certain Albert Meyer lifted the phone seconds after it had begun ringing. He listened for a moment, said understood, then replaced the receiver. 'That was the go-ahead,' he told Chaim.

'He may be coming out – there's a Mercedes pulling up outside the house . . .'

Chaim was sprawled out on the table as Albert opened the window and then moved out of the field of fire. The closed doorway filled the telescopic sight, came up so near he felt he could reach out and touch it. Albert was at the back of the room, packing the Primus stove inside a canvas satchel. When they left, there would be nothing to show they had ever been there.

The black Mercedes turned in the street, parking a dozen yards from the door with its nose pointed the way it had come. Chaim waited, the rifle nestled against the sandbag, which would also be taken away. The door opened, became a shadowed opening. Sheikh Gamal Tafak came out. The door closed behind him.

His head and shoulders filled the telescopic sight. In Arab garb he was hardly recognisable as the Oil Minister for Saudi Arabia; all the newspaper photographs showed him in European dress. But it was Tafak: the magnification of the 'scope was powerful enough to identify him to Chaim who had studied every photograph he could find of the Arab. Tafak was about to go down the first step when Chaim pressed the trigger.

The magnified image of the Arab blurred. Chaim fired again. P-l-op . . . The head disintegrated, thrown back and plastered all over the closed door in a welter of smashed bone and brain and flesh and blood. The upper half of the door was now a reddish smear. The Arab's body toppled down the flight of steps and rolled in the road. The Mercedes drove off at high speed, disappearing in a cloud of dust which settled on the still form lying in the road. The Year of the Golden Ape had ended.